# Castaways

Craig Schaefer

Demimonde Books

# Contents

# Chapter One

Turning invisible was easy. Amy had been doing it her entire life, without a wand or a book of spells in sight. It all started with the stance: shoulders tight, her hand-me-down glasses catching the reflections of faded linoleum and dirty, cigarette-stained carpets, her lips pursed like a lock. She shuffled through the days like a seasoned convict, watching her back and doing her time.

Her sentence was almost up. One more year. She could do one more year.

She stocked a shelf with off-brand candy bars, tumbling their faded wrappers into a plastic bin and shoving the older candy toward the front. The work took on a pleasing, quiet rhythm, underscored by the music — some old acoustic guitar balladeer from decades before her time — that drifted from the convenience store's tinny speaker system.

"Amy. Saturday? Please?"

She hadn't even noticed as Claire popped up behind her, but now the girl in the red apron was clasping her hands together and putting on puppy-dog eyes. Claire was bright, blonde, bubbly, probably Amy's twin from a mirror universe.

"Saturday?"

"My shift?" Claire said. "Please, can you cover me? If I miss one more game I'll get cut from the squad."

"Horror of horrors," Amy deadpanned. "Imagine not being able to cheer the Spartans to victory."

"Okay, the team sucks this year. Not my fault. Still. Please?"

Amy nodded, resigned, and crouched to grab another handful of candy bars.

"Gotcha covered," she said. "No worries."

Claire squealed and bounced on her heels.

"Best friend ever. Want me to take one of yours next week?"

"Nah, it's fine, I need the extra money. Graduation's not that far off."

Claire scrunched up her brow. "Didn't you get a scholarship?"

"Not a full ride," Amy said. "Still have to come up with a big payment up front or Columbia's not letting me in. It's fine, I've got it figured out. Mostly."

Miles — Mr. McCavendish — came around the aisle and pointed like he'd caught them in a conspiracy. His puffy lips hid under a walrus mustache and his toupee was frizzed at the edges.

"Ladies, how about a little less jaw-flapping and a little more work? I don't pay you to stand around and gossip."

Amy's face turned to the floor. An acid retort rose to the tip of her tongue. Then it died there, her jaws locked tight, and she kept stocking the shelves.

"You know," he added, "the sign out front might say 'Miles to Go'—"

"But you're not going anywhere," Claire and Amy echoed together.

"Correct." He pointed two fingers to his eyes. "I see all, I know all."

In her head, Amy was on a beach in California, listening to the waves wash against pristine white sand. She had never actually been there, or anywhere far outside of Holybrook, but she had seen pictures in magazines. It was easier, sometimes, to just burrow inside her own imagination and go Somewhere Else. Safer that way, especially as Miles eased closer to Claire, close enough to breathe down the back of her neck.

"Come by my office later," he purred. "Need to go over some scheduling changes with you."

In the corner of Amy's eye, one of his hands dropped lower, sliding behind Claire's back. She forced a smile, wincing, and gently squirmed free. Always gently, like their boss was made of nitroglycerin and might explode at the slightest nudge.

"Yes sir, Mr. McCavendish," Claire said. "Um...I told Kyle I'd work the register while he took his break, though, so—"

"Later," he said. "You know where to find me."

He vanished, off to police another side of the store.

"Why don't you stand up to him?" Amy whispered.

And even as the words came out, her brain fired back: *Why don't I stand up for her?*

Claire shrugged. "What could I do? There are only like, three places in town that hire teenagers, and the owners all play golf together. This is the best it's going to get for me."

She was smiling, playing blithe and bubbly, but the light in her eyes was gone. Drained away, stolen. Not for the first time, Amy wondered what it would feel like to kill a man.

"That's life in Wholly Broke," Claire added. "It is what it is. At least you're getting out of here."

"You can too," Amy started to say, but Claire cut her off with a look.

"Let's be realistic," she replied. "I know what I am. I'm my mother. And I'm her mother. Maybe I won't get sucked into the same traps they did. And maybe I'll win the lottery. Anything can happen, right?"

She turned to go, then paused.

"But you never belonged in this town in the first place."

*\*\*\**

Amy's bike was a vintage ten-speed, reclaimed from the back of a thrift store. It rode with a wobble and always felt one jolt away from throwing its chain, but it wasn't like she had far to go. Life in Holybrook was a crooked line through the forested roads and backcountry, from high school to the convenience store to home and back again, a warped record stuck on repeat. She gripped the handlebars tight, leaning into the curve as her bike bounced along the gravel-paved stretch at the mouth of the trailer park.

The sun shimmered behind the tall woolly pines, and a sickly plume of gray smoke twisted upward in the distance. The mingled smells of charcoal and hamburgers blew in on a crisp wind, squeezing Amy's empty stomach into a tight ball. *Should be leftovers in the fridge*, she thought. *Unless he ate them all.*

Her father's truck was parked in front of their double-wide, polished like a diamond. She wasn't surprised to see him at home; he usually was. She hopped off, walked her bike the last few steps, and tied it up with an old, battered chain through the front spoke. She didn't notice she was clenching her jaw until it started to ache. Bad habit.

Her nights were ruled by her father's mood, and her father's mood was ruled by his own bad habits. Beer made him maudlin, wine made him angry, and whiskey made him dangerous. A few months ago he'd made a new friend down at the only bar in town, and the little white pills started showing up. The little white pills mostly made him sleep.

Or, like now, she'd find him sitting in his recliner with his mouth hanging open, his bloodshot eyes fixed on the television screen. She closed the trailer door behind her with practiced silence, slipping off her ratty gym shoes so she'd make less noise on the paper-thin carpet. Lost in chemical bliss, he didn't even look her way.

"Dad?" she asked, voice soft. "Did you eat dinner?"

He answered with a noncommittal grunt. Cartoon characters with rubber-hose arms pranced across the television screen.

"I'll fix you something in a bit, after I do my homework, okay?"

No answer. Amy hoped that was a yes. She padded behind him and escaped into her room. More of a closet, really, with a folding bed and a rickety dresser and not much space for anything else, but it was hers and the door had a tiny lock on it. She rested her backpack on the bedspread and rummaged inside, coming up with a thin envelope. Payday, and one step closer to freedom.

An old butter cookie tin hid at the bottom of her dresser, nestled under a folded sweater. She tugged it out and eased open the lid.

Then she stood, frozen, as ice water flooded her veins.

"No," she murmured. "No, no, no."

Her fingers pressed against the empty bottom of the tin, as if her eyes were just wrong and she could banish her sudden terror with a touch. Reality had other plans. In her experience, it always did. She took slow, deep breaths.

"Dad?"

She stood in her open doorway, staring at him from across the room. The din from the television almost swallowed her voice, but he gave her a bleary-eyed look.

"Where is my money?" she asked.

"What money?"

"My — my *school* money," she said, waving a flustered hand at the empty tin on her dresser. "You know? My savings? For college?"

He looked back to the television, already dismissing her.

"Truck needed new tires," he said.

His most prized possession. His baby. Never mind that he barely drove it and didn't have a job to drive it to. A jumble of words collided in Amy's throat, backed up and trapped inside of her, and all she could manage was to blurt out: "But that was *mine*."

He looked at her again. His eyes narrowed to angry, piggish slits.

"And I pay for the roof over your head and the food in your belly, and I get nothing for it but the shit end of the stick. Ain't gonna kill you to help out with the bills around here."

She didn't think, after all these years, that he could find a new way to hurt her. But she had his full attention now and one of his hands was starting to curl like he was thinking about reaching for his belt and there wasn't anything inside of her but fight or flight. She took a sideways step toward the trailer door, handling him like a wounded, cornered animal.

"I'll...go pick us up some dinner," she said. "Maybe...pizza? From Rizzo's? Would you like that?"

Appeased, he returned his attention to the television screen.

"Pepperoni," he said.

***

Amy pedaled through the gathering dark, blinking hard to clear the tears from her eyes as she rolled down a gloomy forest road. She wasn't going to Rizzo's and she wasn't going back, and if "pepperoni" was the last word her father ever said to her then that would be just fine.

*Stupid*, she told herself. *And where are you going to go? No tuition, no college. No way out.*

*There was never really a way out.*

She knew she wasn't thinking clearly. The casual, callous betrayal hurt like a fist, and she was still reeling from having her future yanked out from under her feet like a cheap rug. This town was a cage, and she had to get out. Tonight.

For that she needed money. She was still searching for a plan when she pulled up outside the dingy glass doors of Miles to Go. She glanced at it, noted a couple of cars out front, and rode on before anyone noticed her.

She circled back once the store had closed for the night.

Amy had never stolen anything in her life. But she needed money, and Miles had some. *And he's a pervert who gropes underage girls and gets away with it because his brother's the sheriff*, she reminded herself, psyching herself up. *He deserves a whole lot worse than losing a couple of nights' profits.*

She wouldn't even have to break in. Last year he had given her the key for the back door and the alarm code when he needed her to cover for his usual closer. He'd never asked for the key back, and there was a good chance he'd forgotten she had it by now. She'd be in and out in five minutes. Easy.

Inside the back doorway, she held her breath as she keyed in the code on a panel while it counted down the seconds with angry electronic bleeps. Then it chimed twice more, flashed a green light, and went silent. She exhaled.

She flicked on the light in the back office. Her boss's filing cabinet was unlocked, and she knew what she'd find there: a pair of stacked cash drawers, flush with green, each carefully counted and notated with a receipt for Miles to review when he rolled in tomorrow morning.

She took the paper money and left the coins. The rumpled wad of cash was intoxicatingly fat in her hand, though she knew it was mostly singles and fives. Maybe enough to get her to the coast, maybe not. She'd figure it out on the road. She just needed to be anywhere but here.

She froze in the doorway.

She couldn't do it. Amy wasn't a thief, and she wasn't going to become one now. *What else can I do?* she thought, staring at the money in her hand. *I can't go back.*

She was wrestling with herself, arguing herself into taking the cash then arguing herself back out of it again, when a muffled rumble turned her head. She slipped out of the office, crouching low behind the shelves as she crept through the shadows.

The sheriff was here. His cruiser slowly rolled past the front of the store. Amy ducked, her heart pounding, just before the beam of his door-mounted spotlight glowed against the windows and cut a swathe through the dark. She bit down on a sudden surge of panic. Was there a secret alarm? Some kind of high-tech— No. She caught her imagination before it spiraled out of control. Nobody in Holybrook had anything that fancy, and hardly anyone bothered to lock their doors at night. Just the local lawman, doing a routine welfare check on his brother's business. There was only one problem.

Nobody was supposed to be here this late. And the light from Miles's office could be seen from outside the store. The sheriff knew someone was here. She watched the cruiser roll to a stop. The big man behind the wheel got out and fixed the windows with a scrunch-faced scowl.

He walked out of sight, either checking the front from another angle or circling the building to test the back door. Where he would find it unlocked and wide open, right next to her bike.

She couldn't slip out the back without getting caught. Couldn't risk the front door, either: squeaky hinges and the jangling bells over the door would bring him running. In the space of a heartbeat Amy watched her entire future implode. She'd be arrested. Miles would press charges. Columbia would yank her admittance offer and her partial scholarship. She wouldn't graduate high school; the best she'd be able to manage was a GED from behind bars and a felony on her resume once she got out.

*Did you hear about Amy Nettle?* they'd say. *She actually thought she was going somewhere in life. Guess all those books she read didn't make her any smarter.*

She understood why an animal would chew its own leg off to get out of a trap. She would have done the same, then and there. *Run*, she told herself, fighting through the swell of panic. *Just pick a door, pick a direction, and run.*

She listened, crouched low with her ears perked in the shadows, waiting to see which way the sheriff would go. Then she heard wind chimes. They echoed down the beer aisle, strident and crystal. Amy blinked.

*We're inside the store*, she thought. *There's no wind.*

That was swiftly followed by a second realization: *We don't sell wind chimes.*

The sound lured her closer. The beer coolers were unlit, their motors humming in patches of darkness that were too thick, too *angular* to be real. Amy couldn't see the far end of the aisle — it was lost, swimming in shadows. The stale odors of the convenience store faded, vanishing under the scent of fresh-cut roses.

A black envelope, the size of a greeting card, lay upon the scuffed tile floor. It was directly in her path, as if unseen hands had placed it there for her and her alone. The fear, the imminent threat and danger, faded as she crouched and scooped it up. Her rational mind screamed at her to run, to escape while she still could, but her feet stayed planted and her fingers tugged at the flap of the envelope.

The card inside bore a strange heraldic crest, like something from an old European castle, and four words in formal, baroque type.

"*Your presence is required,*" Amy read, whispering the words aloud.

***

Moments later, the sheriff's fat steel flashlight swept its beam across the aisles, hunting for intruders.

The light fell upon an empty black envelope. The sheriff wrinkled his nose, catching the scent of something strange in the air, but it was already fading.

There was no one else in the store.

# Chapter Two

The world ran like melting wax.

Solid ground fell out from beneath her and Amy plummeted into a spiral abyss, wind whistling in her ears, while the chimes grew louder, thundering like the peals of a massive grandfather clock. She counted twelve in all.

Her sense of time vanished. Then her sense of self. She was bodiless, a being of pure thought moving at impossible velocity, living data firing faster than lightning along a cosmic cable.

And then, suddenly, she was back. But her world hadn't come back with her.

She stood, stunned into silence, in an open courtyard under the light of a full moon. She had never seen the moon so close to earth, so big and bright in the night sky, like she could reach up and touch it with her outstretched fingertips. The sight froze her where she stood, until she figured out what the panic-flutter in the back of her brain was trying to tell her.

Amy knew a few stars. The North Star, Orion's Belt, the Big Dipper — she could always pick those out from the canopy of constellations, the legacy of a half-remembered camping trip when she was a little girl. Not here, though.

These weren't her stars.

She wasn't alone. The courtyard, ringed with high, gray stone walls and wrought iron gates on both ends, held around two dozen strangers. Mostly teenagers, a few even younger than that, every last arrival looking as confused and shocked as Amy felt. And like her, each one of them clutched an invitation in their hands. A freckled, redheaded girl with paste-pale skin dropped onto the pebbled ground and hugged herself, staring into the distance.

Amy's first instinct was to go and check on her. She nearly collided with a tall, lanky boy who dressed like the pictures she'd seen of "mods" back in the sixties. Tight black suit, loose skinny tie, artfully mussed hair and dangerously sharp cheekbones. He looked her way and his dark eyes flashed a warning.

"Don't buy any of this," he murmured. "It's all holograms and hallucinogens. They do it to soften you up before the interrogation starts."

"Excuse me?" Amy said.

He pointed up, past the walls, over the far iron gate. A winding road curled up a hill beyond the courtyard, the darkness broken here and there by the warm glow of floating paper lanterns. And at the top of the hill stood a house.

*House* was a grotesque understatement. It was a vast, brooding fortress of faded stone, with long frosty windows whose arches pointed to the ice-white moon. Flying buttresses, great ornate arcs of stone, swooped around the house's bones, and sleeping gargoyles lined the rooftop crenelations. The sight reminded Amy of an old English manor from a murder mystery, the kind of place where amateur sleuths found corpses behind locked doors.

West of the main house, curling walkways shrouded beneath canopies of stained glass linked to an extension vast enough to be a cathedral in its own right. Light sparked behind its tall, narrow windows as Amy watched, a tiny flicker of sapphire blue that kindled into a distant, cold flame.

"None of this is real," the boy told her. "We're sitting in a holding cell at MiniTrue right now. I knew this was going to happen; my boy Tre boosted some Talon tech and they've been busting everyone who ever met him, trying to claw it back. I told him you don't rip off the OL, and everything out of Talon is stamped *Property of the OL* for a reason."

Amy could barely follow him. "The...OL? Talon? I don't know what those are."

"Seriously? How? Where are you *from*?" he said, boggling at her.

"Holybrook."

"What sector is that in?"

The frozen light from the cathedral bloomed across the glass, bleeding out across wild, tangled grass and the winding footpath up the hill.

Another teenager wandered over. The new arrival had bright brown eyes and a strange feline grace; she wore her dark hair in tight, glossy coils and sported a garment that looked like a sari in raw bronze silk, though it was adorned with metallic curving ruffles that encircled her body like a snake. The ruby around her neck, set into a dangling brass pendant, was the biggest gemstone Amy had ever seen.

"You two don't seem like angels," she said.

"I am definitely," the boy replied, "not an angel."

Amy curled her fingers in a tentative wave. "Pretty sure we're not dead. Hi. I'm Amy."

"Bahati. And yes, before you ask, I'm *that* Bahati."

"Never heard of you," the boy blurted while Amy was still searching for a diplomatic way to say the same thing. "But...I wouldn't mind getting to know you a little better. Name's Dalton. Dalton Three-Four-Eight."

Bahati cast a gimlet eye around the courtyard. "I wondered why nobody was looking at me."

The swell of sapphire light from the cathedral windows glowed in the corner of Amy's eye. The beams sang from the high arched windows, icy fingers grasping out and painting the night sky in a glimmering aurora. Everyone turned to look, distracted by the show. Everyone but Amy. The unfolding scene felt like the setup for a magic trick, fooling the audience into looking left while an illusion unfolded on the right.

Her suspicion was rewarded. A lone figure atop the courtyard wall rose to its full height as the light-show played on and waves of azure neon swept across the lawns. Amy couldn't make out anything but a silhouette from where she stood, but she still felt noticed, *seen*. The shape put one finger to its shadowy lips.

*Shh*.

The waves of sapphire flickered and died. For one uncertain, restless moment, the gathered strangers could see by nothing but moonlight.

A spotlight erupted from the center of the courtyard, a clear crisp beam shining from the soil and stone. It slid up the wall and captured the figure there in a glowing halo. She was mature, though Amy would have been hard-pressed to guess her age; her almond eyes looked older than her face, capturing a sense of wisdom and a certain small, dark amusement. Her voluminous robes, woven in the same shifting blue shades as the cathedral windows, fluttered freely despite the absence of any wind.

Her azure hat rose to a peak and curled to one side, like the bend of a crescent moon, and its wide, floppy brim dangled low over one eye. She offered the gathered throng a smile of approval.

"Good evening," she called down to them.

The murmurs and whispers stopped dead. She held the silence for a moment, letting the chirps of crickets flood the empty space, before she spoke again.

"Every one of you has been singled out," she said, "for a very special purpose. And a special education. I am your headmistress, Chen Lan, and it is my great honor to welcome you to the Saunders Academy."

A wisp of a boy, maybe fourteen, raised a pale, shaky hand. She acknowledged him with a glance.

"I'm pretty sure I'm in the wrong place." He fumbled with his glasses, thin and rimmed with sleek silver wire, unlike Amy's chunky hand-me-down pair. "I don't get...picked for things, and I'm not sure how I even got here, and—"

"Let's put those fears to rest," the headmistress said, scrutinizing his face. "And test my memory while we're at it. You are Mr. Colin Woodrue, yes?"

He lit up at that. Amy wasn't sure why, but he reacted to his own name with wide-eyed surprise.

"That's me," he said.

"Then you're in the right place, considering I signed off on your invitation myself." Lan studied the gathering, all the upturned faces, as if marking them to memory. "All will be made clear shortly. Just know, for now, that you were chosen for your aptitude from a very large pool of potential students."

Amy wanted to stay small and quiet. Vanish in the crowd. That felt safe, felt smart. All the same, she couldn't stay silent.

"Chosen, okay," Amy shook her head. "But where *are* we? And what are you going to teach us?"

The headmistress answered by taking one step forward, off the side of the courtyard wall. She dropped like a stone amid a chorus of gasps, but as one student cried out her voice was swallowed by a hard gust of cold wind. *Wind and salt*, Amy thought, tasting the sea, as Chen Lan pirouetted mid-plummet. The gust caught and lifted her, the trailing sleeves and train of her robes billowing like a living, tattered shadow.

The headmistress hovered five feet above the courtyard stones, her expression placid.

"Magic," she said. "I'll teach you magic."

She slowly descended to earth, drifting like a feather until her toes touched the courtyard path.

"And just in case it wasn't clear, I'm not talking about card tricks and bunnies in hats," she said. "Under our tutelage here at the Academy, you will receive a thorough instruction in occult history and practice. You will learn to traffic with certain clandestine powers, and you will face many ordeals — severe ones, I promise — but you will emerge stronger than you have ever been. I'll change your life forever...if you'll let me."

Amy had a million questions, and she was far from the only one judging by the faces all around her, but life had taught her the most important question to ask up front: "How much does it cost?"

"An understandable concern, Ms. Nettle—" Lan's pointed look said *for you in particular*— "but we aren't interested in money. You'll be welcome at this school so long as you earn your keep here. And that goes for all of you."

*Nice dodge*, Amy thought. *I didn't ask about money, I asked what this would COST.*

Did it matter, though? Minutes ago she'd been staring down the barrel of a botched robbery and a ruined future. Now she was standing under strange stars and watching a woman float in midair. A woman who implied she could teach Amy how to do the same, and more.

*Spontaneous psychotic break? Maybe I'm sitting in a padded cell right now, imagining all of this.*

*Then again,* Amy considered, *things could be worse. I might as well go along for the ride.*

One of the courtyard gates let out a metallic clunk and a high-pitched squeal as it began to swing wide of its own accord. The pebbled path, lined with floating paper lanterns to light the journey, waited just beyond the ornate black iron bars. And at the end of that winding road, the house.

"If you will please follow me," the headmistress said, leading her impromptu pack of twenty-odd confused and disheveled students toward the open gate. Amy moved with the flow, then paused. The girl she'd noticed earlier — the freckled redhead who looked like her entire world had fallen apart — still sat on the ground, clutching her forearms, slowly rocking back and forth. Amy got closer and waved to catch her eye.

"Hey," she said. "Can you walk on your own? Probably shouldn't get left behind out here."

She offered a hand without thinking. The sitting girl flinched, curling in on herself, and Amy pulled her fingers away. The girl gave Amy a vague, uneasy nod.

"Sorry. I mean, yeah, I can walk. I can do it myself. Thanks."

She pushed herself to her feet and shadowed the other students, a ghost in their wake.

At the head of the pack, the headmistress held court. The still, cool night carried her voice as the air filled with the scents of wet peat and wildflowers.

"Let me be clear. The Saunders Academy operates on a strict pass-or-fail basis. You will live up to our expectations, or you will be removed."

"Removed?" echoed a small voice from the pack on her heels.

"Expelled," the headmistress said. "In which case you will be re-turned to your point of origin. *Without* your memories of this place, and without anything you may have learned in your time with us. It will be as if nothing ever happened."

The voice had a face, though she was too short for Amy to pick her out of the crowd at first. As she stepped forward, Amy understood why: she was a tiny thing in a gingham coat, maybe twelve years old at most, with big moon eyes. The kid was one bad moment from bursting into tears.

"When can we go home?" she asked.

A single violet spotlight, buried in overgrown, tangled grass, shone upon a clearing just east of the path. An archway stood there, made from three rough slabs of chalk-white stone. It reminded Amy of Stonehenge, but she couldn't miss how the air beneath the arch wa-vered and rippled like a heat mirage in the dark.

"You can leave now, if you like, or any time at all," the Headmistress replied. "Though you won't be coming back again. This is the Arch of Resignation. Pass through it, and you'll be returned home. A one-way trip, without your memories, but if you can't hack it here..."

Home, except home wasn't home anymore. All Amy had waiting on the other side of the gateway was a jail cell and ruin.

Nothing, and no one, was going to make her walk through that arch.

Dalton had silently fallen in beside her. She gave him a sidelong glance.

"Still think we're hallucinating?" she whispered.

He rubbed the back of his neck and gazed toward the house at the end of the lane. "Let's say I'm reevaluating my rush to judgment."

"Yeah," Amy agreed. "I thought I might be losing it, but we're all seeing the same thing and that's not how crazy works."

"Let me be clear," the headmistress warned the crowd of new students. "Our invitation is given once, and once only. You're free to leave at any time, for any reason, but you won't be coming back. I certainly hope you'll stay."

Bahati, the girl in the bronze sari, took a step forward and raised a graceful hand. One of her eyebrows rose, skeptical.

"Miss...Chen? Look, there's no way I can say this without sounding like a total diva, but I have to know." She put her hands on her hips. "I'm one of the most famous people on the planet. Why doesn't anyone here recognize me?"

A mischievous glint twinkled in Chen Lan's eyes. She took a moment, looking out across the tangle of upturned faces. All of them different to the core, united only in their fear and confusion.

"You're one of the most popular people on *your* world, Miss Bahati. As it happens...each and every one of you was hand-selected from a different parallel Earth. If it helps, think of yourselves as ambassadors."

The headmistress twirled her hand, gesturing to the house at the top of the hill.

"It's late, and you must all be hungry. Let's get some food in you, hm? Nothing settles the nerves like a good meal."

# Chapter Three

The doors of the great house opened wide, and a terrible silence gusted in.

Following the headmistress like a pack of skittish ducks, the conjured and stolen children fanned out across the waxed parquet floor of the academy's main hall. No one spoke. The house was a Victorian relic, austere and cold, but the bronze-rimmed gas lamps along the hall's sculpted pillars burned with violet flame. A long carpet in zig-zag shades of cold ivory and black cut along the heart of the room and up a sweeping, curling staircase.

Amy's head was too full for her to find her voice. Magic, parallel worlds — it was too much to process. But she was here, and this was happening, and she was going to have to deal with it. She pushed her shoulders back, took a deep breath, and hunted through the crowd for the listless, pale freckled girl she'd spotted earlier.

"Hey, Dalton," she murmured.

He turned her way. She nodded at the pale girl, who was leaning against a pillar. Her gaze was off somewhere, a million miles away.

"She look okay to you?"

"Uh-uh." He shot a veiled glance across the room. "She's either sick or she's on something. Or she's not on something and that's why she's sick, if you get my meaning."

*Drug withdrawal?* Amy thought. Preparing for veterinary school required getting her hands wet with a little human medicine, too, just enough to know how dangerous that was. *She should be in a clinic, or a hospital. She could DIE. What are these people thinking?*

The rhythmic tapping of a cane turned her head. A new arrival emerged from the double doors at the back of the hall, hustling along with the aid of a crude hickory walking stick. He was an older man in homespun clothes and a worn leather vest, and his bright glass-blue eyes shone from a wisdom-wrinkled face.

"I thought the new bunch was going to be here first thing in the morning," he said.

"So did we all, but the portals..." Chen Lan gave a dismissive shrug. Apparently not everything at the Saunders Academy was in full functioning order. "Ladies, gentlemen, this is Mr. Orris, our caretaker and groundskeeper. What do you think, Mr. Orris? Can we put some food in these young bellies?"

"No one goes hungry on my watch. I'll have to open up the kitchen, but I'm sure I can throw something together."

To Amy's left, Bahati stood alone with a curious look on her face, somewhere between surprise and muted pleasure. Amy neared her, curious.

"Not sure what you're famous for back home, but this must be hard."

Bahati fluttered her eyelashes, then broke into a grin.

"Are you kidding me? It's been years since I've been able to set foot in public without getting mobbed for autographs. This is kind of amazing."

The short, slight boy with silver-wire glasses, the one the headmistress had called Colin, drifted over to them.

"You're all seeing this, right? Big haunted-looking mansion, purple flames..."

"We are officially off book and out of sector." Dalton crossed his arms and shot a look over his shoulder. "Lace up your boots, kiddies."

***

"I mean, parallel worlds? For real?" Colin walked into the dining hall at Dalton's side, barely tall enough to reach the lanky teenager's shoulders. "It's like the KCU."

Dalton gave him a blank look.

"The Kirby Cinematic Universe? You don't have those movies on your world?" Colin's shoulders sank. "They're...they're really cool."

Amy was focused on the pale, freckled girl, who stumbled along listlessly with the rest of the pack. Careful not to touch her, Amy stayed close, just in case she needed help.

What kind of help Amy could offer, she had no idea. But she had to try.

Tables ran the length of the cavernous dining hall, the old lacquered wood scarred by knives and time like well-loved butcher blocks. The hall smelled of mothballs and rich aged cedar. Amy noticed that there wasn't any high table, no place set aside for leaders or faculty, only long, even, equal rows of benches stretching to the gaping mouth of a soot-stained granite fireplace. Lit, the hearth would be big enough to warm the entire chamber, Amy had to imagine. She felt a sudden chill from a gust of icy night wind that had slipped through a crack in the stained glass windows that lined one side of the gallery.

"Hey." Amy stood at the freckled girl's shoulder. "I'm Amy."

"Vail."

"Like a—" Amy gestured at her face.

Vail shook her head. "With an *a*." Her voice slurred like she was half-asleep.

"Are you going to be able to eat?" Amy asked.

Vail didn't answer. She dropped herself onto a bench near the end of one table, and Amy invited herself alongside. Dalton, Bahati and Colin filled in on the other side, gravitating toward one another.

"Do you think they're serious?" Colin asked. "About that strict pass-fail thing?"

"I wouldn't test 'em just yet," Dalton replied. "Gotta know the rules before you can break the rules."

Colin seemed to fold in on himself, ducking his chin, arms tight, making himself look even smaller than he was before.

"I can't go back there," he said. "That's not home."

Amy knew how he felt.

Shutters rolled up on a long serving window that looked in on the school kitchens. Behind the gap, Mr. Orris was firing up an industrial stove and tugging a flour-stained apron on over his leather vest. Meanwhile, the little moon-eyed girl stood in the middle of the aisle like a deer in a truck's headlights. Amy waved and caught her eye.

"Hey. I'm Amy. What's your name?"

"Nora," she replied in a small voice.

Before Amy could reply, Dalton beat her to it. The lanky, suited teenager scooted to one side and patted the bench beside him.

"Hey, Nora. C'mere and sit between me and Bahati. She's famous on her world and I'm kind of a badass on mine, so we'll keep you safe."

As Nora came over and slid between them, Bahati gave Dalton a dubious look.

"Kind of a badass, huh?"

He ran his fingers through his wavy hair and flashed a cocky smile. "Can you prove otherwise?"

She let him have that.

Dinner slowly rolled out as Mr. Orris filled trays along the serving window with stout wooden bowls and thick-handled spoons. The food was some kind of porridge, quick and simple but clean in a way that filled Amy's stomach with a warm, fuzzy glow. She tasted raisins, notes of cinnamon, all natural and fresh, none of the processed junk that made up the lion's share of her diet. As impressed as she was, across the table it looked like Dalton was eating real food for the first time in his life.

"Try surviving on nothing but standpipe water and Triumph protein bars," he said, catching her look as he wolfed the porridge down. "If they feed us like this every day, I'm definitely sticking around."

"So if we're from different worlds," Colin said, furrowing his brow, "how are you all speaking Tangusti?"

The headmistress drifted past. Her azure hat drooped low over one eye as she leaned in behind him.

"You are all speaking, and hearing, in your native tongues, Mr. Woodrue. We wove a tiny trick into the air of the island to make communication possible. Think of it as your own personal dubbing service."

He started to ask a question but she was already in motion, gliding — literally gliding, her toes dangling half an inch above the parquet — to the front of the room. Heads turned across the hall as all of the new arrivals looked her way.

"After dinner, you will be assigned dormitory rooms on the first floor. Do not venture upstairs: that's where the older, more advanced students reside, and I can't guarantee your safety from their...experiments. You'll be given your uniforms in the morning, before your first classes begin. As you may have gathered, this isn't how we intended to time your arrival here, but I think you'll all feel refreshed after a good night's sleep."

\*\*\*

One by one, the stolen students placed their empty bowls along the serving window, gathering for the march to the dormitories. Chen Lan watched, checking a clipboard and jotting down notes with a peacock-feather quill.

"Excuse me? Headmistress?"

She turned. Amy stood off to her side, keeping a careful distance.

"Ah, Miss Nettle." The headmistress offered her a smile. "I have to say, your suspicion speaks well to your instincts."

"When I asked you about what this is going to cost? I...thought I might have offended you."

"Hardly. We whisked you away to a strange world without so much as a by-your-leave. If I was in your shoes, I wouldn't trust me one bit. A little skepticism is a healthy thing. But don't worry: this is your new home, I promise. You'll embrace that soon enough."

"I didn't come over to talk about me." Amy shot a glance back at the crowd of students by the double doors. "That girl over there, Vail? She's sick. Like...really sick. She needs medical attention."

Chen Lan didn't answer at first. Her gaze was unreadable, distant, like she was hearing and seeing things Amy couldn't perceive. Then she locked eyes with her new student and gave her a look of quiet challenge.

"Some would say," the headmistress replied, "that the best and kindest thing you could do for Vail is to walk her down to the Arch of Resignation. And push her through."

Amy's voice was a whisper of disbelief. "What?"

"Some would say that she'll get medical aid back on her own world. That she'll live, thanks to you. Some would call you a hero for that."

A hero. For pushing a girl going through the throes of withdrawal through an interdimensional gateway right back to the place she came from. The place where she got hooked on drugs in the first place, and Amy couldn't even guess what other horrors might be waiting for Vail back home. She only had her own life to compare, and it would take a team of horses to drag Amy through the Arch.

"*I* wouldn't call myself a hero for that," she said.

"Well, then." The headmistress's smile grew wider, almost Cheshire-esque. "I suppose you'll have to figure it out for yourself. Goodnight, Miss Nettle."

***

The students were quickly broken into two ragged groups. Brandishing her clipboard, Chen Lan led one pack of teenagers to the dorms on the north wing, while Mr. Orris took Amy and the stragglers to the rooms on the opposite side of the house.

"She told you about the stairs, right?" the old man asked as he led his charges past the broad, curving staircase in the great hall.

"Not to go up there?" Nora piped up, safely ensconced between Dalton and Bahati.

"Quite correct, young lady. First-years stay downstairs. Second-years on the second floor, third-years on the third—"

"Let me guess," Dalton said. "Fourth-year students on the top floor?"

Mr. Orris gave him a long, silent look.

"There are no fourth-year students," he said.

After that, he didn't talk at all, not until they reached a corridor lined with violet gas lamps and closed doors with cold brass handles. He traced down his own clipboard, calling out names and pointing to the appropriate rooms.

"Bathrooms and showers are down the hall, by the way," he added. "I don't suggest wandering any further on your own. Not on your first day, and not after sundown."

"Is the first floor...safe?" Bahati asked.

The caretaker crooked a hand over his weathered brow, peering up and down the hallway.

"The dorms are," he said.

***

Amy was assigned to a rustic room at the end of the hall, where dust bunnies clogged the corners of the cold wooden floorboards and luminous gas flames bristled along the rim of a dangling bronze chandelier. The lights, cast downward, turned the room into a jigsaw puzzle of shadows. Single beds fitted with starchy-looking white sheets lined the walls, while a few old, cheap rugs led to a cold, dead hearth.

"This," Bahati declared, "is a fixer-upper."

Outside a window that looked out over the academy grounds, the night wind drove a stray tree branch to knock and scratch against the glass.

They'd been assigned the room along with Nora, Vail, and a girl — maybe sixteen or seventeen, her dark hair twisted into a long, severe braid and her lips painted black — who Amy hadn't met yet. The new arrival watched Vail stumble across the room and fall onto a bed, face-first.

"Is she okay?"

"That...remains to be seen. I'm Amy, by the way."

The girl turned. There was something hungry in her deep green eyes, like coming to this place had unlocked a treasure chest piled high with her heart's desire.

"Olivia. Olivia Renn. Can you even believe it? We're going to learn *magic.*"

When it came to belief, Amy was on the fence about everything right now. Besides, she saw a more immediate need. She skirted Vail's bed and crouching down beside her. Vail was sweating through her street clothes and starting to tremble.

"Vail?" Amy said softly. "Listen, hon. I'm not judging you, okay? But I need to know what you took, so we can figure out how to help you get through this."

The tall, freckled girl muttered something before rolling over and curling herself into a fetal ball. *What'd she say? "Ink"? Of course. Different planet, it's not like they're going to call drugs by the same names. C'mon, Amy, think. Basic triage.*

"Okay, she needs... towels, wet towels." She looked to Bahati. "Can you check the showers and see if there's anything we can use? If not, we'll use the sheets from my bed."

"On it," Bahati said, already heading for the door.

"She'll need fluids so she doesn't get dehydrated. Water...broth would be good, if there's anything in the kitchen—"

"They locked everything up after we left," Nora said.

Amy bit her bottom lip.

"What about the Arch?" Olivia suggested. "I mean, just push her through, they'll probably patch her up on the other side."

Vail rolled over again. Her breath was shallow now, her bloodless skin like wax. She grabbed Amy's hand, suddenly squeezing with steel-grip force as she looked up into Amy's eyes.

"Don't," she breathed. "Don't make me go back there. No matter what."

"Vail, you're going through withdrawal. You could die—"

"I'd rather die," Vail said.

***

Amy knocked on the door across the hall. It opened just a crack, and Colin peeked out at her.

"Hey," Amy said. "Is Dalton rooming with you?"

The lanky, suited teenager joined her out in the hall.

"Remember what you said back there about learning the rules before you can break them?"

"Sure," Dalton said.

"Is that a motto you live by?"

"Not even a little bit."

"Good," Amy said. "I need to sneak into the kitchen. Want to help?"

"Crime? On our first date?"

"This isn't a date."

"Sweet," he said, "because I don't pull crimes with a chick until the second date, even if she's hot. Anyway, let's go do some breaking and entering."

Amy raised an eyebrow. "You don't even want to know why?"

"Figure it's for a good cause. You can tell me on the way."

# Chapter Four

"That's a new one on me," Chen Lan murmured. "Though if the students couldn't surprise us every once in a while, there wouldn't be much of a point to this project."

The fingernails of her left hand dripped with dark paint, the color of a stormy autumn sunset. The paint drizzled down into a shallow basin, carved from carnelian stone, filled with still water and mounted on a tripod of iron.

The paint turned the water's surface into a dark mirror ringed by roiling clouds of smoke, like a living oil slick. In the reflection, Amy kept nervous watch while Dalton crouched before the dining hall doors, working a pair of dull metal hooks inside the lock. He stepped back, pocketed the improvised picks, and dusted off his hands. The door clicked and swung inwards.

"Two expulsions before the first day of classes," Mr. Orris said, standing at Chen Lan's shoulder. "First time for everything, I suppose. The boy looked like trouble from the start, but I thought she had a good head on her shoulders."

"Let it ride," she said.

He tilted his head. "Ma'am?"

"We're going to turn a blind eye to this little infraction," the headmistress said. "I want to see what they do next. If they haven't cleared out in ten minutes or so, go downstairs, stomp around and make some noise. But don't catch them, just scare them back to their dormitory."

Orris was silent for a long moment, watching the animated reflection. In the paint-smeared waters, Amy and Dalton made their way past the serving-window shutter and sneaked into the darkened kitchens.

"On a related subject," he finally said, "and I ask this with all due respect—"

"Vail Curran," she replied.

"Yes, ma'am. She's not in any condition to be here. The girl is some kind of..."

"Junkie?" Chen Lan's eyes glittered dangerously, catching reflections from the painted pool. "Ms. Curran is grappling with a rather severe addiction to Ink."

That couldn't be right. Orris double-checked his clipboard, running an old, broken fingernail along his handwritten notes.

"Says she's from Parallel Twelve."

"Mm-hm," the headmistress said.

He lowered his clipboard.

"There's not supposed to *be* any Ink on Parallel Twelve," he said.

"You spy the conundrum."

"I spy that you're up to something." He glanced from the painted pool to the headmistress. "Did you plan all of this?"

Her chuckle was a light, lilting thing.

"Perish the thought, Mr. Orris. Free will is a core principle of our Academy, as our founders and investors command."

She leaned closer to the shallow carnelian bowl. Light from the moving, rippling images cast a cold pumpkin-orange glow across her face.

"But sometimes," she said, "when you combine the right factors, in just the right way, interesting patterns emerge from the chaos. So we'll let it ride. For the moment."

***

It was the little things, Amy realized as she explored the drafty kitchens, that proved she was a long way from home. Like stove burners with fourteen heat settings, or the claw-footed, bulbous porcelain refrigerators that chugged like they were powered by steam. Or the dangling pots and pans, seasoned cast iron and brass, with manufacturers' marks she'd never heard of.

"So there we were, throwing down with the Hudson Boulevard Crew." Dalton crouched, rummaging under a stainless steel sink the size of a bathtub. "And it was going great until it turned out one of 'em grassed. All of a sudden, police skimmers are cutting off every way out of the park. They even brought in a Valkyrie to try and smoke us out; I had to crawl through a quarter-mile culvert on my belly to get home in one piece."

Amy had been cool and collected at the start of this plan, but now she had a fire under her heels. If they got caught here— *So don't get caught*, she told herself. *Focus and figure it out.* She rummaged through one of the cabinets and found a clean, empty pitcher.

"All that fighting," she said, distracted. "Over a park?"

He shrugged and stood up, showing her a bucket he'd found under the sink. She answered with a nod of approval.

"Sure," he said. "Because where I come from, you either fight to protect what you've got, or somebody's going to take it away from you. They don't even need a reason — some of these cats'll steal your teeth and bones just to prove they can."

Amy thought about the old butter-cookie tin, snug at the bottom of her dresser drawer, where she kept her college tuition fund. Gone now. It had taken her three years of high school to build up hope, and one afternoon for her father to crush it under his careless heel.

"We should hurry," she said. She shot a glance at the serving window, a bridge to the silent, cavernous dining hall. Shadows kept moving in the corners of her eyes, only to stubbornly vanish when she tried to focus on them.

Dalton raided one of the pantries. He leaned back, holding up a long cardboard tube. It rattled as he shook it from side to side.

"Hey, chocolate biscuits."

"Leave it," Amy said. "We're only taking what we need for Vail."

His eyebrows lifted as he read the label. "Real chocolate. And they just leave it out like that, where anyone can find it?"

"Do you...not have chocolate where you come from?"

"Only if you're rich. We have chocolate *product*, which is to the real thing what a dirty dish sponge is to a prime cut of steak. You can eat it, but you'll never delude yourself into enjoying it." He gave her a sidelong glance. "Explain something to me."

"Shoot."

"The opportunity of a lifetime just dropped right into our laps. We're gonna learn magic. So why would you risk throwing it all away for a girl you just met? You don't even know anything about her. That's crazy to me."

Amy stared at him, dubious. "Crazy, huh?"

"Doesn't make a lick of sense," he muttered, going back to ransacking the cupboard.

Amy crossed her arms and replied in a deadpan monotone.

"Yes, Dalton. It's completely irrational that I'd stick my neck out for a stranger in need, especially if she's some girl I just met. I know that you would never find yourself in a situation like that."

He slowly looked over at her. He blinked.

"It's different when I do it," he said.

"Uh-huh."

"It's *cool* when I do it," he muttered under his breath.

*** 

A lonely oil lamp shone in the corner of the dorm room, casting a yellow, dusty glow across the warped floorboards. Nora was already asleep; the little girl had collapsed under the weight of the day, submerged and silent under her blankets. So was Olivia Renn. Their new black-lipped acquaintance let out a long, lilting snore as Amy crept back into their shared quarters.

Bahati was crouched at Vail's bedside. She looked up at Amy, pursed her mouth, and gave a tiny shake of her head. She got up and met Amy halfway across the room.

"Girlfriend's in bad shape," Bahati whispered.

Behind her, Vail's face looked like a waxy moon, and her clothes and sheets were a sodden, freezing puddle of sweat.

"I've been trying to keep her cool," Bahati added, "but now she's shivering and her teeth are chattering and I'm afraid she's *too* cold—"

Amy squeezed her shoulder. "You did great. Thank you. Why don't you get some rest? I'll take over."

"You sure?"

"Yeah. First thing tomorrow morning, we start learning real magic. At least one of us should get a good night's sleep first."

Vail's freckled skin was mosaic of old, faded needle tracks, a constellation of pinprick scars that spiraled outward from the crook of her arm up to her wrist. Her gaze was fixed somewhere between the ceiling and worlds beyond, distant and lost while her body labored for breath. Amy mopped the sweat from her forehead with a damp hand towel.

"Let's get some fluids in you. And I brought a bucket, in case—"

Vail rolled over, lurched toward one side of the bed, and emptied her stomach onto the floor.

"That's why," Amy said. "Let's...aim for the bucket next time, okay?"

***

The hours of the night were long and thin, like a strangled vein trying to pump blood into a dying heart. Amy marked the time by the scratching of a tree branch against the dormitory window and the rustling howl of the cold night wind beyond the glass. Vail's bedsheets were frozen ropes, twisted into knots by her constant tossing and turning. She stretched like a corpse fighting off rigor mortis, her limbs jerking, cramping, then she reached for the bucket and coughed up another trickle of stomach bile.

"Can't," she said, sometime after midnight. It was the first word she'd spoken in hours.

"This is the worst of it," Amy whispered, listening to their dorm-mates snore in the dark. She folded her hand towel and wiped beads of glossy sweat from Vail's cheeks. "Just get through tonight, and everything will be better in the morning."

She had no idea if that was even true, but Amy had to be optimistic for both of them.

***

Pipes rattled and chugged behind the thin wooden walls as a shower head sputtered to life. They were somewhere south of dawn and it took a lifetime to help Vail down the hall, but she made it on her own two feet.

Now Vail sat on the yellowed tile of a shower stall, head bowed, arms wrapped tight around her legs, and she let the rain pour down. Steam wreathed her body as the hot water sluiced away sweat and dried vomit, sending the night swirling down the drain between her toes. Each of the stalls had a rickety, scuffed door. Amy mirrored Vail on the other side of the wooden panel, sitting on the floor, leaning close and sharing the silence.

"I need you to watch me," Vail finally said, her voice nearly swallowed by the sound of water pouring down. "Make sure I don't crack. Don't let me go back there, not until I'm good and ready."

*I'd rather die*, she had said to the prospect of walking through the Arch of Resignation. Amy had been nursing a pet suspicion, and she finally gave it voice.

"You didn't do this to yourself, did you?"

Vail didn't answer right away. She said something, her voice dreamy and lost, but Amy couldn't catch it. Her next words drifted, muffled, through the thin wooden door.

"...going to have words. Me and him. And he's going to listen. But not yet. Gotta heal up. Get rested. Get *strong*."

Pipes shook behind the walls as the shower's flow slowed to a trickle, then died.

"I'll help you," Amy said.

It was a spontaneous offer, the words escaping her lips before she had a second to think twice, but she meant it all the same. She figured they could both use another friend right now. Dawn was coming fast, and with it the first day of classes. The first day of their new lives was about to begin.

# Chapter Five

Somewhere in the small and secret hours before dawn, when the rest of the world was silent and the first stirrings of color touched the edge of the slate-black sky, Vail finally fell asleep. The endless night had wrung her out like a wet, tattered dishrag. She had nothing left to fight and nothing left to fight with, only a bone-deep exhaustion that left her no option but surrender.

*She'll make it*, Amy thought. Vail would make it. She could rest. Then she was falling, and her flat, starchy pillow rushed up to greet her.

She woke to crowsong.

*Song* was a generous word for it. At some point between hitting the pillow and being dragged, unwilling, back to the land of the living, someone had opened both windows flanking Amy's bed. Cold morning air gusted in, tinged with the taste of ocean salt, and a dozen fat, glossy-feathered crows lined the windowsills. They exploded into a frenzy of wing-flapping caws, each crow seemingly determined to be louder and more obnoxious than the one beside it.

"Oh god," Olivia groaned, pulling the covers over her head. "Make it stop."

In the bed next to her, Nora had made a fort of her blankets. The little girl's nervous eyes peeked out from under a lump of fabric. "Why are they *doing* that?"

"Because we all died and we're in hell," Bahati grumbled, trudging across the room. "Amy? How's our girl?"

Vail answered before Amy could, her voice tired and soft. Tired, but not weak: there was a flickering current of strength in the freckled girl's eyes, a fortitude none of them had seen last night.

"Feels like my head is going to explode if my eyes don't pop first." She sat up in bed, winced, and rubbed her knuckles against the small of her back. "Skin's raw, bones ache...and I haven't been this clear in ages. I can think again. Our morning chorus notwithstanding."

Amy fumbled with her chunky glasses and pulled them on. She stood between the open windows, waving her hands at the crows, trying to calm them down.

"You made them louder," Olivia groaned. "How did you make them louder?"

She tried again. On an impulse, she brandished an imaginary baton, flourishing it like a conductor before her orchestra.

The crows fell silent. Two dozen glittering eyes all focused on Amy, staring and rapt.

"Okay," Bahati said. "And you did that...how?"

"Love to know." Amy took a halting step backwards. The crows kept staring at her, silent, fluttering and jostling each other on the sills for room. "We should probably—"

A knock on the door interrupted her. Mr. Orris's voice, muffled by the antique wood, drifted through from the other side.

"Ladies? This isn't normally how we start the first day of classes, but the morning chimes aren't working."

"Agree to disagree," Bahati said, casting a dour eye at the crows.

"Breakfast is in twenty, so I'd suggest you all get a move on," Orris added. "Got your new uniforms, too."

The widest, glossiest crow, his feathers so dark and radiant that they shone purple in the morning sun, hopped down from the sill. The others stayed behind while he waddled after Amy, intent on following her into the hallway.

"Shoo," she whispered, waggling her fingers at the bird. "Go on. Go outside and do crow things."

He glared up at her, holding his ground.

The halls bustled with students, traveling to and from the showers and gathering around Mr. Orris, who pushed a library cart piled with clothing wrapped in tight plastic bags. He crouched, scooped up a few bundles in his arms, and passed them out.

"Got all sizes here," he said, then paused as Nora appeared in the doorway. "Almost all sizes. Sorry, young lady, you're going to have to get a little taller. Let's hope for a growth spurt over the summer, huh? Gather round, gather round. Some of these have skirts, some trousers. Pick whichever you're comfortable moving around in. We've got what the headmistress calls an 'active curriculum.' You will be walking. A lot."

"What about running?" Dalton asked, stepping out of his dorm room with Colin in his wake.

"Only if you're very bad at your studies," Mr. Orris said. He tossed Dalton a plastic bag, and the lanky teenager snatched it out of the air with one hand.

The glossy waddling crow followed Amy down the hall, all the way to the showers. He waited outside, possibly observing some sort of bird decorum.

Amy opened her bag, fingers gliding over thick, warm fabric in shades of rich chocolate and ivory. She hesitated. Just clothes, but Amy had never belonged to anything before. Never belonged anywhere. Never been a part of anything. The headmistress's words from dinner the night before came back to her: *This is your new home, I promise. You'll embrace that soon enough.*

She was reserving judgment, for now, but she could wear the uniform.

She had to admit, after toweling off her unruly hair in a fogged-up mirror and getting dressed, that it didn't look half bad. The Academy style was a chocolate tweed blazer over a crisp Oxford shirt and deep purple school necktie, paired with a long, pleated plaid skirt and stiff, flat dress shoes. At the sink to her left, Vail had opted for the pants. Her trousers matched her jacket, which she wore in an off-kilter slouch. Amy's tie was perfectly knotted and centered; Vail's dangled loose with what felt like a gesture of carefully measured defiance.

Amy frowned at her own reflection. Her fingertips brushed her tie. Vail caught something in her expression and looked over at her.

"What's wrong?"

Not...wrong, as such. Just *off*. Amy didn't speak right away. She wanted to gather her thoughts and put them in the right order before they reached her mouth.

"I figured, magic school, so everything would be...magical," she said.

But their uniforms were mass-produced. Someone had designed them, contacted a company, put in a work order, and paid for the product. She felt like she'd stolen a glimpse of the machine behind the fairytale. This academy couldn't exist in a vacuum: it had to have organizers, hands moving all the pieces around, money and power propping it up from the other side of the curtain.

Which meant, to Amy's way of looking at things, it had an agenda. She just wasn't sure what was on it yet. Or what part they'd brought her here to play.

\*\*\*

The crow let out a strangled squawk of outrage as Amy emerged from the showers. He fell in with her and Vail, waddling behind them as they joined a pack of students and made their way to the dining hall.

"You've...got a bird," Colin said to Amy, in the same tone of voice one might use to tell someone their pants are unzipped.

"We're aware of the bird," Vail told him.

The crow preened, picking at his wing feathers.

The new arrivals were, again, the only attendees in the cavernous hall. The upper-year students had made other plans, apparently. Breakfast was a reprise of last night's impromptu supper. More porridge, though this time it had a nutty, maple-syrup flavor to it, served alongside flame-charred sausage links. The sausage had a gamy, sweet aftertaste, and an oddly crumbly consistency; the more she tasted, the more Amy suspected they weren't actually made of meat. At least, not the meat of any animal from *her* Earth. At her side, Vail picked at her food.

"How are you holding up?"

"Don't want to eat," Vail said, "but I've got to try. If I can actually keep something down, we'll call it a good start."

The headmistress drifted along the aisles, silently measuring her new charges. Amy couldn't miss how Chen Lan's gaze kept landing on Vail. When she came near, Amy held up a tentative hand to catch her eye.

"Ma'am?" Amy said. She pointed to the parquet floor. "We have a crow situation."

Chen Lan crouched, studying the irritated-looking crow with almost childlike delight. She beamed at Amy.

"He seems to think you're in charge of your dormitory room."

"Not sure why," Amy said.

"Regardless, he and his compatriots did provide you a valuable service this morning."

Amy stared at her, not following.

"So pay the man," the headmistress said, rising with a shrug as if it was the most obvious thing in the world.

She moved on without another word. Amy broke one of her sausages in half, pinched it between two uncertain fingers and reached down, offering it to the crow. He cawed once, snatched it in his beak, ruffled his feathers vigorously in her general direction, and waddled away.

\*\*\*

The first class of the year was in the eastern wing of the main house. The lecture hall looked to Amy like something out of a Dickens novel. Dust and history clung to the stiff-backed wooden chairs; the rafters of the room curved inward like the ribcage of a great white whale. Old, faded words clung to the black chalkboard, too cloudy to read, and a quartet of globes lined the windowsill. None of them resembled the world Amy knew.

They settled into their seats. The room was only about three-quarters full by the time the last few stragglers trickled in.

Then they waited.

People coughed. They squirmed, antsy in the stillness. Whispers echoed here and there, then fell silent as the classroom doorknob rattled.

The door opened, bounced on something on the other side, fell shut, then opened once more. The new arrival struggled inside, balancing a fat alligator-skin messenger bag along with two poster tubes and a heavy-looking cardboard moving box. Somehow he managed to make it to his desk at the head of the classroom, dumping his cargo with a red-faced sigh of relief. He was a bright-eyed man in his early thirties with boyish good looks and dark, tousled hair, and he wore leather patches on the elbows of his long herringbone jacket.

"So," he said, smacking his palms together as he looked over the gathered students. "Here we are. Introduction to Occult Philosophy. We should start with...oh, right!"

He hustled to the blackboard, picked up a tiny nub of chalk, fumbled it, and went hunting for a longer piece to write with. He scribbled his name in the upper corner of the board, writing over an old misty diagram, while he talked.

"I'm Professor Lanca, that's L-A-N...well, you can read the board." He turned back to the class. "You're new! And so am I! Bit awkward, really, my predecessor had to leave the academy over the summer break and this is my first actual teaching job, so I guess we'll all be learning together."

"What happened to him?" Dalton called out, slouching in the back of the classroom.

"Oh, I don't think we need to worry about that. Now, then: you're here to study magic, yes?"

He dug around in the cardboard box, coming up with a deck of playing cards. He shook them out of the pack as he approached Nora.

The little girl sat in the front row, right in the center, looking up at him like a deer in a truck's headlights.

"Pick a card," Professor Lanca told her. "Show everyone else, but don't tell me which one you picked. Just remember it, and put it back in the deck."

Nervous, uncertain laughter rippled across the room. Nora furrowed her brow, not sure if she was being teased, and took a single card. She flashed it to the other students before sliding it back into the deck.

"Let's see if I remember how this works," the professor said. "And do pay attention, students, this is the most important part of the trick."

He threw the deck into the air.

It exploded, cards spinning in all directions like sparks from a firecracker. They fluttered and winged around the room, defying gravity, dancing in a storm of chaos. While they flooded the air over the students' heads, Lanca raised one hand high and snapped his fingers. A card appeared between his thumb and middle finger, the Three of Hearts, and he dropped into a graceful bow as he held it up for Nora's inspection.

"Is this your card, miss?"

It was.

"Very good," Professor Lanca said.

He held up his open palm. The flying cards rocketed into his hand, slapping into place in a riffle of pasteboard until the last one landed home.

"Now, let's *really* get to work."

# Chapter Six

"We'll start with the lay of the land," Professor Lanca said, brandishing a piece of chalk.

He drew circles on the blackboard, uneven and mismatched, as he spoke.

"We live in a multiverse. Each of these circles represents a parallel world, in a parallel galaxy. Worlds that evolved on different tracks. Many are so similar that if you accidentally slipped from one Earth to another, you might not even realize anything had changed. Others are...different."

He paused, eying his handiwork.

"A more accurate model would have all of these circles overlapping, like frequencies on a radio dial," he added, "but there's something to be said for visual clarity."

Amy raised her hand. She felt a little bashful about it — being the first student to ask a question was never, in her experience, a gateway to popularity — but her thoughts were piling up like derailed cars in a train crash and she had to get some of them out. Lanca acknowledged her with a nod.

"How many parallel worlds are there?" she asked.

"Excellent question, but the answer is always expanding. We've charted ninety-three parallels so far, around seventy of which can support human life. My former employers knew of even more. Then you have what we call 'pocket dimensions' — smaller worlds, stranger ones. Sometimes they're weird cosmic aberrations, sometimes they're entirely artificial. Worlds spun from whole cloth by ancient magicians, for reasons mostly long forgotten."

Lanca walked over to the row of dusty globes on the windowsill, contemplating them with his hands clasped behind his back.

"Our new home, case in point. This is a very small planet, and Firebreak Island — where the Academy stands — is one of the only actual pieces of dry land. It's all water out there. Deep water." He turned to face the classroom, his friendly manner vanishing. "I hope you've already been told, but under no circumstances should you leave the shore. There are mermaids in the water, and worse things."

A student Amy hadn't met yet, broad-shouldered like a high school linebacker and hair so blond it was almost white, cracked a cocky grin. "Mermaids? Hot."

"I'm sorry to disappoint you, Mr.—" The professor leaned over, checking a list of names on his desk. "—Anders, but this is a prime lesson in how myths and legends mutate across time and even across worlds. Mermaids will not sing sweet songs while shaking their shell-covered bosoms at you. They will, however, drag themselves onto your boat in the dead of night and haul you into the water, where they will devour you down to the bones. Slowly, because the only thing a mermaid loves more than the taste of human meat is when it's still alive and screaming."

The room had gone dead quiet. The professor stared at his classroom for a moment. Then he twirled a finger in the air and broke into an awkward smile.

"*Moving on*," he said. "Across the worlds that still remember the older ways, people have spent eons learning to harness the powers of magic. They've devised systems, techniques, entire religions and philosophies. But these are all just methods of accessing the same primal source."

He tapped the middle of the blackboard with his stick of chalk. It left a tiny, almost invisible pinpoint in the middle of all the lopsided circles. Then he took a second glance at his list of students.

"Miss Curran. What do you see here?"

Vail shook her head, not following. "Nothing?"

"Close! This...is everything. The infinite space outside of the multiverse as we know it. Each world is a pearl, and this is the bath that they float in; we call it the In-Between. Imagine an endless expanse of potential energy, just waiting to be tapped. It's the essence of creation and of creativity."

The professor gazed across the lecture hall. His eyes fell on Amy, and it felt like he was addressing her and her alone, like they were the only two people in the room. She still saw the old ghosts of half-erased symbols on the board, now floating in the In-Between, echoes of forgotten incantations.

"Some people call it the Blood of God." He chuckled, gently. "I am not so mythically inclined. But all you really need to know is that the power to manifest your dreams is out there. It's our job to teach you how to command it."

"Why?" Amy asked.

She hadn't raised her hand. Hadn't even planned to speak again, but the word slipped past her brain and straight to her lips. Professor Lanca didn't answer right away. When he did reply, he sounded like he was tiptoeing through a minefield.

"Because you were chosen for this. Each and every one of you has shown tremendous potential."

"Sure, but...why? Why teach us at all? What does the Academy get out of this?" Amy asked. At the desk beside her, Vail nodded in weary agreement.

"Nothing in life is free," Vail said.

"Wisdom from the mouths of babes," Professor Lanca muttered. He perched on the edge of his desk, crossing one leg over the other. "I'll make you all a deal. Give me one semester. Study hard, work harder, and let me show you what you're really capable of. All your questions will be answered in due time. Fair?"

People were staring at Amy.

She saw them in the corners of her eyes. Expectant glances. She realized that the other students were waiting for her to answer him. Maybe just because she was the first to speak up, to voice the question they were all silently asking. Whatever the reason, they were deferring to her. It felt wrong. Amy had never been a leader of anything or anyone. Didn't matter. She was now, for the moment at least, and she had to decide whether she was going to push the issue or let it rest.

"Fair," she said.

*I can investigate on my own*, she thought. *After class.* Vail nodded, agreeing with her: she wasn't alone. Lanca clapped his hands together as if to seal the pact.

"Excellent," he said, jumping down from his desk. "And with that out of the way...how would you like to learn your very first spell? I'm going to teach you a technique called the Lamp Without Oil. It's small, simple, but surprisingly useful."

Erik, the burly teen who had spoken up earlier, raised a casual hand. He didn't wait to be called on. "So do we get wands or something?"

"Wands?" Professor Lanca smiled and pushed the sleeves of his herringbone jacket back a bit. He ducked under his desk, coming up with an old, splintery wooden crate. "Never use the things, myself.

A bit too ostentatious. Trust me, you'll find there are times to show your power, and times to keep it hidden safely away until you need it most. You can't do the second thing if you're walking around like Merlin the Reaver, waving a wand at people and wearing pointy hats. That said, seeing as you're all beginners, there's nothing wrong with artificial assistance to put a little pep in your step. Training wheels, you know?"

He rapped his knuckles against the side of the open-topped crate.

"So come on down, ladies and gentlemen. The best way to learn is with a focus, and I've got one for each of you."

Amy rose, filed uncertainly across the lecture hall, and looked down into the crate. It was a treasure trove. Crystal prisms, each about the size of her thumb, glittered in a kaleidoscopic rainbow of colors beneath the dusty overhead lights. Vail stood beside her, her brow furrowed.

"Which one do we take?" she asked.

"The one that speaks to you," Lanca replied. "There's no wrong choice, but some choices are more right than others. Take your time, but don't think. Feel."

He looked sharply at the classroom door, as if he heard something — or felt something — that no one else could.

"If you'll excuse me," he said, "I need to step outside for a moment."

Amy glanced over the crate of crystals and tried to take the professor's advice to heart. "Not thinking" was not one of her best skills. If he needed someone to lie awake at two in the morning, overanalyzing every detail of her day and her life, she'd be perfect for the job.

"Leap of faith," Vail said.

Amy gave her a sidelong glance. "Hm?"

"It's a leap of faith." She reached into the crate, digging around as the crystals clattered and chimed, and came up with a prize. Her choice of focus was the color of burgundy wine, with tiny pinpoint sparkles that glittered like a lost constellation of stars. "Go for it. Be spontaneous."

*Great*, Amy thought. *Now I have to be spontaneous AND trust my intuition. My first day of magic school and I already suck at everything.* Vail's crystal had a long, jagged crack along one face. Amy pointed it out, and Vail contemplated the scar before answering with a shrug.

"I still like it," she said. "This one is for me."

Amy tried to clear her mind, or at least fade back from the swirling jumble of thoughts that dogged her every step. She took a deep breath, relaxed her shoulders as best she could manage, and reached into the crate. Her fingers closed around a random crystal, the one that just felt *right*, and she pulled it out to take a look.

It was a chunk of dark purple stone, almost metallic, and it drank in the light without letting anything escape. She held it up to her face, curious.

*Are you the one?* She asked. Her thoughts were answered by a pulse. A tiny kick from the dark crystal, making her fingers tingle and her wrist burn.

"Okay," she whispered. "You're mine. Let's do this thing."

***

Out in the hallway, Chen Lan leaned against the wall next to the classroom door, silent, listening. Professor Lanca stepped out, closed the door behind him, and crossed his arms.

"Really? Spying on me?"

"*Monitoring*," the headmistress said. "I watch everyone and every-thing under this roof. Besides, it's your first day of teaching. I wanted to be close in case you needed a helping hand."

He tilted his head, almost grudgingly, but the look in his eyes said he wanted to know what she thought.

"Your assessment so far?" he asked.

"Bold choice, teaching them the Lamp Without Oil on their first day. Straight into the deep end?"

"Sink or swim," Lanca said. "These are teenagers. Well, except for the really short one, I think—"

"That's Nora. She's twelve."

"Whatever. They're young. You can't force them to do six months of esoteric mathematics and meditation before they cast their first spell. Got to give them a taste of the good stuff right away, so they know what they're working toward."

"It's dangerous," the headmistress said. "But our arrangement stands: if you really think you know what you're doing, I'll allow it."

Lanca's eyes narrowed and turned hard. He took a step closer to her, invading her personal space.

"I know better than you. That's the whole reason I'm here, isn't it?"

"Careful," she said.

"Besides," he added, "let's not pretend we don't know what's really going on here."

He pointed to the closed classroom door.

"In one year, half of those kids are going to be dead. Only half, if you're lucky."

"You promised you could raise our batting average."

"You should let me tell them the truth," Lanca countered. "This is wrong. It's cruel."

Chen Lan let out a sharp bark of a laugh.

"Since when do you care about right and wrong?" she asked. "And as far as cruelty goes, you're something of an expert in the field. Let me be clear, Professor: this batch is going to *live*. And you're going to give them the tools to survive what's coming for them, or you and I are going to have a problem. A bigger problem than the one we already have."

He gave her a wan look. "Penance for my sins?"

The headmistress dropped her voice to an icy whisper and looked to the lecture hall door.

"There is no penance in this world or any other that could wash your hands clean. Now get back in there and do your job."

# Chapter Seven

The lecture hall was silent, save for faint, anxious rustling and the whisper of a cold ocean wind that made the dusty classroom windows rattle in their frames. Amy stared down at her hands. Her dark crystal prism nestled in the palm of her right hand. In her left, just like every other student in the room, she held a tiny bulb of frosted glass.

"Remember. You draw power with your weak hand, and project with your dominant one." Professor Lanca strolled down the aisles, double-checking each student's poise and posture. He paused, glancing down at Amy. "You're a leftie?"

She nodded. He wriggled the fingers of his left hand at her in a wave, winked and moved on.

She felt a tingle in her palm. Nothing more.

The professor's instructions weren't the issue. More that she was exercising muscles she didn't know she even had until today. She had to learn new ways of moving, of feeling. Thinking. Lanca had chalked an elaborate mandala on the blackboard, an elaborate tapestry of spirals and petals and cubes, a concentric vortex in ghostly white. Staring into the heart of the mandala made Amy feel like she was falling, as if the lecture hall was tilting onto its side and stealing solid ground out from underneath her feet, but it didn't bring her any closer to success.

"This is a basic exchange of energy," Lanca told the classroom. "You're snatching a bit of raw power from the In-Between and converting it to light. Think of your body as a conduit, an electrical wire."

More silence, more rustling, then a high-pitched gasp broke the silence like a gunshot. Heads turned as a pinpoint of light blossomed in the corner of Amy's eyes.

Nora had done it first. The little girl stared in silent awe at the frosted bulb in her hand as it took on a shimmering, golden glow from within.

"That's it," Professor Lanca said, his voice barely above a whisper. "You're getting it."

Amy wasn't. Her bulb was as cold and dark as the crystal in her other hand, stubbornly lifeless. The harder she tried to force it to work, the more it bucked back against her, the power refusing to flow.

"You have to compartmentalize your mind."

She turned. Lanca had circled the lecture hall and returned to stand over her shoulder. He tapped his temple with a fingertip and flashed a roguish smile.

"The spell isn't fighting you," he said. "*You* are fighting you, because there's a part of your brain that says none of this is real. Slipping past that, accessing your subconscious directly, is what the mandala is for, but maybe we need to find you a different technique. Keep at it for now."

He started to walk away, then paused.

"I'll tell you a secret, Miss Nettle." He leaned closer, conspiratorial now. "This world wants to be filled with magic, and magic wants to fill the world. Every magician is a gateway. An open window to the In-Between. And that includes you, whether you believe it yet or not. Work with the current. Don't force it, don't wrestle it, *allow* it. Keep an open heart; that's where the real power is."

He moved on. She thought it over. Normally having an analytical mind whose gears never stopped turning was a good thing, but here it was tripping her up, making her second-guess her every move. Didn't mean she couldn't use logic to her advantage, though. She could work through the problem like it was a mathematical equation.

*Task at hand*, she thought, *slip past the parts of my brain that are getting in my way*. It felt like a stage magician performing a trick in the mirror: somehow, she had to fool herself. Impossible, but Nora's glowing bulb — and two others, lighting up across the lecture hall now, one after the other — said otherwise.

The rattling windows and the cold draft from the old, warped frames were a constant distraction, tugging Amy's attention away every time her bulb even threatened to ignite. *If I could be somewhere else*, she started to think. Then she caught herself. She could. She'd been doing it for years, a survival technique she'd learned to handle her father's drunken rages and her boss's wandering hands.

And just like that, for a moment, she was gone.

Her body sat in the lecture hall and her mind went to her old escape, her postcard picture vision of a California beach. She pictured the warm sand under her back, the ruffle of a hot breeze in her hair. Her anxiety and her fear of failure, her constant companions, stayed behind in the real world. She could split herself off, if only for a minute or two. She could be Elsewhere.

A connection sparked. A pulse flowed through her, from the core of her dark crystal and up her arm, flashing through her chest and striking her heart with a raw shock of lighting. It kept moving, down her other arm, her veins burning like gasoline.

The filament inside the frosted bulb sparked and flickered. Then it began to glow. Softly at first, a sunrise at dawn, then brighter as it warmed the lecture hall.

*I can do this*, Amy thought, staring at the light. *I can really do this.*

"Hey," Vail whispered, sitting at her side.

Amy turned. Vail's own bulb was glowing, soft and slightly pulsing, the light tinged with a faint golden glow.

"Twins," Vail said.

***

There were moments in everyone's life, Amy knew, when you crossed an invisible border and nothing would never be the same. The first time someone looks into your eyes and says "I love you" and you know they mean it. Your first heartbreak, and remembering what it feels like to be alone again. The moment she decided she was never going back to her father's trailer, and never going back to Holybrook.

And now...magic. The students walked through the halls of the Academy in stunned silence, some still clutching their bulbs — the spell long worn away, the filaments cold, but a reminder of what they'd just managed to achieve. They were united in a shared secret.

A shared power.

"Number one MVP right here," Dalton said, ruffling Nora's hair as they walked to the dining hall. "First one out of all of us to learn the trick. This kid's a natural."

The girl ducked her head, blushing furiously. On her other side, the broad-shouldered blond, Erik, stared into the amber depths of his own crystal focus.

"It's incredible," he said, to himself as much as to them. "If we can do that...then we can do *anything*. We could be like *gods*."

"We probably shouldn't get ahead of ourselves," Colin said, trailing behind the group.

"No, he's right." Olivia Renn, Amy's black-lipped new roommate, folded her arms and nodded in sharp agreement with Erik. Her eyes glittered with hunger. *Or greed*, Amy thought, but she knew she wasn't being kind. She was still irritated about Olivia's casual dismissal of Vail's pain last night. That said, under the circumstances, she couldn't blame anyone for acting weird.

Vail stayed close to Amy's side, craning her neck to look at the small crowd behind them. "Anyone seen Bahati?"

"I think she went exploring," Colin said.

Vail arched an eyebrow. "That thing we're not supposed to do?"

"And yet," the slight teenager said with a shrug. "And yet."

There were new faces in the dining hall. Pockets of students here and there, isolated in cliques. All in the school uniform, but with modifications. At one table, a pack of ten or so students wore ocean-blue ties instead of the first-years' school purple, along with matching scarves that they draped over shoulders or tossed, with casual care, around their throats. A few older-looking students, isolated at the farthest corner of the cavernous hall, bore glittering stickpins on their blazer lapels.

"Wardrobe change," Vail said. "You think every grade has a different look?"

Dalton looked around the room, taking more notice of the empty benches than the filled ones, and shook his head. "Where's everybody else? All the other students combined aren't much bigger than our class alone. And Old Man Orris said there's nobody up on the fourth floor. Like, at all."

"Maybe they stagger lunch schedules," Amy suggested. "My school used to do that."

Vail waved a hand at all the empty seats. "It's not like they're short on room."

Lunch, lined up along the serving window on plates that kept appearing, refreshed, every few minutes like clockwork, was a lightly toasted cheese sandwich and a fruit salad. At least, Amy assumed it was a fruit salad; the strangely colored, misshapen little nuggets sat in a pale syrup that smelled vaguely of pears. Tasted a bit like them, too, with an aftertaste like a slightly sour cherry. The cheese was almost familiar, but just a little too smooth, a little too eager to melt on her tongue, to resemble the kind she knew back home.

It tasted fine, though, and it would fill her up and fuel her for the afternoon's lessons. That was all she needed right now. That and some friends around her.

Bahati strode up to the table, leading a new face. The new face was dark, like Bahati's own, with sea-blue eyes that matched her necktie and the silk shawl she wore draped across her slender shoulders.

"Guess what?" Bahati said. "Made us a new buddy. Everyone, this is Anahera. She's going to tell us what's up. Turns out she's from my world."

"I had to pick my jaw off the floor." The new arrival's voice was breathy and her moves soft, like she was a cloud in the shape of a girl. "Do they know—"

"They know I'm amazing," the diva said, preening a bit. "That's all I ask, at least until they can hear my jams for themselves."

"I was told of your coming," the new arrival said to Amy. She didn't sit down with them so much as drift onto a bench, alighting like a feather. "I warned the headmistress you'd be arriving a day ahead of schedule. I'm glad I did, or you would have spent the whole night out in that courtyard. Probably catch a cold. Not good. Not optimal for learning. There were seven potential outcomes where you would have gotten sick."

"Back up," Amy said. "You were told of *our* coming, or *mine*? And who told you?"

Anahera answered with an enigmatic smile. Her eyes were glassy, swimming in and out of focus as if she was gazing into two worlds at the same time.

"Girl's a third-year student," Bahati said, giving Anahera the side-eye. "She sees things...a little differently. Anyway, sounds like we've got good news, bad news, and dangerous news. Which do you all want first?"

# Chapter Eight

"**B**ad news first," Amy said. She was overruled by Vail and Dalton, who blurted out their answers a split-second ahead of her.

"Good news first."

"Dangerous first," Dalton said.

Bahati waved her open palms, pressing them down against the table. "Okay, okay, we'll get into all of it. First thing I wanted to know about was the deal with the different uniforms. Don't look at me like that, I've got a passion for fashion."

Anahera was gazing at something a million miles away. It took her a few seconds to come back to reality. She flashed a shy smile at Bahati and addressed the table in a faint, breathy voice.

"As I told Bahati, after your first year — assuming you pass the final exam — you'll have the opportunity to join one of our school's septs. A sept is a..." She paused, frowning. Apparently the translation spell that let them all share a unified language had flaws here and there. "...it's like a camp? A camp at a learning-mount. Not something the school itself created, more like a...a club of like-minded students."

Amy furrowed her brow, trying to draw a line to her own experience and her own Earth.

"You mean, a sorority or a fraternity?"

Anahera's glassy eyes brightened. She nodded, enthusiastic.

"That sounds right. We have four: the septs of Coins, Cups, Staves, and Blades. It's my honor to represent the Sept of Cups. We are interested in knowing things, and seeing things. We see and we know."

At the end of the table, Erik and Olivia had become fast friends, comparing notes about the morning's class in hushed whispers. As Anahera spoke, Erik casually twirled one finger around his ear, then covered the gesture by scratching the back of his neck. Amy shot a hard look his way. He didn't even notice.

"You see the students with the brass medallions pinned to their blazers?" Anahera nodded to a neighboring table. The students there were boisterous, and most of them had modified their school uniforms in slight but chaotic ways, everything personalized. Most had eschewed the school-issued dress shoes in favor of well-worn boots, some caked in road dust. "Sept of Coins. They travel, venture, and blaze the trails. Good people. Just not our way."

"Always did want to travel," Vail murmured.

"So we can join any sept we want?" Dalton asked.

Anahera giggled. "No, no. You may *ask* to join. Normally we spend the first year scouting for the best prospects, and tap them after graduation with an offer. We only want the most perfect fits."

*Like you're scouting us right now*, Amy realized. Bahati hadn't "found" a new friend, Anahera had found all of them.

The Staves you won't often see in the great hall," Anahera said. "They keep their own counsel and dine apart from the rest."

"And the Blades?" Amy asked.

Anahera didn't respond, but began to count down under her breath, faintly whispering from five to one. On the last number, the dining hall doors swung wide.

"Don't make eye contact," she told them.

Amy still looked. The newcomers were a gang of eight students. A wolf pack, tight and lean and hungry. Their scarves and ties were two-toned like old heraldic banners: half dark metal, like brushed stainless steel, and half a checkerboard pattern of scarlet and black.

"Sept of Blades," Anahera breathed. "They *protect*."

That last word dripped with soft venom.

The leader of the pack was a girl of nineteen or so. Her snow-white hair was black at the ragged tips, as if she dipped it into an inkwell, and she had the thousand-yard stare of a hardened convict. She wrinkled her nose as she strode past the first-year students like she smelled something foul, but didn't say a word. A couple of her minions fanned out, beelining for the other cliques. Amy watched, her eyes narrowing, as students grudgingly slipped envelopes and folded letters into the Blades' open palms.

Dalton said what Amy was thinking: "Looks like a shakedown. What's up with that?"

"The white witch in front is Jellica Barnes," Anahera said, studiously staring in the opposite direction. "Do not speak to her. Do not look at her. You do not want her attention."

The snow-haired teenager imperiously snapped her fingers and pointed to the serving window. One of her hangers-on, a tall but slight girl wearing bottle-thick glasses and a dark lace choker around her pale throat, scurried over and began loading up her arms with trays for the entire group while Jellica and the other Blades took their seats.

Colin hunched low on his bench, as if he could make himself disappear with enough effort. He kept shooting fleeting glances at the new arrivals, then staring down at his lunch. "So, uh, what's their deal?"

"If you stay," Anahera said, "and I certainly hope you do, you will learn a great many things in these old halls. My friends in the Cups use magic to plumb the mysteries of the universe; the Coins walk across worlds. The Blades, on the other hand, are war-weavers. They are very good at hurting people. And they like hurting people. With the lack of staff and security around here, they've taken it upon themselves to enforce school discipline, which is largely an excuse to do whatever they like to whomever they choose."

"So...they do curses and stuff? I want to learn *that*," Erik said. Olivia nodded in firm agreement.

Amy held up a finger. "Hold on. They put all the jerks in school into one big club for jerks? That...doesn't make any sense. I have to think the faculty would do something about that."

"A fish rots from the head down," Anahera replied. "Most of the Blades are quite lovely people, if you catch them alone, but united they all dance to Jellica's tune. And honestly, we need them."

"Need them for what?" Dalton asked.

She didn't answer him.

It wasn't long before something strange started to happen. Little commotions from the other cliques, scattered across the great dining hall. The sounds of plates cracking, and veiled snickers from the Blades. Amy imagined the energy of the room shifting around her, turning erratic and fractured like winter ice.

*Wait a second*, she thought.

It wasn't her imagination. She *felt* the flow all around her, currents of magic riding invisible winds. It was as if her morning lesson had opened up a sixth sense she never knew she had before, a power dormant her entire life.

Distracted, she stabbed her fork at her fruit salad. The bowl slid sharply to the left, dodging.

"Your bowl is—" Colin started to point out.

"I'm aware," Amy said.

She tried again. The bowl zigzagged to escape, rattling across the dining table. Then it bounced, launched up like it was spring-loaded, flipped in the air, and spattered the table as it landed. More faint snickering. Amy turned. On the far side of the hall, Jellica was staring at her, the girl's eyes bright with eager malice.

"*Really?*" Vail said.

"Don't take the bait," Anahera breathed. "She's testing you."

"You can't expect us to just put up with that," Dalton fired back.

"I can and I do. For your own safety. Please."

"It's okay," Nora said. The little girl got up from the bench. "I'll bring you another one, Amy. I wanted to ask if I could get seconds anyway."

"Dang, girl," Bahati said. "Where are you putting all that food?"

Nora lifted one leg. Her uniform skirt fit her like a tent, dragging behind her.

"You just have to learn magic," Nora said. "I have to learn magic and get at least three inches taller."

Dalton had a question in his eyes, but he waited until Nora was out of earshot to ask.

"Tell us something," he said. "If this is a four-year school, why aren't there any fourth-year students?"

"Who told you that?" Anahera asked.

"Old Man Orris. He said there's nobody up on the fourth floor."

"Mr. Orris has a very good heart, but he is sometimes less than judicious with his choice of words. You don't need to worry about the fourth floor."

"Yeah, but—"

She cut him off. "Later this week, work assignments should open up. You'll find them posted in the foyer. The Academy operates on a skeleton crew, so they use students to help with cleaning, taking care of the grounds and whatnot. Purely optional, but if you think you can balance a little work with your studies, I highly suggest you take the opportunity."

"You're changing the subject," he said.

"Yes," Anahera replied. "I am. As I was saying, it's a good way to show school spirit, if you want an invitation to the Septs. Also a chance to see more of our fascinating little island. And most importantly..."

She reached into her blazer and drew out a small silver coin, holding it up for the new students to see. It was old and tarnished, like a piece of some ancient pirate treasure.

"...you do get paid. The Night Market comes through twice a year, bringing supplies for the Academy, and they set up shop outside the walls. You can find some really nice things there, and most of the merchants only take gems and precious metals. Paper money, not so much."

"Got a White Card with an unlimited balance in my pocket," Bahati muttered, "and I can't use it because my bank's on another planet."

Nora was returning with a pair of bowls, carrying them gingerly. In the corner of her eye, Amy saw Jellica move. Just a quick, furtive gesture from the back of the room, a twirl of her white-painted fingernails.

She didn't see the fall. She just heard it, a distressing *thump* as Nora hit the dining hall floor, tripping and landing face-first in a bowl of fruit salad.

Amy jumped up and ran over to her, Colin at her side, helping the little girl up while a chorus of giggles wafted over from the Blades' table. Dalton shot from his seat like a rocket and clenched his fists.

"Oh, *hell* no," Bahati said. Vail nodded in grim agreement, getting up from the table.

"Three dudes, five chicks," Dalton said, doing a head count. "I don't mind those odds, but I'm going to need a little help because I've got a rule about not hitting girls."

"Got your back," Vail growled.

"Stop," Anahera said. "Please. You're giving them exactly what they want."

"A good beating?" Vail pointed to Nora. Colin had found a napkin and was gently mopping the girl's face while Amy checked her elbows for a bruise. "She's *twelve*."

"Listen to me," Anahera said. "Jellica Barnes eats, sleeps, and dreams of war-magic. She does not take weekends off. She does not take holidays. And she has been under this roof, mastering her arts, day in and day out for years. She demands the same of her followers. This is not a fight you can win."

"So?" Dalton shrugged off his blazer and started to unbutton the cuffs of his shirt. "Where I come from, we call this a heart check. When somebody gets in your face, you have to throw down, win or lose, or everybody knows you're nothing but a little—"

He paused as Amy and Colin led Nora back to the table.

"—word I'm not going to say. Whatever, you get it."

"And if you start a brawl in the dining hall, you'll likely be expelled," Anahera said. "If you aren't crippled, or worse. Is that what you want?"

"*They* started it," Colin protested.

"Good luck proving that." Anahera pointed to her own blue-glass eyes. "Please trust me when I say there is no outcome here that ends in victory."

"So that's it?" Vail said. "We just have to take this garbage?"

"No," she said. "You have to learn. And grow strong."

# Chapter Nine

Anahera calmed everyone down — eventually, more or less — and the Blades turned their attention elsewhere. Dalton and Vail still wanted to go over and start throwing punches, but she convinced them to let the payback wait.

"At least take your first class with Professor Chalk," she told them. "His specialty is occult self-defense. Sit with him for a while and you'll understand what you're really up against."

"Lanca had us powering light bulbs," Olivia said, brandishing hers.

Anahera pursed her lips.

"Did he warn you about leaving the grounds? And the mermaids?"

"I thought he was kidding," Erik said.

"Not a joke. This is a small island in a vast ocean, and nothing in that water is natural or good. You know Professor Lanca is new here, yes?"

"He said we're his first class," Amy replied.

There was a curious glint in Anahera's glassy sea-blue eyes. She tilted her head, focusing on Amy, as if she could hear something no one else could. Amy's visions of magic winds grew stronger: she saw currents winding around the girl's body like a coil of smoke making its way up her spine.

"Did he tell you," she asked, choosing each word with delicate care, "what happened to his predecessor?"

They answered her with blank stares and shaking heads.

"He went for a midnight swim one night, and never came back," Anahera said. "One week later they hired Professor Lanca to take his place. Isn't that...curious?"

***

No lights burned in the lecture hall, a few doors down from the classroom they'd started the morning in. Only the overcast afternoon sun, straining through storm clouds and dusty windows, could push back the shadows. The first-year students found seats and waited in an uncertain silence.

"Still don't believe we have to put up with this," Vail grumbled, sitting next to Amy.

"Like being back at my old high school," Amy said. "We need to keep an eye on Nora, okay? Bullies are bullies. I don't know what their problem is, but you know they're going to keep going after her."

"Not while we're around." She gave Amy a sidelong glance. "Besides, I'm watching *you*."

"Me?"

"In case you've forgotten the magic dancing bowl of fruit salad, Nora wasn't the only one they went after. They targeted you first. And did you see the way Jellica was staring at you? Creepy as hell."

"I'm used to being a target," Amy said. "I can take it. Nora shouldn't have to."

Vail gave her a long, silent look.

The slow, steady rap of a cane heralded a new arrival. The professor was a tall man, dark, bald but sporting an immaculate goatee. Latex gloves sheathed his hands, and he walked with a slight hitch in his step. Amy would have guessed he was somewhere in his fifties, but he had the bright clear eyes of a twenty-year-old. Old hairline scars flecked his neck and one cheek.

His cane was a rod of ebony, capped in bronze on both tips. He turned to face the room, resting both hands on his cane, and surveyed the faces before him.

"So this is what I'm working with," he said. "Very well. I am Professor Abraham Chalk. I will spend the next few months teaching you the basics of occult self-defense. This is the most important class you will ever take. You will listen, you will learn, you will meet my expectations, or you will be expelled. I have never taught a class without making at least three expulsions by the year's end, and judging from the looks of you...you lot will not be the first to break that trend."

Somewhere behind Amy, Erik murmured, "Guy thinks he's a hard-ass."

Chalk's head snapped up, his eyes focused like a laser.

"Yes, Mister Anders. I am indeed a..." The professor curled his lips into a humorless rictus. "...*hard-ass*. Or, to put it in a more civilized way, I have exacting standards. The techniques I will teach you in this classroom are dangerous. You will learn methods that can maim and kill if mishandled, and I demand absolute respect for the weapons I'll be putting in your hands. I will not allow you to endanger yourselves, your classmates — or me, for that matter — with foolish behavior."

He paused, started to turn away, then looked back at Erik.

"That was your one strike, by the way. You only get one."

"Maim and kill?" Colin shifted nervously in his seat. "I don't want to hurt anybody."

"And yet there are people and forces who very much want to hurt you, Mr. Woodrue, a fact of which *you* are well aware. Magic is not an art for pacifists."

The professor took out an antique pocket watch, fixed to a golden chain slipped through the buttonhole of his coat, and checked the time. He nodded to himself and snapped the watch shut.

"Excellent timing. There's a demonstration I want you all to see. Out of your seats, and follow me. We're taking a field trip."

\*\*\*

The class emerged into the afternoon haze. A storm was on the horizon, the western sky a blot of darkness feeding the endless ocean with thunder and rain. Amy rubbed her arms under her school blazer. A chill hung in the air and brisk winds whistled through the copses of stout, ashen trees that surrounded the academy's courtyard.

A long gravel walk wrapped around the moldering stones of the great house, winding through dour, dying gardens and past a thick iron gate. Along the way they passed a granite statue posed atop a small burbling fountain. The statue was of an elderly woman in a cardigan and slacks, cradling a notebook and a pen close to her chest. No heroic pose, no grand gestures — she could have been anyone off the street. A simple inscription, stained rust-brown by the fountain water, read *Carolyn Saunders.*

"As in, the Saunders Academy?" Amy asked, staying as close to Professor Chalk as she dared. "Is she in charge here?"

Chalk's cane rapped along the path as he led the way. He answered without looking at her.

"No. She was a friend of one of our investors. She died, years ago, on some backwater parallel Earth. The sacrifice she made that night laid the foundations of the institution we are today. The name was a nod of respect."

"So who *is* in charge here?"

"You've met the headmistress," he said, striding along.

"Sure, but who does she answer to?"

"Miss Nettle," the professor replied, "at this moment in time there is one, and only one authority figure you need to worry about. Me. Focus up."

Their path ended at a clearing behind the manor house. They weren't alone: a good two dozen students were already gathered, all higher-years, some who Amy recognized from lunch and a handful of new faces as well. *No Jellica*, she thought, searching the crowd for the steel-and-checker heraldry of the Blades. *Good*.

At the heart of the gathering stood a fighting ring. At least, that was how it looked to Amy: it had five sides, a pentagon instead of the square boxing rings she knew from back home, and the "floor" was rich dark soil, packed and stamped down tight. Stout, rustic wooden pillars served as ring posts, linked by a trio of vines — dripping with autumnal leaves and clusters of fat berries — that wrapped around the arena.

"There are times," Professor Chalk announced, his deep voice turning heads, "when students encounter irreconcilable differences. This is where we settle those differences."

He nodded toward the wide-eyed pack behind him.

"I think the first-year students might benefit from this demonstration. Mr. Parr, Mr. Garcia, have you resolved your conflict?"

"We have not," called a gruff voice from the crowd.

"Very well. Into the ring with you."

Parr was a twitchy, feral kid, and Amy recognized him as one of Jellica's enforcers. His scarf glittered in the gloomy light as he clambered into the ring, hauling himself up and over the vine-ropes. Garcia was a new face, older, but he wore the same uniform the first-years did.

Vail watched, close on Amy's left. Amy suddenly noticed Anahera on her opposite side, standing just at her shoulder.

"Garcia should have joined us when we tapped him last year," Anahera said in her breathy, faint voice. "He said he didn't need a Sept, that he could do it all on his own."

"This will be a one-fall duel," Professor Chalk announced, raising his voice above the rustling, chilly wind. "The fight will proceed until one contestant submits or is rendered unable to continue. There will be no lethal techniques, no irreversible transformations, and all conjurations must remain inside the ring at all times."

Parr climbed up onto one of the ring posts, mugging for the crowd. Garcia stood dead still on his side of the arena, fists clenched, staring dead-eyed at his opponent.

"On my command, begin." Professor Chalk's latex-gloved hand shot into the air, a finger pointed to the stormy ocean skies. "*Fight.*"

Parr jumped from the post, launching into a backwards flip, and landed on his feet in the middle of the arena. The flashy move won a smattering of hoots from the crowd but almost cost him the fight: Garcia ran at him like a freight train, cocking one beefy fist back as he charged.

"Less showmanship and more efficiency, Mr. Parr," the professor called out.

A length of golden thread dropped from Parr's sleeve as he landed and his arm swung with the momentum from his flip, all in one smooth motion. Blue lightning crackled along the thread, and it lashed out like a whip. Garcia changed plans, threw up a forearm to protect his face from the lash, and spat a breathless incantation. A crystalline shield blossomed upon his forearm, then shattered under his rival's attack a second later, sending Garcia tumbling back across the arena's black-soil floor.

"Kinetic alchemy, Professor Chalk," Parr shouted back. He flashed a cocky grin. The professor leaned into his cane and grunted.

"Jerk club for jerks," Amy whispered to Vail.

She wasn't certain but just for a moment, in the corner of her eye, it looked like Professor Chalk quirked a tiny smile.

Garcia dropped to one knee, thrust his hands out with his palms turned to the stormy skies, and curled his fingers in a beckoning gesture as his lips moved in a furious, silent chant. The black soil of the arena floor boiled and burst. Green vines as thick as fists, lush and seething, fired up from the dirt and stood almost as tall as the two teenagers. They licked at the air, snapping, filling the space between the fighters. Garcia stood, motionless now, his eyes fixed on the Blade across the ring.

"Catch what he's doing?" Vail murmured, her breath ghosting across Amy's ear. "Parr has to run the gauntlet. Those vines are going to beat the hell out of him. Smart."

Amy saw. Not the strategy, like Vail, but the movement and the flow. Her focus crystal tingled in her clenched hand and sent sparks of static electricity kicking along the veins of her arm. Her senses were heightened, the world coated in a strange haze that was sharp but edged in fog. Every movement in the ring left neon outlines in Amy's vision, along with sparkling gemstone glitter-trails that traced the weave of Garcia's spell. She watched as Parr assessed the battle-field...and leaned back, pushing himself against the ropes. More glitter-trails followed him, a spray of rubies in Amy's eyes, but then the glitter went hard and packed tight; it formed lines and arrows, a lethal trajectory.

"You can *see*," Anahera hissed at Amy, her glassy eyes bright like the sun on winter ice.

Vail turned her head. "See what?"

She saw the spell Parr was casting. Before he finished casting it.

"He just won the fight," Amy said. The words came to her lips unbidden. She couldn't back it up, couldn't rationalize why she thought so. She just knew she was right, as if she'd stolen a flicker-fast snapshot of the next thirty seconds.

"No chance," Vail said.

"Watch."

# Chapter Ten

*K*inetic alchemy. That was the phrase Parr had used when he fueled his golden thread with the momentum from his opening
leap. Now Amy saw it all: he pushed himself back against the ropes,
straining, putting his entire back into it. As they hauled against him,
the opposing forces amplified one another, becoming a hard-packed
core of potential energy in the pit of Parr's stomach.

*And every action has an equal and opposite*— Amy started to think,
a vaguely-remembered snatch of her high school science class, before
that dense core of energy *burst*. Parr flew across the arena like a torpedo, legs blurring, dodging past the whipping vines as they snapped
helplessly in his wake. Garcia only had time enough for his eyes to go
wide before the Blade plowed into him at full speed, throwing a brutal
punch square into his chest. Garcia hit the dirt and Parr pounced on
him like a cat, flipping him onto his belly, and yanked one arm behind
his back. He gave Garcia's wrist a savage twist and pulled even harder,
straining his elbow to the breaking point while the teenager yowled in
pain.

Garcia's other hand hammered the black soil, tapping out. The
brass tip of Professor Chalk's cane came down with the sound of a
thunderclap.

"Match point goes to Mr. Parr, representing the Sept of Blades. Well done."

Amy glanced to her right to see Anahera's reaction. The older girl was already gone.

Parr stood over Garcia for a moment. Then he held out a hand. Garcia reluctantly took it, and the other boy hauled him to his feet.

"Grudge resolved?" the professor asked. He waited, holding a stern silence, until both of the fighters nodded. "Good. I expect it will stay that way. Any further disruptions from either of you and you'll be dealing with me directly. Mr. Garcia, see me after your classes today. I have notes on your performance."

*** 

*Is anyone else seeing the magic winds? The glitter-trails?*

Amy asked the question in her head as they filed back into the unlit classroom, fresh from the demonstration outside. A cold rain started to drizzle down, flecking the dusty windows along one wall and casting deeper shadows across the lecture hall.

"I do."

Amy started. Nora was staring at her, her small face grim.

"I see them too," she said.

"What you witnessed today," Professor Chalk said, "was an example of the abilities you'll command by your third year of studies. If you make it that far."

Nobody missed the look he shot at Erik. Except maybe Erik, who was more interested in Olivia's chest. Colin held up a hand, waiting silently until Chalk acknowledged him.

"That...thing with the vines growing really fast," he said. "Will we learn how to do that?"

"I think your particular interests will be better served in Professor Mallory's class. And the answer is perhaps, but not this year. Your first-year studies will be entirely centered around self-defense. Once you learn to protect yourself, you can learn to protect others. Once you learn how to protect others, *then* I will teach you how to fight."

The professor walked along the aisles, slapping a book down on every desk, casting an eagle-sharp glance at each student before moving to the next. At Amy's seat, the book came down hard enough to make her jump in her chair. It was small but thick, with a hand-sewn cover in onyx black. A sigil in gold leaf, swirling like a vortex, adorned one corner of the cover along with the title, *Liber Scutum*.

He held her gaze just a second longer than the others. Then he moved on.

"I do assume you can all count," he said, "so please open your texts to page twelve. If you cannot count, fake it. I can only endure so much disappointment in a single day."

Amy opened the cover and leafed through the old, yellowed pages. The spellbook smelled of musty libraries and secrets. A single diagram dominated the entirety of page twelve and just looking at it made her eyes water. Two concentric circles nestled inside of a triangle, each shape ringed by squirmy, scratchy runes that made Amy think of animal claws.

"This is a basic layered circle of protection," Chalk explained as pages riffled across the gloomy classroom. "Obviously not something you'd ever use in a pinch, given its complexity, but we can break it down into pieces and explore the foundations of shielding-magic together. You may have noticed Mr. Garcia manifesting a shield during his duel; that's a more advanced technique, and it builds upon this one."

The last book handed out, he returned to the head of the class.

"Over the next month, we will focus exclusively on this method of protection, so that you can learn how each piece works and why. This will culminate in your first exam: I expect each and every one of you to construct your own circle of protection and power it appropriately."

Olivia held up her hand. "How will we know if it works?"

Professor Chalk's lips pursed in the faintest ghost of a smile.

"I will be testing your circle's effectiveness myself. While you are standing in it. If anyone doesn't think themselves up for the task, I'll be happy to show you the way to the Arch of Resignation. Anyone leaving? Not yet?" He paused, expectant. "Good. When next we meet, I expect each of you to have read the preface along with pages eight through twenty-three. Also, commit the correspondence chart at the beginning of chapter two to memory. You will be quizzed on this."

***

Dinner was slices of credible turkey, a sauce that tasted like someone's vaguely-remembered description of a cranberry, and bright, waxy beans that popped, hollow and wet inside, between Amy's teeth. Most of the upper-year students were absent, off on their own strange errands, and the Blades didn't put in a second appearance.

Later, as the night swept in and the hours stretched into silence, Amy curled up in her bed and studied by lamplight. A cold rain rattled the dormitory windows, transmuting the panes into glistening black mirrors. She barely heard the rolling thunder or the scratching of wild branches against the wall behind her head, too engrossed in the old, brittle pages of the *Liber Scutum*.

It was a puzzle, of a sort.

Diagrams referred to other diagrams before circling back again, like an ouroboros of many parts: a snake eating its own tail, but sectioned off and connected only by trails of symbol and thought. The simplest parts of the spell had been walled off behind bricks of metaphor. Amy hunted along the word-mortar, feeling for a crack, a seam, anything to dig her fingers in and grab onto a bit of understanding.

Later, the lamps doused, she lay restless, staring at the ceiling in the dark. Bahati was long asleep, snoring, and Nora was a tiny lump swallowed by her blankets. Olivia was buried under her covers too, but the little swaying glow of a penlight said she was even more driven than Amy to figure things out.

Then there was Vail.

"You up?" Amy whispered.

Rhetorical question. Vail had been tossing and turning for an hour now. She rolled onto her side in the neighboring bed, facing Amy in the darkness.

"You okay?" Amy said. "You barely touched dinner."

"Stomach lining's all raw. Having a hard time keeping anything down."

Made sense. Vail's body only wanted one thing, Amy figured, and it wasn't food.

"Hanging in there?"

"Don't worry about me."

"Hey," Amy said. Their eyes met in the gloom. "The real answer."

The freckled redhead shrugged, shifting on her pillow.

"Better than last night by a country mile. But there's layers to this stuff. First it grabs onto your body. Teaches your brain that it *needs* the junk. But then you fight your way past the need, and break through, and..."

Vail rolled onto her back.

"...and then you're left *wanting* the junk, craving it, and that's its own new flavor of pain. It helps that I'm literally a world away from my supply, but if someone walked up to me right here, right now, and put a needle in my hand—"

"That's not going to happen." *I won't let that happen.*

"—or a year from now? Two years, five years, ten? Am I going to be fighting this monster for the rest of my life? Amy...I'm not that tough."

"You're tougher than I am. You and Dalton were ready to throw down with Jellica and her whole gang at lunch."

Vail twitched her nose. "That's just a matter of principle. But who am I kidding? You started reading Chalk's textbook, right? Does it make any sense? At all? And this is supposed to be the simple stuff. I'm going to get expelled."

"Okay, first of all, Professor Chalk is trying to intimidate us."

"He's good at it."

"But we have a month before the test," Amy said. "I'm not giving up, and neither are you. We'll work together, okay?"

They fell into shared silence. Lightning flashed outside the dorm windows, casting a shadow across the old floorboards, turning beds and coatracks into misshapen beasts.

"Because," Amy said, reluctantly finishing her thought, "I can't go back to my world. I'm dead if I go back. And I think you're in the same boat."

Vail didn't answer right away. She gathered her thoughts in the dark.

"The thing about Ink," she said. "The thing about Ink is, it makes you feel...connected. No matter how alone you feel, suddenly you're joined at the heart and soul with everyone else who takes it. You're floating, part of this big, warm hive-mind, and everything is going to be all right. Once you get used to that feeling, it hurts to go without. Like part of you has been carved away, left all raw and bleeding and gone."

She paused.

"Of course, it's all a lie. Never trust the needle."

"Well, I can't compete with a warm fuzzy illusory hive-mind," Amy said.

Her arm flopped over the side of the bed. She stretched her hand out to Vail, in the space between them.

"How about a real connection, instead?"

Vail's hand found Amy's in the dark, and gave it a squeeze.

"That sounds like a plan," Vail said.

# Chapter Eleven

There was a crow on Amy's chest.

She opened her eyes, feeling a strange scrabbling sensation along her bedsheets. The fat, glossy crow perched on top of her, leaning close, garnet eyes glinting as it tilted its head.

"Please don't," she said.

The crow erupted in a wing-fluttering, ear-splitting *caw*. Another dozen or so crows lined the open windows, and they joined in, screeching to the heavens as a frigid morning wind whipped through the dormitory and ruffled the blankets.

"Why is it so cold in..." Olivia sat up, rubbing her eyes. "Who keeps opening the windows?"

"Our wakeup service," Bahati moaned, pulling a pillow over her face.

"They can't open windows, they're birds."

Amy gently nudged the leader of the band. He pecked at her hand, irritated, until he finally hopped to one side and allowed her to pull the covers back.

"Try telling this one he can't do anything he wants to do," she said. "And good luck with that."

"Ladies?" Mr. Orris's voice sounded from outside the dorm-room door, accompanied by a soft knock. "Morning bells are still broken, so—"

"We have our own, thanks," Vail called back.

The glossy crow chased Amy from the showers to the dining hall, unrelenting until she bought him off with a chunk of blueberry muffin.

Amy noticed a few extra empty spaces. A couple of missing faces at the edges of the breakfast table, people she'd noticed yesterday but hadn't had the chance to meet yet. Of course, Bahati had the details.

"Want tea with your breakfast?" she said. "That kid with the scraggly baby-mustache headed straight for the Arch of Resignation after Chalk's class yesterday. Meanwhile, did you meet Korine? Doesn't matter: she got caught snooping around upstairs last night, and now she's gone."

"They expelled her?" Colin asked, popping a crumbly bit of muffin into his mouth.

"Just like that," Bahati replied. "They're not messing around. Anahera says they loosen up on the rules about a month in, once they figure out who's going to stick around for the long haul."

"So after we get to draw a circle on the ground," Dalton said, "and trust that it's magical enough to stand in it while Professor Chalk throws knives at us. Not the weirdest thing I've ever done, but it definitely makes the top five."

Colin gave him a nervous look. "You don't think he's really going to use knives, do you?"

"Nah. He'll probably throw snakes at us. Venomous snakes." Dalton paused. "Or maybe bears."

"You can't throw bears," Nora said, with the full and unflappable confidence only a twelve-year-old can possess.

"After the stuff we saw and did yesterday," Dalton said, "I'm keeping a more open mind than usual."

"You're going to be eating our dust." Erik smirked at the end of the table, all swagger. Olivia sat next to him, closer than yesterday, and she flashed a black-lipped smile.

"Do tell," Dalton said.

"We jumped ahead in the assigned reading last night," Olivia said, talking over Erik as he started to reply. "Chapter three is filled with techniques to make your circle stronger."

"But we're still in chapter one," Amy countered.

"*You* are."

"The chapter with all the safety techniques. And the bits that it says you need to never, ever skip."

"Surprising," Olivia said.

Amy narrowed her eyes. "What is?"

"Thought you'd be eager for some extra credit. I mean, you just seemed like the overachieving teacher's pet type."

*I am*, Amy almost angrily fired back. Then she realized that wouldn't be the defiant flex she hoped.

"I want to do things the right way," she said. "This stuff is dangerous. It deserves respect."

"It deserves to be *understood*," Olivia said. "I don't get you. A whole world of magic at our fingertips, and you want training wheels."

"Just until I learn how to ride," Amy said.

\*\*\*

"Hope you're ready to work some of that food off," Mr. Orris said, leading a gaggle of students out into the pale morning light. "Got a bit of a hike ahead of us. Professor Mallory prefers to keep to herself."

"A hermit," Dalton mused. "Great quality for a teacher."

"It's not that. Well, not just that. The Academy's got wards on top of wards, just in case a nasty so-and-so comes a-knockin'. The professor says the protective spells muddy up her experiments. Something about the different flavors of energy not playing nice together."

The courtyard gate whistled wide, opening the way onto the wilds of Firebreak Island.

Stout wooly pines, tall and proud, forested the land all the way to the west, where hazy sunlight sparkled silver against the endless ocean waters. The crisp air smelled of sea salt and pine needles. Amy's breath licked the air with a curlicue of frost, and stiff, frozen grass crackled under her footsteps.

At least there was a path to follow, more or less, well-trampled but weedy, winding down between the trees. Rough-hewn wooden posts marked the way every twenty feet or so, each post carefully positioned within sight of its neighbors to keep travelers from getting lost.

"I'll lead you down and back the first few times," Orris told the students, "but eventually you'll have to hoof it without me. Just stay on the path, keep in sight of the markers, and you'll never go wrong. And always get back to the Academy before sundown."

"Do we need to worry about 'nasty so-and-sos'?" Vail asked.

"By day, I'm more worried about the local wildlife," Orris said. "Damn fool student nearly lost a hand last year. Thought he could pet a bobcat."

"And after dark?" Amy asked.

"The nice thing about following the rules, you'll find, is that it sharply reduces the number of things you need to worry about in life. And you won't ever be out after nightfall, will you?"

She knew a rhetorical question when she heard one. She kept walking.

A leaning wrought-iron fence, barely clinging to the muddy soil, encircled a garden. The air smelled of violets and sickly-sweet sap, fat flies buzzing, and the black arch of the fence crested above the gate with an unmissable symbol: a skull and crossbones, suspended in the chiseled outline of a potion vial.

"Professor's private garden," Mr. Orris explained in passing. "Never set foot in there without permission and an escort."

"Why's that?" Olivia asked, leaning close to the fence and craning her neck to see.

A chipmunk streaked along the garden path, fleeing in a mad panic from something in the bushes. It shot toward the fence, dashing blind. Then tendrils whipped from the side of the path, the undergrowth bursting open and flashing jagged teeth set into a mound of matted rot. The thin vines snared the chipmunk, hauling it off the path and out of sight faster than Amy could blink, leaving only the echo of a strangled squeak behind.

The garden belched. Rodent bones, stripped to the ivory, spat across the path and rolled like dice.

"Because everything in there'll kill you stone dead," Orris replied. He kept moving, seeing no need to elaborate.

Spiders flourished in the verdant wood. Webs stretched from tree to tree, frost-touched and glistening with frozen drops of morning dew. Ahead, through the trees, old crumbling buildings loomed. There was a greenhouse, or the broken shell of one, the glass shattered and boarded over with rotten planks. And beyond it, linked by the overgrown shadow of a spiral path, was the hut.

It didn't stand so much as squat, slouching, the tilt of its rotting shingles resembling the bend of a peaked hat. Like the fallen greenhouse, all its windows were plastered over with worm-eaten planks of wood, hammered into place with rusty spikes. Dragonflies flitted in the matted, overgrown grass, one humming past Amy's ear as she batted at it.

Orris knocked on the hut's door. It rattled, the wood cheap and splintered, under his weathered knuckles.

"Come in, come in!" called a voice from inside. "We're late as it is."

Orris pulled the door wide and gestured to the students to enter. Amy couldn't miss that he was pointedly staying outside.

She held her breath and walked in. Amy passed beneath an overhang and a patch of thick shadow — and then emerged into light. On the outside, Professor Mallory's hut was a sagging corpse of dead wood and rot. Inside, it was made of glass. Sunshine streamed in through the octagonal crystalline walls and the dome of the roof, flooding the place with light and warmth and feeding the lush, vibrant plants that overflowed a clutter of tables and shelves. Vines clung to the one-sided windows, coiling up across bookcases, snaking around burners and alchemical devices, all while birds with vivid rainbow plumes took fluttering wing overhead. A parrot, crested with the orange of a simmering flame, perched on the edge of a workbench and screeched a greeting.

"In, in, keep it moving, room for everyone," said the welcoming voice. "Let's get a good look at you."

Professor Mallory looked to Amy like she'd stepped out of time somewhere in the Sixties. She wore a hand-woven caftan bound with a sash, strands of lacquered wooden beads, and a headband to keep her hair — long, stringy, and gleaming silver — out of her sharp blue eyes. Her feet were bare, caked in black soil that matched the gardening stains on her fingertips. She smelled faintly of sweet patchouli oil.

"Well," she said, "I told them to send me a batch of promising students, and they performed above and beyond my expectations. I hope you'll all perform above my expectations, too. I'm Professor Mallory, and this is your introduction to the foundations of natural magic. There are worlds for us to explore out there, and while this must all seem fantastic at the moment, I promise you: reality is far stranger than you think. Stick with me and I'll show you some things."

# Chapter Twelve

"Let's begin with a question," Professor Mallory said. "Nature. What is it?"

The students sat on the earthen floor, cradling their focus crystals in their laps as they looked up at the professor. She strolled around the hut as she held court, rainbow-plumed birds fluttering past her. Even the plants and vines responded to her presence, potted wildflowers lifting their petals as she drifted past.

"Trees?" Colin said.

"Trees, growth, yes, and?"

Vail shrugged. "Animals?"

"And? Keep going."

"Healthy food," Olivia piped up.

Something glinted in the professor's sharp eyes. "Healthy. Interesting. Expand on that."

"Well, like...organic food. It's organic, so you know it's good for you."

The professor paused at a cluttered table, her hand slipping between coiled vines to pick up a tiny vial. It was a faceted globe of stained glass, glittering like a blood-wet stone, and it cradled a few drops of some dark, syrupy liquid inside.

"This is an extract of cyanide from my garden. Perfectly organic. Would you like some in your afternoon tea?"

"I...don't think so," Olivia said.

"Indeed. But this nasty little substance has a number of positive uses, from industry to medicine, so long as you employ it correctly. Nature is not good, or evil. Nature is a *quality*. A quality, I should stress, that cares nothing for human notions of ethics. Or cares for humans much at all, really."

The vial caught the sunlight, glistening. She set it back on the table.

"But the seed of every world in the multiverse is an act of pure creation. A moment of concentrated divine power, creating a tether to the In-Between. And this, handily for our purposes, is how natural things take on magical properties. This is why, to draw a couple of random examples, blue-spiral stones are handy for psychic defense, and the powdered root of a hensprig plant can soothe nightmares. Or consider those focus crystals you're all holding: they were chosen specially for their power to heighten your magical consciousness. None of these things will do the magic for you, that's your job, but they can give you the boost you need...or paper over a gap in skill."

Amy raised her hand. Professor Mallory acknowledged her with a glance.

"But if every world is a little different, do those properties match up? Is a rose a rose wherever you go?"

"And by any other name would smell as sweet," the professor said. "But only the smell is the same. Objects with magical properties take on the tone and timbre of the world they came from. The most ancient earths are full to bursting with occult potential, while newer and half-formed worlds might struggle to produce a spark. And how do we know? Research, experimentation, and more research."

She stroked a sagging flower's petals. The flower raised up on its stalk, lifting its head, petals unfurling and reaching for the sunlight.

"Some say that nature encompasses what *is*, while magic is an expression of intervention and transformation. Magic is the reality we *impose*, by force. And if imposing your force upon the universe is what gets your engine revving, I suppose it's a workable analogy, but I prefer a harmonious partnership with my surroundings. I'm going to teach you ways of working with natural forces, hand in hand. I think you'll find it makes for a much smoother and far more effective ride. Now I'd like to show you a little trick. Let's go outside."

***

Amy's nose itched.

*Stop. Deep breath. Back to the beginning.*

Eyes gently closed, she sat in the tall grass and let the sunlight glow against her face. The crisp breeze felt like a cold silk scarf trailing along her arms. She mentally whispered the mantra she'd been given, sinking into a meditative trance. She thought about how people back home must have noticed she was missing by now, and she wondered how her father would react. Or if he would care.

*Stop. Deep breath. Back to the beginning. I'm never going to get this.*

"Be kind to yourself," Professor Mallory told the students gathered in the forest clearing outside her illusion-cloaked hut. "Meditation is hard work. Your thoughts will drift: this is normal, this is fine. Breathe and begin again."

Amy's newly awakened senses struggled with her restlessness. She wanted to be thinking, moving, doing, not sitting in the grass and repeating nonsense words while dragonflies buzzed past her ears—

*Stop. Deep breath. Back to the beginning.*

"You've learned how to call unformed power from the In-Between," the professor said. "Grounding is very similar, except you're going to draw in the physical energy of the world beneath you. Think of it as...getting a taste of your environment, like a snake licking the air."

Amy reached out, downwards, one hand pressed to the dew-damp grass and the other clutching her focusing crystal as it tingled against her palm. Something in her mind jiggled, like a piece of loose glass in the corner of a broken window, and tumbled free. It fell and she plunged with it, down into stone and soil, bramble and root, the cold and wet and dark.

She was in two places at once: sitting cross-legged in the grass under a hazy sun, and hidden, snug, deep beneath the world. She sensed water. It ran along her thought-body's skin in icy trickles, carrying black dirt and a brackish, stale odor.

She wasn't alone down here.

Something moved on the edges of her perception. Something in the water. Amy sensed blubber and rot, some vast dead thing decaying on the ocean floor. She pushed her newborn senses toward it.

It opened one baleful yellow eye and stared back at her. Down in the crushing, drowning dark, a tentacle unfurled.

Amy's eyes snapped open. She patted the wet grass with her hand, tilted her head back and inhaled the cold wind, anything to remind herself that she was back in her body. Professor Mallory dropped onto the grass beside her, stretching her legs and flexing her muddy toes.

"Saw it, huh?" the professor whispered.

"What was that?" Amy hissed. "And how do you know what I saw?"

Mallory pointed to her wizened eyes. "All in the look, kid. When somebody meets the Corpse for the first time, it shows."

She gestured, inviting Amy to look around. Her fellow students seemed like they were still in the "try, fail and repeat" stage of meditation, silently mouthing their mantras.

"It's not a corpse," Amy whispered. "It's alive down there."

The professor shared an impish smile. "I know."

"It *looked* at me."

Her smile vanished. "That... I did not know. You're sure?"

"Big eye." Amy stretched a hand over her head, pantomiming. "Real big."

Mallory eased over in the grass, sitting in front of her. She took Amy's hands in her own.

"All right. Listen to me. You are not to repeat the grounding exercise until I say otherwise. Not under any circumstances, understood?"

"The...totally safe grounding exercise?"

"It's safe for them," the professor said, nodding to the other students. "You're going to need a modified curriculum. You're a very bright girl, Amy."

"I mean, I did get straight A's in my old high school..."

"No. You're a *bright* girl." Mallory made ripples in the air with her fingers. "Like a light bulb. Or apparently, more like a spotlight. We have to work on that."

"Oh. What is that thing, anyway?"

"The Corpse? It was here long before we arrived. The founders of the Academy didn't create this world; it was built by ancient hands, long dead and gone, and we adapted it to suit our needs. There's an entire laboratory down on the ocean floor, but it's flooded out and we can't get to it. Not that there's anything worth having from that place. My personal theory is that they *made* the Corpse, along with all the other horrors in that ocean."

"What happened to them? The people, I mean."

Mallory let out a tiny chuckle. "I suspect they learned not to screw with Mother Nature. Of course, again...just my theory."

***

At the session's end, most of the students hadn't gotten much farther than the starting line. A couple had fallen asleep, snoring softly in the forest clearing until Professor Mallory clapped her hands sharply above their heads.

"Personal experience is half of mastering natural magic," she said. "The other half is research. Cracking the books and studying what other, more experienced magicians have already learned will save you time, trouble, tears, and blood."

Vail leaned close to Amy and whispered in her ear. "Did that meditation do anything for you at all? Didn't work for me."

"It worked," Amy whispered back. "Kinda wish it didn't."

"Let's find you a challenge." The professor paused, deciding the assignment on the spot. "I fear I might be coming down with a headache. Sooner rather than later. So for our next class I want you all to research a natural curative for me: a headache cure that grows and can be cultivated in this exact island climate. All the information you need can be found in the school library, and just so you know, I do give extra credit for creative solutions. Feel free to work together — but you'll pass or fail together accordingly. Happy hunting, kids."

# Chapter Thirteen

A my's first refuge on dark and stormy days had been her local library. The one in Holybrook was cramped and money-starved and used to be a Pizza Hut, but she loved it just the same, spending endless hours haunting the stacks and learning about whatever random slice of the world caught her eye. The library was her sanctuary, a place to take shelter when it was too dangerous to be at home.

Upon her first look at the Academy's library, though, she realized what she'd been missing her entire life. *This* was home now.

Shelves stretched to the vaulted ceilings on both sides of the long, baroque gallery, crammed with dusty hardcover books and peppered with rolling ladders. Study tables and private carrels lined the heart of the chamber, flanked on both sides by a sprawling maze of bookshelves. Violet lights licked and burned under globes of frosted glass, casting long, shifting purple shadows across the parquet floor.

The faint, clean scent of sandalwood incense hung in the air. This place was a temple. Amy's words escaped in a faint, reverent whisper.

"Let's find somebody in charge. Maybe they can point us in the right direction."

"No computers," Vail noticed, walking in at Amy's side. "Guess they're keeping it old school."

No computers, but Amy couldn't miss the film projector perched on a polished wooden platform behind the empty front desk. It was a brass-hulled antique, dull and unpolished, with a fat film reel loaded and ready to play...to nothing, and for no one. There wasn't a screen in sight, and the projector was aimed at the library itself instead of a nearby wall. She approached the desk, curious.

The film reel clacked, and the projector spun to life. Amy threw a hand over her eyes as a beam of hot light sizzled from the projector's lens. And now, standing on the other side of the desk, was a prim-looking woman.

She was encompassed by the projector's light, her body translucent in parts, as if she had been born from celluloid and dreams. She wore a bonnet and a Victorian dress with a tight-laced corset and wide, flared skirts, and she greeted Amy and Vail with a pleasant nod.

"Ah, new faces. Welcome! I am Adelaide Constance Tiptree, your librarian in residence. How can I help you today?"

"You're, um—" Amy pointed to the film projector.

"*Inconvenienced*," Adelaide replied with a chipper smile.

"Are you a ghost?" Vail asked.

"I prefer the term *un-dead*," the librarian said. "I had a bit of a mishap that separated me from my physical body."

Amy looked to the projector. "So you...live in there now?"

"And to think, some people dream of a life in the movies." Adelaide shrugged, cheerful but resigned. "I can't really leave the library, but my goodness. I've barely read half of these books and once I finally reach the end it'll be the perfect time for seconds. Why would I want to go anywhere else?"

*She has a point*, Amy thought.

"We need a book," she said. "For our natural magic class."

Adelaide's ghostly eyes gleamed with an impish look as they flickered in the projector's light.

"Professor Mallory always issues the most interesting trials. Some of your fellow students are already on the hunt." She gestured to the study tables, where Colin and Dalton huddled over a hefty tome, pointing at paragraphs and debating in low whispers. Other students, most of whom they hadn't met yet, drifted in and out of the labyrinth of shelves with books piled in their arms. "I suggest you start by getting familiar with our card catalog. I will be happy to help you find any book you need...except for one."

"Which one?" Vail asked.

"You'll know," the librarian said. She folded her hands gracefully on the desk.

Nora stood by the card catalog, a long wooden antique filled with dozens of drawers, each one marked with a yellowed, typewritten label. The little girl waved.

"Did you see it?" Nora asked in a low, curious voice.

"See what?" Vail asked.

Amy just nodded. She knew what the precocious budding magician meant: the Corpse. A sudden concern latched onto her.

"It didn't see *you*, did it?"

Nora shook her head. "Sometimes being small and quiet has its advantages. Professor Mallory told me not to do it again, though. Have you used the card catalog yet?"

"No, but my old library back home had one before they put everything online."

"Probably not like this one."

Nora proceeded to demonstrate, pulling open a drawer and rifling through rows of meticulously organized index cards. Each card bore a book and its author in mismatched, jagged type. Most of them were coffee-stained, dog-eared, or faded with age. Nora plucked out the card she was looking for and rapped it, three quick taps, on the antique wood.

A pair of fireflies flitted from the open drawer, taking flight. They danced in the air in front of Nora's face, their abdomens glowing in a warm, soft welcome. Then the lightning bugs began to drift away in lazy spirals, leading the girl along.

"They show you where to find your book," Nora explained, starting to walk along with the glowing insects. "Except for the one."

"Which one?" Amy said.

"You'll know."

The fireflies led her away. Vail rubbed the back of her neck, her expression harder than usual.

"Starting to feel like a mushroom here."

Amy asked a question with her eyes.

"Feeling like I'm being kept in the dark and fed a whole bunch of—" Vail took a breath. "I'm trying not to get panicky, but we've got one month to build a cast-iron circle of protection for the scariest teacher I've ever met, and I can...make a light bulb slightly glow if I try really hard. You and Nora are *good* at this."

"I'm a long way from being good at anything," Amy said.

"Not true. And at least you can focus." Vail stared down at her own hand, like she could see something there. "Got ants crawling inside of me. You can't imagine how badly I want to get high right now. The Ink always made my problems go away for a while, you know? Like getting wrapped in a nice warm blanket. Course, it didn't solve anything, not really. Just me kicking the can down the road and killing myself in slow motion. I can see that now. The nasty trick of it all is that I can see it's poison, I know it's poison...and I still *want* it."

Amy took hold of Vail's arm. She gave it a gentle squeeze.

"Every day you stay clean is going to get a little easier. You're through the worst of it." She had read that somewhere once. She hoped it was true. "And I'll get you through the rest. Neither one of us is getting sent home. Hey, how about we polish off Professor Mallory's homework first? It shouldn't be too hard, and then we can compare notes and see where we're at on the magic circle?"

They set out on the hunt. *Good old Dewey Decimal System*, Amy thought, thrilled at being in her element. *I guess some things really do stay the same, even on different planets*. She played a hunch and when it paid off, a wide grin spread across her face.

"Oh, too easy," she said. "She really threw us a softball for our first lesson."

"Whatcha find?" Vail asked.

Amy tugged a card from the drawer, turned it in her fingertips, and showed it to her.

"*An Examination of Curative Flora Native to Firebreak Island*, a monograph by Professor Josephine Mallory," she read aloud. "She literally wrote the book on this place. The herb we need has to be in here."

She mimicked Nora's earlier move, tapping the card three times. But this time, drawers jolted open all along the card catalog and a sudden swarm of lightning bugs took to the air, flowing and swirling like a marching band taking the field. They flashed their abdomens at the same moment, their bodies spelling out an unmistakable message.

*NICE TRY.*

"Oh," Vail said. "That's the one book."

"And now we know."

The swarm dispersed, fireflies hopping back into their nests, card drawers rumbling shut as if shoved by invisible hands.

\*\*\*

"So what changed?" Amy asked.

They were lost in the maze of twisting, bending library shelves, somehow bigger on the inside than it looked from the outside. A firefly danced along, leading them on a slow chase, its body flaring with amber light.

"How do you mean?" Vail replied.

"Yesterday, you were able to do the Lamp Without Oil trick, just like me. But today you stalled out in Mallory's class. Is it just the meditation thing? Because I'm not good at it either, but with practice—"

Vail pursed her lips, thinking as she browsed the towering stacks.

"No. And she didn't mean it, but something she said just landed wrong with me. The whole grounding thing, tasting the physical world, bringing it inside you."

"But you already did that once in Professor Lanca's class."

"That was just energy-stuff from the In-Between," Vail said. "Abstract. And I wasn't really clear enough to overthink it. Now I'm thinking."

"Is it the danger that's putting you off?"

"No. The idea of it. Bringing the world inside of me."

Vail's fingertip trailed along a row of hardcover spines, their titles worn away. Her next words were almost too soft to hear, as she turned her face from Amy.

"I don't want anything inside of me," Vail said.

They browsed the stacks in silence for a bit. Exploring, close.

"Hey," Amy said. "Day one, you passed the light bulb test, same as me. You can do this: we know you can. Do you think...maybe it's a trust thing? The magic seems to flow a lot easier when you move with the current. If you're uncomfortable, that's probably tripping you up."

"I'm fighting it," Vail said with a sigh. "I know. Trust is not something I'm good at."

"Disagree," Amy said.

Vail lifted an eyebrow. "Oh?"

"You trust me, don't you?"

Vail stared at her for a long, quiet moment.

"I do," she said.

Amy moved closer to her, closing the gap between them.

"If you can let me in," Amy said, "you can let the magic in. And I'm the queen of overthinking things. We'll figure this out together."

# Chapter Fourteen

A my laid out her plan over dinner. Practice.

"We're all on the same deadline," she said, "and we've got one month to crack Professor Chalk's challenge or we're out the door. I don't know about you, but I'm not leaving."

"Whatever you're thinking, I'm down," Bahati said.

Sitting next to her, Dalton chewed thoughtfully on a mouthful of potato stew, the sauce thick with sliced mushrooms in an odd, cheesy gravy.

"I don't get it," he told her, swallowing. "Most of us either *can't* leave, or at the very least our prospects back home don't look so hot. But you're rich and famous."

"Not all it's cracked up to be," she said. Her tone was light. Too light, even flippant, and she changed the subject before Amy could get a question out.

The question stayed with her, growing along with her suspicions. After dinner, she watched for her opportunity and caught Bahati alone in the hallway outside their dorm room.

"Dalton wasn't wrong," Amy said, her voice soft. "If I get sent back home, I'm screwed on more levels than I can count. Dalton's got warrants out for his arrest, and he doesn't talk about it much, but we all know Colin's got some really lousy parents. Then there's Vail. She says she'll die before she goes back, and I believe her."

"The way she looked on that first night?" Bahati shook her head, her eyes tinged with anger. "I don't blame her."

"Everyone thinks you're the odd student out." Amy paused. "Everyone but me."

Bahati stared at her for a long, quiet moment.

"Just between you and me," Bahati said.

"Of course."

"You remember Anahera, from yesterday."

"Sure," Amy said. "With the Sept of Cups. She's from your world."

"But she's been here for a few years. Out of touch. Incommunicado with the home front."

Amy tilted her head, leaning closer.

"What happened, between then and now? This isn't just about you. There's something you don't want Anahera to know about."

Bahati glanced behind her. Turning back, her gaze settled somewhere over Amy's left shoulder.

"I spent the last decade watching some very bad people reach for power. And they were honest. They always said, right up front, what they'd do once they were in charge. Then...they went ahead and did it. We had a quick coup, an even shorter civil war, and a brand new president for life. And the free world I took for granted was just gone one morning." Bahati's lips curled in a bitter smile. "I couldn't even pretend to be surprised. They told us who they were every step of the way. Anyway, the new president is a fan of my music. My messages, not so much. So he made me an offer: I can either retool my lyrics to be 'appropriately patriotic and supportive of the new regime,' or I can be silent. Forever."

"I'm sorry," Amy said. "I had no idea."

"I'm not going to spend my life in a cage being some fascist's pet songbird. A lot of my music's about self-respect, and I like to practice what I preach. So no. I'm not going back either." She paused. "That's not what I'm keeping from Anahera. My old stomping ground, Beltway City, is Anahera's home town. It's also one of the last pockets of resistance against the new guard. Two days before I got yanked over here, the city was hit."

"Hit?"

"A dirty bomb hidden in a delivery van," Bahati whispered. "Dynamite and contaminated radium. The death toll was..."

She trailed off. A sense of dread sank into Amy's spine, heavy and cold, dragging her down.

"Anahera's family?" she asked.

Bahati shook her head.

"I'm not hiding anything from her. I need you to understand that. I *want* to tell her."

"But that's not the kind of thing you just drop on somebody," Amy said. "I get it."

"I'm figuring it out. Just keep this between us for now, okay?" Her eyes darkened. "It's funny. I was talking to Olivia earlier, and you don't even want to know what her deal is. Suffice to say she can't leave either. And I find this whole situation just a tiny bit sus."

Amy had been thinking the same thing. "This many students with their backs up against the wall? That can't be a coincidence. Can't be."

"Well, my agent has a saying when he's negotiating deals for me: put the other guy in a corner, make sure he has no other options, and he'll sign any contract you put in front of him. So. Practice time?"

"Absolutely," Amy said. "Vail and Olivia are in. I just have to find Nora. Have you seen her anywhere?"

Colin swung by, the short boy leaning close as he walked past them.

"Eyes up," he breathed. "Those jerks from the Sept of Blades are roaming around the first floor. Pretty sure they're not supposed to be. I'm going to go get Mr. Orris."

"Have you seen Nora?"

"Uh-uh," Colin said, breezing past them. "But considering how they treated her at lunch yesterday..."

"Let's split up," Bahati said. "Whoever finds her first, bring her to the dorm room so the Blades can't mess with her, and we'll meet back there in five."

Amy couldn't find Nora, but she did catch Vail, who was stalking through the Academy's halls like a woman on a mission.

"Blades in the first-year dorms—" Amy started to say.

"I know. C'mon. Looking for Nora. Let's find her before they do."

"Great minds think alike."

"Thing about bullies is, they're predictable. Hey, do you have puckslam on your world?"

Amy shook her head. "What's that?"

"My favorite sport." Vail showed her teeth. "It's *really* violent."

***

"You're going to die here," Jellica said.

The white witch leaned in, the tips of her wild winter bangs dipped in black ink, and towered over Nora. The little girl pressed her back to the mildewed tiles in the far corner of the showers, the air thick with steam heat and the brackish scent of dirty water.

"You're going to die here," Jellica said, "and no one will ever even know. They'll bury your body in an unmarked grave behind the school. Is that what you want?"

Tears welled in Nora's eyes. She fought them back, clenching her jaw and puffing out her bottom lip. Jellica had a pair of her toadies with her: a tall, broad-shouldered boy in a Blades scarf and the strange, quiet, bespectacled girl in the black lace choker who had served Jellica's table at lunch. They didn't touch Nora, but they flanked her, keeping her pinned in the corner, giving her nowhere to run. Jellica crouched down, almost kindly, and stroked Nora's cheek with her frost-painted fingernails.

"It's not your fault," she said. "You never should have been brought here. You're just not good enough, sweetie. You'll never be good enough. And if you don't walk through the Arch and go home while you still can—"

The door to the showers flung open, hitting the wall hard enough to bounce off with a slamming jolt.

"Finish that sentence," Vail said, walking in with Amy at her side. "I dare you. No. I double dare you."

"Let's go straight for the triple dog dare," Amy suggested.

Jellica rose and turned, regarding the two of them like a hungry hyena spotting zebras on the run.

"Oh, look. It's the bookworm and her friend, the junkie whore."

Vail's hands balled into fists and she took a step closer. "What did you just call me?"

Jellica ignored her, looking at Amy. "So...is she attached at your hip because she thinks you're going to get her high, or do you have to pay her by the hour?"

Amy hadn't been in a fight since she was Nora's age, if she could even call some playground hair-pulling a real battle. She didn't think about it. Vail launched herself across the hard, wet tile floor like a rocket, and now Amy was moving too, bracing herself, charging into the fray.

The burly boy jumped in front of his mistress. He threw up a forearm, knocking Vail's punch aside before it could land, and plowed his fist into her gut like a sledgehammer. She dropped to her knees, winded and breathless. He didn't waste any time, grappling her to the floor, yanking both of her arms behind her back and pinning her wrists while shoving her cheek against the grimy shower tiles.

Amy didn't even see the other one move. She just felt a sudden explosion of pain across the small of her back, a whistling and falling sensation, and then she was on the floor next to Vail with the girl in the choker perched on her spine like a cat from hell. Hot breath washed across the back of her neck and tiny, sharp teeth, like bone needles, grazed her skin. Her attacker didn't speak. She just hissed, a raw, hungry sound.

Jellica slowly strolled to the heart of the shower room, turned, and regarded her new catches with pleasure in her eyes.

"I thought we were just going to lose one piece of dead weight today. Instead we get to drop three. None of you — not one — is worthy of this school."

"You don't get to decide that!" Amy said. The girl in the choker twisted her wrist savagely, bending it to the point of nearly snapping, and Amy bit back a squeal of pain. Chuckling, Jellica crouched in front of her. She cupped Amy's chin in her fingers.

"You're cute. The pathetic thing is, you've got more raw potential than most of these losers. Might have even made something of yourself if you had the right priorities and made the right friends."

"At least I have friends," Amy snapped.

Jellica contemplated her for a moment, then held up a finger.

"Change of plans," she said.

She leaned closer to Amy, their faces just inches apart, Jellica's eyes burning.

"I'm going to punish that mouth of yours."

Amy glared at her. Terrified, her heart slamming against her ribs, but damned if she was going to show it. It probably wouldn't even be the worst beating she'd ever taken. She could find some solace in that. Pain was just pain. It faded, even when the memories didn't.

"Do your worst," she said.

"Oh, I will." Jellica looked to the girl in the choker. "Prentise? Hold her arms tighter. And break her wrist if she tries to squeeze her eyes shut. See, Amy... I'm not even going to touch you. What I am going to do is beat the hell out of your friends here and make you watch every second of it."

She leaned in, putting her lips to Amy's ear.

"I bet you didn't think I knew how to hurt you," she whispered. "But I'm very good at what I do, and you're an open book to me. Now sit back and enjoy the show. You earned it. This is all for you."

She rose and gestured to the boy.

"Get Vail on her feet. I haven't had my evening workout and I need a punching bag." Jellica flashed a feral smile at Amy. "She'll do, don't you think?"

# Chapter Fifteen

The boy in the silken Blades scarf hauled Vail to her feet and pinned her arms roughly behind her back, swinging her around so Jellica could go to work on her. Nora stayed in the corner, trapped and small, while Amy lay flat on her belly on the grimy, spotted tiles with the girl in the choker — Prentise — perched on her back and growling in her ear like a wild animal. The pressure on Amy's trapped wrist made her eyes water, the pain like a knife in her lung, stealing her breath away.

Jellica pulled back a clenched fist, locking eyes with Vail, taking her time and savoring the moment.

Amy couldn't move. Couldn't fight. Her mind raced. Had to be a way, something she could do, something she could use. She struggled to let her vision slip sideways, calling on her visions of the magic winds. She didn't know any combat magic, couldn't do anything more dramatic than make a light bulb glow, but her instincts told her there was still something left in her tiny bag of tricks.

There was a secret hidden in the twisted knot of Jellica's words. Time dragged to a slow-motion crawl as she worked to untangle it with raw fingertips. And suddenly, she saw it.

She had never spoken to Jellica before. The things the older girl knew about her didn't make any sense. Like calling her a bookworm:

guilty, Amy would happily admit, but Jellica had never even seen her in a classroom. Or the way Jellica knew that hurting Amy's friends would cut her on a level that frightened her even more than the Arch of Resignation. Could have just been lucky guesses, but...

...but there it was, in Amy's second sight. A tether, like a rippling stream of icy water, running from Jellica's left hand to the hollow of Amy's throat. *She put something on me*, she reasoned, *some kind of occult whammy. Left hand is the hand of receiving. Jellica didn't figure anything out, she just cracked my brain open and looked inside, all so quiet that I didn't even notice. And if she's still connected...*

*I've got a weapon after all.*

"I hope you appreciate this," Jellica told her.

Amy suddenly saw her mind as a set of parallel bars in darkness. Her soul spun, flipped, launched free of the bars, then fell. She plummeted into the cold wet nothing, past stone and soil and down into the crushing depths of the ocean beyond the shores of Firebreak Island.

Jellica's hand twitched. Her head jerked.

"What are you doing?" she demanded, suddenly suspicious.

Amy's astral body torpedoed through the brine, firing toward a vast terrible shadow.

"Professor Mallory says I'm bright," Amy breathed. "Apparently more of a problem than one might think."

In the waters beyond the island, down in the crushing, lightless depths, the Corpse opened a vast yellow eye.

She felt it more strongly the second time around. It was alien, truly alien, and its thoughts were blurred musical notes played on a child's toy piano to score a hundred distinct odors of rot. Amy didn't follow, and for the first and only time in her life, she didn't want to. Nothing in that monster's brain was meant to be understood. All she grasped for certain, beneath it all, was a single and undying constant: *hate.*

The creature didn't just *see* her from the other end of their psychic conduit. It *wanted* her. The sudden shock of the connection nearly blinded Amy, jolting her out of her vision and sending her physical senses reeling, vertigo squeezing her stomach in a fist. The communion flashed down the tether and hit Jellica twice as hard. Unlike Amy, she hadn't seen it coming. One moment she was on top of the world, and a second later an ancient mad leviathan was pouring static and rage into her brain.

Jellica squealed, staggering back, the connection between her and Amy tearing like wet paper. That was the opening Vail needed. She raised one foot and brought her heel down on the boy's instep hard enough to make bones crack. He lost his grip on her and she spun, grappling with him, as the door to the showers flung wide open.

Colin was back. He hadn't found Mr. Orris, but he'd brought reinforcements. Bahati, Olivia, Dalton, and Erik ran in with him, spreading out as the door swung shut behind them.

"Look at that," Bahati said. "Eight against three. How do you like those odds?"

Jellica curled her lips back, defiant. "Three warriors against eight untrained, untalented runts. I'll take those odds with a smile and I won't even have to use magic."

"Cool. Cool, cool, cool." Dalton had his hands jammed in his pockets. He leaned forward, casting an exaggerated look at the scene around him, and wandered to the other side of the room. "But, uh, if we're going to throw down, I want to bring in a little flavor from back home."

Jellica propped an unsteady hand on her hip, still recovering from Amy's psychic shock. She gritted her teeth. "Meaning?"

"Oh, just that I spent most of my childhood in custody in juvie hall. Now, where I come from, we've got a tradition when somebody in juvie gets out of pocket. We call it a shower party."

He tugged one hand from a pocket, reached out, and yanked down a handle. A shower head spat and then started to spray, filling the room with the hiss of slowly spreading water. Dalton nodded, approving, and moved to the next showerhead. Then a third, opening each tap as he slowly closed with Jellica.

"First thing you do, see, is you get all the showers running at once." Now he had to raise his voice over the rattling pipes. "It gets nice and loud. Muffles any sound of trouble, so the screws don't come snooping around."

He paused, leaned his head back, and sniffed deeply. Steam billowed around them, drifting through the shower room like wisps of fog.

"There we go. Next you get the water good and hot. Get the steam rolling. I'll tell you, there's nothing like beating some punk into paste in the middle of a free-for-all, and all you see around you are shadows. Don't know who's a friend or who's a foe. That's when the adrenaline really starts pumping."

Dalton tugged another pair of shower handles, approaching the trio of Blades. Then he dropped low on one knee, running his hand along the grimy tile floor before standing tall once more. He showed Jellica the wet beads on his fingertips.

"But the best part of a shower party? The water. Everywhere. People start slipping, falling, breaking bones left and right, and nobody's safe. And the water doesn't stay water for too long. Not when the knives come out." Dalton grinned, ferocious. "At the end of a really good shower party, it's all cherry-red. I've left at least a pint and a half on the floor of every juvie hall I've ever been locked up in. I don't mind. It's all part of the fun."

"You don't have a knife," Jellica said.

"Don't I? Babe, I've spent the better part of my developing years getting my ass kicked in the worst hellholes you've ever seen. I've been in a hundred brawls and I've lost at least fifty, so look me in the eyes. Look me dead in the eyes and tell me the truth: do you really think there's any situation, in this world or any other, where I *didn't* start carving a shiv on my first night here?"

"And passing them out to his friends," Colin said, crossing his arms in defiance.

Jellica and Dalton locked eyes, staring each other down. Amy felt something shift in the air, a teetering balance beginning to slip. Then Jellica shot a glare at her followers. The three Blades made a slow retreat, falling back to the door as one, staying tight, eyeing the first-years all around them.

"You're going to regret this," Jellica told them.

"Agree to disagree," Amy said.

"You especially," the witch in white told her. "You just became my special project for the year."

Prentise bared too-sharp teeth and chomped the air in Amy's direction. Jellica grabbed the scruff of her neck and administered a sharp, hard yank, as if she was a wayward pet, pulling her toward the door. The boy in the Blades scarf limped at her other side, wincing every time he put weight on the foot Vail had stomped.

"Thanks for coming," Bahati said, wriggling her fingers in a goodbye wave. "Drive safe, and have yourselves a lovely evening."

***

Amy caught up with Dalton outside the showers, Vail not far behind her.

"I have to ask," she started to say.

"Why, yes," he said. "I am the most handsome bachelor at the Academy. Glad to confirm."

"No, I mean…do you really have a shiv?"

Dalton chuckled and shook his head.

"Eh, I whittled one just to stay in practice. I gave it to Colin. The kid's scrappy, but he's barely taller than Nora and I think that's as big as he's going to get. Me, I don't need one."

He reached into his left pocket, tugging out the slim, black plastic handle of a switchblade. He only pulled it out far enough to show Amy, then pushed it back into hiding.

"This was already in my pocket when I came across. Only school I've ever been to where they didn't search me at the front door. Suckers."

"You bluffed, when you didn't have to?"

"I've got some rules," Dalton told her.

"Like not hitting girls?"

"That's more of a guideline, and I'm having a little heart-to-heart with myself at the moment. Stay tuned. More importantly, I don't draw a weapon unless I plan to use it. Only lunkheads wave their steel around as a threat: you're just begging for somebody tougher and faster to take it away from you. If you ever see me pull this knife all the way out of my pocket, somebody is getting cut and they're not getting back up again. That's my court of final appeal."

"You like to fight," Vail observed. He answered her with a cocky grin.

"Takes one to know one. And I like to *brawl*. I'll go fists and boots all day long, any time, any place, but I've never killed anybody and I'm not looking to start."

"Want to come over?" Amy asked, nodding over her shoulder toward their dorm room. "We're going to practice the circle of protection before bed."

"As enticing as an invitation into my two favorite ladies' boudoir sounds, I should go check on the pipsqueak."

"Nora's rooming with us," Vail said.

"The other pipsqueak," he said. "Colin's not good with confrontation. Gonna make sure he's okay."

Vail stared at him.

"What? I never had a kid brother before. We're all finding our own lanes here."

# Chapter Sixteen

"Y ou're holding the book upside down," Olivia said.

Down on the floor, clutching a stubby piece of chalk, Nora gave her cheeks an exaggerated puff.

"I'm holding it upside down," she said, "because I'm drawing the bottom part of the circle."

"You can't read the runes that way."

Nora's shoulders slumped. She paused, halfway through drawing an impossibly curling sigil that looked like a fusion of eight letters at once.

"I can't read them upside down. I *also* can't read them right side up. Not seeing a problem here."

"You know, in chapter three—"

"Oh my god," Bahati said, kneeling next to her and carefully drawing the slow, steady curve of the outer circle, "stop talking about chapter three. We're still on chapter one."

Nora was shaken after being cornered in the bathroom, but she didn't want to talk about it. She wanted to study, a coping mechanism Amy could wholeheartedly get behind, and a visit to the library yielded an old box of ghost-white chalk. The wooden floorboards at the heart of the dorm room were their canvas, a magic circle slowly unfolding as they worked together to draw one from the designs in the *Liber Scutum.*

"Looks like we need two circles on the outside," Vail said, holding up the open book. "What do you think? Maybe three inches of space between the rings?"

"Worth a try." Amy squinted at the diagram. "Book says the top glyph is supposed to point toward magnetic north. Are we sure we've got the facing right?"

"In chapter three there's a technique called the Regardie Shunt—" Olivia started to say.

"In this dorm," Bahati said, "we're on chapter one."

"Why? He's making us use training wheels. We're better than that. We could get this done so much faster if we jump ahead and cut a few corners."

"Because Professor Chalk is scary," Nora said, putting the finishing touches on a sigil. She frowned at it, licked her finger and smudged a little notch at the tail of a curling line, a more perfect match to the diagram in the book.

"I think," Amy told Olivia, trying to be diplomatic, "that we're handling some really dangerous stuff here, and the professor is an expert. I know what it's like to want to pour everything into your brain at once; I feel it too. But I want to learn things the *right* way. Besides, he's a stickler for people following the rules. What if he gave us the whole book to see who would do the assignment the way he said, and who would skip ahead without permission?"

"He's hot to expel somebody," Vail muttered, stretching out her legs on the floor. "You're lucky he didn't make an example out of your boyfriend."

Olivia's nostrils flared. "Erik is not my boyfriend."

"And yet, you knew exactly who I was talking about."

"What if he wants to see who the most ambitious students are?" Olivia countered. "What if the test is that you're supposed to go above and beyond the assignment?"

"Then the rest of us will all feel really dumb, while you'll be crowned the queen of the first-year students and the high grand pooh-bah of the mystic arts," Bahati said. "We'll give you a funny hat and everything. Now can we please focus? I'd like to sleep at some point tonight."

As the circle grew, their sticks of chalk stroking against the wood and leaving ghostly curls in their wake, Amy's perception began to shift. Tilting, like a camera slowly losing frame and focus only to find a new perspective in a new direction. The circle wasn't a circle. The circle was a word. Each glyph within its concentric rings was a letter, a concept, a sound feeding the melody of the whole. Each individual symbol was powerless itself, a spark at best, but joining the lines formed a circuit. Combustion.

She didn't feel the combustion, though, as the final line was drawn into place. Just a battery with no power.

Amy had admonished Olivia for jumping ahead just like everyone else, but she was drawn, almost guiltily, to some of the expanded definitions in the next chapter. The individual seals ringing the circle were signs of home, of sanctuary, of safety. *It is meant*, the writer urged, *that the skilled magician feel these signs as they are drawn, and invest them with the appropriate energies.*

She couldn't do that. She was working with a different dictionary. *Home* had never been anything but a nightmare and while she understood the concept of *safety*, at least in her head, she couldn't invoke an emotion she'd never felt before.

All the same, their first circle of protection was drawn, and now it had to be put to the test. Amy suddenly noticed everyone looking her way, waiting for instructions.

"Why am I in charge?"

"Because nobody else wants to go first," Bahati said.

"I don't want to go first either."

Bahati put a hand on Amy's shoulder.

"But you must," she said. "Because you're in charge."

They scrounged up a collection of half-melted soap bars from the showers and gathered around the circle while Amy took her place inside the concentric rings. Her bare feet were light on the cold, waxed wood, careful not to smudge any of the careful linework with her toes. She crouched, her focus crystal in one hand. She reached out with the other, following the book's instructions, and touched her fingertip to the sigil drawn at magnetic north.

*And now...ignition.*

She felt nothing.

"I don't think this is going to—"

She ducked and covered her head as a hailstorm of soap flew in from all directions, pelting her and bouncing off her shoulders and back to skid across the dorm room.

"Not in the face!" Amy said. "Hey! C'mon, not cool."

Olivia threw her chunk of soap last. It hit Amy's arm, fell, and spun on the floor at her feet. Amy stared at her.

"Really?" Amy asked her.

"Had to be certain," Olivia said. "For science."

Nora had her book open, squinting at the diagrams, and held her copy up for Amy to see.

"Did we mess up the lines?"

"No." Amy frowned, resting her chin against her knuckles as she compared the ornate design on the floor to the one in the book. "The circle is perfect. I'm firing it up wrong. Someone else want to take a shot?"

Bahati was next, after they spent nearly an hour re-drawing the circle, arguing over fine details and re-drawing half of it for a third time. Sleep weighed on Amy's shoulders like a thick blanket, and her lumpy mattress sang to her in a siren's voice, promising a balm for her aching muscles. She wasn't alone; Nora stared like a zombie, and Bahati and Olivia couldn't talk without snapping at each other.

"And...*fire*," Bahati whispered to herself, touching the northern sigil. She had barely gotten to her feet before the hurricane of flying soap began. She threw both arms over her face, curled into a fetal position, then snatched up Olivia's chunk and threw it back at her. Olivia squealed and threw herself behind a bed, thumping hard against the floorboards on her belly.

"Okay," Amy said. "Okay. That's it, we're calling it for tonight. Everybody is tired and cranky and we're not getting anywhere."

"I want to try," Vail said.

"Come on," Olivia said, "if *they* can't do it—"

Vail turned on her. "What's that supposed to mean?"

"What does it sound like it means?"

Vail looked back to Amy. "I want to try."

Amy relented, gesturing for her to step into the circle. They took some time to redraw smeared edges and questionable curls. More of the night slipped away.

Nora had checked out. The little girl sprawled on her bedsheets, dozing with her mouth hanging open. The others finished their work, and Vail stepped into the circle. Bahati and Olivia threw their chunks of soap a lot harder than they needed to, but Vail didn't flinch as they pelted her. Amy tossed hers underhand.

"What was that?" Vail said.

Amy blinked. "What was what?"

"That wussy throw. You don't think I can take it?"

"No, I just—"

*I just knew the circle wasn't going to work*, Amy thought. *And now she knows I didn't think she could pull it off. Small world, and I'm officially the biggest jerk in it.*

"Again," Vail said.

"Come on," Bahati said. "It's past midnight and we've got class in the morning."

"*Again.*"

The other girls spread out around the circle and picked up their fallen chunks of soap. Vail locked eyes with Amy, her jaw clenched with frustration, sending a silent message: *Do it right this time.*

*Trust me this time.*

Amy pulled her arm back and flung the soap. The last thing she wanted to do was hurt Vail, but she realized that holding back had stung her so much deeper. She didn't make the same mistake twice. She watched helplessly as the chunk of soap flew effortlessly over the powerless circle of protection, straight toward Vail's face.

A sudden fire-flash blinded Amy. She threw one arm over her eyes, staggering back. As her vision cleared, spots wavering in front of her eyes like volcanoes frozen mid-eruption, she saw everyone else reeling too. Everyone but Vail, who stared at her empty hands in bemusement. The air smelled like burnt popcorn.

Chunks of soap lay scattered on the floorboards around her, half-black like charcoal briquettes.

For a heartbeat, Amy was elated. They'd cracked the code. Finally, one of them had mastered the circle of protection. Then she looked across the floor, and realized the truth. Some of the soap-bars had fallen well inside the concentric rings before they burst into flames. Others, like Olivia's, had erupted a split-second after they touched the open air.

She crouched down, putting two timid fingers to the outer circle. Cold. Inert. Powerless. Vail hadn't mastered the circle, any more than the rest of them. She had just forced the soap-chunks to spontaneously combust.

"Uh, Vail?" Amy said. "How did you do that?"

"I have no idea. I was just... I've been so frustrated. We ran into the Blades in the shower and I couldn't *do* anything."

"I think you broke that kid's foot," Bahati pointed out.

"Not what I mean," Vail said. "I'm the runt of the litter in this class. We all know it."

"I'm not letting you fail," Amy said.

"You can't take the test for me, Amy. And you haven't figured it out either, so it's not like you know anything."

She paused. They locked eyes. Amy bit her bottom lip, hard.

"I didn't...mean for that to come out like it did."

"No," Amy said. "I get it. It's okay."

Bahati stepped between them, hands raised.

"That's it, we're done. Bedtime for everybody."

*Which is what I said before everything got tense*, Amy thought, biting back a sigh. *Why do people keep putting me in charge and then not listening to anything I tell them?*

The mystery would keep until morning. Getting everyone — including herself — through this test was more important, and as an unsteady sleep rose to subdue her in its shadowy grasp, one fact chased her into the darkness: what they were doing wasn't working. They needed to find a new approach, and fast. The clock was ticking.

# Chapter Seventeen

Walking back from breakfast, in the middle of a crowd of students, Vail's hand found Amy's. She gave it a tight, quick squeeze, then let go.

"I'm sorry," she whispered. "About last night."

Amy shook her head. "That's on me."

"Let's not do the blame thing, okay? We were all tired and cranky, and it's a new day. Listen, do me a favor. Don't tell anyone about my...pyro incident. I'm asking the other girls to stay quiet too."

"Vail, you conjured *fire*. Without even trying. That's the most impressive thing any of us has managed. Maybe that's exactly what the professors need to see to prove you belong here."

Her expression darkened. "'Without trying' is the part I'm worried about. You know, some drugs can rewire the pathways in your brain, to make you more dependent. What if the Ink...ruined me? What if I'm defective?"

Up ahead, a crowd had gathered around a corkboard in the foyer, studying some tacked-up sheets of parchment lined with spidery, uneven writing. Amy touched Vail's arm as they made their way to the front of the pack.

"First of all," Amy started to say, "there's no such thing as a defective person—"

Colin walked past in the other direction, holding a torn ticket from one of the tacked-up pages. "Work assignments, and they're first come, first served. Get 'em while they're hot."

"You're in a good mood," Vail said.

"Professor Mallory needs help in her greenhouse."

"One of her plants ate a chipmunk," Amy said. "I mean, we all watched it eat a chipmunk."

"I'm sure she'll start me out on the non-carnivorous ones," Colin said, beaming. "I was never allowed to have a garden back home."

The crowd slowly churned and pushed Amy and Vail to the front of a misshapen line. Half of the work opportunities were already gone, but that still left a dizzying amount of jobs: from kitchen staff to maintenance, it was clear the Academy left most of the mundane work to the student body, handling anything and everything Mr. Orris couldn't manage on his own.

"Brought us here on the wrong night, bells still don't work, the staff is a skeleton crew..." Vail tilted her head and gave Amy a sidelong look. "Get the impression this place is run on a shoestring budget?"

"Well, they're not charging us anything."

*Yet.* The word hung between them, no need to speak it out loud.

"I'm also thinking..." Vail smiled and tore a dangling ticket from the bottom of the sign-up form. "...volunteering in the library will give me some face time with Adelaide, our resident ghost."

"You think you can sweet-talk her into letting us see that book Professor Mallory wrote?" Amy asked.

"I know I can try. Besides, sounds like we're going to be doing wall to wall research this year, so I might as well get familiar with the place. Not like I ever set foot in a library before I landed here. How about you, anything catch your eye?"

Nothing at first, despite the long list of possibilities, but then Amy paused. She smiled, pointing to a neglected entry toward the end of the page.

"Mr. Orris wants help in the stables. I didn't even know we had stables here."

"You're doing it wrong," Dalton said, looming over Amy's other shoulder and leaning in to study the postings. "You're supposed to pick the easiest job with the best rewards."

"I think those are already gone," Vail said. "You should have gotten up sooner."

"Hard to do without an alarm clock. We don't even get a chorus of crows to wake us up. We have to listen to *your* crows."

"They're Amy's crows."

"They're not my—" Amy shook her head. "Anyway, I like working with animals. I was going to be a veterinarian. Before my sudden change of plans, I mean. Still might. Not like we know what's going to happen after graduation."

Dalton jammed his thumbs in his pockets and shot a pointed glance at the forbidden stairway. The curling steps winding up to the second- and third-year dorms...and the empty fourth floor.

"Indeed we do not," he said.

*** 

The first-year students had one more professor to meet. One more taskmaster to satisfy, one more gauntlet to run to prove they belonged at the Saunders Academy. He was already there when the class shuffled into the drafty lecture hall. The windows all yawned open along one wall, flooding the room with a gusty salt-tinged ocean breeze that ruffled papers. A distant dark line painted the horizon, thunder over the black and bottomless sea.

His dapper suit aside, the man behind the teacher's desk was a mile from Amy's notions of what a professor should look like. He was a slab of muscle who dwarfed his own chair, tall and wide and chiseled from stone, with a shaved head and a cocky lantern-jawed smile. His jacket slid back just far enough to show the start of tattoo sleeves on both arms, with whirling geometric patterns that twined from under his shirt collar and adorned his neck as well, all the way up to the hollow of his throat.

"Come in, come in, grab a seat," he said, waving a casual hand at the open chairs. "They're all good, you can see me from anywhere in the house. Hey you. Short stuff."

Nora froze, staring up at him. "Me?"

"Yeah, you. Why are you tiny?"

"Why are you huge?" she asked.

"Protein, vegetables, and exercise." He pointed to an open chair in the first row. "You'd better sit up front, where I can keep an eye on you. Short people. I don't trust 'em."

He sounded anything but serious — Amy suspected he just wanted to make sure she didn't get lost behind the bigger students — but Colin still gave him a dubious look as he walked into the classroom. The professor turned, pointed two fingers at his own eyes, then stabbed them at Colin.

"That's right. You sit next to her. I'm keeping an eye on both of you."

"This feels vaguely like harassment," Colin deadpanned.

"Sorry, did you say something, little man? I can't hear you from up here." The professor rapped a sheaf of loose pages on his desk. "All right, everybody in? Let's get to work. Name's Kamaka, and I'm here to teach you the basic principles of navigation."

Erik raised his hand. Amy struggled not to roll her eyes. Next to her, Vail didn't bother holding back. He didn't notice.

"We're here to learn magic," Erik said. "What does navigation have to do with anything?"

"I'm glad you asked," Kamaka said. "Because it's not like I was just about to explain that to the entire class."

Vail leaned over and whispered into Amy's ear. "I like this one."

The professor walked over to the blackboard. He paused, gesturing at the vast expanse of black slate, marred by the half-erased ghosts of seminars past.

"You already got the multiverse lecture, right?"

"From Professor Lanca," Nora said.

"Figures he'd steal my act. Okay, good, saves me some time. My family are island-people, and where I come from we make our living from the sea." Professor Kamaka nodded toward the row of open windows. "Not a deathtrap like *this* ocean, but the sea doesn't know mercy, or pity. You meet her on her own terms and you ride the waves she throws at you, or you sink and you drown. It's that simple."

He drew as he spoke, sketching a map on the chalkboard. Not a map of the countless planes of existence, dimensions within dimensions, but something more humble and closer to home: islands, their jagged shorelines drawn from memory, separated by the scalloped waves of ocean currents. Amy couldn't miss the similarity to the tattoos on his neck, the way the lines formed, rippled, and broke like water lapping against a beach.

"We had to keep sailing, flowing with the annual migrations. The fish taught us where to go. And my forefathers and their fathers quickly learned that every island in the archipelago was a world unto itself. Different languages, different cultures." He tapped the board. "Caricopa has music and dance and sweet coconut rum. One day's sail to the southeast, if the wind is good, you end up in Tormalin, where they'll hang you for laughing. My people had to learn to fit in wherever we went — to fit in while still being true to ourselves. Knowing where you want to go, and how to get there, is only part of the art of navigation. You also have to know how to blend. And how to disappear when you really need to."

Amy had a hard time imagining the huge, statuesque man pulling a disappearing act, but she didn't doubt him, either. She already knew this lesson. She'd been learning it her entire life, donning a different mask for every occasion: one for school, one for her lecherous boss, one for her violent, drunken father — whatever mask would keep her safe. What started as a survival technique became a life habit. Sometimes, in the small hours of the night, she contemplated all her masks.

If she took the last one off, she wasn't sure there'd be anything underneath it. Nobody worth knowing, anyway. Nothing worth seeing.

"Magicians are just like sailors," Kamaka said, "but we work the waters of the In-Between, and we have a thousand ports of call, all just a wish and a heartbeat away. And just like sailors, we've invented some special tools to get us where we need to go."

He scooped up an old, battered leather pouch from the edge of his desk and tugged it open. A deck of cards dropped into his beefy palm. They were antiques, old and yellowed, with rounded corners and a design on the back like a star chart carved from rustic driftwood.

"This," he said, "is called the Navigator's Tarot. Once you master it — *if* you can master it — you can pull off some impressive tricks. Like so."

He picked three cards off the top, turning them in his hand to flash them at the lecture hall. The Chariot bore a stoic conqueror, his carriage pulled by a pair of exotic, roaring sphinxes. A woman in jade-green armor, wounded but rising and brandishing a two-handed sword, marked the card of the Knight, and the Eight of Staves depicted a galleon in full sail bearing eight sturdy oars. Kamaka murmured an incantation under his breath, then traced a trackless pattern with his thumb against the backs of the cards while he walked to the classroom door.

He slapped the cards against the door. Amy's ears popped. The room shifted, a pressure front rolling in, pinching her sinuses tight.

The door swung wide. Behind it, instead of the hallway they'd come from, gleamed a tropical beach. Elegant wooden houses protruded along the shore, built upon pylons and a maze of raised piers, while skiffs and fishing boats sailed on glass-smooth water. A sweet scent, like barbecue, wafted through the doorway on a warm breeze, clashing with the cold sea-salt smell from the open windows. Temperatures crashed and melted into one another, while the room flooded with even more pressure, as if the entire lecture hall had just been flung to the top of a mountain. A metallic groan echoed through the hall, rattling the floorboards under the students' feet, like a rusty gear on an old machine struggling to turn.

Professor Kamaka slammed the door shut and returned the trio of cards to his deck, shuffling it in one practiced hand. The pressure vanished, the grating, shrill sound fading fast. The tremors jolted to a sudden stop.

He opened the door a second time, showing them the hallway outside.

"Not a first-year technique," he said. "But stick around long enough, and I'll show you how it's done."

# Chapter Eighteen

"That tiny earthquake, by the way," Professor Kamaka said as he strolled back to his desk, "was the school lodging a serious complaint. Firebreak Island is warded to the gills to keep anyone from opening a door and popping in without an invitation. I figure the headmistress will be down here in about—"

A fast, insistent knock sounded at the classroom door.

"Excuse me a second," Kamaka said. "I need to get yelled at."

Vail leaned closer to Amy. "Where did you just go?"

"Huh?"

She poked Amy's forehead. "You just went away. Like you do sometimes."

Amy hadn't realized. She was fixated on the lifeline they'd just been handed. Those cards could open doorways...elsewhere. If she could learn that trick and get her own deck, it wouldn't matter if the school expelled them. She could open a door, take Vail — she'd just included Vail in her plans, she realized — and they could just *go*. Anywhere.

Anywhere but home.

*Except I can't open a door here, and they take your memories when you pass through the Arch of Resignation*, Amy realized, remembering Chen Lan's introduction when they first arrived. *And your magic, and everything you learned here.*

Just like that, an idea offered hope, escape, freedom, before going down in flames. And just like before she was facing the same immutable problem: graduate or die.

"Just had a thought," Amy whispered back. "But it wouldn't work."

Vail looked to the classroom door. It hung open a crack, and they could see the huge professor backed up against a wall in the hallway outside while the headmistress jabbed a finger against his chest. They couldn't hear her, but with body language like that, they didn't need to.

"You were thinking we could swipe those cards and jet," Vail said.

"You and me." Amy caught herself, quickly adding: "And anyone else who wants to go."

Vail's tired eyes held a question. "You feel like quitting?"

"Heck, no. Not even a little bit. I'm not giving Jellica and her pals the pleasure of seeing us fail. But I like to have a just-in-case up my sleeve. You know. Just in case. What about you? You feel like quitting?"

"A lot less than I did last night," Vail said. "And for pretty much the same reason. She doesn't get to beat us. Not as long as we've still got a shot at making it here. The look on Jellica's face when we graduate will be worth all the frustration and then some. That said..."

"That said?" Amy asked.

"Nothing wrong with having a backup plan."

The professor returned, shooting a glance over his shoulder as he pulled the classroom door shut.

"Unpleasant, but so very worth it," he said. "Okay! So as you've seen, the Navigator's Tarot can open doors for you. It can close 'em, too, and sometimes that's even more useful. For this class we'll focus on the basics. My job is to teach you the most powerful skill in any sailor's arsenal."

The tarot cards leaped from his left hand to his right, flowing through the air in a perfect horseshoe of flickering cards before the last one landed, falling into place with a snap of cardstock.

"How to get home," he said.

"Never been there," Vail murmured.

"I'll be teaching you orienteering — both the magical and mundane varieties, because they work together better than you might think — and some good old-fashioned living off the land, just in case you find yourself stranded in hostile waters. But everything circles back to the Navigator's Tarot. By the end of this year, I'll need each of you to have a grounding in the basics of cartomancy before I can let you graduate. That's a fancy word for 'card magic.' See? You've already learned something new today. You're welcome."

"Do we get our own decks?" Amy asked, eager.

"You're adorable, but no. You get a *book* about the tarot. These decks are rare birds. Beyond mine, which is mine, and came down from my granddad's granddad, the school only has three of 'em, plus a smattering of lost cards kept under lock and key. Upper-year students can check them out for research projects."

Olivia's hand shot up like a flare, her eyes hungry and bright. "Lost cards?"

"There's one in every class," Kamaka said, shaking his head as he walked back to the blackboard. "Okay, listen up. Your basic Navigator's deck — what we call a 'complete' deck, though it's anything but — holds all fifty-six cards from the Low Suits: Staves, Storms, Fathoms, and Salt. Those are the bare essentials you need to get anything done."

He drew a pair of boxes on the board and numbered them, *fifty-six* and *forty-three*.

"Then there's the High Suits. The High Priestess, the Salesman, the Wheel of Fortune, and so on. We think there are another forty-three of those, but most haven't been seen in centuries outside of private collections. See, the Navigator's Tarot started popping up around a thousand years ago. First on one parallel world, then another, then a third. The exact same cards, but by different artists."

Professor Kamaka turned, his gaze targeting Amy like a laser.

"What does that tell you?" he asked her.

Amy squirmed a little in her seat, uncomfortable in the spotlight, but the answer was obvious enough.

"Its creators were travelers. Magicians, like us," she said. "They carried their cards from world to world and left bits and pieces for other explorers to find."

"You're feelin' it. Well, except that last bit: we don't know their motivations, only that they did leave traces behind, and people have been trying to put together a full collection — a master deck — ever since."

The professor tugged a card from the middle of his deck, not looking down. He found the card with his fingertips alone, guided by instinct. He twirled it in his fingertips, showing the class the rugged countenance of the Reaver, a feral buccaneer standing upon a storm-tossed ship's deck. Then he let go. The card hovered in the air, floating of its own accord, before Kamaka rapped his fingertips against the deck. The Reaver did a backflip, slipping in with the rest of the cards.

"These are your power cards," he said. "They can open doors and minds if you know the trick. A collection like mine, with any cards from the High Suits, is called a pilot's deck."

"How many do you have?" Olivia asked, leaning forward in her seat.

"Nine. Inherited five, spent my whole life searching, and came up with the other four on my own, just in case you're wondering about your odds of finding a whole set. Hey. Pay attention here. This is important."

Kamaka's easy, jovial nature faded. He regarded the class in silence for a moment, his eyes stony, as he rapped his fingers on the deck.

"People kill for these," he said. "Thanks to centuries of trial and error, not to mention blood, sweat, and tears, we know how to create a basic deck. But there's a reason the Academy only has three: they take years of intensive labor and craft, and the reagents cost more money than your average person will ever see in a lifetime. We *don't* know how to replicate High Suit cards. The methods are lost, so the only examples left are the ones that already exist, and just about all of those are in private ownership. The High Suits are powerful, they're priceless, and there's no shortage of magicians out there who would gut you like a fish just to get their hands on a single one of them."

The big man shrugged, smiled wanly, and tucked his deck back into its battered leather pouch.

"So if you find one, give it to me! But that's not something you'll have to worry about for a long time. I'm going to start by having you memorize the names, meanings, and core symbolism of all fifty-six cards in the Low Suits. Master that and I *might* even let you touch my deck. Maybe. No promises."

***

The winding paths behind the Academy led Amy past the fighting ring. Empty now, its well-trodden soil floor bore scuffs and scorches from recent bouts, and it smelled of sweat and anger. She swept past, making her way to the rustic stables that overlooked a small walled-in pasture. Grass rippled in the shadow of the tall, wool-gray stone that kept the island wilderness at bay. Mr. Orris met her outside, waving a weathered hand in greeting as he looked her up and down.

"One volunteer, huh? Well, it's a three-person job, but we should handle it just fine. Where's your friend?"

*Are we really that inseparable?* Amy thought. She blinked, almost flustered. "Um, Vail decided to volunteer in the library."

He gave her a knowing smile. "Thinks she's going to get test answers out of Adelaide, huh?"

"Not going to work?"

"Better luck squeezing blood from a stone. You got any experience with horses?"

Amy thought about her mother. Just a fleeting echo. A half-remembered face, a muffled but proud voice.

"When I was little," she said. "I rode when I was a little girl. Not so much since then. But animals seem to like me."

"That's a good sign in my book. They're better judges of character than most people are. C'mon, I'll introduce you to the locals."

The "locals," housed in side-by-side stalls, were a pair of saddle horses named Comet and Prince. Comet was a golden palomino with smears of ivory along his mane and tail, while Prince had a dark, lustrous coat and stood taller at the shoulder than Amy. Comet leaned into Amy's hand, savoring her touch, as she scratched behind his ears.

"Made a friend already," Orris said, approving. "Prince is a little more standoffish, but he'll get to know you. Here, give him this."

He passed her a stubby carrot, fresh from the dirt. Comet happily ate from the palm of Amy's hand.

"Weird question," she said, "but why does a school have horses, anyway? Why not use cars?"

The old man flashed a yellowed smile. "You see any gas stations around here?"

"In hindsight," Amy said, "I guess that should have been obvious."

"Nah, I mean that's part of it, but we could import fuel if we really needed to. Real reason is, the founders meant for the Academy to be as self-sufficient as possible. We grow as much of our own food as we can and shore up our stocks with canned goods when the Night Market comes through twice a year. Horses get sick, but they don't need exotic replacement parts or oil changes. Then there's the Vapor-Lock."

Amy tilted her head. "What's that?"

"Ah, right, you won't touch on that for a few months yet. Chalk'll probably teach ya. It's a golden oldie. Goes a little something like this."

Orris pulled a faded matchbook from his hip pocket. His lips moved, reciting a silent spell as he struck the match and made it sizzle to life. His other, empty hand passed over the flame.

The match froze in time. The flame just *stopped* mid-flicker, reduced to a three-dimensional photograph clutched in the old man's fingertips. He tapped the fire and it shattered, falling apart in a shower of sparks, leaving a naked, scorched matchstick behind.

"Like so many machines, car engines operate on the principle of combustion. A basic, straightforward chemical process. And one that's easy to interrupt with a tiny jolt of magic in just the right spot. A competent second-year student can stop an engine cold just by getting close enough. Horses, not so much."

"What if someone attacked the horses directly?" Amy asked. "Like, cursing their hearts to stop or something."

"Not impossible, just a lot harder to do." He flicked ash from the dead matchstick and shoved it back into his pocket. "Any magician worth their salt can tell the forces of nature to stand back and take a break for a minute or two. Taking command of someone's heart, though...that's tricky."

# Chapter Nineteen

The horses were healthy, but the stables had fallen into neglect. Orris clearly spent his time doting on the animals and didn't have time for much else given his hundred other duties at the school. So Amy pitched in, pulling on a pair of sturdy gloves to help with the cleaning. She didn't mind the hard work, and besides, he'd given her a lot to think about.

She climbed a ladder to the loft and sorted through old tack and pony gear, trying to organize the sprawling mess. One object, perched high on the knotty pine wall, caught her eye.

"Mr. Orris?" she called down.

"Ayuh?"

"Why do you have a gun?"

He chuckled at the foot of the ladder.

"Firebreak Island's not that big, not compared to all the water around it anyhow, but three-fourths of the land is forested. We get bears every once in a while, wolves sniffing around looking for handouts, and there's a bobcat living near Professor Mallory's shack but I've never caught a look at it."

"But... that spell you told me about. The Vapor-Lock?"

"What about it?"

"Don't guns work by combustion, too?"

The rickety ladder groaned under Orris's muddy boots. He clambered up to the loft, joining her, and took the long-barreled rifle down from its hooks.

"They do indeed," he said. "And that's why you never bring a gun to a mage-fight."

Up close, the rifle was even more intimidating. It had five barrels. Four smaller ones, all slightly different calibers, crested a single cavernous barrel wide enough to fire shotgun slugs. The arrangement of the barrels resembled the imprint of an animal's paw.

"Back home, we call this a catspaw or a *fünfling*. It's a hunter's tool: each barrel is chambered for a different game. Pheasants to elk, she can do it all."

"Can you fire all five barrels at once?" Amy asked.

"Only if you want to completely destroy whatever you're shooting at. But if a dangerous animal gets too close to the school, I just fire warning shots in the air and make 'em run. Our local critters demand respect, like all wildlife, but they're pretty mundane."

"The things in the water aren't."

He studied her for a long, contemplative moment.

"The things in the water," he said, "were already here when our founders arrived."

Amy read between the lines. "So the bears and wolves and bobcats...weren't."

"I didn't say that."

"I think you did."

He grinned. "Let me guess: Professor Mallory's got you on a scavenger hunt. You know, one benefit of being an old man is that I can prove I wasn't born yesterday. You're going to have to work harder than that to get a free hint."

"I'm just learning all about the island and its flora and fauna," Amy said, innocent. "Which is exactly what I'm supposed to be doing, isn't it?"

"Uh-huh."

"And I'm doing research," she said. "Primary research includes conducting interviews with people who have first-hand knowledge of the subject."

"What were you gonna be before you ended up at this school? A lawyer?"

"A veterinarian."

Orris rubbed the bristle on his chin. "I think you missed your true calling. But all right, fair enough. What do you know about the island?"

Amy had been sitting on a hunch. She decided to test it, here and now. She'd get all she needed from his reaction.

"I know it shouldn't be here," she said.

Something mischievous entered the caretaker's eyes, younger than his years. He put the five-barreled rifle back up on its perch and waved for Amy to follow him to the edge of the loft. He sat down on the lip of the overhang, his legs dangling over the stalls below.

"And you think that because?"

She joined him, settling down on the dusty, scattered hay and the splintery floorboards.

"It doesn't make sense. This entire planet is completely covered in water. On my world, we have a place called the Mariana Trench. It's so deep that only two expeditions in history have ever reached the bottom, and compared to this place the Trench looks like a kiddie pool. So how would this vast water-world have one single, solitary island? One island that just happens to have its own balanced ecosystem, fertile soil, and everything humans need to survive, on a planet that is otherwise not in any way, shape, or form survivable?"

Orris kept his lips tight as he listened. "Meaning?"

"Meaning," Amy said, "this island isn't natural. It was built, just like the Academy itself. And if that's the case, then every plant, tree, and animal here had to be imported from another world. If I can figure out where they were brought in from, I can get the perfect answer to Professor Mallory's homework problem."

"Ayuh." He nodded amiably. "Sounds about right."

"Thank you."

"For what?" He turned to glance at her. "I didn't tell you anything at all. Just listened while you put it together on your own."

"I guess...I really needed that," she said. "I'm not used to people listening to me."

She took a deep breath and let it out as a tired sigh.

"And now I'm apparently in charge of my dorm room, an honor I didn't want or ask for, and that'd be stressful enough but nobody actually hears me. They want me to lead and then they don't want to follow. Like somebody stuck me with a job herding cats."

"Ah. You didn't volunteer, you were volun*told*. Happens to the best of us, and the worst. Sometimes people need to be led, and you don't get a say in that. The real trick is to be a person worth following."

"But I'm not," Amy blurted.

He fixed his gaze on her, silent, waiting.

"I keep thinking about the day before I got here," she said. "My boss was a real piece of garbage. And he kept hitting on this girl I worked with and I...didn't stand up for her. I could have. But I was afraid. So I didn't. Then Jellica and her pals started making trouble at breakfast and I should have stood up to them right then and there, and I didn't. Maybe if I had, they wouldn't have gone after Nora in the showers—"

"It's funny," Orris said, cutting her off. "All I hear is 'don't' and 'can't' and 'afraid' from the student who risked her enrollment and broke into the kitchens on her first night here, all to help a girl she had just met."

Amy stared at him. Her eyes went wide.

"You...know about that?"

"Nope. If I knew about it, I'd have to report it to Chen Lan, and if she knew about it, she'd have to expel you." He winked. "But I'm just a doddering old fool and my eyesight isn't what it used to be, so neither of us knows anything. As far as Jellica Barnes goes, unfortunately, she's going to be a thorn in your side for a while."

"I can handle her," Amy said. "I've been dealing with bullies my entire life. I can take it. Nora shouldn't have to, and neither should Vail. What's Jellica's problem, anyway? It's like she's appointed herself the Academy's gatekeeper, and she's mortally offended that anyone but her and her friends even *goes* to this school."

Orris stared down at his hands. He steepled his fingers and contemplated them, putting his thoughts in order before he spoke again.

"Things aren't always as they appear, kid. Especially here. One thing you can be certain of, though: whether they've been here for three days or three years, everyone at this Academy is fighting their own private war. I know it's hard, considering Jellica doesn't exactly invite any kind of warm feelings, but...try to kindle a little bit of compassion in your heart for her. It will matter. I promise."

"Can I feel compassionate while I'm beating her face in? Because if she keeps picking on Nora, I don't see this going any other way."

Orris cracked a smile. "You know Jellica is Professor Chalk's best student, right?"

"Is that why she gets away with murder?"

"No. But it's something you should bear in mind while keeping that temper of yours in check."

"So I can't fight her, or at least I can't win if I try," Amy said. "How am I supposed to protect Nora, protect Vail, juggle four classes, and learn magic, all at the same time?"

"Seems like a mountain blocking your path, doesn't it? But that's because you're used to doing everything alone. Have you ever had anyone watching over you? Anyone covering your back?"

Amy thought about her mom again. Her voice was muffled in Amy's thoughts. Her face a blur. She caught bits and pieces, glimpses and echoes. She wasn't sure how much was real, and how much was a figment of her imagination.

Didn't really matter, in the end. Her mom was gone.

"Friends?" Orris added. "I don't mean on your social media. I mean real friends. The kind of friends who'll help you bury a body. Metaphorical or otherwise."

"No," Amy whispered, feeling lost.

"Well now you do. Those ladies back in your dorm room didn't put you in charge just because they didn't want the job. They *like* you."

"I...can't imagine why," she said.

"You should find out. You might just learn that you like you, too. I know, it's a scary prospect. Point is, it's only a losing battle if you insist on fighting all alone. A very wise man once said that when he was a boy and saw scary things on the news, his mother would tell him to look for the helpers."

"The helpers?" Amy asked.

"Sure. Because when disaster strikes, there are always helpers. People looking to pitch in and make things better."

"And...what if I don't see any helpers around?"

Orris rose, stretched, and walked over to the cluttered jumble of tack and tools. He rooted around and pulled out an old three-tined pitchfork.

"Then *you* must be there to help."

He held out the pitchfork.

"You can start by mucking out the stables. Comet and Prince appreciate your service."

\*\*\*

Dusk was a couple of hours away, Amy reckoned, though the distant, hazy, cold orb of the sun moved with a mind and rhythm of its own, shrouded behind clouds of wet, dirty silver. The walls of the Academy towered behind her, fading in the growing distance as she hiked the forest trails.

"First-years aren't supposed to leave the grounds, with the exception of going to and from Professor Mallory's gardens," Orris had told her, "but that's a guideline, not a rule. Just stick to the marked paths, use the buddy system, get back before sundown, and don't go into the woods. Between here and Mallory's place is safe enough. By which I mean it isn't *safe*, but I walk those trails on the regular and I haven't had to scare any bears off for a couple of months now."

"Can I borrow your rifle?" Amy had asked him.

"Nope." He held up an extra pair of thick canvas work gloves, the fingers stained black with gardening soil. "But you can borrow an extra pair of gloves for your friend Vail."

"I'm that obvious, huh?"

"Don't touch any plants with your bare skin, especially if you don't know what they are. And don't eat anything you find out there."

"Come on," she said. "I'm not dumb."

Mr. Orris had shrugged, gazing off into the distance. "Last year, a kid tried to pet a bobcat. I learned on that day that magical aptitude is no measure of intelligence."

Now Amy trudged under the slowly setting sun, hands firmly gloved, cradling a thin library book in the crook of her arm as she and Vail filed from one wooden marker to the next along the curving dirt trail. Strong, thriving pine trees rose around them, their boughs blotting out the sky, the air thick with birdsong. Amy's shoulders and back ached from hours of working in the stables, but the excitement of discovery pushed her onward.

"For a Victorian ghost," Vail was saying, "Adelaide is *sassy*."

"Yeah, Mr. Orris said you weren't going to get anything out of her. I guess somebody tries that every year."

Vail craned her neck, gazing up at the trees.

"Well, since you wanted to go play with the horses," she said, "I got stuck working with Olivia in the library."

"Ouch."

"She's not a bad person, she's just annoying on a level that wounds me in my very soul. So what's our plan out here?"

Amy brandished her book. She opened it, ruffling through pages covered in diagrams of plant life and floral anatomy.

"Mr. Orris confirmed my theory."

"That everything here came from somewhere else," Vail said.

"Exactly. Now, this book is about the healing properties of medicinal plants commonly found in temperate forest biomes. The author was a magician who traveled to six or seven different worlds, studied the plant life, and wrote this thesis to compare and contrast what he learned."

"Roses by any other name," Vail said, repeating Professor Mallory's remark from class. "Even if we find a match, it might not work the same way."

"Sure, but we have to start somewhere." Amy's eyes shone bright behind her glasses. "I figure we can study the local flora and see if anything is a perfect match to the examples in this book. The founders wanted to build a self-sustaining ecosystem on Firebreak Island—"

"So everything they brought here would have come from the same place," Vail said, catching on. "Invasive species wreak havoc all the time. They wouldn't have taken a chance on throwing weird stuff from different worlds together. Safer and smarter to recreate an environment that already exists."

"You got it. We could narrow it down even more if we figured out what worlds our professors originally—"

A long, deep growl from the underbrush froze the words on her lips.

# Chapter Twenty

The bushes rustled, parting to make way for the growling voice and the beast it belonged to.

It was a bobcat. A well-fed bobcat, nearly two feet tall, with tufted ears, a thick glossy coat of spotted tan, and fur that drooped at the sides of its wide face like muttonchops. Its paws resembled big, fluffy pompoms tipped with steel knives. It stopped, stood tall, and fixed the girls with an expectant stare.

"Well," Vail said, backing away slowly, "at least it's not a bear."

Amy scrambled to remember everything she knew about wild cats as she copied Vail, edging back to the far side of the hiking trail.

"Don't make direct eye contact," she said. "She might consider that aggressive."

"I consider her aggressive."

"Cats are territorial. We're probably in her spot. Let's just...very nicely and gracefully leave."

Vail showed the bobcat her empty hands. "See? We're walking away now. You stay. Good kitty."

They eased further down the trail. The bobcat followed them.

"Don't look now," Vail whispered, "but Murder Mittens is stalking us."

The cat kept a careful distance, but made a point of squatting in the middle of the trail as she followed them, claiming her turf.

"I think she's just curious," Amy said.

"You're not going to try to make friends with it, right?"

Amy stared at her.

"You're becoming the weird animal chick," Vail said.

"I am not."

"Amy? Every morning a gang of crows shows up in our dorm room and screams at us until we get up and you feed their boss."

"I wouldn't say *gang* — I would use more of a musical chorus analogy—"

"Of course you would. Because you're the weird animal chick. You had posters of horses in your room back home, didn't you? On second thought, don't tell me." Vail pointed to a patch of wildflowers with thick, grassy stems, comparing it to a diagram in the field guide. "Hey, these look promising."

She crouched, reaching for the flowers, and the bobcat stopped her cold with another throaty growl.

"Are these...her flowers?" Vail asked.

Amy flipped through the field guide's pages, her brow furrowed.

"Wait. Those have four points on each petal. The drawing in the guide only had three, and the colors look off."

"Swing and a miss."

"Maybe not," Amy said. She could have sworn she'd seen something just like those flowers the first time she paged through the book. Finally, toward the back, she found it. A perfect match. She showed Vail the entry.

*Bittertear. Harvested from latitude 47.6062N, longitude 122.332 1W on Parallel Five. Known for its highly toxic sap, which will induce irritated, itchy skin and weeping sores for up to two weeks. Ingesting trace amounts may lead to hallucinations, seizures, or death.*

Vail looked at the book. Then back up the trail to the cat, who was glaring at both of them.

"She knew. She warned me off before I could grab it."

Amy waved. "Thank you, Murder Mittens!"

The bobcat yawned expansively and leaned into a stretch, poking its stubby tail in the air.

"You are so weird," Vail said.

"What? You named her."

"Also, why would they bring this stuff here?" Vail wrinkled her nose at the wildflowers. "Bittertear sounds *awful*."

"Ecosystems are fragile. Remove one thing and they can fall apart just like that. Even wasps have a purpose."

"They do not," Vail said, shuddering, "and I want you to never say that again."

***

"Okay," Professor Lanca called out, "everybody in, take your seats, we've got a full day ahead and a lot to accomplish."

Amy noticed on the spot that something was off. The professor's boyish charm clashed with his bloodshot eyes, and dark stubble clung to his cheeks.

"Let's see those focus crystals," he said. "A couple of you weren't getting it last time, so we're going to work on the Lamp Without Oil until everybody has the method down. I know, it's a glorified parlor trick and you're all eager to get to the *good* stuff, but you have to learn to walk before you can fly."

"We're going to learn how to *fly*?" Olivia gushed.

Professor Lanca took a deep breath and pinched the bridge of his nose.

"Absolutely not," he said. Then he shot a quick, furtive look at the closed lecture hall door. "So before we get to practice today...we need to have a little talk."

He sat down on the edge of his desk, the toes of his penny loafers dangling over the parquet floor.

"We have visitors coming. In two weeks, the Night Market will make its first trip to the island. The Academy has an arrangement: the Market visits twice a year, they keep our pantries stocked, and they open up their grounds for a single night. Think of it as...half open-air market, half carnival. The Racani run the show. They're a tribe of travelers, traders and performers who wander from world to world. I've been advised that it's a school tradition to allow students, including our first-years, to visit the marketplace."

Lanca rapped his knuckles on the desk, his feet swaying, while he frowned at something. He gathered his thoughts and went on.

"Last night I had a very long discussion with our headmistress about the matter, and asked her to cancel the practice. We did not see eye to eye on this. So, yes, you will all have the *option* of visiting the Night Market when it arrives."

"But you don't want us to," Vail said.

"Look, I'm as new as you are, I just started teaching here, but I'm familiar with the Night Market. I don't like it, I don't like the folks who run it, and some of the things that go on there are...not appropriate for people your age."

*That was dumb*, Amy thought, watching her peers react to that last comment. *Now everyone is going to go. You can't tell a teenager*

*something's too mature for them to handle and expect them to NOT*
*want a closer look.*

"What I can do," he said, "is lay down some ground rules for your safety. I can't trust the Market to watch out for you kids, so me and the rest of the faculty will have to pick up the slack."

"You're saying it's dangerous there?" Olivia asked.

"I'm saying they don't have their house in order, and I don't have a lot of respect or trust to spare for people who can't get their houses in order." Lanca hopped down from the edge of his desk, strolling across the lecture hall as he spoke. "But our headmistress made clear to me, in prolonged and forceful detail, that we depend on the Racani for supplies. Unfortunate consequence of building a magical academy in one of the most toxic armpits of the multiverse, but what do I know? I'm just a lowly expert, no reason to listen to me."

He held up one finger.

"Take notes on this. Rule one: use the buddy system. Go in pairs at least, and larger groups are better. Don't let us catch any of you wandering around the Market alone. Oh, and Professor Chalk will be there, so...yeah. The worst *I'll* do is tell you how disappointed I am. Abraham's ideas about school discipline are a little more intense than mine."

Vail leaned close, her breath a warm puff of air against Amy's ear.

"We're totally going though, right?"

"Of course we're going," Amy whispered back.

"Rule two," he said. "Enter into no agreements, arrangements, contracts, or bargains beyond exchanging cash for goods. If anyone offers you a job, walk away. If anyone offers you a quest...don't be flattered, just run. And never, ever give your word if you don't intend to keep it. The Night Market has its own ways of correcting such problems, and you aren't ready for that kind of trouble. As a magician, your word is your bond, so act like it."

Lanca stopped pacing. He turned to regard the class, focusing on Vail in particular, like this last part was just for her.

"Rule three, nothing's free. Racani culture is rooted in the principle of reciprocity: like for like, goods for goods. Every exchange must be a trade. Not necessarily a fair trade, mind you, but a trade. They believe that this reciprocity feeds the flow of the universe, and that taking something for free, or giving it, creates a sort of...spiritual pollution. An imbalance that can harm everyone involved."

Olivia's hand shot up.

"The answer to the question you're about to ask is no," Lanca told her, "it's utter hogwash. Unfortunately, as you will learn, learning to tolerate odd cultural peccadilloes goes with the territory of being a working magician. The bottom line is this: if anyone at the Night Market offers you anything for free, even something as small as a single roasted peanut, do not accept it under any circumstances. They're trying to trap you in a one-sided deal, and whatever the real price is, I promise you won't want to pay it."

After that they worked on the Lamp Without Oil for a while. Last time, manipulating the winds of magic and making a light bulb glow without power had felt to Amy like she was testing out a new muscle, one she didn't even know she had. Now it was more like slipping into a comfortable, well-worn jacket. She didn't have to think too much; her heart knew the path.

"Let's break for lunch," Professor Lanca told the class. He glanced at the antique watch on his wrist, adorned with a rough, faded leather strap. "We'll meet back up at one-thirty sharp, okay? Hey, Ms. Nettle. Come here a second, let me talk at you."

Amy and Vail shared an uncertain glance as the other students rose and shuffled out of the room in loose, ragged groups.

"I'll save you a seat in the cafeteria," Vail told her. Amy nodded and walked over to face Professor Lanca. He waited, amiable but concealing his thoughts until her classmates had all left and the two of them were alone in the lecture hall.

"Like I told the class," he said, "I can't order you not to go to the Night Market. Chen Lan says it's tradition, and traditions are the grand backbone of something or other, I wasn't really listening at that point and I don't care. But you have two weeks to decide, and I want you in particular to think really hard about it. Will you do that for me?"

"Why...me in particular?" Amy asked.

"Because professors talk. I overheard Mallory telling Chalk about your encounter with the Corpse. You're a bright girl."

"That's what she said," Amy replied, "though at the time, I thought she meant—"

"You're also highly intelligent and capable. I could use a few more Amy Nettles and at least one fewer Erik in this room. And a much less ambitious Olivia. I swear she's going to make me start drinking again."

Amy raised an eyebrow. "Aren't professors...not supposed to talk about their students like that?"

He shrugged and spread his open hands as he leaned back against his desk.

"Beats me. I mean, do I look like a man who has a legitimate teaching degree?"

"Yes," Amy said.

"Well, I'm a good liar. I'm figuring things out as I go along, same as you. One thing I do know, though, is that you've got a little more of a natural...spark, than your fellow students. And, sad but true, that means you've got a little more to fear, at least until you learn how to protect yourself and pull a lampshade over your noggin."

Amy's lips parted, a question frozen on her tongue.

"No," Lanca told her. "You won't have to wear a literal lampshade."

"Just making sure."

"All things considered, a perfectly reasonable concern." Lanca reached back, snatched a folder from his desk, and checked his student roster. "Ah. I've been to your world, quite a few times actually. Nice place."

"Is it though?"

Lanca waved a hand toward the lecture hall windows and the dark, frothing ocean in the distance.

"Have you seen the *rest* of the multiverse?"

"Fair point," Amy conceded.

"I'm curious now. Ever read Shirley Jackson?"

Amy's eyes lit up. "Oh, I love her! *The Haunting of Hill House* was great."

"*No live organism,*" the young professor quoted, "*can continue for long to exist sanely under conditions of absolute reality.*"

"*Even larks and katydids,*" Amy replied, lost in a memory, "*are supposed, by some, to dream.*"

Professor Lanca was silent for a moment, holding her gaze.

"This house," he said. "This island, this world...it is not sane."

"But we can fix that," said Jellica, standing in the classroom doorway.

# Chapter Twenty-One

"Nothing a little winter cleaning can't fix," Jellica said, strolling into the lecture hall. "Taking out the garbage, that kind of thing."

In the corner of Amy's eye, Professor Lanca's body went tight as a drum. He pushed himself away from his desk and turned to face Jellica, putting himself between her and Amy.

"Miss Barnes," he said. "I believe you're supposed to be in Professor Chalk's class right now."

"And I believe you're supposed to be burning in hell right now. I guess nobody's where they should be." The white-haired witch leaned to one side and fixed Amy with a hungry, predatory stare. "Of course. I shouldn't even be surprised. *You* put her up to it."

"Whatever you're accusing me of," Professor Lanca said, "choose your words carefully. And watch your mouth. I can have you expelled."

"No," Jellica said. "You can't. Chen Lan doesn't trust you with that kind of authority and she never will. Besides, this school needs me. It doesn't need you, *Red Lanca*. You're an impotent, spineless worm, which is why you sent Amy to attack me."

Amy blinked. "What? Are you talking about the fight in the showers? You started it by picking on Nora. I was just defending my friends!"

"Exactly how he wanted it to look. But now that I know the two of you are conspiring against me, I'm going to have to take harsher measures. He did tell you, didn't he? That we know each other? Professor Lanca and I go way back, long before either of us came to this school."

"No," he said firmly, "we don't."

Jellica ignored him, lost in a growing fury, seething, manic.

"He wants to finish what he started, and I suppose you're his obedient little patsy. So let me make one thing clear: neither of you is going to take me down. I'll dance on your graves before that happens."

"That's it." Lanca swiped the air with the flat of his hand. "*Enough*. Get out of my classroom."

She took a step back, then held her ground.

"It's going to be you or me," she hissed. "Only one of us is leaving this island alive."

The air shifted between them as a chill draft gusted through the lecture hall, prickling the flesh of Amy's arms. Lanca's face wasn't the same. Or maybe he wasn't the same man. It was like a switch had been flipped behind his eyes, transforming him into something cold and calculating and quiet and hard.

He closed the space between himself and Jellica and stood before her, close enough to touch. He stared into her eyes, taking her measure.

"Miss Barnes, I have no interest in killing you. If I did, you would be dead now. I would not challenge you to a duel, and I would not play any of Professor Chalk's silly games involving arenas and sportsmanship and *rules*. I would not give you any warning, or any indication that your death was imminent, or any chance to defend yourself. You would simply...die."

Then he leaned close and whispered something into her ear. Just a few words, the space of a breath, for Jellica's benefit alone. Amy couldn't hear what he said, but Jellica suddenly recoiled, staring in shock, like he had backhanded her across the face.

"You...*bastard*," she breathed.

"I believe I told you to get out of my classroom," Lanca replied.

\*\*\*

"So why does Jellica think Professor Lanca wants to kill her?"

In their dorm room, the lights extinguished and the air thick with snoring, Vail and Amy whispered, nestled in their side-by-side beds. The night wind rattled a skeletal branch against the frost-licked window.

"All he'd tell me is that 'she's a very disturbed young woman who needs counseling.'"

"Well, duh," Vail whispered.

"Right? This, we already confirmed."

"So do you think there's anything true about what she said? Like that thing about them knowing each other before they came here?"

"I think Jellica's elevator doesn't go all the way up to the penthouse," Amy said. "I just don't know why she gets away with everything. I mean, Professor Chalk almost expelled Erik for making an offhand comment in class. Meanwhile, Jellica can make death threats and walk around campus like she owns the place."

"Didn't Mr. Orris say she's Chalk's best student?"

"This is not a typical teacher's pet situation," Amy said. "Sure, overachievers can get away with a little more than slackers can—"

"You would know," Vail murmured.

"Hey now."

Vail rolled onto her side, flipped her pillow over, and watched Amy in the dark.

"Tell me I'm wrong," Vail said.

"I can say that your characterization of my outlook lacks critical nuance."

"But not that I'm wrong. Teacher's pet."

"What I mean is, a little favoritism is one thing, but Professor Chalk is a disciplinarian to the core. Letting Jellica run riot all over campus doesn't make sense."

"Opposites do attract," Vail suggested.

Amy stared at her, not following at first. Then she got it.

"You think..." she dropped her voice, breathing out the words. "Jellica and Professor Chalk? No. No way."

"The last time I bothered showing up at my old high school," Vail said, "my biology teacher was banging three of my classmates and even knocked one of them up. Everybody knew. Nobody did anything. You have to admit, as explanations go, it's plausible."

"We have to look into this," Amy said.

"Uh, no. We have to stay far, far away from Jellica Barnes and her entire circus of suck. She already thinks you're in cahoots with Professor Lanca. She sees you sniffing around, it'll feed her paranoia like jet fuel."

"'Cahoots'?"

"Cahoots," Vail said firmly.

Amy drifted under the covers, somehow exhausted and restless at the same time, swimming in and out of the waking world. She thought

Vail had fallen asleep in the neighboring bed, but then the freckled girl spoke up once more.

"I figured it out," she murmured.

"Jellica?"

"No. Remember when Professor Lanca was laying down the law about the Night Market? Did you notice how he kinda fixated on me, at the end?"

"Okay," Amy said, "so he *was* staring at you. I thought I might have been imagining things."

"No, he was, it was weird. But I get it. He really doesn't want us to go."

"I know he doesn't want me to go—"

"Us," Vail said. "That third rule, about nothing being free? That was for me. And I didn't understand at the moment because I was like...yeah, obviously. I know that lesson better than anyone, so why is he telling me?"

Amy didn't have anything to say, so she listened instead, her eyes keen in the dark.

"See, once upon a time, I was at a house party, and this guy...god, he had great hair. Isn't that stupid? Out of all the things to get stuck in your memory. But he said he liked my style, and he had something that would light my world on fire."

Vail's lips curled into a bitter smile.

"First hit is always free," she said. "Lanca knew. I think he didn't want to embarrass me or call me out in front of the class, but...Professor Lanca is watching out for us. He wanted me, in particular, to know exactly what kind of people we might run into out there."

*And what kind of temptations are waiting for you*, Amy thought.

"He's right," she said. "We shouldn't go."

"He's wrong," Vail countered, "because we've been studying and working our butts off and we deserve a night out."

"But..."

Amy's voice trailed off into silence.

"You don't have to tiptoe," Vail said. "I'm an addict. That's not a judgment. Just facts. But what am I supposed to do, turn into a hermit and hide in this dorm for the rest of my life? I can't live like that. There are *worlds* out there, and I want to see them."

Vail slid over to the edge of her mattress. She held out her arm, bridging the distance between their two beds.

"Come with me?" Vail asked.

Amy's hand found hers in the dark.

# Chapter Twenty-Two

When she was back in high school, nothing tested Amy's resolve like a blank piece of paper. She was a research machine who wrote essays like she was born in a library, but that first paragraph, that first line, that first *word* danced away until she finally managed to catch it, always feeling like she'd stumbled onto it by awkward blind chance.

Now she knelt on the stone pavilion behind the Academy, staring down at a wide sheet of butcher paper stretched out and held down by smooth round stones, edges rippling in a cold breeze. Her pen, a stubby little thing straight out of a nineteen-fifties office, zealously hoarded its last few drops of ink.

"Normally," Professor Chalk said, stalking between the rows of sitting and kneeling students, "drawing this kind of protective seal on paper is ill-advised. At the very least, it's far less effective and easier to defeat. That said, in the interests of preserving our school's flooring, this is how we practice. You will proceed to sketch out the basic circle of protection, from memory, with your textbooks closed."

The professor's ebony cane rapped with each step he took. He paused, his expression severe, at the small chorus of groans.

"To be clear, I don't expect any of you to have fully memorized the glyphs," he said. "I mean, you would if you were truly dedicated to the art, but I've learned to temper my expectations lest I suffer even more disappointment. This is simply an examination to check your progress and correct any bad habits before they become permanent."

He paused beside Erik, lowering his voice as he leaned in.

"It is not enough to learn. You must learn correctly. Flaws in your fundamental practice can dog you for a lifetime. I will break you of your bad habits, or you will not graduate my class. I can't make it any simpler for you people."

Memory wasn't Amy's enemy; dexterity was. Her concentric circles looked weak and deflated, like sad balloons. In the book, the first sigil was a writhing, powerful mass that made her think of some great tentacled sea-beast. Her version looked more like a fistful of undercooked spaghetti.

As she lost herself in the labyrinth of her growing anxiety, a shadow fell over her. Professor Chalk loomed, imperious, his cold gaze unreadable as he studied her sheet of butcher paper.

"Is that magnetic north?" he asked, pointing to the sigil at the top of the circle.

"It should be," Amy said. She felt like she'd just given the worst answer possible, and the way he glanced from the paper to her, his latex-gloved hands clenching the head of his cane, drove it home.

"Did you *check*?"

"Well, when we came out here everyone just started facing the same way..." She looked around at the uneven rows of students, all sitting in the same direction, each with their own page. "And I just, um..."

"Say the word," he told her.

It came out as a small, shamed whisper. "Assumed."

"You did." The professor took a deep breath, letting it out as a slow, tired puff of air. "In the art of magic, assumptions kill. Do you know the difference between a leader and a follower, Miss Nettle? A leader — if there were any to be found in this class, and I'm nearly out of hope —

would have asked questions, verified the facts, and formulated a plan for successful action. A follower…does exactly what you just did."

He turned his back on her.

"Disappointing," he said. "Do better."

While Amy's heart sank into her stomach, he started to walk away. He took two steps, the brass cap of his cane rapping against the gray stones of the pavilion, then paused. The professor turned his face, deliberating about something. He came to some quiet decision, then spoke again.

"You should consider apologizing."

Amy's mouth hung open.

"Sir? I…I mean, I understand what I did wrong, and going forward—"

"Not to me." His stiff shoulders slumped a little. "Get up. Walk with me."

Amy's heart slammed against her ribs as she followed him to the pavilion's edge, away from the other students. *This is it*, she thought. *He just decided to expel me for messing up. He's going to make an example out of me.*

*No. I'll fight. They're going to have to shove me through the Arch, and I swear I'll take at least one person with me. I'm never going back. I'll throw myself into the sea before I go back.*

Her hands curled into small, powerless fists. She didn't know what she was going to do with them.

"I heard what you did to Jellica Barnes," Professor Chalk said. He eyed her, expectant, waiting for her response.

*That's what this is*, she thought.

*I'm expelled. It's over.*

The professor's eyes flicked downward. She had never seen him smile before, but there it was, just the tiniest hint of amusement on his tight, thin lips.

"Why, Miss Nettle, this is surprising. Are you having violent thoughts?"

"I'm thinking," she said, "that I am sick and tired of everyone either coddling that bullying jerk or letting her walk all over them. I'm thinking I don't *care* that she's your favorite student, and I'm thinking that if you're about to kick me out of this school...well, I can't actually stop you, but I'm going to make a lot of noise before I go."

He scrutinized her, studying Amy like she was a painting on a gallery wall. His fingers stroked his thin goatee.

"You continue to disappoint, Miss Nettle."

She stared at him, speechless.

"In battle," the professor said, "momentum is key. Once you turn the tide of a fight and seize control of the momentum, you must hold it at all costs. You stunned Jellica when you opened her mind to the Corpse, but did you see how quickly she recovered?"

Chalk gently took hold of Amy's wrist and lifted it up, her fingers still balled in a confused fist. He tapped her knuckles, then leaned close and looked her in the eye.

"You *should* have broken Jellica's nose while you had the element of surprise on your side. That would have taken her out of the fight. I won't be teaching battle-magic until your third year with us, but you're never too young to learn an important lesson: a magician, just like everyone else, has fists, feet, and teeth. Learn to use them. Your enemies certainly will. You should take a note from your friend Miss Curran. She fractured two bones in that boy's foot. Simple, effective, and no spells required."

This was not what Amy expected.

She stood there, brow furrowed, trying to figure out how a rug had just been yanked out from under her.

"Professor Chalk? I...I think I might have misunderstood some things about you."

"In the art of magic..." he said, pointedly. He waited for her to finish the rest.

"Assumptions kill," Amy replied, her voice soft.

"Whoever told you that Miss Barnes is my favorite student should come and say that to my face. She is my most successful, effective, and lethal student. I also find her company loathsome and her general demeanor about as appealing as expired milk. I'd be more than pleased to see someone take her down a few notches. But you, a first-year newcomer still struggling to master a basic spell of protection, are not going to be the one to do it."

"I'm trying to avoid her."

"She's not trying to avoid you, though. Quite the contrary, from what I've heard on the grapevine. Do you even realize what you did to her?"

"I kinda just...repeated my meditation exercise and tapped into the Corpse's brain and then I..." Amy bit her bottom lip. "I threw it at her. Metaphorically speaking."

"In other words, with no training in combat magic, you improvised an entire attack technique, on the spot and under pressure, and successfully deployed it against a superior opponent." The corners of his lips quirked. "An impressive performance, let down only by your lack of follow-through."

Amy stared up at him. She swallowed hard. She had the feeling Professor Chalk didn't say the word "impressive" very often.

"She should have blocked," the professor continued, "but *someone* was arrogant and thought you weren't worth even minor defensive precautions. She won't make that mistake twice. It's been a very long time since anyone's managed to slip through Miss Barnes's armor, and even longer since anyone made her look foolish. I shouldn't have to tell you how she feels about being made to look the fool. She wants a pound of your flesh, and she's not going to let this drop."

Amy spread her hands, feeling helpless.

"What can I do? If I can't beat her and I can't hide from her, what options do I have left?"

"Apologize."

"Apologize," Amy echoed. "For not letting her beat my friends."

"Yes. And anything else she wants you to apologize for, whether you did it or not. I would suggest bringing her a gift, as well. She enjoys chocolate."

"You can't be serious."

"Humor," Professor Chalk said, "is not part of my skill set. Solutions are."

He reached into the breast of his tailored jacket and drew out a thin box covered in snakeskin, about the size of an eyeglass case. His latex-gloved fingers flipped it open.

The device was a projector. Tiny discs set into its interior glowed like small, steady points of candlelight, while thin beams wove a holographic image in the air above the professor's hand. It was a city of wrought-iron bridges and grand canals, of bright frescoes and grand mosaics, arrayed under baroque, brass-hulled zeppelins that watched from a starry night sky.

"This is my home," Professor Chalk said. "Nalajara, the City of a Thousand Princes. The name is barely an exaggeration, given the expansive, magically preserved, and horrifyingly inbred aristocracy. Dueling is the national pastime, and that's where I found my calling: I was a champion for hire. Nearly once a week, some fop would pick a fight but find himself lacking the stones to step into the ring, so he'd hire me to be his legally appointed stand-in."

"Were the duels...to the death?" Amy asked.

"Sometimes. Sometimes to the blood, sometimes to submission. Sometimes I'd have to beat a man down, carve him up, boil him in arcane fire. And of course, they were trying to do the same to me." He winced a bit as he flexed his gloved fingers. "I have fought, and won, over three hundred sanctioned duels. Each and every bout left me with a scar and a story. At the peak of my career, before the injuries crept up on me, I once took a victory without lifting a finger. My opponent heard he'd be facing Abraham Chalk in a fight to the death and he quit on the spot, swearing never to touch a blade for the rest of his life. That was fortunate for me, because I believe he would have easily won."

"And you're telling me that Jellica is just that good."

"She could make a comfortable living as a professional killer, but that's not the point. The point is, do you know how many of those duels were over anything *real*? No. Insults, perceived slights, social cuts. I have murdered good men and good women to soothe the wounded pride of an overgrown infant in a coronet. I have filled a graveyard in the name of pride. None of it was necessary. None of it should have happened."

He snapped the hologram shut and slid the case back into his breast pocket. Placing both hands on his cane, he leaned in, towering over Amy.

"The pain of wounded pride is nothing compared to the pain of death. A wounded pride can teach, and a wounded pride can heal. So swallow yours before this feud escalates completely out of control and someone gets hurt for real. Go to Jellica and grovel. On your knees, if that's what it takes. That should get her off your back for a while. And then..."

"And then?" Amy asked.

"You come to me," Professor Chalk told her. "And you *learn*."

# Chapter Twenty-Three

"Yes, sir." Amy said, staring up into Professor Chalk's cold, unblinking gaze. "I mean...I'll think about it."

"Do so. Oh, and one other thing. That maneuver you improvised, forging a connection to the Corpse and then shunting it to Miss Barnes? That was inventive, clever, and proved to me that out of this entire first-year batch, I have at least one student who shows genuine promise."

She started to reply, but he cut her off by rapping his cane against the stones at the pavilion's edge.

"And if you ever do it again, for any reason," he said, "I will expel you on the spot with no questions asked. You could have been killed. Or worse. That abomination has devoured the minds of far stronger magicians than you, Miss Nettle."

"What do you think it is? Professor Mallory says it might have come from a lab or something."

"Or something," Professor Chalk said, his tone dark. "What you need to know is that the Corpse is the psychic equivalent of a leaking nuclear reactor. Toxic beyond measure. And it knows we're here. It can sense us, the school, but it can't haul itself out of the water. I suspect it must be as if... Imagine if you were starving. Not for hours, or days, but for centuries. Nothing but the agony of hunger, and there above you, an academy filled with the most delicious morsels you can possibly imagine. Just out of reach. You know that Professor Lanca is a new arrival, yes?"

"I heard something happened to the last Introduction to Occult Philosophy teacher, not long before we got here," Amy said.

"The man was obsessed with the Corpse. He wanted to write his masterwork thesis on it. He opened a door, and it wormed its way into his brain like a maggot of obsession. Then, one night, he went for a swim." Chalk raised his mahogany cane, gesturing at Amy. "The Corpse knows your name. It knows the taste of you now, understand? And it will take far more than a taste if you give it the chance. Conduct yourself accordingly."

"Speaking of Professor Lanca..."

She let the question hang, hoping he'd fill in a few blanks from there. Instead he stared at her, dispassionate, waiting for the question.

"What's the deal between him and Jellica?" she asked.

"She believes," Chalk said, choosing his words with care, "that Professor Lanca committed a very serious crime against her, many years ago."

"Believes," Amy echoed. "But he says they never met before coming to this school. So who's right?"

He gave her a long, measured look. A thought jumped into Amy's head, unbidden. It sounded like the professor, speaking into her inner ear while his lips remained still.

*They both are.*

"Miss Nettle," he said, using his voice, "my job as a professor is to guide your magical development. I know you may find this hard to believe, but I want each and every one of you to succeed. That means deciding what you will learn, and when and how you will learn it, because I have the experience to guide your education properly. So when I say that something is none of your business and not a situation you want to be involved in, I hope you'll take it to heart."

He leaned closer.

"It's none of your business, and you don't want it to be. Drop it. And let me remind you that your circle exam is in two weeks. You may be promising, but you'll pass or fail — and be expelled — just like anyone else in this class. If anyone told you I play favorites, they lied. So keep your eyes on your own work."

***

Violet flames licked and shivered behind globes of frosted glass in the Academy library. The smell of dry incense clung to the air, like an offering made to some ancient temple. Amy and Vail sat side by side at one of the study tables, leaning over a shared copy of the *Liber Scutum*. Amy had leafed ahead of the classroom plan. She felt guilty that she was following in Olivia and Erik's footsteps, but she promised herself she wouldn't be reckless, not like them. She just needed to understand. She needed *more*.

Vail, meanwhile, sank steadily deeper into her own morose world. She answered Amy in monosyllables, staring blankly at the diagrams in the book while Amy tried to explain the symbolism of the north-eastern rune.

"And I'm...talking your ear off," Amy said, deflating.

"It's not you. It's me." Vail gestured at the book. "I'm never going to get this. Look, I understand the...the metaphors, and the symbols. I'm not dumb."

"I would never call you that."

"But everything else just slides in one ear and out the other. I froze up back in Chalk's class. I could barely remember how many circles to draw, let alone half a dozen intricate seals with a hundred steps each."

Amy thought for a moment, then it came to her. She snapped her fingers.

"You didn't spend a lot of time in school, did you? I mean, before coming here."

"As little as possible," Vail said, "and that was before...before I just couldn't go anymore. For other reasons. You know."

"Nobody ever taught you how to study, did they?"

Vail scrunched up her brow. "Isn't that what we're doing right now?"

"Your problem isn't grasping the theory. Your problem is memorization, that's all. It'd be the same if we were taken to...I don't know, alien math school."

"This is all alien math," Vail said, glancing down at the exotic symbols on the yellowed page.

"Exactly my point. Memorizing things is its own skill, and you never had to learn. So let me teach you. I mean, I'm just as lost as you are here, but I used to do tutoring for a little extra money, and I'm told I'm pretty good at it. Oh! Flash cards. I could whip up some flash cards."

"Can't ask you to do that," Vail said. "We both have to nail this test or we're out, and you're a lot closer than I am. Last thing I want is to see you get expelled because you wasted all your study time on me."

Amy slapped both palms flat on the lacquered wood of the study table, loud enough to draw a glare from Adelaide. The ghostly librarian, flickering in the light of her film projector, pressed a finger to her lips, then went back to reading a faded book of poetry.

"Okay, stop it," Amy snapped at Vail. "Just stop."

Vail lifted an eyebrow.

"This can't be a waste of my time," Amy said pointedly, "unless you're a waste of my time. And you aren't. There are more than enough people at this school who *want* to put us down. Don't make their job any easier for them, and don't be an accomplice to jerks who want to hurt you. You're better than that."

Vail leaned back a little, studying Amy in silence. She blinked.

"Damn. When did you grow claws?"

Amy hooked her fingers and wriggled them. "Rawr," she said, deadpan.

"Sorry, just not used to you kicking into top gear like that."

"Well," Amy said, her voice softer now, "I...I think you're cool. And when you talk down about yourself, you're basically saying that I'm a lousy judge of character. So be nicer to yourself and stop insulting me."

Vail flipped a casual salute. "Okay, captain, message received."

They worked together for a while, going over the glyphs and their meanings, while Amy devoted the back of her mind to coming up with a study plan. She could do this. They both could.

"I have to ask..." Vail said, apropos of nothing.

She didn't need to finish the thought. "I can't bring myself to disagree with anything Professor Chalk said to me. Yeah, I'd rather have a battered sense of pride than a busted arm or worse. Can't argue with his logic."

"But you're still not going to apologize to Jellica," Vail said.

"Tell you what," Amy said. "If the Corpse rises up from the ocean depths wearing a top hat and tails and performs an interpretive tap dance, I'll consider it. Anything short of that doesn't move me. She's a third-year student, and she won't be here forever. I've got plenty of experience hiding from bullies. I don't like it, but I like it a lot better than the idea of throwing myself on a violent psychopath's nonexistent sense of mercy. We just have to outlast her."

"We just have to ace this quiz," Vail said, gesturing at the book, "or Jellica and her gang won't have to lift a finger to get rid of us. Professor Chalk will do it for her. You...really think you can help me figure it out?"

"Learning how to learn is a skill, one most that people never really grasp. Anyone can stuff their head with facts and trivia, but it doesn't mean they really know how to dig deep into an idea, or make connections, or prove things with research. You can already do the hard stuff, you just need the techniques to *retain* it. And like I said, I've done this before." Amy paused. "I don't want to badmouth any of my after-school tutoring clients, but...let's just say, if I could teach them, I can definitely teach you."

"You're forgetting an additional problem," Vail said.

She held her right palm over the table, open and empty, facing upward. Then she concentrated. A vein throbbed near Vail's left eye, pulsing, as her jaw went tight as a steel cable.

Amy fell back, almost slipping from her chair and hitting the library floor, as a puff of blue-hot flame burst from Vail's palm. It rippled, roared and died in the space of a heartbeat, leaving nothing behind but a wisp of smoke and the acrid smell of brimstone.

"Even if I learn how to draw the most perfect circle of protection ever...circled," Vail said, "my magic is still busted. I can't control it. Hell, when it works, it's great, but making it happen is a total coin-flip."

Adelaide's ghostly voice carried across the vast chamber, her tone arch, the projector lending it a soft crackle.

"I do hope I don't need to tell any students present that starting fires in the library is strictly prohibited. And if the reasons for this rule are not patently obvious to you, I will be greatly concerned for your mental wellbeing. This has been a public service announcement directed at no one in particular. Carry on."

Vail turned, curled her fingers, and gave the librarian a sheepish wave of apology. Adelaide stared at her, then tapped the side of her nose with a slender, bony finger. She returned to her poetry book.

# Chapter Twenty-Four

The Saunders Academy didn't do holidays. At least not as Amy understood them. There were no Christmas celebrations on the school calendar, no Easter or Thanksgiving. It briefly puzzled her, until she connected the dots. Olivia — in the middle of late-night circle practice in the dorm — finished drawing the picture for her.

"I don't get it," Olivia was saying. "It's not like I've ever been all that devout, but I'm surprised the school doesn't have a proper chapel. I think we should at least be able to walk the Vigil of Twelve Hours and leave some martyr-lights. You know, for confidence."

Bahati, already tired and annoyed, narrowed her eyes as she crouched on the opposite side of the circle. "What are you talking about?"

"Uh, obviously, I'm a Branch Redemptionist. It's the biggest religion in the world."

"Your world," Bahati said.

"Right, but...you all have it on yours too, right?"

Bahati, Vail, Nora and Amy all offered blank stares.

"It's...the revealed truth," Olivia said. "You know, absolute scriptural truth? How could it only exist on my world, and not on any of yours?"

"I'm gonna tell her," Vail whispered darkly.

Amy nudged Vail's ribs with her elbow. "You will *not*."

"Dalton says his world only has four holidays," Nora piped up, changing the subject, "and if you don't celebrate, you go to jail."

"Festive," Bahati said.

Days went by, the Night Market looming closer, and the discussion stuck with Amy. One morning, as Chen Lan made her rounds through the dining hall, she managed to steal a second of the headmistress's attention.

"So, Adelaide is a ghost," Amy said, approaching her question from an oblique angle.

"She prefers the term *inconvenienced*, or *un-dead*," Chen Lan replied.

"But this implies the existence of the human soul, and an afterlife."

The headmistress flashed a small, charming smile.

"Precision, Miss Nettle. It *establishes* the existence of the human soul — seeing as you've spoken to Adelaide and witnessed the evidence yourself — and suggests that there may be one or more means of preserving said souls in a post-mortem state. Not necessarily what people think of when they hear the word *afterlife*, though."

"And...God?"

The headmistress's lips tightened. Her eyes still held a twinkle, though, as she regarded Amy.

"Our official policy is that, given that our students come from a vast array of worlds and cultures, the Saunders Academy makes no statement on religious practice. Students are encouraged to continue whatever practices they've brought from home, especially if such practice is soothing or centering, provided they aren't disruptive about it."

"That's not what I asked," Amy said.

"But it was the question I chose to answer," the headmistress said. "Good luck in your studies today."

That didn't mean the Academy didn't do holidays at all. Two days later a notice appeared on the announcement board in the school foyer.

"*Professor Mallory's class for first-year students is postponed until seven p.m. tonight*," Colin read out loud.

"Free afternoon." Dalton rubbed Colin's shoulders like a boxing coach. "Sweet, we could use that time to bone up on Chalk's homework. Or just hang out and not. Whatever."

Vail eyed him sidelong. "You are taking this seriously, right? We pass that test or we go home. Professor Chalk doesn't offer do-overs."

"Relax, babe. I've got no intention of going back where I came from." The corner of Dalton's mouth twitched. "Next week is Lady Martika's birthday bash. The parades are mandatory and go on for two days straight."

"Who is—" Nora started to ask, looking up at him.

"Dead chick. Super dead. You still get five years in a cube if you don't show up."

Colin looked back over his shoulder. "Can I finish? I was just getting to the good part. Mallory's treating us all to a cookout on the beach. Hot dogs, hamburgers..."

Vail grabbed his other shoulder and leaned in, her eyes wide.

"Say that again," she told him.

"You can read it all right there on the flyer."

"Yeah, but that was the best thing I've heard since we got here, so say it again."

***

Mr. Orris led the first-years out into the dark of the night. He gripped a lantern, holding it out before him like a crucifix to ward off vampires. Its bullseye beam sizzled against leaning trees and ghostly white spiderwebs glistening with dew. The path veered from the route to Professor Mallory's hut, turning east. A hand-carved sign nailed to a post at the side of the trail pointed the way to Hemlock Beach.

"We've got two beaches on Firebreak," Orris told them. "Hemlock to the east, and Gadfly over on the western end. That's where Professor Kamaka sets up his obstacle courses, though, so you'll be sick of the place pretty fast."

"His obstacle what now?" Colin said.

"Every year," Orris muttered. "Every year I mention that too soon."

They smelled the beach before they saw it. The salt wind was so strong Amy could taste it in the back of her throat, but there something else rode in with it. Something oily, unhealthy. Polluted.

"That fresh ocean air," Orris said, leading the way. They emerged from a narrow trail lined with overgrown trees onto an open expanse of dirty white sand that stretched north and south along the island's coastline. Dark water lapped against the edge of the beach, leaving whirls of slimy foam as it receded from the glistening shore. Brambles and branches littered the coast, the sand at the far edges giving way to dirt and clumps of tangled crabgrass.

A trio of paper lanterns, lovingly wrapped in shades of saffron yellow and black, hovered in the night air and cast globes of light across the shadowy beach, sending hermit crabs scuttling for safety beneath the sand. The lanterns slowly bobbed up and down, drifting but held in place, like balloons on invisible tethers. And at the heart of the beach, in the sphere of the middle lantern's glow, Professor Mallory stood at a wide charcoal grill with a spatula in hand.

Her apron was black with streaks of violet, and bore a firm admonition: *Do Not Attempt to Kiss the Cook*. She twirled the spatula in her hand and used it to wave the first-years out onto the sand.

"Come on down," she called out. "The sand is safe. It's the water that'll kill you."

Vail kicked off her dress shoes and peeled off her socks, letting out a happy sigh as she curled her toes in the sand. Amy was more hesitant. *If I keep my shoes on, would that be weird?*

"C'mon," Vail said. She took Amy's wrist and gently pressed her palm to the silky white sand.

"It's...warm," Amy said.

"Warm sand, cold night air, stars in the sky. Love to see it."

Vail took a deep breath as the ocean breeze caught a wisp of smoke from the grill and sent it their way, the air suddenly rich with the smell of barbecue and home-cooked hamburger patties. A cooler sat with its lid propped open, piled high with ice and what looked like cans of soda, the logos strange and unfamiliar.

"Originally Hemlock Beach was off limits to all students," Professor Mallory said, "especially after a mermaid crawled up onto the shore and tried to eat a sunbather. We doubled down on our warding-spells after that."

Amy could see the wards. When she let her vision slip just out of focus, looking to the water's edge and the *No Swimming* sign hammered onto a post in a puddle of tidewater, she made out the frozen ripples of an occult barrier. It was as if they'd conjured a ghost of the ocean, froze it into crystal, and flipped it onto one side, the water becoming a wall.

"Then we noticed our new students were showing a bit too much fear of the sea," the professor continued.

"Fear of...the massive and incredibly deep ocean filled with sea monsters," Bahati said. "I mean, reasonable?"

"There is a vast gulf between fear and respect," Mallory said. "Fear can be a powerful, life-saving tool — it's that little voice in the back of your mind, telling you that you're in a bad situation and you need to get out — but it can also make you freeze at the worst possible moments. Respect is when you see the danger, you understand the danger, and you protect yourself with equal amounts of rationality and intuition. So, I started these little get-togethers to let you spend time up close and personal with the water under appropriate supervision. Mr. Orris, would you be so kind as to open up those bags and find the plates? The burgers should be nearly ready."

Amy sat at the edge of the beach and reluctantly took off her shoes. She rolled her socks into them, put her bare feet on the sand, and curled her toes.

"See?" Vail said. "It won't bite. Feels nice, right?"

Olivia's squeal turned their heads. "I want to rub its belly! Can I rub its belly?"

She and several other students had gathered around a jumble of rocks down by the water's edge. Murder Mittens was stretched out on a boulder, preening, her steady, unblinking gaze like a promise of malice in the dark. She was keeping a distant but watchful eye on Amy.

"Of all the stupid—" Professor Mallory grunted, stalking toward them. She pointed her greasy spatula at the bobcat and hissed a short, hard incantation. A jolt of orange-streaked lightning surged along the jagged bend of the spatula and projected from its tip in a flat, long, and crackling beam. It shot harmlessly over the bobcat's head, but the sudden blast of light sent Murder Mittens running. Only a faint, furious hiss and the rustling of bushes remained.

"What am I even doing with my life?" the professor grumbled. "*Come out to the island,* she told me. *Teach at my school, we'll get together, have a few laughs.* Didn't bother mentioning that half of my students would be suicidal lemmings."

While Amy got used to the feeling of her toes in the sand, trying not to fret about getting it into her clothes, Vail went and grabbed a pair of paper plates.

"Cheeseburger?" she asked, offering one to her.

"Cheeseburger," Amy said.

Dalton walked by, holding up his plate in both hands as if to show them an amazing discovery.

"*Cheeseburger,*" he said.

"Cheeseburger!" Vail replied, showing hers.

As they ate, a foghorn bellowed in the distance. Amy's head jerked to one side, peering in the direction of the school through the thick forest boughs, but that wasn't where the sound had come from.

It was out on the water. Out on the horizon line, where a dark mass skimmed along the waves. It was coming their way.

Colin took a tentative step toward the shore, framed in moonlight, squinting into the gloom. "Is that...a ship?"

The galleon — closer now, with three rippling sails that looked like leather and a belly clad in sheets of rusted, tarnished brass — cast a spotlight upon the waters before it. The spotlight wobbled and dangled from the topmast in a way that reminded Amy, queasily, of an angler fish.

Professor Mallory stood beside Colin, clutching the spatula in her grip like it was a sword.

"That, Mr. Woodrue, is a thing that likes to play at being a ship. A perfect object lesson, right on schedule."

# Chapter Twenty-Five

As Amy watched, the ship melted.

Its leather sails ran like candle wax, the colors of skin and gristle shading to bubbling, drooling pus. Then its belly began to unfurl. It came apart like a mass of painted worms all joined in one terrible, hungry, writhing knot, spilling across the water as the illusion collapsed. Then, with a squelching, suckling rasp, the last remnants of the serpentine creature vanished beneath the jet-black waves.

"Rule of thumb," Professor Mallory told the first-year students. "They can't come up here, but we can go down there, at least if we're stupid and looking to die. The local aquatic life knows this. It has a hundred ways to lure you into that water, and a thousand ways to make sure you never surface again. Our saving grace is that most of these creatures don't really understand how humans think, making their efforts at temptation...slightly lacking."

"Most?" Amy asked.

"Have you heard the expression *Never play chess with a mermaid*?"

"If I had, I definitely would have remembered that."

"Well," Professor Mallory said, "it's a good proverb to keep in mind."

The headmistress drifted down from the forest trail, literally, her slippered feet dangling just above the sand as her long skirts ruffled in the night wind. She carried a doumbek, a hand-drum whose goblet-shaped curves were embellished in baroque engravings, and it wasn't long before a drum circle started on the beach.

"Excuse me," Bahati said, walking past Amy and Vail. "Music is happening. I need to get in on this."

Amy and Vail sat alone together, side by side, at the far fuzzy edge of a globe of paper lantern-light. The growing rhythm of the drum slid a beckoning finger around Amy's mind, quickening her pulse.

Vail asked a question with her eyes.

"We could," Amy said, looking over at the drum circle, "but I'm fine right here for now."

"Me too," Vail said.

After that they didn't need to say anything at all. They just sank into a companionable silence and the afterglow of a good meal, lounging on the warm white sand as a crisp wind ruffled their hair. Amy spotted Professor Mallory making the rounds from clique to clique, sharing a few words with each of her first-year students. They were next on her list.

"How are you both holding up?" she asked, though Amy felt like she directed it mostly at Vail.

"We're still here," Vail replied.

"Quite. You know, we have a saying back home," Professor Mallory said. "*I am awake and not crying. It is a good day.*"

"Checks out," Vail said.

"Can you give us any hints for the circle test?" Amy asked, hopeful.

"Start by studying the class materials," the professor advised her. "Then, and this is an important step not to be skipped, learn them."

"I was hoping for something a little more specific."

"I'm sure you were. Abraham and I have agreed to disagree about some aspects of his teaching style. I think he's crazy to start you off with such an advanced technique."

"The circle of protection isn't for beginners?" Vail asked.

"Oh, heavens no. The Lamp Without Oil is for beginners. Meditation and communing with the land is for beginners. Building a barrier to ward off curses, maelstroms, and flame is a *bit* more advanced, no matter what Professor Chalk tells you. I think some students need a little more time to blossom than others, but he's a firm believer in trials by fire."

"Culling the wheat from the chaff," Amy said.

Mallory nodded. "I won't say his class gets any easier after this, because I don't enjoy lying, but if you can pass the circle test it means you've got the right stuff to graduate. Doesn't mean you will, just that you *can*. So, what's your malfunction?"

"Ma'am?" Amy asked.

"Both of you have potential, and you're learning the foundations just fine." Professor Mallory pointed a sharp green fingernail at her own eyes. "Trust me. I've got the eyes of an old bird and they can see things that you can't...yet. So if you're still having trouble, you're dealing with some kind of external blockage."

Vail shot a warning, pleading glance at Amy. She understood: Vail was terrified of being found out, judged for her explosive bouts of uncontrolled pyrokinesis, banished for being a defective witch. Amy didn't think she had anything to worry about, especially not with Professor Mallory, but she cradled her friend's secret close.

"I can't make it flow," Amy said quickly, taking the Professor's attention onto her own shoulders. "I understand the principles, I understand the theories, but the power still fights me if I try to do anything more demanding than ignite a light bulb."

"Might take a little more diagnosing," the professor said, studying her, "but if my hunch is right, and it usually is, you're overthinking things. You have to trust the magic. Let it inside you. Let it flow where it will, and trust that it knows the way. The winds of magic aren't our masters or our servants: they're our partners, and this is nothing but a very intimate dance."

Vail bit her bottom lip, wincing in silence. Mallory shot her a pointed look, then turned back to Amy. It was clear to both of them who she was really talking to.

"You can't treat magic like a math problem. Magic requires closeness, trust, and when you've been burned before that doesn't come easy. Otherwise, you're trying to pour liquid gold into a clogged pipe."

"So how do I...fix that?" Amy asked.

"Most likely by small opportunities and baby steps," Professor Mallory replied. "If there was a one-size-fits-all panacea for pangs of the heart, I would have dosed you all upon arrival. You can solve this problem by realizing, first and foremost, that it isn't *about* the spell-craft. It's about trust, which requires vulnerability. Magician, heal thyself."

She started to drift away, then paused, looking back. She locked eyes with Vail.

"You are *allowed* to be vulnerable here," she said. "You are not allowed to fail."

Then she moved on, over to another group of students sitting down by the shoreline.

***

"I'm gonna kill her," Bahati said.

Sitting cross-legged on the dorm room floor, Nora leaned forward to drawing the curve of a circle for another late-night practice session. She gave Bahati a skeptical look.

"So first you don't want Olivia here, now you do."

"Not the point," Bahati countered. "We started these practice sessions as a team. She should make kissy-face with Erik on her own time."

"Allegedly," Amy said, focused on her work as she drew a serpentine glyph, "they decided to study together from now on because they're both so much more advanced than the rest of us."

Bahati glared at the half-finished circle, overlaid across the faint, still-visible lines of failed and erased sessions past.

"It's like I told my second touring manager," she said. "'I don't want to fire you, I want you to suck less and stop making my life more difficult than it already is.'"

"Did it work?" Vail asked.

"Ask my third manager."

"Night Market's coming tomorrow," Nora said.

"You got someone to go with?" Bahati asked.

"Not yet."

"You're with us, then. I'm going down with the guys. Amy, Vail? Plenty of room."

Amy was lost in thought, holding her copy of the *Liber Scutum* next to the glyph she'd spent the last twenty minutes drawing. All she could see were the differences, the flaws, her handful of limp spaghetti compared to trellises of arcane power.

"Academy to Amy," Bahati said, waving a hand to catch her attention. "Hi. Um, look, I don't want to criticize, but we've all moved on to our second or third glyph and you're..."

"It isn't right," Amy said, frowning at her handiwork.

Bahati glanced between her copy of the grimoire and the floor. "Looks fine to me."

"It's not perfect yet."

"I didn't say perfect. I said fine, and fine is what we need if we're gonna get this done tonight and get some experiments in."

"Perfect is the enemy of the good," Nora added, her voice small but authoritative.

"You're twelve," Bahati said, staring at her. "Where do you even hear this stuff?"

"Books."

Amy curled her lip and added a few more strokes of chalk to the sign on the wooden floorboard, fleshing out a tail here and a curl there.

"*Amy*," Bahati said. "Let it rest like a good cut of steak and move on, okay? We need you with us here and now, not five minutes ago."

\*\*\*

The next afternoon, Mr. Orris found Amy outside the dining hall and told her to stop by later. She found him on the edge of a tangerine sunset, chopping wood behind the stables, bringing the ax down with the strength of a man half his age. He stopped to catch his breath, ruffling his sweat-stained shirt while a crisp gust of wind rolled through.

"Got something for ya," he said, holding up a leather pouch that smelled of old, stale tobacco. "Assuming you're going to the party tonight."

Amy took the pouch, curious. She tugged the drawstring and shook it out into her hand. A scattering of silver and pewter coins, their regal faces worn down by corrosion and time, tumbled into her open palm.

"It's a little more than the pay we agreed on," the caretaker said, "but you're doing a good job and the horses like you, so...call it a luckpenny."

"Thank you," Amy said, rubbing her thumb across the coins. "Are you going too?"

He set his ax down and wiped the back of his hand across his brow, gazing at the sunset on the horizon.

"Nah, the critters always get riled up when the Market opens a portal onto the island. I think they feel the pressure shift, and it makes 'em anxious, so I stay behind to soothe their troubles."

"Do you need help? I could stay with you—"

"And miss your first time at the Night Market?" He broke into a weathered smile. "Hey, do me a favor. You know what stick candy is?"

"Candy...made of sticks?"

Orris's shoulders slumped. "Youth is wasted on the young. Just look for the confectioner's tent and tell 'em you want some of the root-beer flavored candy sticks. I look forward to those things all year."

"I could stay and you could go."

He scratched the back of his sunburned neck. "You're that nervous, huh?"

"I'm not nervous for me," she said.

He seemed to understand, taking her in as he nodded slowly.

"That's what the buddy system is for," he said. "You watch out for her, she'll watch out for you."

"We're... I'm...going with a whole bunch of first-years, I think. Just a big...group outing."

"Sure," he said, in a tone that could have meant anything.

"Professor Lanca says the Night Market could be dangerous."

"If Professor Lanca tells you the sky is blue," Mr. Orris chuckled, "you'd better stick your head out the window and check if you know what's good for you."

"So he's wrong?"

"No. The sky *is* blue, and a broken watch tells the perfect time twice a day. Guard yourself at the Market. The people running that show don't want to hurt you. They want to impress you and wriggle into your good graces, which is arguably worse."

"Impress me?" Amy shook her head. "Why? I'm nobody."

"Today's fledgling is tomorrow's bird of prey. Considering how much of their business involves catering to dimension-walkers and magicians, the Racani make a point of knowing who's who in the occult underground."

"So they can sell stuff to us later, once we graduate? That doesn't sound so bad."

Orris gave her a wan look. "Only if you don't mind a band of roving merchants keeping a dossier on you. They sell more than relics and books. They sell information. You got the lecture about not taking anything for free, right?"

Amy nodded. "Professor Lanca drilled it into our heads."

"A broken watch at the right time," Mr. Orris said, still gazing into the distance. "Always remember this, kid: if you get offered anything for free, that means *you're* the product."

# Chapter Twenty-Six

A t last, the Night Market was here.

It arrived with a pressure front that bit down on Amy's sinuses like an alligator clamp, forcing her to pull her glasses off and lie down until it passed less than a minute later. Passing, over them and through them, a sensation like an invisible soap bubble expanding to envelop Firebreak Island all the way from beach to white-sand beach.

In a great clearing a ten-minute hike from the Academy gates, the Market's vendors and performers arrived in their eccentric homes: caravans and wagons, some painted peacock colors and embellished with gold leaf like circus stagecoaches, others rusted out, wobbling on patched tires, pulled by draft horses in lieu of dead engines and dried-up oil lines.

The caravans formed a rough circle, looping around the great clearing's perimeter and forming walls against the gathering dark. Then the vendors set up booths and tents, erecting a midway and an open-air bazaar with practiced efficiency. The air soon filled with the sound of song, jangling music played upon sitars and snares. It was an invitation, the sound washing up through the forest to the school gates, just a few minutes' walk away.

Students were already beginning to arrive, drifting wide-eyed into a wonderland of silken tents, pipe-smoke, and glittering, flowing coins.

Three of those students wore scarves of checkered steel. Tullo was still stinging from the memory of his fight in the showers — emotionally and literally, considering his foot ached with every step he took, reminding him how Vail had gotten the better of him. A first-year student. His jaw clenched so hard it shook.

"I'm going to kick her ass tonight," he said through gritted teeth.

At his side, a girl with a shock of pumpkin-orange hair, piercing green eyes, and a sneer gave him a dubious look. She wore a safety pin as an earring, and thick mascara lined her eyes in a hawk-winged swoop.

"And did the boss give you permission to do that?" she asked.

"Shut up, Gecka."

Prentise followed them, loping two steps behind, wearing her silk chessboard scarf and black lace choker. The pale teenager said nothing, just flashed too-sharp teeth at anyone who came too close.

"I mean," Gecka said, "if we're talking about deserving people getting their asses kicked, you going behind Jellica's back should really make it happen. Maybe she'll even let me do it."

"Shut *up*, Gecka. Why are you even walking with me if you don't want to get in on this action?"

She stuck a thumb back over her shoulder, at Prentise.

"Jellica told me to feed her cat."

Tullo froze in his tracks. He slapped Gecka's shoulder and pointed. She stopped too, following the tip of his finger.

"Look who we have here," he said with a wicked smile. "Oh, we are *going* to feed the kitty tonight."

***

*It's a carnival*, Amy thought, stepping onto the midway with Vail at her side. She looked up at the brightly colored tents and the paper lanterns as a stilt-walker loped between market booths and a dancer spun burning hoops on her wrists, drawing whorls of flame in the night air before spitting fire up at the stars.

"They said they were going to meet us here." Vail narrowed her eyes, hunting through the crowd for any sign of their friends. "I thought they left the school before we did, though."

"Did Adelaide give you anything for helping out in the library?" Amy asked.

"Better believe I earned it, too. I had to clean her projectors." She shot a sidelong look at Amy. "Projectors. Plural. And they have *goop* inside of them, like egg yolk."

"I had to muck out the stables."

"Don't know what that means," Vail said, "and I don't want to."

"You see, horses—"

She cupped her hands over her ears. "Nope, nope. This is our night off. Nobody can make me learn anything tonight. Come on, let's go look for the guys. Dalton's tall enough to stand out in any crowd."

Amy did spot a familiar face, and she caught Vail's eye with a sharp, hard nod. Three Blades were making their way across the marketplace with violent intent.

"Don't know who they're hunting," Amy started to say.

"But it's not you."

"They're going after somebody, though," Amy said. "Don't like that."

Vail craned her neck, checking all around them.

"Remember the showers? We should get some backup first."

"Should," Amy said. She watched the three students infiltrate the churning crowd, almost slipping out of sight. "But whatever they're up to, they're doing it right now. How about this: I'll follow them and try to stall. You go find our friends and round up a posse."

"Uh, no?"

Amy turned to face her. Vail shook her head, firmly.

"That's not how we do things," Vail said.

She walked with Amy, hot on their targets' heels. Together.

They found the unfamiliar teenager, Gecka, keeping careless watch near a roped-off storage tent made of brightly colored quilt patches. She sauntered up to block their path as they got closer.

"Got a message for you," Gecka said. "From Jellica."

Vail stalked right past her, rounding the corner, and peered into the narrow alley between the storage tents. Tullo and Prentise had cornered Nora, backing the tiny girl up against the rippling side of one tent.

"Same song, new verse," Vail said. She clenched her fists at her sides, elbows curling back.

"A message...for you," Gecka said to Amy. "Not her."

"I don't care about anything Jellica has to say, to me or anybody else," Amy said. "You can tell her I said so."

Gecka had a habit of licking her lips, her mouth slightly parted, her tongue flickering out now and then to taste the air between words.

"She wants to talk to you. To...settle some business. Come up to the third floor sometime. Come alone, though." Gecka slowly reached out. Her finger trailed idly along Amy's shoulder, before Amy angrily yanked it away. "Hey, why so hostile?"

"Why do you think?" Amy snapped.

Behind Gecka, the other two Blades turned to square off with Vail. Prentise dropped into a crouch, curling her sharp fingernails and hissing, while Tullo kept an iron grip on Nora's shoulder.

Just for Amy, Gecka's wet lips curled into an eager grin.

"Want to see something awesome?" she asked. "Watch this."

Gecka raised two fingers to her mouth and whistled, two short, sharp whoops. Prentise's head turned, and the girl's eyes flashed in the dark. She turned her back on her former prey and loped over to crouch at Gecka's side, completely abandoning Tullo.

On his own now, Tullo stood face to face with Vail. He let go of Nora's shoulder and took a hesitant step back.

"Won't tell anybody if you stomp him into the mud," Gecka told Amy. She stroked Prentise's hair and scratched behind her ear. The feral girl shut her eyes and leaned into Gecka's hand. "See? We're not all terrible. I promise."

"*Not cool, Gecka*," Tullo snapped. He edged away as Vail closed on him.

"You should run," Vail told him. "If you can manage it."

***

Amy and Vail kept Nora close between them as they wove through the churning, delighted crowds on the carnival boulevard. Vail rested her hand on the back of Nora's neck, a bit of quiet reassurance, while they steered her to safer climes.

"He actually ran," Vail said.

"He hobbled," Amy said.

"Away from me. And what's the deal with Choker Girl?"

"Prentise?" Nora looked up at her. "Did you see her *teeth*?"

Amy pointed, spotting a happier sight up ahead. Just as Vail had predicted, Dalton stood head and shoulders above the crowd. He turned, saw them, and held his arm high, waving them over.

Amy was thinking about Jellica. First and foremost, wondering where she was, if she was lurking somewhere, watching them, getting ready to strike from the shadows of the Night Market. She shook off her paranoia, reflecting on what Anahera told them during their first lunch at the Academy: *A fish rots from the head down. Many of them are quite lovely people, if you catch them alone, but united they all dance to Jellica's tune.*

The other girl, Gecka, had shown a moment of unexpected mercy. Or, at least, she'd been more interested in humiliating her fellow Blade than in hurting the first-years. Amy knew she couldn't expect a gift like that twice, especially if Jellica was there to see it.

"We were supposed to meet out front," Vail said, clasping Dalton's arm and drawing him into a quick, tight hug.

"Someone got distracted," Colin said, nodding at Bahati. She clutched a paper cone half-filled with what looked like long, baked bread sticks glistening with amber crystals. The crumbs of already-devoured treats clung to the rolled paper.

She thrust the cone at the new arrivals. "Eat one of these. Seriously."

Amy gingerly took one between her fingers, irked by the sensation of crumbs and stray sugar on her fingers, and gave it a tentative bite. A burst of flavor hit her mouth, a blessed union of fresh-baked bread still hot from the oven, cinnamon, and sugar, all with a gooey, molten core that tasted something like cheesecake.

"Right?" Bahati said.

"Oh yeah," Vail said, nodding vigorously as she gobbled hers down. "We need more of these."

"And if my white card worked on this planet, I'd hire an in-dorm chef for all of us." Bahati let out a tiny sigh. "More money than a small nation and I can't spend any of it."

Dalton laughed. He held up a pair of tarnished silver coins, rolled them across the back of his knuckles, then flipped his hand around, snatching them out of the air and making them disappear under his curled fingers.

"For me? This is flush, babe."

"Who is that?" Nora asked, staring ahead.

A wandering merchant had attracted a crowd, mostly first-year students Amy recognized from outside their little clique. He was a stoop-shouldered man dressed in heavy swirling layers of robes and rags, so many swatches of earth-brown and black that it was hard to tell where any piece of clothing began or ended, all of it caked with days of road-dust. The robes almost swallowed him, with sleeves that drooped low on his hands and a hood that cast his eyes in shadow, revealing only his bulbous nose and the bony spear of his chin.

He walked with the aid of a staff-turned-sales-display, with deer antlers jutting from its gnarled wooden length, the bone draped with glittering silver chains and talismans. The old man leaned into the staff, one of his legs shorter than the other. His torso was squat, his arms long but uneven. His head oscillated as he walked, in a tic Amy could only interpret as something...reptilian.

The wandering merchant had already captured Erik and Olivia's attention. The two teenagers were holding hands, breaking contact only long enough for Erik to slip something into his back pocket. It looked like a small, thin-covered book.

"Now for aid in studying," he was saying to Olivia as the other students approached, "I have amulets aplenty. For you...something attuned to the rhythm of Caduceus and the fourth house in the fourth hour, I think."

As Amy neared, the merchant's head snapped toward her. His crooked nose wrinkled, as if sniffing the salt-tinged air, and his blood-less lips curled in a smile.

"More customers, more and more, delightful. Gather round, chil-dren. I'm Elmer, but they call me the Jangly-Man, and I promise, I have everything you need. You, there, young lady — what's your name?"

"Amy," she said. She noticed that Vail wasn't at her side. The freck-led redhead stood by her shoulder, two careful paces back.

Now Amy had his undivided attention.

The Jangly-Man approached her, sliding into her personal space, and leaned his staff forward. The rows of talismans draping from the antlers clinked and chimed.

"Amy," he said, tasting the name on his lips. "You look to these ancient eyes like a budding cartomancer. Is that so?"

She wanted to be.

She couldn't argue that Professor Kamaka's class had grabbed her imagination in a way the others couldn't quite match. But she hadn't told that to anyone, not even Vail.

"Y-yes," she stammered.

The world, the lights and flames and music, all faded into a dull roar. In that moment, they were the only people in the Night Market. Alone, face to face, on the carnival boulevard.

"And how is your practice coming along?" he asked.

"Well, we don't really use the cards," she said. "Yet. We're studying them in a book, though—"

He clicked his tongue and shook his head.

"That won't do. That won't do at all. Now where did I..." He trailed off, pondering, then snapped his fingers. "Ah, yes. As it so happens, I have a very special treat for a very special girl, and I've been saving it until I meet the perfect recipient. That could very well be you, my dear lady."

He reached into his robes and withdrew a fat deck of cards. He fanned them in his hands. It was a Navigator's deck, all fifty-six of the Low Suit cards. Faded, their rounded corners worn with time and wear, but perfectly intact.

"If you really want to learn," the Jangly-Man said, conspiratorial as he draped his arm around Amy's shoulder, his staff nudging against up her body like a shepherd's crook, "you *should* have a deck of your own."

# Chapter Twenty-Seven

They were the only two people in the world, the faces and lights around Amy and Elmer, the Jangly-Man, fading into a blur of mist.

"You deserve your own deck," he told her. "You're competent. Capable, aren't you?"

"I am," Amy whispered, staring at the cards.

"These 'teachers' are holding you back. Imagine what you could do with these cards. How much you could learn. The places you could go." His smile was a waxing crescent moon, widening by the word, and his breath smelled like rotting flowers. "An escape clause, just for you and someone special. You could feel secure. Safe. Have you ever felt truly, genuinely safe in your life, Amy? It's a wonderful feeling, and it seems so wrong to me that you've never had the pleasure."

She was beyond questions. The sight of the cards, the opportunities right in front of her eyes, mesmerized her, while his arm tightened around her shoulder.

"How much?" she breathed.

"Surely more than you could afford, but...oh, who am I to stand between you and greatness? I'll tell you what. You can have it. Gratis.

But I'll need something from you in the future. Just a little favor, nothing onerous—"

Professor Lanca's warnings about the Night Market came back to her in a flash. Amy edged back, squirming out of Elmer's grip.

"Not interested," she said.

He waved the cards, making them sway like a snake charmer's cobra.

"Don't take this the wrong way," he said, "But you're not very good at lying."

"You can keep the deck," Amy said, inching away from him. "Sorry. Not for me."

His smile curled into a tight, petulant frown.

"A shame. To think of it: you could have been the greatest graduate the Saunders Academy had ever known. A paragon, and a mistress of the cards. And you decided...*Not for me*."

He flicked his fingers out. The deck had vanished, leaving an empty, wrinkled hand behind.

"But there's still hope, my bright girl. Maybe not as grand as the future you *could* have just chosen, but one of power and light nonetheless. With this."

Now he held a single card. *The Psychopomp*. A triumphant woman in a witch's robes strode forth from a cloud of billowing gas. Sparrows took flight all around her, one landing upon her shoulder while another perched on one outstretched hand, a crackling and jagged crystal clutched in the other.

The woman on the card looked just like Amy. Maybe ten years older, with a lifetime of experience and all the winds of magic at her command.

"A taste of the High Suits," the Jangly-Man said. "A single taste. The spells you could weave with this one card...oh, the doors you could open. You could go anywhere. Do anything. Taste true freedom for the first time in your life."

*People kill for these*, Kamaka had told her.

Amy bit her bottom lip until she tasted copper.

"You could have been the best and you refused me. But you can still be second best, and my next offer will be nothing at all. Take the card and take my hand, Amy. It's going...and it's going..."

Vail's hand clamped down on the scruff of Amy's neck.

The world snapped back into focus. They weren't alone, they were standing in the heart of a crowd, and Amy's friends were all around. The music and the din of the marketplace washed over her.

"And it's gone," Vail snapped, pulling Amy back like a mother cat protecting her kitten.

The Jangly-Man snapped his fingers closed, as if crushing the priceless card, and showed his empty hand.

"Indeed it is," he said. "What a pity."

"Vail, what are you—" Amy stammered.

Elmer watched them go as Vail pulled her away, hauling her around the corner of a silken tent in the colors of a peacock's tail, breaking their line of sight. She turned Amy around and leaned close, their noses almost touching.

"Do you trust me?" Vail asked.

"Of course."

She dipped around the corner, shooting a look up the carnival boulevard, then back to Amy.

"I know a pimp when I see one," Vail said.

They kept walking.

That wasn't the last time they saw the Jangly-Man. Over the course of the night, as they drifted from booth to booth, savoring the smell of popcorn and fresh toffee and street food from a dozen different worlds, Amy kept hearing the distant rattling-coin sound of his staff just behind them. Always out of sight, echoing from the shadows.

"We need to stop by the confectioner's tent," Amy said, trying to keep her nerves in check. "Mr. Orris wanted me to grab some stick candy."

"Is it made of sticks?"

"That's what I asked."

Amy wasn't sure what she expected, but the confectioner's tent, lit by floating lanterns beneath a circus canopy of a dozen wild colors, was the laboratory of some mad alchemist. Serums dripped from alembics while burners hissed with blue flame and a vat of green fluid, which smelled like Key lime pie, bubbled behind glass. Racani chefs moved like a drill team, ferrying trays from ovens to coolers, spinning out long gooey stretches of caramel and slicing perfect squares of hot, freshly baked fudge. A thin trickle of smoke tickled Amy's nose, filling the back of her throat with the taste of pink bubblegum.

Amy held up a faded coin the size of her thumbnail to the nearest clerk. "Excuse me, sir? I'm supposed to buy some root beer-flavored stick candy."

The Racani behind the counter looked like any other human: olive-skinned, green-eyed, with tight short-cropped curls and an apron adorned with tied silk sashes. He gave a tiny laugh and looked back over his shoulder.

"Hey, *gromma Orris sichati, kai-kai*." He clapped his hands twice, as if dusting them off, and looked back to Amy and Vail. "We pick some up just for him every time we come through. You're new, though. Not the student he usually sends."

"First-years," Amy said.

One of the other chefs brought over a glass jar capped with an airtight seal. It was filled with dark brown sticks of sugar candy. The man behind the counter passed it to Amy.

"Take it. It's already covered, but tell him his account's running low."

Amy reached for the jar, then hesitated. She still held the coin in her other hand. Deliberately, pointedly, she held it out to the clerk.

"Despite that, sir, you're giving the jar to me. I'm going to need you to accept this payment."

The clerk broke into a gold-toothed grin, snatching the coin from her outstretched fingers and tucking it into his apron pocket.

"Teaching you right," he said, handing her the jar. "Always nice to see. Give my regards to the old man."

They ran into Colin and Dalton outside. Dalton wore a shark grin, and Colin looked shell-shocked.

"Bahati and Nora went to check out the music pavilion," Dalton said. "So, uh...have you seen the striped tent?"

Vail looked from him to Colin and back again. "Not sure I want to."

"Today," Colin said, "I am a man."

Dalton ruffled his hair. "You literally peeked under a tent-flap for three seconds before security chased us off."

"That was all it took," Colin said, still wide-eyed. "It's a rite of passage. You'll understand someday, when you have worldly experience like I do."

"Yep," Dalton deadpanned, "I can only dream of being a player like you, stud. Someday I might even go on a date with a real girl and everything."

The night stretched on and the crowds began to thin, the Academy's students drifting back up the trail in twos or threes, making their way back to the dorms before lights out. Vail stared up at the great house on the hill in the distance and frowned.

"Penny for your thoughts?" Amy said, holding up one of her last coins. "Or...whatever these are? I tried figuring out where they came from, but the island's translation spell doesn't want to cooperate."

"Just having fun. With you. Don't want the night to end, but we should probably..." She trailed off, glancing over her shoulder.

When she turned back, Elmer the Jangly-Man was standing in their path.

The crowds surged around him, parting like waves, though they barely seemed to notice him. He gave his deer-antler staff a rattle, silver talismans catching the lantern-light and glowing like fire.

"Miss Vail Curran," he said. "I can't believe I didn't recognize you at first. It's our job, you see, to tailor our wares to suit the very specific needs of our individual clientèle."

"I'm not your client," Vail fired back, "and we don't want what you're selling."

"Are you sure about that? You must be lonely, so far from where you came from."

He reached into his ragged, dirty robes.

"Could I interest you in...a little taste of home?"

Vail froze. Her mouth gaped, no words coming out, as he pulled a small plastic baggie from his inside pockets. Its contents glistened, dark and wet.

Amy grabbed her arm and pulled, hard. She dragged Vail along until they'd slipped through a gap between the tents, found another path, and lost themselves around a string of twists and turns. Vail still didn't say a word. Her skin was cold to Amy's touch, and her parted lips twitched.

"Hey. Hey, look at me." Amy grabbed Vail by both forearms and tugged her close. "It's time for us to go back to the dorm. Okay?"

"Yeah," Vail said, shaking it off. "Let's, um..."

"We'll find a different way back."

That proved to be easier said than done. The edge of the Market was a labyrinth of tents and sleepy caravans, some with candles gently flickering against the dark behind cheap patchwork curtains. *It should be this way*, Amy thought, leading Vail toward the path she was certain would connect with the main boulevard.

She stopped as a metallic jangle echoed her next footstep. She ducked into the shadows behind a rusted-out mobile home, pulling Vail with her. They crouched there, side by side.

Elmer hobbled past them. He paused, raising his hooded head and sniffing at the air. Amy held her breath. Her cheek started to itch. She fought the urge to scratch it, wincing, forcing her hands to stay perfectly still.

From the other direction, Professor Lanca approached. He stopped in front of Elmer. The two men stared in silence, taking each other's measure.

"Lovely night for it," the Jangly-Man said.

"For?" Professor Lanca asked.

Lanca turned his head, and locked eyes with Amy in the dark. Then Vail. He kept moving, one smooth motion, before Elmer could follow his gaze and spot the girls.

"A grand and wondrous show." Elmer raised his deer-antler staff high, making it rattle as he swept it out, taking in the marketplace. "Tell me, good sir. I'm looking for a pair of pretty young ladies..."

*Don't tell him*, Amy thought, desperate. *Please*.

"Try the striped tent," Lanca replied.

# Chapter Twenty-Eight

The Jangly-Man's lips curled into an unamused rictus at the professor's jest.

"Not the sort of female company I'm seeking, I'm afraid."

"Well," Professor Lanca said, "they say you can find anything you desire at the Night Market. You should keep searching."

Lanca turned to go, then hesitated. He looked back at Elmer.

"The girls you're looking for. One a mousy type, with cheap glasses and a cheaper haircut? The other taller, a redhead with freckles?"

"Yes," he hissed, leaning into his staff. "Those are the ones."

"Just saw them over at the music pavilion. You might still catch them if you're quick."

Elmer's staff rattled with excitement, his hand trembling. He thrust his other hand, empty for the moment, from his robes and offered it to Lanca.

"My thanks, good sir. Elmer the Jangly-Man, at your service."

Professor Lanca eyed him for a moment.

"I'm sure you are," the professor said, and walked away without another word.

Elmer watched him go, sniffing the air one last time. Then he shambled slowly in the professor's wake. Amy and Vail didn't dare breathe until he was gone.

***

All good things come to an end. One by one, the floating lanterns above the Night Market snuffed themselves out, inviting darkness and starlight. Tents came down, shutters locked tight, and the performers and vendors of the bazaar made their way back to their caravans for a night's sleep before heading to their next port of call.

Toward the southern edge of the clearing, a Winnebago camper from the Seventies sat on four concrete blocks, tires stripped, the RV's front hood scorched by the remnants of an old engine fire. Its door rattled on its rusty hinges and fought, stubborn, as it squealed open.

Elmer shambled inside, nose wrinkling at the sudden odors of sour milk and rot. He leaned into his staff, and the door swung shut behind him on its own.

"It's only me," he announced. "You can come out now."

A tattered, moldy curtain separated the back bedroom from the rest of the camper. It ruffled, then yanked wide, jolting on half-broken rings. The creature that emerged wasn't human.

It wore a musty, heavy cloak of black wool over a garment of rough tanned leather and brass studs, every piece mismatched and asymmetrical as if he'd picked his outfit from a armorer's rubbish bin. The face that stared down at Elmer, shrouded under a hood, had beady scarlet eyes and a long, snaggle-furred snout dripping with whiskers and drool.

The rat-man was more than twice Elmer's size, wide enough to fill the camper. And like Elmer, a low metallic clacking followed him as he walked, but it came from the weapon dangling at his side: a length of rusty rebar affixed to a wooden grip, bumping against the brass studs on his high, muddy boots. The rebar curled at the tip like a fisherman's hook, sharpened to a deadly point.

"I believe I asked you to bathe," Elmer said.

The rat-man, looming over him, spoke in a vicious growl.

"Your religion is literal filth."

Elmer twitched his nose again. He frowned, plucking at his patchwork robes, suddenly fastidious.

"Indeed. And yet, somehow, I still manage to practice basic hygiene. If we're going to be living together in tight quarters for the next six months, I expect—"

The rat-man moved with terrifying speed. One second, Elmer was standing before him, putting him in his place. The next he was gasping, turning red, as a long-clawed, black-furred hand grabbed him by the throat and hoisted him into the air.

"The client said you were one of their top men."

"I...am," Elmer stammered.

"Then you should be accustomed to obeying your superiors."

Elmer's feet dangled, spasming and kicking as he struggled to breathe. He glared, clinging to his spite.

"As soon as I see one, I will," he managed to croak. "Hands off, or your contract is canceled."

The rat-man let go. Elmer fell, crashing to the camper floor as his knees buckled under him. His staff toppled, silver talismans slipping loose and scattering under the cupboards. He lay prone for a second, rubbing his throat, swallowing hard.

"I think we're on the same page now," Elmer said, pushing himself back to his feet. "I can happily say, Mr. Shaddock, that your reputation for ferocity precedes you."

"When I desire a compliment from a human," Shaddock grunted, "I will tell you what I want you to say. Did you have any success at all out there, or was this trip yet another waste of time and fuel?"

"Better than success." The Jangly-Man's eyes glinted with eager mischief. "The advance scouts were right. It's *here*. On this very island. And while I didn't snare all the little beauties I wanted, I believe I've made a new friend for us. Who should, if my intuition is correct..."

A single, firm knock sounded at the camper door.

"I always know the weak ones when I see them," Elmer said, rubbing his hands together. "Back behind the curtain if you would be so kind, Mr. Shaddock. Let's not frighten our new friend. Not until they understand just how badly they need us."

***

Vail had gone to the washroom. She never came back.

Amy wanted to give her space and time. But as the minutes crawled by — the old mansion groaning, settling, the distant lights of the Market all doused and cold — she knew something was wrong. She slipped out of the silent dorm room and started to search.

The first-floor washrooms were empty.

Amy took deep breaths, trying to keep her rising anxiety in check. The showers were empty, too. She went from stall to stall, softly calling Vail's name. The grand foyer stood desolate, the violet braziers dulled to a faint firefly glow. The dining hall was locked, along with the library. Amy poked her head into empty lecture halls, straining to catch sight of a friendly face in the gloom.

She walked outside, alone.

The Arch of Resignation was a parasite, a constant fear feeding on Amy's brain, stoking her terror, but she didn't have to walk that far. Vail was in the courtyard, the same place they'd arrived on their first night at the Academy, sitting on the ground all alone with her back to the wrought iron gates. She looked up, greeting Amy with an unreadable, vacant look.

"Thought about climbing it," Vail said. "Wouldn't be all that hard."

"And going back to the Night Market."

Vail stared down at the pebbled path.

"Can I sit with you?" Amy asked.

"It's a free country. Planet. Dimension. Whatever."

Amy sat beside her, putting her back to the gate's bars, shoving a clump of pebbles aside with her heel.

"Would have been so easy," Vail said.

"But you didn't. You stayed."

Vail didn't answer.

***

Under his bedsheets, by the jack-o-lantern glow of a weak, flickering penlight, Erik studied his prize from the Night Market. It was a book, slim, its covers almost threadbare, the gilding on the title worn down to flecks of dirty gold.

*The Seventeen Tablets of Song*, the frontispiece read.

He flipped through the pages, drifting past exotic charts and tables of concordances. Incantations, twisting and barbarous, tantalized with promises of clandestine power. *A Spell to Plague the Unbeliever*, promised one chapter. *A Most Effective Charm for Conquest, to Make a Maiden's Heart Your Own*, offered another, right next to *A Method for Conjuring Most Pleasurable Apparitions*.

*I'm ready for this*, he thought. *Hell, I deserve this. Just wait until they all see what I can really do. They'll wish they'd shown me more respect.*

His finger rapped against a section buried deep in the tome. *Methods of Strengthening Protective Circles and Other Defensive Operations.* Exactly what he — and Olivia, he supposed — needed to pass Professor Chalk's class.

It was like the book had been written just for him.

\*\*\*

The door of an RV squealed in the night, rattling shut.

The Night Market was over now, quiet, slumbering, nothing to see or do. Professor Lanca stalked through the darkness, furtive, shooting quick glances over his shoulder.

He stopped short. Fifty feet away, at the end of a row of shuttered and empty booths, Jellica emerged into the moonlight. She froze, caught on her own midnight errand.

They stared each other down. Jellica's hand slowly eased toward the white velvet handbag resting against her hip. Lanca reached into his jacket pocket.

They stayed that way for a moment.

Then Professor Lanca took a half-step to his left. She mirrored him. And slowly, never taking their eyes off one another until they'd broken line of sight, they slipped into the maze of tents and caravans and went their separate ways into the dark.

# Chapter
# Twenty-Nine

D ays passed, and the Night Market fell into memory, the forest clearing stripped of anything but long, jagged scorch-marks through the overgrown grass. Nights came and nights went.

Amy dreamed of drowning.

Something gripped her ankle. Something like a steel cable wrapped in wet, rancid fat, dragging her down into ink-black water. She saw murky clouds, slithering sharp shadows, streaks of billowing red all around her.

She saw Vail, asleep and lost in the black, tethered by strands of seaweed that groped at her legs, her wrists, her hair. Amy reached for her. Vail's eyes snapped open and she let out a muffled scream, the last of her air escaping in a stream of bubbles, before the ropes hauled her down into the dark.

And all the while the pressure grew, building, squeezing Amy's head like a vise while her tortured lungs burned. She could make out something below her now. A chasm, vast and deep, drawing her in.

*Not a chasm*, she realized. She wasn't looking at the seabed at all.

It had teeth.

***

Amy's eyes snapped open.

She was in her bed, shivering, tangled in sheets drenched with icy sweat. The dorm windows were still dark, not a hint of sun on the horizon.

Her bare feet touched down on the cold floorboards. She padded to the door and out into the hall, heading to the washrooms. She clicked on the light once she stepped inside, and the overheads hummed to life. Cool water poured into the closest sink. She leaned down, scooped it up with both hands, and splashed it across her face. She focused on that. Real sensations, real things, to drive away the nightmare.

She looked up at the mirror, into her reflection. Someone had daubed a single word on the glass in rust-red ink.

*amy.*

Slowly, moving in slow motion as if still lost in a dream, she looked to the next mirror.

*aMy*, it read.

She took a few steps down, to the third mirror.

*AMY.*

And upon the fourth and final bathroom mirror, one last message, scrawled in a rough, eager hand.

*i know your name.*

Her paralysis broke. She grabbed a hand towel, soaked it under the tap, and scrubbed wildly at the mirror. She smeared the trail of words until they were a faint scarlet blur, then she moved to the next. And the next, until the last of the message was gone.

***

Amy fell back asleep at some point, though she didn't know how. She woke to crow-song and a very agitated band leader stomping on her chest with his little bird feet as he squawked in her face.

In the bathroom, not even the smeared memory of the words she'd erased remained. *Did I dream the whole thing?* She wondered. *A nightmare inside a nightmare. But it felt real.*

Stress, she figured. She wasn't the only one feeling it. Breakfast was like a slow march to the death chamber: the circle test was tomorrow and nobody, not even the most confident overachievers in the first-year batch, felt ready for it. Colin and Nora sat folded in on themselves, and Dalton couldn't even manage to crack a joke.

Amy had a plan. Sort of. She'd been working it out in her every spare hour since the Night Market, quietly resolved that she'd burn this school to the ground before letting Vail get sent back to the nightmare she'd been plucked out of. It didn't matter that the Arch of Resignation would steal her memories and make her forget that she'd ever had a fleeting chance at a second, better life. She'd still be back in hell.

There was a cruelty to this place. It was baked into the gray, mossy stones of the Saunders Academy, woven into its proud school banners and the pages of its textbooks. Gatherings after class had grown steadily testier, patience wearing thin, even her own friends starting to turn on each other or simply — like Olivia abandoning the dorm study group for private time with Erik — drifting apart.

Amy couldn't shake the feeling that it was all by design. The cruelty was the point, a crucible designed to test, burn, and break.

And that was the best motivation she could have asked for.

"They want to send us home," Amy whispered to Vail, sitting together in the cavernous library. "It's like...it's like a game. They're trying to beat us."

Vail curled her hands into fists of utter frustration. "Then why did they bring us here in the first place?"

"My guess is because they only want the best of the best. They might be able to tell from a distance that we've got potential, that we *could* learn magic, but they won't really know until they put us through the wringer. And I have made a decision about that."

Vail gave her a sidelong glance.

"*Challenge accepted*," Amy said. "I still don't know why they chose us or what the long-term plan is, but their system sucks. So we're going to beat it. Then we're going to change it."

"You...really think we can?" Vail asked.

Amy gestured at the book between them, the *Liber Scutum* with all its riddles and mysteries.

"What's it for?"

Vail shook her head. "Passing the test?"

"No, I mean, the big picture. Magic. If we can't use it to *change* things, to make the world — the worlds — better, to *help* people, then what's the point? I grew up in a small town in the middle of nowhere, and my entire life people have been telling me, 'Well, that's just the way it is.'"

"The status quo," Vail said.

"The rich and the powerful get to do what they want, and take what they want, and hurt whoever they want." Amy picked up the book. "This. This is our chance to change things."

"Will they let us? The Academy, I mean. We still don't even know why we're here in the first place."

"If we learn everything this school has to teach," Amy said, "who's going to be able to stop us?"

She set the book down and reached for a small stack of index cards, rapping them on the lacquered wood of the study desk.

"You've been getting better at drawing the sigils for the circle of protection," Amy said. "A lot better. Right now your main problem is keeping the order right."

Vail leafed through the pages of the spellbook, gesturing at a curling monstrosity of a twenty-angled glyph.

"Not easy when they look like...that," she said.

Amy beamed at her. Vail slowly inched back in her chair.

"You worry me when you get excited," Vail said. "Have I ever told you that?"

Amy slapped the index cards down one after another. Each bore one of the special seals meant to be inscribed along the rings of the circle. She scrambled them, fast and loose.

"Put them in order," she said.

Vail got the top one right. She faltered placing the second, and froze on the third.

"I mean, I recognize them, I just..." she trailed off, more frustrated than before.

Amy tapped the second index card. "Name it."

"*Essi*," Vail said.

"Easy," Amy said. "See? You didn't hesitate. You *know* this stuff."

"Okay, but—"

Amy put her fingertip on another index card, sliding it into place below its companions. "Name it."

"Pehh...*Peisaay*?"

Amy added another card. Vail shook her head.

"I can't even pronounce that one."

"You won't have to," Amy said with an eager glint in her eye. Her fingertip traced the treelike structures of the magical seal, a network of thirsty roots digging into symbolic earth and drawing forth magic, feeding its offspring. It dripped with geometric shapes and twists. "What does this look like to you?"

"Kind of a tree, sort of." Vail squinted. "I mean, if we want to treat it like an inkblot test."

"We do. And this part right here?" She tapped her fingernail.

"Like fruit? Oblong, like a lime, I think."

"Close."

Amy added another index card to the growing ring.

"This one I can pronounce," Vail said, "I can even draw it from memory pretty good by now, I just can't remember where it goes. I keep trying to put it on the wrong side."

"And that's why we're going clockwise. Now, see this corkscrew-looking part?"

"Sure," Vail said.

"See how it's pressing the runes against the curve of the sigil? Almost like it's...squeezing them."

Vail stared at her, speechless.

Amy stared back.

"No," Vail said.

Amy nodded. Then she pointed to each card in order, making her way around the ring.

"You see, Vail, casting a proper circle of protection is..."

"Don't say it."

"Easy...peasy...lemon...squeezy."

"That," Vail said, "may be the dumbest thing anyone has ever said to me. And yet."

"And yet you're never going to forget again, are you?"

Vail smiled.

"You...really figured all this out, just to help me?"

"Yeah, well, I'm trying to be more of a helper than I used to be. Speaking of, we should move this party to the dorm. Bahati's on her last nerve, Nora's terrified, and I don't want anybody to have to be alone tonight."

***

"Hi," Olivia said.

She stood in the bedroom doorway, looking small, her shoulders clenched. The other girls, joining forces to etch one last practice circle on the chalk-stained floorboards before bed, looked up from their work.

"Back early from Erik's side of the dorms," Bahati said, wrinkling her nose. "Let me guess, he's kind of a...*quick* study?"

Vail snickered and Nora gave her a blank look.

"I don't get it," Nora whispered.

"Give it a few years," Vail whispered back. "You will."

"He's obsessed with this stupid book he got at the Night Market," Olivia said. She ducked her head and kicked the toe of her dress shoe against the floor, grinding out her anxiety. "Listen, I...I'm sorry I ditched you guys. It was a real jerk move and...if you don't want me around, I totally get it—"

Amy brandished a piece of white chalk. Then she held it out to Olivia.

"Get over here," Amy said, "and join in. We're already running behind schedule. With you in the mix, we should be able to make it happen and still get some sleep before the test."

Bahati grumbled but scooted aside, making room. The five girls worked into the night, most of it with books firmly closed. They drew glyphs from memory, catching and correcting each other, weaving the grand design.

A glimmer flashed in the corner of Amy's eye. Olivia had a new necklace: an occult seal, baroque and strange, engraved on pewter and dangling from a delicate chain.

"Where'd you find that?" she asked.

"The Market," Olivia said. "I bought it from that strange old guy with the deer-antler staff."

Amy bit back a surge of panic. Next to her, Vail looked sick.

"You paid him for it, right? He didn't just give it to you?"

Olivia looked at Amy like she'd grown a second head.

"Give it to me? Of course not, I had to pay out the ear for it. But every little bit helps, right?" She proudly tapped the seal. "It's for harnessing concentration and building a strong memory."

"Does it work?" Nora asked.

"Well, I haven't forgotten anything since I started wearing it." Olivia paused. "Unless I forgot that I forgot."

Later that night as she finally bedded down, Amy felt a strange sense of relief. This was it. There would be no delays, no reprieves, no second chances. All her experience at the Saunders Academy would be put on trial tomorrow morning, first thing after breakfast. In the end, everything came down to a simple binary. One of two outcomes.

Do or die.

# Chapter Thirty

"This," Professor Chalk announced, "will be an all-day examination. To prevent collusion or dishonesty, your lunches will be brought to you here. Should we need to run late, dinner will be catered as well."

Erik raised a timid hand. Everyone knew he was on thin ice, having thrown away his only reprieve on the first day of class, but apparently this was important enough to risk the professor's attention. Chalk looked his way, eyes narrowing.

"Yes," the professor said, not waiting for the question. "There will be *supervised* bathroom breaks."

Erik put his hand down.

They weren't in the regular lecture hall today. Professor Chalk had gathered the first-years in a gymnasium on the far end of the manor's east wing. It was tall and wide enough for a game of basketball, with empty, neglected bleachers lining one long wall, and each student had been allotted five square feet of dusty, lacquered floor to etch their circle of protection from memory, books closed.

"You will have three hours to complete the drawing." The professor's brass-tipped ebony cane rapped against the floor, clicking, as he walked between the rows. "Then your circles will be put to a practical test. If it protects you as intended, you pass. If anything gets through the barrier, you fail, and will be going home today. Any questions? No? Good. On my command, begin."

He snapped his latex-gloved fingers.

"Begin."

Amy lurched forward, driven, almost fumbling her stubby stick of chalk. She clenched it tight between her fingers as she began to draw the first inner ring. Slowly. She wanted to push, to race, to get it all over with, but she knew that was a trap. Three hours was more than enough time to get the work done, as long as she paced herself. Better to do it right, to take the extra time to draw a perfect freehand circle. Then another, and a third. Once she managed that, she could tackle the detail work.

The gymnasium fell silent save for the endless rustling, scratching, clicking, scraping of the first-year students staking their claim on the weathered floors, occult diagrams blossoming like connected whorls in some great ghost-white mandala.

"The Regardie Shunt," the professor observed, standing between Olivia and Erik. "Really."

"The book says it's more effective this way," Olivia said.

"Rare that I see a pair of students trying to pass their first serious examination by using more advanced and more difficult techniques than necessary. You've made things harder on yourself for no logical reason. Kudos. Also, I don't give out extra credit."

After that he stood over Vail's shoulder for a while. He said nothing.

He moved on, past Nora — gracing her work with a pointed head-shake — and eventually made his way over to Amy.

"And is that," he said, the brass tip of his cane hovering over the sigil she'd just begun to draw from memory, "magnetic north?"

Amy showed him the eight-sided compass snug in her other palm, borrowed from Adelaide's collection. A silver needle floated on a centimeter of water, gently spinning to point the way.

"I checked," she said.

He nodded, brusque. "Carry on, then."

A few of the first-years weren't so lucky. One had chosen to begin by facing the exact opposite direction, and Amy noticed the Professor leaning against his cane, saying something in a soft, firm voice.

The student rose, pale and shaking, and Chalk escorted him out of the room.

The professor came back alone.

"Sixty minutes remaining," he announced.

Amy wanted to check on Vail more than anything, but she knew she couldn't risk looking like a cheater. The best she could do was glance over and make fleeting eye contact.

Vail lifted one finger, meeting her gaze, and drew a circle as she mouthed four silent words.

*"Easy peasy, lemon squeezy."*

Amy smiled and went back to work. Vail was going to be all right. Now she could worry about herself.

The last sigil daunted her. It wasn't right. She didn't doubt her memory, but it wasn't right.

"Ten minutes remaining," the professor announced. Amy blinked. She thought she'd had half an hour left, at least. She'd gotten drawn into the rhythm, lost in making the circle perfect, when she should have just been getting it done.

She made a touch-up here, an artful smudge there. It still wasn't right. In the back of her mind she heard Bahati's admonition to "let it rest like a cut of steak." Amy was overthinking things again. She knew it. She could work down to the last second and the glyph still wouldn't be right because she wouldn't let it be right and she wouldn't let go.

*Because letting go means trusting it's finished and it works*, she realized. It was never about the lines and loops and jagged whorls. It was about trust.

"Five minutes remaining," the professor called out.

Amy put her chalk down. She folded her hands in her lap and squeezed her fingers tight, forcing herself to stop, here, now.

The professor paused on his patrol, contemplating her, then the circle before her.

"No more additions? No final touches?"

"It's finished," Amy said. She wished she felt as confident as she sounded.

"How do you know?"

"Because I finished it," she said.

He nodded, then moved along.

At the head of the gymnasium, he raised his dark cane with both hands and brought it crashing down, hitting the floor with a peal of metallic thunder.

"Writing instruments down, hands in your laps, all eyes on me," the professor said. "If you haven't finished, you've just failed my class. The rest of you, take a five-minute break, collect yourselves, and we'll begin the real test."

\*\*\*

"So?" Amy whispered, leaning close to Vail.

"Did my best," she said with a nervous smile. "That's all I can do, right?"

Olivia was up first. At the professor's instruction, she stepped into her personal circle of protection. She crouched on one knee, touching her fingertips to the seals and whispering an incantation, firing them with power. There were no special effects, no grand bubbles of force or whirling walls of steel, no indication to show it had any life in it at all. It needed testing.

Professor Chalk held up one closed hand, turned it, and opened it. An emerald-green sphere of hard rubber, about the size of a ping pong ball, rested in his palm. He closed his fingers and opened them again. Now the ball was a short, thin-handled throwing knife, its blade polished to a razor sheen.

"Choose my weapon," he told her.

Olivia bit her bottom lip. The professor turned his hand, changing the knife to a ball. Then back again, as beads of sweat broke out on her forehead.

"The ball...wait. No." She stammered, catching herself. "The knife."

Professor Chalk stared at her.

"Why?" he asked.

"I mean, that's...that's the right answer, isn't it?"

"Did I say there was a right answer?"

Olivia stared at him. "I..."

*Don't say "assumed,"* Amy thought, wincing. *Don't do it.*

"I thought," she said, "it would show that I'm confident in my work."

"So you're telling me that you can't be confident in your work unless you're risking your life, with absolutely nothing to be gained by it." The professor squinted at her. "Is that your final answer, or would you like to reconsider?"

"On second thought," Olivia said, sheepish now, "the rubber ball is probably just fine."

His fingers fluttered. The knife became a ball.

"Never tell me what you think I want to hear," Professor Chalk told her. "Tell me what you think is *correct*. Now then. Are you ready?"

She took a deep breath.

"Ready."

He paced a bit, circling her, walking the outer ring as she braced herself. Then, with no warning, he reared back his arm and let the rubber ball fly, flinging it straight toward her face with the arm of a professional pitcher.

The ball crossed the outer ring of the circle and burst. It was suddenly wreathed in a glowing web of blue-hot flame, squeezing and slicing the projectile in midair and then igniting in a blinding flash. When Amy could see again, all that remained was a scattering of green rubber dust along the perimeter of Olivia's circle.

"And that," Professor Chalk told the class, "is how to make a perfect circle of protection. Well done, Miss Renn, it appears you'll be staying with us for a bit longer at least. You may erase your work and take a seat in the bleachers."

The next student wasn't so lucky. She was a first-year Amy had spotted at the edge of the crowd, always hovering but never quite making a connection to anyone else at the school. Her circle looked even crisper than Olivia's, the linework perfect, but the next rubber ball Professor Chalk produced sailed effortlessly through the invisible barrier, pelting off the girl's shoulder hard enough to make Amy wince.

She was in tears as he firmly escorted her out of the gymnasium, one hand clamped on her shoulder, steering her toward the courtyard. He came back alone.

One by one, the survivors on the bleachers grew in number. Colin fell to his knees as his circle destroyed the professor's missile, the spell devouring it down to a stray scrap of torn rubber. The adrenaline was too much for him to handle, and Dalton had to gently help him up, walking him over to the bleachers and sitting him down where he could catch his breath with the rest of the victors.

"Nailed it, little bro. Told you that you would, right? The real takeaway here is that I'm always correct."

Colin squeezed Dalton's arm. "Your turn."

Dalton wore his usual swagger as he stepped into his circle and prepared for the test.

"Hey," he said, "if the circle doesn't work but I punch that ball right out of the air before it hits me, do I still pass?"

"No," Professor Chalk replied. "That's a failing grade. You'll impress me, but you'll fail."

Amy knew Dalton well enough by now to catch the nervous trapped-animal look behind his eyes. A cocky smile could only cover so much. He settled into a fighting stance, squaring his feet and pushing his shoulders back, and ran his fingers through his slicked-back hair.

"Hit me, prof."

The rubber ball curved in midair, lanced around Dalton's circle, and then whipped back around, careening for the back of his head. It never made it. It burst into flames as it sailed over the outer ring and then *crunched*, crushed with brutal, pulverizing force, as it crossed the second. The ball, now withered to the size of a shriveled pea, landed harmlessly against the side of Dalton's shoe.

"And that's a pass," the professor said. "Good. Clean up and take a seat."

He turned, contemplating the remaining students, his gaze finally settling upon Vail.

"Miss Curran. Your turn."

# Chapter Thirty-One

V ail locked up. She stood at the edge of her circle, not stepping in.

"Time is a factor, Miss Curran," the professor said.

Vail looked at Amy, her expression teetering on panic.

"I can't do this," she whispered.

"You can."

"My busted magic—"

Amy kissed her on the cheek.

She didn't think about it. She needed to give Vail something, something like a lady's favor, to carry into battle. But she didn't have anything tangible, so she just leaned in, fast, and pecked at Vail's freckles.

Vail's face went beet-red. Her lips parted.

"For me, okay?" Amy said. "And I'll do mine for you."

Vail stepped into the circle. She crouched down, touched her fingertips to the northern glyph, and focused. Nothing seemed to change, not even a ripple in the winds of magic, but she stood and turned to face Professor Chalk.

"Do it," she told him.

Some students had squeezed their eyes shut or covered their faces when it was time to prove their skill. Vail stared right at the ball. She clasped her hands behind her back, standing at parade rest, refusing to protect herself with anything but the mystic circle at her feet.

Chalk nodded once and let the ball fly.

It crossed the outer circle and exploded. The ball burst into white flames, burning, crumbling, until all that remained was a tiny finger of soot that puffed and burst against Vail's collarbone, leaving a harmless smudge behind.

"Quality work, Miss Curran. Clean your station and join the others on the bleachers. You're moving forward."

Vail shook as she made her way to the benches. She caught Amy's eye and mouthed something, the words impossible to mistake: *Now you do it.*

It wasn't Amy's turn yet, as much as she wanted to get it over with. Bahati was up. She sang under her breath as her fingertips traced the inner contours of the circle, firing it to life. She glanced up, meeting the unspoken question in the professor's eyes.

"It's called 'All the Broken Pieces,' it came off my self-titled debut, and it spent thirty-eight weeks in the top ten," Bahati told him. "We all have our own ways of getting in the mood, okay?"

"Mood," Professor Chalk said, "is no substitute for technique."

"I can do both," she said.

A moment later she proved it, as the professor's missile went careening like a pinball, making a harsh, discordant noise — the sound of a hand hitting a half-dozen piano keys at once — as it bounced off the invisible circle and ricocheted, burning up in flight.

"Execution is a bit rough," the professor mused, "but you met the requirements to my satisfaction. Clean up and join the others, Miss Bahati. Mr. Anders, you are up."

Erik's confidence could have filled the entire gymnasium. He was already inside his circle before the professor had finished calling his name. Chalk gave him a moment, as if leaving slack for him to open his mouth and hang himself. Erik was just smart enough to stay quiet this time.

"Ready?" the professor asked.

"Sir," Erik replied.

The emerald rubber ball sailed from the professor's hand. It crossed the outer circle without even slowing down. Then the second. Amy's stomach clenched. *He's going to fail—*

Scant inches from Erik's nose, as the missile hit the third concentric circle, it vanished.

It didn't burn or pop or — like it had for one of the first-years Amy hadn't met yet — freeze solid on the spot. It was just *gone*, silently cut from reality itself.

Professor Chalk held Erik's gaze for a long, quiet moment. Something passed between them, a wordless understanding, but Amy couldn't quite catch it.

"Congratulations, Mr. Anders." The professor sounded anything but pleased. "Clean up every last trace of your work and join the others on the bleachers."

The next two students washed out on the spot. One built a totally ineffective circle, and the other could only slow the ball down, not stop it. Not good enough. Professor Chalk walked them to the Arch of Resignation together. He was gone a lot longer this time. Amy realized she was chewing on her fingernail. She hadn't noticed before now.

"Amy," Bahati called out, sitting with their friends on the bleachers. She hammered the seat next to her. "Saving this spot for you, girl. Don't let us down."

"You're gonna make her even more nervous," Dalton said. He cupped his hands to his mouth like a megaphone and called out, "Amy! Kick this test in the balls!"

Colin tilted his head. "Singular."

"Huh?"

"He only throws the one."

"Oh, right." Dalton put his hands back to his mouth. "Kick it in the ball!"

Amy and Vail locked eyes. Vail favored Amy with a smile. She didn't say a word.

Professor Chalk finally returned, alone, grim-faced. His gaze fell upon Amy.

"Miss Nettle," he said. "Into your circle, please."

She stepped over the concentric lines, surrounded by her careful, maybe-good-enough glyphs, and sank to one knee. She contemplated the circle both as a gathering of parts and a whole. A machine that would only work if every piece fired perfectly, in the right order, in the right rhythm. Bahati had found her trigger in a snatch of song, but Amy was still searching.

In the corner of her eye, she saw her friends on the bleachers. Watching, expectant, silently cheering her on. The idea of letting them down scared her more than anything.

And then there was Vail.

Amy recalled something the professor had told them during their very first class, after the demonstration in the fighting ring. *Your first-year studies will be entirely centered around self-defense. Once you learn to protect yourself, you can learn to protect others.*

Maybe she was jumping ahead after all. Because in one heartbeat of reflection, she figured it out.

Her classmates had been treating her like some kind of leader since she'd gotten here. She'd assumed it was just because she was willing to do the jobs nobody else wanted, but now, with all eyes on her, it finally made sense. *I didn't spend all that time in study groups and the library because I was trying to learn to protect myself*, she thought.

*I wanted to protect YOU.*

A tiny spark tingled against her fingertips. She pulled her hand from the floorboards, and rose to her full height, turning to face the professor.

"I'm ready," she lied.

He cocked his arm back. She held her breath and stared it down as he let fly, aiming straight between her eyes.

The ball spattered to the floor half an inch beyond the first circle. It melted like wax, drooling a trickle of black smoke that stank of burning rubber.

"An adequate performance, Miss Nettle. Clean your station and join the others."

Bahati squealed, charging from the bleachers and hauling Amy into a bear hug, Vail right behind her. As they half-led, half-dragged their victorious friend to the bleachers, Dalton held out his knuckles for a fist bump.

"Look at that," he said. "Crew's all here, save for one."

"And she's the one we don't have to worry about," Bahati said. "Nora's probably going to make that ball explode *before* he throws it."

"Nora's a powerhouse," Colin agreed. "And she has to pass. I mean...she has to."

Dalton ruffled his hair. "Yeah. If she leaves, you'll be the shortest person at the Academy."

"Miss Swale, you're up." Professor Chalk waited, pursing his lips as he stared across the few remaining stragglers yet to face the test. "Nora Swale. Stand and deliver."

Nothing. Amy looked to where Nora had been sitting, a few rows behind her. Her circle was drawn, finished, pristine, but the girl was gone. The professor glanced down at his antique pocket watch, dangling from the buttonhole of his waistcoat. Then he sighed and looked to the bleachers.

"I'll continue testing these last few students. You lot, go and find Miss Swale. And tell her that she'd best have a very good reason for leaving this examination without my express permission."

*** 

Nora just needed fresh air.

It was too much. She was twelve. Before now, "high stakes" meant getting grounded for earning a C on a math test. The Saunders Academy offered her magic, a new world, a new life, the freedom to do and become anything she could dream of. Nora was a big dreamer.

Too big, today. All she could see was what she stood to lose. How all her hopes were being dangled in front of her on a hook, ready to be yanked away the second she made a single misstep. So she slipped out of the gym when no one was looking to steal a few seconds of solitude. She was good at that. She'd done it before in school on her own world plenty of times, and no one ever noticed.

Besides, the professor said nobody could even go to the bathroom without being watched, but she'd finished drawing her circle. She figured that looking it up now wouldn't do her any good at all, so nobody could call her a cheater. And she was only going to be gone for a minute. Less than a minute.

Nora was just starting to relax when a hand clamped down on the back of her head, grabbed a fistful of hair, and gave it a rough yank, jerking her backwards. Another hand clamped down over her mouth.

"I don't think you have a hall pass," Jellica whispered in her ear.

She roughly dragged Nora backwards, pulling the girl off her feet, her heels kicking along the old floorboards as Jellica hauled her around a corner and out of sight.

# Chapter Thirty-Two

N ora wasn't in any of the dormitory bedrooms. The showers and bathrooms were all empty. The first-years hunted like a wolf pack, searching door by door, nobody saying what they were all thinking. Not until Dalton charged into an empty lecture hall. He flipped over a chair, brought his heel down hard, and snapped one of its legs off. Then he scooped up the broken hunk of wood, brandishing it like a club.

"Squirt. You still got that pigsticker I whittled for you?"

"You know it," Colin said.

"And the rule is?"

Colin rolled his eyes. Clearly, Dalton had been emphatic about this.

"Fists are for fighting, the knife is for surviving," Colin recited. "Don't escalate until they do."

Bahati glanced down at Dalton's makeshift club. "Mixed messages, much?"

Dalton slapped the splintered chunk of wood against his open palm.

"This isn't escalation," he said. "This is the natural and expected consequence of some very poor life choices. Not mine, for a change."

Nora wasn't anywhere on the ground floor of the house. They checked the courtyard, the stone pavilion, the fighting ring, and came up empty. Amy and Vail shared a glance.

"They took her upstairs," Vail said.

"Where we aren't allowed to go."

"Sure we are," Erik said, his face grim.

Erik had never shown much affection for Nora, or for any of the other first-year students besides Olivia, but he fell into step with the rest of them. This was a rescue mission. And it was tribal.

"How do you figure?" Amy asked him.

"Because Chalk told us to go find her. He didn't say where to look, he didn't say where not to, he just said to get her and bring her back to the gym. So if she's upstairs, we're not breaking the rules, we're following them."

"Brilliant as always," Olivia said, curling a hand over his shoulder. He shot her a look of vague irritation.

They headed for the foyer. Anahera awaited them at the foot of the curling staircase. The older student wore the sea-blue tie and silk shawl that matched her dreamy, distant eyes. She wasn't alone.

Two other students, also dressed in the blue of the Cups, drifted in from the opposite side of the room and moved to flank her. A third Cup perched at the top of the staircase like a gargoyle.

"Tell me something good," Bahati said.

"I would if I could," Anahera replied. "They took her upstairs. Then we lost track of her."

Colin's eyebrows lifted. "Aren't you guys supposed to know...everything?"

"We know what we know. You don't need ethereal insight at the moment. You need an escort." She waved her followers closer. "Cups. Stay close to the first-years. We're going upstairs."

They walked up the curling stairs, and the stairs walked with them. The steps seemed to move under Amy's feet, sometimes sliding beneath her like an escalator moving in the wrong direction, sometimes lifting to meet her heels and carrying her along. She moved with momentum and purpose, her friends and fellow students falling into a silent accord. One way or another, things were about to change around here.

The second floor wore the great house's age with pride. Violet flames under spheres of frosted glass lit long, gloomy galleries where the shadows moved of their own volition. Portrait frames, their gilding long worn away, hung empty on the walls. They framed nothing but the dusty wood behind them, their art invisible.

The first-years kept climbing. The staircase fought them now, firmly in down-escalator mode, and Vail slipped on a step that dodged out from under her foot at the last second. She caught Amy's arm.

"I'm a third-year too, Jellica," Anahera called up, more forceful than the first-years had ever seen her. "You can't keep me out of my own dorm. Stop playing with the stairs."

The Blades decided to meet them halfway.

Jellica descended with her pack at her heels. Her smile was unnerving. *That's not petty cruelty*, Amy thought. *That's triumph.*

"You can go where you please," Jellica told Anahera. "You always do."

"You know why we're here," Vail said.

"Oh, you want your Nora back?" Jellica studied her fingernails. "She's not here. Not anymore. I finished with her."

Amy took a step forward. Anahera put a warning hand on her arm. She shrugged it off.

"What do you mean," Amy said, "*finished*?"

"I just made sure she understood the situation. Namely that she doesn't belong here, she has no hope of graduating and if she keeps going…well, she wouldn't be the first dead student at this school."

"She's just a little kid," Dalton said. "You threatened to *kill* her?"

"I did nothing of the kind," Jellica replied. "I didn't have to. You genuinely have no idea how much danger you're in here, do you?"

"Some of us are in more danger than others," he said, still gripping his chair-leg club.

"You're cute." Gecka leaned out from behind the white witch, looking Dalton up and down. "You single?"

"I don't date psychos. Anymore. Trying to break the habit."

"Where *is* she?" Amy demanded. "It's not just us looking for Nora. Professor Chalk wants her, and he wants her ten minutes ago. Unless you want to deal with him next, tell me the truth."

Jellica tapped a finger against her lips, pretending to think.

"Well, she's not up here, as I said. And if she's not in your dorms, maybe you should check…the planet she came from?"

A wave of terror squeezed Amy's stomach in a fist. She turned on her heel and sprinted back down to the second-floor landing. Anahera ran at her side, her footfalls utterly silent. The dreamy-eyed young woman tugged the sleeve of Amy's blazer, somehow already knowing what she needed to see. She led Amy into one of the second-year dorm rooms.

It was more spacious than the first-year rooms, with its own fire-place, the hearth dark and piled with ashes. More personal — the beds had unique quilts, and the walls and shelves were decorated with keepsakes from the Night Market and journeys beyond. Amy raced to the nearest window.

She could see the Arch of Resignation from here. And Nora. She looked so tiny from here, a lonely, frail thing, as she walked toward the Arch.

"Nora," Amy shouted. She hauled on the window, but it refused to open, lifting a quarter inch and then slamming back down of its own accord. "*Nora!* Don't quit! Whatever she said, she's lying to you! *Don't go!*"

And then Nora was gone.

\*\*\*

The first-years, the Cups, and the Blades were still locked in a standoff on the stairs. Her friends parted like waves as Amy returned, letting her through. She only had eyes for Jellica. She marched toward the white witch like a train gathering steam.

"You don't understand this yet," Jellica started to say, "but that was for her own good—"

Amy punched her in the face.

Her knuckles hit Jellica's cheekbone hard enough to leave a smeared red welt. Jellica staggered back, slipped off her feet, and landed on her ass on the stairs. Her face was a frozen mask of shock. Amy liked that. She wanted to see more of it.

Professor Chalk had told her to press the advantage, and this time she had every intention of following through. She didn't care about the rules. She didn't care about the consequences. She just wanted Jellica to *hurt*.

Amy never got the chance. Arms looped around hers, dragging her backwards, away from the fight. Dalton had one of her elbows trapped, and Vail had the other.

"Not here," Dalton said, "not now. Not on their turf. We'll get even later."

Jellica rubbed her cheek and pushed herself to her feet. Her look of surprise melted into a wide, hungry grin.

"That's right. Run along with your little friends, Amy. I'll see you soon."

Amy had spent her entire life letting things slide. Letting things go. Turning the other cheek and getting slapped across both. No more. One word sprang to her lips.

"Duel," she said.

Jellica lifted a snowy eyebrow. "Duel?"

"You and me."

"Amy," Anahera said, a warning in her tone.

"Time?" Jellica asked.

"*Right now*," Amy growled.

"Suits me just fine. I haven't had my afternoon workout yet. You'll do."

***

The ring was waiting for them.

It looked just like it had when Amy first saw it: an octagon of engraved wooden posts, roped off by thick flowering vines. The arena surface was a thick layer of jet-black soil, freshly raked like a Zen garden. It seemed so much bigger now that she was standing inside it. Jellica entered from the other side, hauling herself up and over the vines and landing lightly on bare feet in the bed of soil. Her toes scrunched, taking in the feel of it.

Professor Chalk spared Amy a glance as he surveyed the ring. And the slightest shake of his head. Then he turned to address the gathering crowd. All of the first-years, the Cups, the Blades, and a smattering of other students Amy had never met had all turned up for the show. Eager voices filled the air, fading to murmurs as Chalk raised one gloved hand.

"Might," he intoned, "does not make right."

His hand drifted down to rest on the head of his cane.

"But when differences between students are irreconcilable, we have the ring."

Jellica started to pace.

She wasn't showboating or playing to the crowd. She barely seemed aware of where she was as she sank into a furious waking trance. Amy thought she looked like a lioness in a cage, stalking, restless, wanting nothing but to burst loose.

"Amy Nettle. Jellica Barnes. Have you resolved your differences?"

"No," Amy said.

"I don't have differences with anyone," Jellica said. "I just have haters."

"This will be a one-fall duel," Professor Chalk proclaimed to the crowd. "The bout will proceed until one contestant submits, or until first blood is drawn. There will be no lethal curses, no irreversible transformations, and all conjurations must remain inside the ring at all times. On my command, fight."

He raised his ebony cane high, then brought it down on the flagstones with a metallic clang.

"*Fight.*"

# Chapter Thirty-Three

I t wasn't a fight. It was a slaughter.

The echo from Professor Chalk's brass-tipped cane hadn't even faded before Jellica launched herself across the ring like a torpedo, propelled by a mixture of magical velocity and athletic prowess. Amy didn't have time to bring her hands up before Jellica pummeled her belly with hard, fast jabs, driving the breath out of her lungs. Then she took Amy's wrist, spun her around, and gave her a shove.

Whatever spell she'd used to accelerate herself flooded down Amy's arm, lighting her veins on fire. Amy was suddenly running, flung helplessly toward the vines that roped off the ring. They stretched like rubber bands, impossibly elastic, and now she was launching in the opposite direction, right back toward Jellica. Her only choice was to keep running or fall as the soil floor became slick as ice, every step threatening to shoot her legs out from underneath her.

Jellica's forearm clotheslined Amy's throat, flipping her off her feet. Amy landed on her back on the arena floor and saw stars. She struggled to breathe.

Jellica appraised her like an exterminator deciding how to kill a roach. She kicked Amy's hip, rolling her over and forcing her onto her belly.

"Which hand do you write with?" she asked. "Never mind, don't care."

She dropped one knee onto Amy's back, sending an explosion of pain rocketing along her spine. Then she grabbed Amy's left wrist and yanked it behind her.

"That sensation in your elbow," Jellica hissed through gritted teeth, "is your arm slowly popping out of its socket. You lose. Tap out."

"Go to hell," Amy snapped, her eyes flooding with tears.

The pain was blistering, searing, flooding out all rational thought. All Amy could cling to was her grief. Her grief and her rage. She'd failed Nora. Picked a fight she couldn't win. Made a fool of herself in front of her friends and the entire school. Her refusal to submit was the one scrap of pride she could still cling onto.

"I will break it," Jellica whispered calmly in her ear. "Tap out, and this can all be over."

"*No*," Amy snapped, her jaws clenched.

"You know, it's been a while since somebody really made me work for it. I'm going to do something special, just for you."

Amy felt Jellica's other hand scrabbling at the collar of her shirt, yanking her school tie like a noose before pulling it loose. Keeping Amy pinned to the soil, Jellica used her body to hide what she was doing from the crowd. And from Professor Chalk.

A lightning-flash of pain seared her collarbone. Amy felt a spreading, sticky wetness, and caught a glint of bloody steel in the corner of her eye. Jellica slipped her hand behind her back, the knife vanishing.

"Professor," Jellica sang out, "Amy's bleeding. Call it for me."

Professor Chalk brought his cane ringing down.

"That's the bout. First blood and the victory go to Jellica Barnes."

Jellica left Amy bleeding in the dirt.

She gracefully rolled over the ring vines, landing on the other side like a ballerina. As her followers flocked to her, she made her way to the professor with a bounce in her step.

"Aren't you going to tell me how well I did?"

"Should I congratulate you for remembering to tie your shoelaces? Perhaps you'd like an award for walking and chewing gum at the same time." Chalk waved a dismissive hand. "Let me know if there are any other trivially easy tasks you'd like to be praised for."

Amy rolled onto her back and squinted up at the hazy, overcast sky while she tried to remember how to breathe. Her clothes were disheveled, her face and hands caked with black dirt. She gingerly touched her collarbone and winced. Her fingers came away scarlet. *She cut me*, Amy realized. *She actually CUT me.*

Professor Chalk stood over her.

"There are no words," he said.

"I don't know what the hell she said or did to Nora," Amy panted, still catching her breath, "but she *left*. She's gone."

"A most regrettable decision on Nora's part. Do not compound her mistake by joining her. Also, you should have tapped."

"What difference does it make?" Amy gestured to her torn blouse and the spreading puddle of blood. "She won anyway."

"Her victory was a foregone conclusion. She knew it, I knew it, and you, Miss Nettle, should have known it. Forcing a win was nothing to her. She wanted your submission. I am afraid you've only managed to make things worse, which is...quite a feat."

\*\*\*

"You should have tapped, kid."

Amy inhaled, sharp, as Professor Mallory pressed a poultice of pea-green herbs against her collarbone. Jellica had given her a keepsake, a long, jagged cut. The herbal remedy smelled of spearmint and burned like pure alcohol as it worked its way into the wound.

"That's what everyone's telling me."

"For once, everyone is right. Vail, hon, grab me one of those strips of white cloth over on the table by the flowering crostium. That'll do for a bandage." Professor Mallory leaned back and eyed her handiwork. "Pretty sure you're going to have a nasty scar, but this poultice will keep the wound from getting infected."

Vail dragged up a stool. They were alone with the professor, in the sunlit window-world of her forest hut. Outside the glass, Murder Mittens napped on a patch of flowers.

"Jellica's gotten worse," Professor Mallory said. "I told the headmistress she was already halfway to being a liability, and Lanca showing his face here pushed her over the edge."

"I need to know." Amy looked at Vail. "We need to know."

Mallory sighed. She tossed up her hands, relenting.

"Fine, you'd hear it all soon eventually, and at least with me I know you're getting the unvarnished and unembellished truth. You've been wondering why there aren't any fourth-year students at a four-year school."

"And why there are fewer second- and third-years than new recruits," Amy said. She was thinking about what Jellica had said to her back on the staircase: *She wouldn't be the first dead student at this school*.

"The Saunders Academy only began operating a few years ago," Professor Mallory said.

"But it looks...ancient," Vail said.

"Its traditions and methods certainly are. But this wasn't even the school's first site. Our first attempt was on a more populated, easier-to-reach world. Sloppy. The whole idea was damn sloppy from its inception. A year later we took the survivors and relocated here."

"Survivors," Amy echoed.

"I'm certain you heard me clearly."

"What happened?" Vail asked.

"There is...an organization, much like our own, but its opposite number. Opposite and more than equal. They sent a hunter. He proceeded to stalk, and murder, every single one of our first batch of students. The students who, had our security been stronger, had we read the warning signs, would have been our first graduates-to-be."

Vail furrowed her brow. "Does this 'opposition' have a name?"

Professor Mallory rose from her three-legged stool and stretched, clasping her hands behind her back. She walked amid her tables of potted plants and greenery, checking on them like they were infants in a nursery.

"They call it by hundreds of names on hundreds of worlds," she says, "but most people call it the Network. An innocuous, harmless epithet for a monstrous cult. We couldn't save the kids, but we could track down the hunter."

Amy's eyes widened. "You're saying that Jellica—"

"What?" Mallory laughed. "No, she's a third-year, she wasn't even here until after it was all over. And I can pin any number of malicious crimes on that girl, but I'm fairly certain she's never murdered anyone. It's the opposite of what you're thinking: Jellica loathes the Network with an absolute passion. They ravaged her homeworld. She's been a first-hand witness to their atrocities."

"Okay, but..." Vail paused. "What do the dead students have to do with Jellica?"

"What I'm about to tell you," Professor Mallory said, "does not leave this room. Are we in agreement?"

Amy and Vail's heads bobbed, nervous but curious.

"As a magician," the professor said, "your word is your what?"

"My word is my bond," Amy said. At her side, Vail repeated the pledge.

"We hunted the hunter. Me, Kamaka, Chalk. We didn't kill him. Don't get me wrong, I wanted to, we *all* wanted to, but Chen Lan had a different idea."

Mallory turned to face them, her hands still tight behind her back.

"She turned him instead. Made him give us a masterclass in the Network's techniques and methodology so we could harden Firebreak Island into a fortress. And, as our headmistress is quite fond of ironic punishments...she handed him a teaching job. So he can replace the students he murdered."

Amy's lips parted. She stared at Mallory, silent for a moment. Vail said what she was thinking.

"Professor Lanca."

"Red Lanca," Mallory said, "was one of the Network's top assassins. His body count is somewhere in the hundreds, but even he doesn't remember them all. Now, we intended to keep this a secret."

"You wanted to let a murderous psychopath teach us, and *not tell us*?" Amy said.

"Believe me, he's on a magical leash. He's harmless. And...well, he's claiming to be penitent, but that and a coin will buy you a cup of coffee at the Night Market. His word isn't worth much else. But if you'll allow me to explain...yes, that was the plan. We didn't expect Jellica to lose her ever-loving mind the second she laid eyes on him."

"But if she wasn't here, and didn't know any of the students he killed—" Amy started to say.

"The Network graced her homeworld well before she was chosen as a candidate for the Saunders Academy. It may have even been one of the reasons we offered her a spot. I couldn't tell you; I don't work in admissions."

Professor Mallory let her hands fall to her sides. She hesitated, just one piece of the puzzle remaining. Then she slid it into place.

"Jellica is convinced that Red Lanca led the death squad that burned down her village and murdered her entire family. She remembers it fairly well, you see. She watched it happen."

# Chapter Thirty-Four

With the horror of what they'd learned still hanging in the air between them, Amy's question almost felt irrelevant. Still, she had to know.

"Did he?"

"To be honest," Professor Mallory said, "I don't think that he did. Red Lanca was a lone wolf. We never knew him to work with a team or lead the Network's grunts and bullyboys into the field. He's...well, it's worthless to ask him because if he *did* do it, he would lie anyway. He claims he doesn't remember, and that I do believe."

"How could you possibly forget doing something like that?" Vail asked, incredulous.

"You have to be a certain kind of person, I would imagine," the professor replied, "but I'm not that kind of person so I can't really say."

"What about Jellica?" Amy asked, feeling sick to her stomach.

"What about her?"

From the moment they'd met, Amy had seen Jellica as a force of pure malice, a sadist who afflicted her fellow students for the pure joy of it — at least, anyone who wouldn't fall in line behind her.

Amy heard Professor Chalk's voice, a memory from when she'd realized how badly she'd misjudged him. *In the art of magic, assumptions kill.*

"She's *hurt*," Amy said. "She's traumatized. She needs therapy, not war-magic. Why isn't the school *helping* her?"

Professor Mallory held a tactful silence for a moment.

"Jellica Barnes," the professor said, "lives and breathes with one desire: to burn the Network to the ground. Our Academy's investors...like that idea, I think."

Vail's lips parted in horror.

"They're keeping her sick," Vail breathed. "So she'll be a better warrior. That's...that's vile."

"Who are they?" Amy demanded. "The investors. I want to meet them."

The professor pursed her lips and shook her head.

"We don't talk about the investors," she said. "And that was more than I should have told you. That poultice will stick nicely. You should go back to your dorms now."

\*\*\*

Professor Mallory had sworn Amy and Vail to secrecy, but in the end it didn't matter. Over the next few days, Jellica and the Blades fed the school's network of whispers, making sure everyone heard a story. Every story ended with *Professor Lanca is the enemy.*

Amy was pretty sure they were right. All the same, she kept thinking about how Lanca had shielded them at the Night Market, sending Elmer the Jangly-Man on a wild goose chase instead of giving away their hiding spot. And she couldn't square the hip young professor who liked to perch on his desk with a bloodthirsty killer who'd murdered an entire class of fledgling magicians.

"Okay," Lanca announced as he strolled into the lecture hall. "Focus crystals down. Before we practice, we need to talk."

He sat on the edge of his desk, hands in his lap. He glanced down at them like he wasn't sure how to begin.

"You've all heard some things about me," the professor said, "or if you haven't yet, you will. It is not what I wanted you to know, and not the way I wanted you to find out, but it is what it is. So cards on the table. Yes, I *used* to go by the name Red Lanca. Yes, I was a contract killer."

He paused, looking down, not making eye contact with anyone in the room.

"And yes, I am the reason this Academy nearly failed before it could even open its doors. I've been on retainer ever since, shoring up Firebreak's defenses and making sure that no one...no one like me can ever do that again."

Murmurs rose, until he pushed them back down with a wave of his hand. He hopped down from his desk.

"If it makes you feel better — and I hope it does, because this thing is uncomfortable as hell — our thoughtful headmistress provided me with an...implant. If I go rogue, well, my death will be colorful and memorable. I couldn't hurt you kids if I wanted to." He caught himself, quickly adding: "And I don't want to."

Erik raised his hand. "What about Jellica? I mean, you're leaving some stuff out, right?"

In a moment, Professor Lanca's entire disposition changed. He stalked toward Erik like a jungle cat, eyes quietly burning.

"I used to kill people for pay. I do not *burn villages*. I do not *assault women*. I am not a barbarian, and if you want to sit there and judge me I must insist that you judge me based on the crimes that I actually committed as opposed to the nightmares of a traumatized teenage girl. Do you understand me?"

Erik stared up at him, poleaxed.

"*Do you understand me*, Mr. Anders."

It wasn't a question. Lanca allowed him no room for anything but a single answer. Erik meekly nodded. The professor stepped away and put his mask back on. He was suddenly all smiles and boyish charm again. He spread his hands wide.

"Well all right! Now that the nasty stuff is out of the way, how about we get some practice in?"

***

"The basic circle of protection," Professor Chalk lectured, "is effective against many threats — as you've seen first-hand — but deeply impractical in a fight. Today, we begin working on something that will build upon the concepts you've already learned in a much more useful way. I've brought in one of my experienced students for a demonstration."

Amy recognized Garcia. He'd been in the fighting ring on their first visit, defending his right to independence. Now he wore a checkerboard Blades scarf around his throat and a hangdog look on his face. He held up one hand, brandishing a wire bracelet lined with rough, misshapen chunks of jet and smoky quartz.

"This is a Spellchoke," the professor said. "Unlike the circle, it is powerless against physical attacks, but an absolute equalizer against a hostile magician. Mr. Garcia, I intend to throw fire at you. If you fail to counter my attack, you will be burned quite badly. Is that acceptable?"

He nodded, no hesitation. "Yes, Professor Chalk."

"And why is that acceptable?"

"Because I will not fail."

"Very good. Let us begin."

Chalk barely moved his hand. His fingers curled, little more than a twitch, and then a lance of roaring, naked flame burst from his fingertips. Amy leaned back in her chair, heat washing over her face as if she was standing in front of a furnace.

Garcia didn't budge. He stood there, staring the burning missile down. Then he casually waved his hand. The fire bent in midair, buckling and flowing like a snake, drawn straight toward the Spellchoke. It hit the bracelet and erupted in a blinding flash, etching flares on the inside of Amy's eyelids.

The fire was extinguished, and Garcia was unscathed. The only casualty was the Spellchoke, which had fallen to the classroom floor at his feet. The wire was scorched black, ripped in half, and its stones lay in shattered, burned-out pebbles.

"One use only," the professor said, "and extremely expensive to make. But if I had been a hostile mage just now, looking to ambush Mr. Garcia with a lethal spell, that device would have saved his life. Thank you, Mr. Garcia, you may return to your scheduled class."

Professor Chalk rested both palms on the head of his cane, fingers curling tight as he addressed the first-years.

"Your next long-term project will be the creation and testing of your own personal Spellchoke. *Your* examination will not involve the use of flames, but I assure you: failure will be painful indeed."

***

Amy lost herself for a week in the pages of the *Liber Scutum*. She was starting to understand. At first the methods for building a Spell-choke seemed impossibly complex. Then she looked back to the circle of protection and started drawing connections. Professor Chalk was right: everything they were learning built on the foundations they'd already hammered down.

"Like, this formula for anointing the bracelet stones," Amy excitedly told Vail, holding her *Liber Scutum* open as they walked down the hall. "Look at the symbols you're supposed to trace on them."

Vail squinted at the old woodcut diagram. Then she saw it too. "Those are the same. Same seals of protection, we're just...applying them differently."

"We already know how to do three-quarters of this stuff," Amy said.

"Must be why he's giving us less time. Not gonna lie, I like the idea of having an early-warning bracelet. Making the circle work was cool and all, but we can *use* these."

*Especially if Jellica decides to escalate things*, Amy thought. Amy had been mousing around, keeping her head down and watching her back, but she knew it was only a matter of time.

She had taken the poultice off. As promised, it fought off infection and healed the wound. Also as promised, now Amy had a long scar the color of a dead fish-belly along her collarbone. A keepsake from the white witch, a memory of Amy's impulsive failure engraved for life.

As they approached their dorm room, Amy and Vail heard crying, soft and muffled. Vail frowned and picked up her pace, walking through the door ahead of Amy.

It was Olivia, hiding under her covers and hiccup-sobbing. Judging by her puffy, red face, she'd been at it for a while. She clutched a wadded-up ball of sodden tissues to her chest.

"Hey," Amy said, "what's wrong?"

"Erik," she croaked, wiping at her eyes, which only seemed to smear the tears around.

Vail clenched her fist. "Did he hurt you?"

"Not...not physically. He's been totally obsessed with that stupid book he got at the Night Market."

"And more obnoxious than usual," Amy added.

"I wanted to practice with him, and...and he said *I'm not on his level.*"

"What?" Vail boggled at her. "You two have been tight since you got here."

"He said that I was—" She sniffed wetly. "'Fun to have around, for a little while.' But he doesn't need me anymore. He doesn't need anybody."

"Okay, first of all," Amy said, "you've got that backwards. He's a creep and you don't need him."

Amy met Vail's eyes. A silent conversation passed between them in sharp glances. Vail sighed in exasperation.

"Olivia," Vail said, "c'mon down to the library. You can hang out with us from now on."

# Chapter Thirty-Five

"We're going to die here," Colin gasped. "We are all going to die."

"Aw, put a cork in it," Professor Kamaka called out through the bullhorn held close to his mouth. "You're just whining because you've got short legs."

"Yes," the boy wheezed. "*I do.*"

"On your left," Dalton called, racing past Colin on the sand. He ran toward a yellow rope dangling down a wall of plywood, grabbed onto the knots, and started to climb, finally hauling himself up and over.

Gadfly Beach was one giant obstacle course, and Amy could only picture it as the invention of a twisted drill sergeant who wanted to kill his own recruits. At least the students had been given athletic clothes — t-shirts and shorts, in the school colors of chocolate, purple, and gray — but she was still drowning in sweat as she jogged the beach and hopped along a row of old spare tires.

"Remember," Kamaka said through his bullhorn, "Strong body, strong mind. Strong mind, strong magic. You can do this. C'mon, hustle!"

At least the view was incredible. Endless sea and storm on Amy's right, the forest and tall rocks of western Firebreak on her left. She noticed, for the first time, that there weren't any gulls. She found their absence odd until she thought about the ocean here. *Birds don't eat fish here,* she thought, *fish eat everything.*

The insight tugged her consciousness downward, down into the brine, without her even realizing it was happening. Not until she felt the Corpse, like a stalker standing just over her shoulder, breathe her name.

She snapped the link, squeezed her lips tight, and focused on the obstacle course.

"I used to be, like, kind of a jock," panted Vail as she fell into step at Amy's side.

"I could have guessed."

"*Used* to be. This is pain."

Kamaka, reclining on a beach chair, lifted the bullhorn to his mouth again. "You don't even know the meaning of the word yet."

Vail shot a sidelong glance at Amy. "How does he keep hearing us when he's all the way over there?"

"Magic!" the professor called out.

On the southern end of the beach, the sand gave way to a jumble of boulders. Then to a sheer, imposing cliff that captured Amy's eye. Her cell phone, just like that of everybody else who'd brought one from their world, had run out of juice months ago. She couldn't call anyone from a world away, but she would have liked to have gotten some pictures of this place.

*The Night Market comes through twice a year,* she thought. *If I save up the money I get from working in the stables, maybe I'll get lucky next time and they'll have an old camera or something.*

She was looking up at the cliffs, trying to distract herself from the burning in her lungs and her legs as she ran the obstacle course, when a glint startled her. It was just a flash, high up on the rocks, like the sunlight strobing off a chunk of glass.

"Did you see that?"

"See what?" Vail asked.

Behind them, Colin gasped, "I see nothing but suffering and regret. No, no, I *feel* nothing but suffering and regret."

Almost too far down the beach to see him now, Professor Kamaka raised his bullhorn.

"Nah, suffering is what you're gonna feel tomorrow morning when you wake up and all those muscles you've been ignoring want to have an important talk about your life choices. But you know what? Second time gets easier. Third time gets easier than that. Dig deep!"

"I'll dig deep in his—" Vail started to mutter.

"I heeearrr youuu," the professor sang through his bullhorn.

After class, as she walked off the ache, Amy circled back around to Kamaka.

"Professor? Got a second?"

"For you I could manage ten or even twenty. Good effort out there. Don't get discouraged because you ran out of gas — the more you put into this, the more you'll get out of it. Hey, see that?"

He pointed at one of the more advanced parts of the course, one they hadn't touched today. It was a balance beam suspended twenty feet in the air by a pair of thin posts. The only way up was a dangling rope. Amy didn't want to think about all the ways down.

"Some of my third-years can do cartwheels on that thing," the professor said. "And none of 'em believed they could at first."

"Is there anyone up on those cliffs?" Amy pointed to the spot where she'd seen the flash of light, among the brambles and brush that littered the rise.

"Better not be. South end of the island's all wilderness — we haven't built the trails that far out yet. And Professor Mallory's our only self-appointed hermit. Everybody else lives in the school proper."

"I thought I saw a light up there. Just a flash."

Professor Kamaka cupped a hand over his eyes to cut the glare and squinted up at the rocks.

"Eh, you probably just got the sun in your glasses."

*But I took my glasses off to run*, she started to say. He was already walking off with another student, giving pointers for next time.

***

Amy couldn't let it go.

Professor Kamaka was right. Glasses or no, she had been sweaty and tired, her head bobbing as she ran, and she could have just caught a flash of the afternoon sun in her eyes. But she couldn't let it go. It was important, even if *why* it was important utterly escaped her. She felt like she had all the pieces of a jigsaw puzzle but she couldn't arrange them into a full picture.

She had more pressing problems. Despite having the basics down, constructing a Spellchoke for Professor Chalk's class was still a daunting prospect. Nerves in the dormitory were wearing thin. The remaining first-years had just survived one of Chalk's pass-or-fail gauntlets, and now he was throwing another at them without so much as a breather.

Erik had all but vanished, spending his free hours deep in the labyrinthine stacks of the school library. Amy suspected he wasn't doing research on anything but that book he obsessively carried around, and that he was only using the maze of shelves to hide from Olivia and the other first-years. But mostly Olivia. *Fine*, Amy thought. His presence wasn't missed.

At least until he emerged from the stacks while the girls were studying at one of the long lacquered tables. Bahati noticed him first and tapped Olivia's shoulder. Vail and Amy were the next to turn their heads.

He did not look well. His school uniform was rumpled, his eyes bloodshot, his cheeks covered in two days of patchy stubble. He strode up to the table and dropped his prize with a *thump*. He had finished his Spellchoke.

"And ahead of schedule," Amy said, her tone less than delighted.

It didn't look right. Or at least, it didn't look like the bracelets they'd been stringing on their own or the one that Garcia had worn for the demonstration. The metal cord was as sickly as Erik, frayed and thin, and the stones he'd chosen to adorn it with were...*oily*, Amy thought. She was relieved when he scooped it up and put it on his wrist. She didn't want it anywhere near her.

"You've got no idea." He pointed to his temple. "The concepts I've been learning, the techniques I'm mastering."

"Yeah," Vail said, "we heard. From you, mostly, over and over again. If you don't mind, we're trying to study here, Captain Ego."

Even after he left, Olivia still stared, sullen, down at the study table. Bahati rubbed her shoulder.

"You good?"

"I just feel..." she said. Her voice trailed off. Then she said, contemplative, "...like I'm a lot better off without him."

"Hear, hear," Vail said.

***

Amy woke from dreams of drowning.

She slipped out of bed, making her way to the bathrooms in the dark. Lights hummed and flickered as she entered.

The writing on the mirrors was back. Only on one, this time.

*aMy*, it read. *Come to me.*

She splashed water on the glass and scrubbed it with her fingers until only a hazy blur remained. Then she sat down in a cramped, cold stall and flinched at shadows.

A relentless sense of *wrong* had dogged her heels since their visit to the Night Market. While she chalked that up to the creepy antics of Elmer the Jangly-Man, the Market and its tribe had only stayed on the island for a single night. They were long gone and wouldn't return for months yet.

*Professor Lanca told us not to go. And he knew someone would offer Vail all the drugs her body wants. He was right about that place.*

*And...Professor Lanca is a retired serial killer. If me and Vail had been in that first class instead of this one, he would have murdered us too without thinking twice. We can't trust him.*

*Not even all that sure about the "retired" part.*

# Chapter Thirty-Six

"Several of you," Professor Chalk said, addressing the lecture hall, "have been having difficulty with the enchantment on the Spellchoke's wire. I must remind you that this is a separate process. Do not attempt to consecrate the wire and the stones at the same—"

"I'm ready," Erik said. He didn't even bother raising his hand.

Chalk stared at him, nonplussed.

"To do...what, Mr. Anders?"

"The thing. The test." He held up his wrist. His Spellchoke dangled, its dark, oily stones swallowing the light around them. "I'm ready to rock. Let's go."

"The test is next week, Mr. Anders. You still have several days of study and preparation time available to you, and I suggest you spend it making your bracelet as strong as you possibly can."

"It's finished," he insisted.

Professor Chalk glanced at Olivia. She mostly sat in the front row these days.

"Miss Renn. As the only person here who seems to have a hold on young Erik — besides Erik himself — could you please persuade your friend to pursue this project with all seriousness?"

Olivia turned in her seat. Her expression was hard to read as she shot a look at Erik. Then she turned back to the professor and made her stance clear.

"He's not my friend."

A few snickers and *ooohs* rose from the back rows, until the professor silenced them with a glare.

"Very well," he said. "If this is really what you want...step up in front of the class, Mr. Anders."

While Erik swaggered up to join him, Professor Chalk picked up a sheet of blank paper from his desk. He folded it, then folded again, then again into precise thirds. Then he crushed it between his hands, scrunching it up into a tiny ball. He held it up for Erik's inspection. And for the anxious classroom, by proxy.

"As promised, I won't be using anything quite so harsh as I did in the demonstration with Mr. Garcia. That said, you will be very unhappy if my spell breaks through your bracelet's ward. And expelled. Are you absolutely certain you'd like to do this?"

"I was born ready."

"Then I suggest you prepare yourself."

Watching, Olivia pursed her lips.

Erik took half a step back, measuring how much room he had to move. The fingers of his opposite hand ran across the stones on his bracelet.

They came away wet. From her seat, Amy noticed how they glistened, and how the stones wobbled like blobs of jelly.

Or eggs, about to hatch.

Professor Chalk was focused on the wad of paper in his hands, preparing the spell he was going to use. He never got the chance.

The stones on Erik's Spellchoke began to melt. Dripping, drooling down in long, ropy strands, spattering the floorboards. Black at first, then a light shade of tan. And scarlet. Erik held up his hand, his eyes going wide.

His hand was melting along with it. His flesh ran like skin-colored wax, and then the blood began to pour. As his fingers began to dissolve, scarlet bone jutting out from beneath, he opened his mouth to scream.

Professor Chalk ran to the back of his desk, faster than Amy knew he could move, and began ripping through his drawers. He yanked out an amulet in the shape of a pewter seashell, tossed it aside, then came up with a syringe. Something cold and green burbled inside.

"Amy! Olivia! Up here, now, we're going to stabilize him. Dalton, run and get the headmistress. Everyone else, stay in your seats!"

Erik collapsed to the classroom floor. Amy thought he'd fallen, at first. Then she saw his empty dress shoe, filled to the brim with liquid flesh. Professor Chalk crouched over him and punched the needle into his neck, driving the plunger in. Then he tossed it aside and grabbed the seashell amulet, waving Amy and Olivia close.

"We're going to weave a suspension field," he told them, as Erik screeched and flopped on the floor, his full-body seizure throwing rivulets of melting skin against the blackboard. "It's a third-year technique, but you're my two best students, so pay attention and deal with it."

Normally Amy would have glowed at a compliment like that, especially from Professor Chalk, but she didn't want this responsibility. She didn't want to be part of the reason that Erik either lived or died. As if he could hear her thinking, Chalk gave her a hard look.

"Second-guess yourself later," he said. "A life is at stake."

They worked fast, Amy and Olivia following the professor's lead, the three of them holding the amulet above Erik's thrashing body with outstretched fingers. He led Amy in a chant, then Olivia, the three of them invoking three different dead languages like a funeral dirge in the round.

Amy felt the power swell between them. It was as if Chalk were a tightrope walker, carefully navigating to Erik's rescue, while Amy and Olivia worked together to keep him in perfect balance. Amy felt the energy flow this way or that, harder or softer, and she kept the professor aloft with tiny nudges from the winds of magic.

Then the balance slipped.

She wasn't sure if it was her mistake or Olivia's, or if they were just too late, but the swell of power buckled and popped like a soap bubble.

"Again," Chalk snapped.

"Professor," Olivia started to say.

"*Again.*"

Olivia pointed to the floor.

Erik was dead.

His body was still melting, a pool spreading like spilled paint on the lecture hall floor, reducing him to nothing but a wet skeleton in a school uniform. He had stopped breathing, probably right around the moment he no longer had a throat or a mouth. Chalk stared at the body.

"Everyone out," he said. "Classes will be canceled for the rest of the week. Go back to your dormitory and wait for further instructions."

He pointed to the doorway, his eyes still fixed on what was left of the dead teenager.

"*Go.*"

***

"This place is going to kill us all," Colin said.

He was sitting on a rock on Hemlock Beach, picking up pebbles and skipping them off the moonlit water. Each one bounced three times before being dragged underwater with a sickly suckling sound.

"Don't say that." Dalton sat next to him with one knee bent, his foot propped up on the stone. "Erik…Erik made his choices."

"I don't think he did," Amy said.

She and the students she had grown closest to, the ones she counted as friends, had all gathered on the beach. They needed some time away from the school after watching their classmate die.

"How do you figure?" Vail asked.

"Professor Chalk is *careful*. Olivia, remember the thing with the knives and the balls? When he got on you for wanting things to be more dangerous than they absolutely had to be?"

"Thanks for reminding me," she sighed, gazing out across the black waters.

"He used a tougher attack on Garcia because he knew he could handle it, and he still asked permission first. He wasn't going to test any of us that hard. He said so. So…if a Spellchoke could do that to a person, do you really think he'd *teach* that to us? As first-year students? He wants to teach us to protect ourselves, not to hurt us even worse."

"But we all saw it happen," Bahati countered. "I mean, I was looking right at his wrist. That's where the…melting started from."

Olivia nodded. "It was definitely the 'choke."

"And we all know Erik's been obsessed with that book he got at the Night Market for weeks. Olivia, I saw him with it when I spotted you both near the Jangly-Man. Is that where he bought it?"

"I don't know where he bought it," Olivia's hands touched the amulet dangling from her neck by a thin silver chain. "All I got from Elmer was my concentration-helper charm. And it works perfectly."

"How do you know?" Vail asked.

"Because I concentrate all the time."

"He didn't have it in the classroom," Amy said, still chasing her hunch. "Dalton, Colin, he was rooming with you guys, right?"

"I mean, I guess we could go through his stuff," Colin said. "It's not like he's gonna mind now."

Amy paced along the white sand. A cold night wind, laden with salt and secrets, washed in from the sea and ruffled her hair.

"If Erik got his techniques from that book," she said, "it means one of two things. He overreached and tried to do something way more powerful than he could handle—"

"That's Erik all right," Olivia said.

"—or it was sabotaged."

"You think that book was *meant* to kill him?" Bahati said.

"I don't think anything. All I know right now is that we aren't safe here. I thought Jellica was the worst problem at this school, but ever since the Night Market came around, things just feel..."

"Like they're falling apart at the seams," Olivia said.

"And let's not lie. None of us liked Erik. None of us wanted him dead, either, but that's not the point. He wasn't part of this...whatever this is that we have here. Each and every one of us on this beach has watched each other's backs since the night we arrived."

"I'd be dead if it wasn't for all of you," Vail said, her voice soft. "Don't think I'm not grateful."

"And here's something else I know," Amy said. "I don't care how dangerous it is here, because I'm not going back. I've got nothing to go back for but a dead-end life in a dead-end town, and probably a jail cell."

Dalton held up his hand, his face wan. "Same. On the cell part. Probably just with a lot more torture involved. I'm wanted for thought-crimes, and also regular crimes."

Colin curled his arms, squeezing them tight as his head drooped.

"They won't even call me by my own name. I'm...I'm not going back. I don't care what it takes or what it costs. I'm not going back. This is the only place in my entire life where I've ever been allowed to be me."

"I'm fleeing a fascist dictatorship," Bahati said.

"Go big or go home," Vail said.

"I always do. But yeah, I go back, I'm nothing but a songbird in a cage for the rest of my life. Not happening."

"You all know my damage already," Vail said.

Everyone turned to Olivia.

"What?"

"We're sharing," Amy told her.

"Oh. Um, I have a lot of debt. For reasons."

"And on your world," Bahati said, "do they...murder you for having debt or something?"

"Of course not, that'd be silly."

"Uh-huh."

"But they do throw you into a work camp until you earn enough to pay it back plus compound interest. Usually takes twenty or thirty years of hard labor."

"Next time," Bahati told her, "that's where you *start* the story. Just a tip."

# Chapter
# Thirty-Seven

The beach was cold at night, cold enough for Amy to catch a wisp of ghost-vapor in the air when she exhaled, but nobody wanted to go back just yet. They gathered driftwood and built a small fire on the sand, down by the black water's edge.

Amy warmed her hands by the fire, the crackling flames casting a shifting glow against her downturned face.

"Nobody ever thought I'd be worth anything at all back home," she said, to herself as much as to her friends. "Nobody ever had any faith in me."

"I wasn't the perfect child my parents wanted," Colin said. "So they threw me out. Like garbage."

"I get it," Bahati said.

He glanced at her, across the fire. "You do?"

"Got yanked out of school and cut off from my friends when I was twelve, because my folks found out I could sing and dance and figured they could make a few bucks promoting my act. Then I blew up, and suddenly I'm dealing with managers and promoters and..." She brushed some sand from her shoulder with a look of disdain. "...they decided who I could talk to, what I could say, what I would wear, the exact amount of calories I'd be allowed each day so I'd keep my bod tight. I've got all the money in the world, but I never felt *free* until I came here."

"Freedom," Vail murmured, gazing into the fire. "If we can keep it."

Dalton walked by and scooped up a rock.

"So we fight," he said. "That's the one thing I know how to do."

He turned and threw the stone as hard as he could, sending it sailing out over the oily black waters.

"*I'll fight the ocean*," he roared. Then he threw an arm around Colin's shoulder and pulled him close. "You gonna fight the ocean with me, little bro?"

"Whatever it takes," Colin said, grim-faced.

"We're not going back," Amy said, raising her face and turning to the others. "None of us are going back, and none of us are dying here. On our own worlds, we're all castaways. The people who should have protected us failed. The people who should have cared for us didn't even bother to try. Here, maybe, if we all stick together—"

"We can be more than anyone bargained for." Vail reached over the fire, took Amy's hand and clasped it tight. "All right. Let's do this thing."

Bahati put her hand on theirs. "You know I'm in."

Colin stood on his tiptoes and reached out, connecting. Olivia was next, grim but determined.

"The Castaways Club has a nice ring to it," Colin said.

Dalton's hand was the last to join the stack.

"Not as cool as the name of my old gang," he said, "but I'll allow it."

"What was your old gang called?" Colin asked, looking up at him.

"The Ash Boulevard Eviscerators."

Bahati let out a little snort. Amy's lips trembled.

"What?" Dalton said.

"So that's, uh…" Vail couldn't keep herself from grinning. "That's considered 'cool,' where you come from?"

"I mean, I didn't come up with the name myself," Dalton protested. "I—"

Whatever he was about to say next, it was swallowed by a sudden roaring wave and a distant voice that called out in a sing-song lullaby.

"*Daaalllton… Come swim with us.*"

Colin tugged on Dalton's sleeve and pointed.

"I think the ocean's here to fight."

A trio of buxom mermaids frolicked in the oily water, barely a stone's throw from the shore. One flipped and rolled, flashing a rotten tail covered in infected, peeling scales. Another floated and stared at the castaways on the shore. Her face — *like all their faces*, Amy realized — was too perfect, too beautiful, too porcelain to be real, and as frozen as a funeral mask.

"*Dalton,*" the middle mermaid cooed, her arms swaying like a belly-dancer as she beckoned him.

"Her lips aren't moving," Bahati said under her breath.

"I don't think that's her actual face," Amy said.

Dalton cupped his hands to his mouth and called out to the creatures.

"Sorry, babe! If I want to make out with a chick who'll probably eat me alive, I'll just go flirt with Gecka. Besides, as of tonight, I've got a renewed commitment to my education. This is no time for love."

The mermaid lifted her hands high in the air and flashed both middle fingers. Then, with a petulant flip of her diseased tail, she and her sisters vanished under the waves.

"Where did they even learn to *do* that?" Colin asked.

"My friend," Dalton said, "we live in an age of wonders."

\*\*\*

Dalton had bought a harmonica at the Night Market, and he played it with the skill of a jailbird. The shrill strains sang out over the water, music rising up to the starry night sky. Amy and Vail sat together beside the dying fire, watching the embers crackle and fade. Murder Mittens was a lump of a shadow further down the beach, the bobcat napping but staying close enough to keep an eye on her self-appointed charges.

"Does she think you're her kitten or something?" Vail asked.

"I...have no idea," Amy said. "I know she won't hurt us—"

"But you're still not going to pet her." It was an order, not a question.

"But I'm still not going to pet her."

Vail was quiet for a moment. She stared at Amy, Vail's freckles cast in firelight, her expression thoughtful.

"What is it?" Amy asked.

"We never really talked about it."

Amy tilted her head, a question in her eyes.

"The circle test," Vail said.

*Nora should be here, with us*, Amy thought.

*I failed her.*

*Never again.*

"I tried to stop her from leaving," Amy said. "I tried."

"I know." Vail's hand closed over hers on the sand. "That's not what I mean."

"What, then?"

"You kissed me."

A hot blush colored Amy's cheeks.

"It was…kind of a spontaneous heat of the moment thing," she said. "I was trying to…"

"Motivate me?"

"I think so."

"It worked," Vail said.

"Even so, I'm sorry. I was out of line, I shouldn't have sprung that on you, I—"

Vail held up a hand, silencing her apology mid-stride.

"I've got one, and only one complaint," she said.

Amy bit her bottom lip, anxious. Then Vail curled her legs underneath her, shifting on the sand, and turned to face her.

She grabbed Amy's school tie just below the knot and yanked her close, hard, so they were nose-to-nose. Vail held the tie tight, gazing into her eyes.

"If you're going to kiss me," Vail said, "do it right."

She pulled Amy in the rest of the way and their lips met, smoldering, velvet-soft, while Amy's heart pounded a staccato rhythm and lightning sizzled through her veins. Vail raised her free hand and pointed to the fading fire.

With a blinding flash the embers erupted back to life. The fire blazed brighter than before, casting jack-o'-lantern shadows up and down the beach and painting the sand with orange light.

Their lips parted, but they stayed close. Vail kept her hand clenched around Amy's tie. They shared shaky, eager smiles.

"I think I understand," Amy stammered. "Might need a refresher later, though."

Colin walked by, staring at them, his eyes wide.

"Today," he said, "I am a man."

Vail threw a handful of sand at him, sending him scurrying. Then she contemplated the renewed fire.

"Maybe I really can do this," she said.

"No *maybe* about it," Amy replied.

They leaned into each other for a while, silent, and watched the flames together.

# Chapter Thirty-Eight

Like Professor Mallory's hut, the Academy greenhouse looked like a wreck from the outside: one side had caved in entirely, and ramshackle boards covered the broken windows. Through gaps in the boards Amy made out long, soil-littered tables cluttered with dead and dying plants.

Colin turned his key in the door — a privilege of helping tend the professor's plants after hours — and opened it wide.

"What do you think?" he said.

The boards, the broken glass and ruin, were all an illusion. Inside, the greenhouse was rich and thriving, the sun burning down through pristine panes of glass, a world of healthy plants and blooming vines. A rich, peaty smell filled the air, mingled with the scent of fresh wildflowers. Colin led the others to the back of the greenhouse, where he'd dragged tables aside and cleared out a space of open floor ringed with mismatched chairs.

"I figured we'd need a place to study."

"A place Jellica and her goon squad don't know about," Bahati murmured, her big eyes wide and glittering. "Amazing."

Dalton rapped his knuckles on one of the windows. It chimed at his touch, like a crystal flute.

"Outdid yourself on this one, little bro. Where'd you find the chairs?"

"Around," Colin said, ducking his chin a bit. "Nobody'll miss them."

Vail walked past Dalton, scrunching her nose at him. "You're a bad influence."

"My divine calling."

"Space, security, great lighting," Olivia murmured, taking in the greenhouse. "This is everything we need. Well, that and a lot of hard work."

"Speaking of," Colin said.

He held up his half-finished Spellchoke, one stone strung along a steel wire. The wire caught the sunlight, softly glowing.

"Shall we?"

***

They relocated dozens of herbs in tight clay pots to other nooks and crannies in the greenhouse, making room for their supplies. The stash grew as the days passed, textbooks and grimoires and vials of pungent oils and pouches of exotic stones joining the growing hoard.

"Not the same time, remember?" Amy said, catching Dalton in the middle of anointing his Spellchoke with a tattered rag and a tiny drop of oil. "The wire and the stones are two different spells."

"They look exactly the same."

She leaned over his shoulder, pointing to a single line in the *Liber Scutum*, in the middle of an incantation that ran for two pages.

"This part right here. See? It substitutes *Essi* for *Logimus*. Think about it like this: the bracelet is the early-warning device, like a smoke alarm for magic. That kicks the stones into action, and they do the heavy lifting of taking the hit for you. The Spellchoke isn't one thing — it's two different parts, working together in perfect union."

"Bullet and a gun," Dalton said. "Okay. That, I get."

On the other side of the greenhouse, Olivia worked with Colin, both of them painstakingly sliding more wires through minuscule holes in chunks of jet and smoky quartz.

"If you ask me," Olivia was saying, "we already know who did it."

"Fill me in," Colin replied.

"Think about it. Erik smarts off to Professor Lanca—"

"Lanca did get kinda scary for a second there."

"—and then Erik dies. It's not like he has a problem killing teenagers, you know? By his own admission."

Colin looked up from his work, brow furrowed.

"But he's got that...implant thingy. He's not supposed to be able to hurt anyone anymore."

Olivia threw a flustered hand in the air. "Come on. They couldn't even teleport us here at the right time. It's been months and the school bells still don't work, and they don't have anywhere near the staff a place like this needs, which is why they use students to do half the work. Are you really going to tell me, after everything we've seen, that you trust Chen Lan to do *anything* right?"

He thought about that for a second.

"Le Guin's Razor," he said.

"Never heard of it."

"It's a...thing from my world. Never mind. Means that in the absence of confirmed truth, it's logical to go with the view that holds the preponderance of evidence." He shrugged. "The headmistress and all the other professors know exactly who and what Professor Lanca is and how dangerous he is. I can't buy that they'd *all* let him slip loose and nobody would notice anything."

"You're forgetting something," Olivia said.

"Oh?"

"What if one of them is in on it, covering for him? It'd only take one turncoat, like...Professor Chalk, maybe?"

***

"*Stand and deliver*," Professor Chalk intoned, rapping his brass-capped cane on the lecture hall floor. "As before, this examination will be pass-fail. Miss Curran, you're up first."

Vail and Amy shared a glance and a quick, furtive hand-squeeze before Vail rose from her chair.

"Ready, Professor."

Chalk gestured to the open floor before him.

"Then please, Miss Curran, prove it. By the way, have you ever had food poisoning?"

"Once. Thought I was going to die."

The professor twirled his empty fingers. They manifested a small rubber ball, like the ones he used during the circle test, but this time it was a garish, sickly shade of puke yellow.

"Good," he said. "Then you know what will happen if this manages to connect."

Vail took a deep breath, looked across the room, and fixed her eyes on Amy.

"Do it," she said.

The ball whipped through the air, sailing toward her.

Her Spellchoke ignited. It erupted in an inferno, a single blinding second that washed the world in colors of molten steel. When Amy could see clearly again, Vail was still standing. The torn scraps of the ball and the twisted, smoking ruins of her Spellchoke lay on the floor at her feet.

"A bit flashier than I would prefer," the professor mused, "but clearly a success. Well done, Miss Curran. Return to your seat. Next...Mr. Woodrue, if you would be so kind."

Colin stepped forward, rubbing the onyx stones of his bracelet with trembling fingers. Chalk took aim and threw.

When the puff of smoke cleared, flooding the lecture hall with the scent of burnt hickory, Colin stood untouched.

One by one, the other castaways rose to take the professor's challenge. And one by one, they made the grade.

*** 

As the weeks passed, their greenhouse stash grew and transformed. There were more books, more oils and half-worked talismans, and Colin had started to tack charts on the walls, as Professor Kamaka challenged them to learn the constellations of three alien worlds. Today they were roving the island trails, racing the dying light while the sun drooped behind a thick copse of trees.

"We need, and I quote," Bahati announced, reading from a scrap of parchment, "*one sprig of jester's remorse, one clump of deadnettle moss, one cutting of the blue poppy flower, all properly harvested and dried to my satisfaction.*"

"Already got the drying rack set up," Colin said. "Trust me, I work with Professor Mallory every afternoon. She is *particular* about things, but I know what she wants."

"Deadnettle grows on a patch of trees just south of here," Olivia called out. "I saw some the other day while I was out hiking! Consider it done."

"Found the blue poppies," Dalton shouted from just off the trail. Murder Mittens, stalking the first-years as usual, let out a throaty growl.

Amy ran to meet Dalton, carefully easing her way through the brambles, watching where she put her feet. She held a tiny knife with a curved, white-steel blade.

"We have to harvest it just right or the sap-pod will pop and we'll get nothing," she said. "If it bursts hard enough, it'll take out that entire patch and probably burn your hands. Chain reaction. Want me to do it? I've been practicing."

Dalton showed her his own identical blade and flashed a smile.

"How about I do it, and you let me know if I'm about to slip up?"

He didn't slip once.

***

"Night Market's coming back around," Mr. Orris said.

Amy's shoulders ached as she rammed a pitchfork into another bale of hay, but she couldn't deny that after months of working side by side with Mr. Orris in the stables — or in the Academy's musty storage rooms, or out on the courtyard lawn, or anywhere else he needed a helping hand to keep the place in order — she'd gotten stronger. At least, she felt stronger, and that was good enough to keep her moving.

"Root beer stick candy?" she asked.

"You know me well."

"Last time," Amy said, "the man at the confectionery said your account's getting low."

"Ayuh, sounds about right. I'll give you some cash to top it off for me."

Just like that. No hesitation. No distrust. A small smile touched her lips. Orris stood back a moment, pondering.

"The horses are taking a shine to you."

The big black stallion nickered and flicked his ears.

"Comet is," Amy said. "Prince, not so much."

"Aw, he likes you more than most. Professor Lanca came by the other day, askin' about the horses, and Prince was fixing to kick him straight into the ocean."

Amy paused.

"Why did he want to know about them?"

Mr. Orris shrugged. "Above my pay grade, as I'm so often reminded around here. I'm on the staff, but that doesn't make me a professor of anything."

"Huh? But...you *do* magic. You showed me the Vapor-Lock spell and we haven't even started to learn that yet."

He chuckled and waved an idle hand.

"Mighty kind of you, but I'm an enthusiastic dabbler at best." He scrutinized the horses. "You know, we don't have a whole lot to do this afternoon."

He led Amy over to the wall of tack, saddles and bridles hung up and oiled with care.

"How about you take Comet out for a bit, put him through his paces?"

Amy's eyes went wide. "Really?"

"Sure. You're responsible and you know how to handle yourself. That's all I need to see."

"It's been a long time," she said.

He took down a bridle, the supple leather curling around his weathered hand, and held it out to her.

"Like riding a bike," he told her.

\*\*\*

Amy and Vail sat across from one another at the long, polished study table in the library. For a while they worked in silence, books open, taking notes, only sometimes sharing furtive glances. In the corner of her eye, Amy saw Vail bite her lip.

"You want to talk about it?" Amy asked.

"We're really doing this. Magic. Plumbing the mysteries of the universe."

"Right now," Amy said, "we're learning how to make a poultice to heal fungal itch."

"Everybody starts somewhere."

Amy tilted her head, studying Vail's face.

"There's something else."

Vail dipped her head a little. A faint blush colored her cheeks.

"I've been working on a project."

"Alone?" Amy said. "We're all in this together. If you need help—"

"You already did."

"How do you mean?"

Vail slouched back in her chair. Her fingers drifted across a spidery diagram in the open book before her.

"You know how jammed up I was."

Amy still remembered how she nearly set fire to the library out of pure frustration.

"You've been improving every day, though," Amy protested. "You're acing everything, even Professor Chalk is impressed—"

"That's a step too far. Nothing impresses that man."

"Fair."

"But you know, I had a lot of problems letting the magic in. Didn't trust it."

*And didn't want anything touching you*, Amy thought. *Can't blame you one bit.*

"But you showed me," Vail said. "You showed me...it could be okay. So I've been practicing."

She reached across the table, her palm upward. Concentrating, lips pursed, she curled her hand until her index finger pointed in the air.

A plume of scarlet fire blossomed from her fingertip. It curled, hissing, and sprouted shadowed wings, a dragon in miniature. Their faces silhouetted by the flame, Amy and Vail shared a smile.

The librarian cleared her throat from the other side of the library.

"It is clearly time for another public service announcement," she declared. "*No fire in the library*. In case you aren't aware, celluloid is highly flammable, and I would very much prefer not to die a second time."

Vail curled her finger and snuffed the flame as she winced and mouthed an apology.

Not long after, Adelaide, flickering and transparent, drifted past them in her corset and bustle. A projector swiveled to frame her in its light.

"You know," she said, conspiratorial, "there is an unlocked broom closet in the east wing, if you two really need a place to go and make out."

"*Adelaide*," Amy gasped.

The ghost put a hand to her bodice.

"What?" she said. "I was born in the eighteen hundreds. It was *far* more common than you might think, especially for unmarried young ladies."

Amy sank in her chair. "Never mind me, just going to die of sheer embarrassment now."

"Don't die in here," the librarian said. "This haunt is mine."

Amy and Vail locked eyes until she was out of earshot.

"So," Vail said.

"Yeah," Amy said.

"You want to…take a walk with me?"

Amy quirked a nervous smile and rapped the cap of her pen against her notepad.

"*After* we finish this assignment."

"Priorities," Vail agreed. But just barely.

# Chapter Thirty-Nine

Professor Kamaka promised the obstacle course would get easier. Amy couldn't call him a liar. After a month of running the beach, she felt faster, fitter, than she ever had before. She just didn't anticipate that the course would never be the same twice. New obstacles started popping up between visits, as if the beach was stretching to fit them all in.

"Notice we never see *him* running the course?" Colin panted, his athletic uniform soaked with sweat.

Down the beach, almost too small to see, the professor raised his bullhorn to his lips.

"That's because I do my training in the temple of *pain*, little man. That's another word for a gymnasium. Someday you'll see one."

Up ahead, Olivia tumbled as she tried to hop from tire to tire. Bahati caught her before she could faceplant in the sand.

"What are you doing?" Olivia squinted as Bahati helped her up to her feet. "You're faster than me, go!"

A few months ago, they could barely stand each other. Bahati just dusted the sand off Olivia's shirt and got her steady on her feet.

"We all finish, or nobody finishes," Bahati said, glaring back at Professor Kamaka. "We're not trying to beat each other. We're all trying to beat *him*."

"Music to my ears," Kamaka's bullhorn rang out. "Now hustle!"

As Amy hopped from tire to tire, keeping her balance and watching her footing, she glanced up in time to catch a distant flash of light.

It came from the southern cliffs. Just like last time.

"Vail—"

"Hold on." Vail looked back, waiting until Professor Kamaka's attention was on some flagging runners at the back of the pack. Even with magically-enhanced senses, he could only focus on one voice at a time. "I saw it, too. I knew you weren't imagining things. I've been keeping an eye on that spot every time we come out here."

"Professor Kamaka is all the way down the beach behind us. We know it's not Professor Mallory, because we just left her class and she's back in her hut. And Mr. Orris told me he didn't need me to come around after school because he's got some kind of all-day meeting with the headmistress."

"And Professor Chalk's a powerhouse, but I've never seen him leave the school grounds. Not sure if he can climb with that cane."

And that left Professor Lanca — *who had been asking about the horses*, Amy remembered — or some upper-year students slipping off the trails and out of bounds. She suspected Jellica for a moment, but Vail had the same thought and cut her off before she could say it.

"It's not the Blades. Come on, an obstacle course with this many opportunities for someone to get hurt? They wouldn't be able to resist messing with us."

"They aren't subtle," Amy panted in agreement, as she dug deep to reach the finish line.

\*\*\*

They were supposed to head back to the Academy after the obstacle course to hit the showers and get ready for the afternoon's classes. Amy and Vail had other ideas. Colin and Bahati ran interference, trailing Professor Kamaka until he was a safe distance away. Colin, barely a stick figure in the distance, gave Bahati a quick wave. She turned and passed on the gesture, jumping in the air to make sure Amy and Vail spotted her.

"That's one nice thing about the gym class from hell," Amy said as she scrambled up a harsh incline. "Now I can do this without breaking my neck. Probably."

The thick, shifting soil threatened to slide out from under their feet with every step. Gnarled roots rose up from the dirt, twisted and dead. Vail grabbed them like handholds on a climbing wall, using each one to haul herself a little closer to the top.

When the land finally flattened out, Amy fell on her belly for a second in the wet, dirty grass and caught her breath. When she pushed herself up, she saw Vail just ahead, standing in frozen awe.

"Look at it," Vail breathed.

Amy stood beside her, gazing out over the crumbling cliff as the hazy sun began its slow descent through the muggy gray clouds.

They could see everything from here.

Gadfly Beach stretched out below them, a long ribbon of white sand between the island forest and the merciless, eternal sea. Bits and pieces of the trail network stood out, peeking through the dense foliage, and in the distance, ominous and grand, stood the gray stone curtain walls and dour manor-house arches of the Academy itself. To the south lay a rugged, untamed expanse, no paths or trail signs to mark the way.

They couldn't admire the view for long. They had work to do, and no excuse if they were caught here with nothing to show for breaking the rules. They carefully edged closer to the cliff, the death-drop directly overlooking the obstacle course far below.

Someone had been here. A folding camp chair had been knocked over and abandoned, along with a few stray wooden stakes, some twine, and a patch of cleared ground bearing the impression of a makeshift tent.

"I was right," Amy said, crouching low to run her fingers along the indentation in the dirt. "That flash we saw. It was the sunlight catching the lens on a pair of binoculars."

"Or a scope," Vail said, frowning at the campsite.

"Either way, someone's been up here watching us. For months now. Maybe not every day, maybe not every time, but..."

"I see the evidence," Vail said, "I see the camp, I just don't see the reason why. We went over the list. The most likely suspect is Professor Lanca. What's he going to learn about us that he can't already figure out just by seeing us in his own classes?"

"How fast we can run a mile?"

Vail gave her a sidelong glance.

"What?" Amy said.

"It's only a quarter-mile course, Amy."

"Is not."

Vail grimly pointed over the edge of the cliff, down to the obstacle-littered beach.

"Evidence," Vail said.

"I'm changing the subject before I get depressed." Amy turned, hands on her hips, and studied the fallen camp chair. "We have to talk to somebody about this. I mean, somebody in charge."

"Somebody who won't bust us for leaving the trails."

"So not Chalk," Amy said. "Obviously not Lanca. Chen Lan?"

"She's a wild card," Vail said. "I still can't figure out what's going on in her head half the time."

Amy thought back to the night of their arrival, when Vail was strung out and fading and needed help. The headmistress told her to walk Vail down to the Arch and push her through. Amy had rejected that option, and later came to think of it as just another show of the Academy's survival-of-the-fittest mentality.

These days she wasn't so sure. In hindsight, it felt like some kind of test, but Amy didn't know if she'd passed or not, and Chen Lan wasn't in the business of giving out hints. In any case, they couldn't predict how she'd react.

"Mallory?" Amy suggested.

"Colin thinks she knows about the greenhouse gatherings, and she's letting it slide so long as we don't make a big deal about it. We've finally got a good thing going here, and I don't want to push her hospitality."

*Fair*, Amy thought, though that left only one option.

*** 

"I'll give you kudos for this much," Professor Kamaka said, the big man rubbing the back of his suntanned neck as he examined the abandoned campsite. "It's not often somebody proves me wrong. You said you saw something up here, and you did. Good one."

He gave them an expectant look. Amy and Vail stared at him, faces blank.

"Well?" he said. "You can thank me now."

"*Thank* y—" Amy started to say, confused. "No. What? Why?"

"Well," the professor said, "how'd ya even get up here?"

"Obviously we weren't going to try to climb that cliff face," Vail said, "so we followed the trail until it stopped, used the sun to chart our way through a patch of woods, circled around and found a safe route to the top."

The professor stroked his chin, putting on an exaggerated face of scrutiny.

"Ooh," he said. "So what you're telling me is, you put together a navigation plan just like I taught you, you used the orienteering skills I taught you, and you pulled off a none-too-easy root climb on rough soil, just like the angled climbing wall on my obstacle course?"

The girls shared a helpless glance.

"Um..." Vail said.

Kamaka spread his hands wide and grinned.

"Yeah, I *am* the best professor ever, and thank you both for saying so. Okay, let's see what we've got here. Great vantage point, signs of a tent, the chair says somebody left in a hurry or at least they weren't planning on coming back. What's missin'?"

Amy had never been camping in her life, so she had no idea. There were plenty of tracks, but they were all scuffed and unreadable. She wasn't sure if that was because of the treacherous soil, or if whoever was spying from this perch made sure to muddy them up on their way out. Vail, on the other hand, instantly spotted the missing piece.

"No campfire," she said. "Firebreak gets cold at night. I can't imagine someone sleeping in a tent out here and not getting frostbite."

"Good eye," the professor said.

He quirked one corner of his mouth, turning from the camp to the girls.

"Now, as for you two. Technically I'm supposed to write you up and refer you to the headmistress for going out of bounds. That said, technically I'm supposed to do a lot of stuff — like writing staff reports

— and I just, y'know, don't. My life's easier that way. So let's make a deal: you leave this to me, and I'll keep your names out of it."

"Thank you," Amy said.

"*There* you go. Okay, kids, get back to your dorm, or another class, or...whatever! Just don't be here when I turn around. I'll give you a two-minute head start. Careful climbing back down."

# Chapter Forty

Dying amber light shone through the arched windows of the Academy's faculty lounge, casting long, bony fingers along the polished floorboards. The lounge didn't offer much in the way of creature comforts, just a couple of old sofas with olive vinyl upholstery, a few stiff wooden chairs, and a pantry next to a brass-fauceted sink and a plastic Mr. Coffee machine.

The folding camp chair from the cliff above the beach slapped down on the middle of the lounge floor. It sprang open at a touch, metal piping unfurling a black canvas seat and back.

"This," Kamaka said, "is a problem."

"And you're still not going to tell me who led you to it," Chen Lan said, her expression inscrutable.

"What, and make you do extra work? You think I'm a jerk or something? Forget it, doesn't matter. This matters. Somebody's peeping on my kids, and I want to know who and why."

"That's not ours," Professor Mallory mused, studying the chair. "I just had one of my student helpers take an inventory of all the camping gear in storage last week. Nothing is missing."

Professor Chalk pointed the tip of his cane at it, stopping just short of nudging it over.

"Simple," he said. "Let's get some psychometric readings from it. A bit of applied magic should tell us exactly who it belongs to."

Kamaka raised one disdainful eyebrow.

"Hey, Abe? I know you're not my biggest fan, and vice versa, but give me a little credit for having a brain? First thing I did before I brought this to y'all. It's been wiped. So was the entire camp. Whoever did this managed to erase their entire magical signature."

"No student did that," Chen Lan said. "We don't even teach that technique until the fourth year of study, and..."

She didn't need to say the rest. There were no fourth-year students. Not anymore.

"I can't help but notice," Mallory commented, "you invited all of us to this shindig but Red."

"Please don't call him that," the headmistress said.

Kamaka looked over at Mallory. "Don't tell me I gotta say why I didn't want him here."

The elderly woman pursed her lips, eyes still fixed on the chair. "Indeed you do not."

The headmistress held up a warning finger.

"Speak of the devil, and..." she said, just as the lounge door slammed open.

Professor Lanca stood in the doorway, bug-eyed and seething.

"Private meeting, pard," Kamaka drawled.

"Did *you* do it?" Lanca demanded.

"I do a lot of things. Wanna be more specific?"

"Someone," Lanca said through gritted teeth, "*urinated* on my office floor."

Kamaka barked out a laugh. "Ha! That's great! But no. Wasn't me."

Lanca circled the room, approaching him in a slow spiral.

"You sure? I know where you come from, Kamaka. This insult feels..."

They stood toe to toe, Lanca glaring up at the taller man.

"*Tribal*," Lanca spat.

"Somethin' I'll never understand," Kamaka replied. "Countless worlds in the multiverse. Infinite kinds of people, infinite ways to live. And yet somehow, despite all of that, you still manage to be a racist."

Lanca blinked. He took a halting step back, suddenly deflated.

"I'm...I'm not a racist!"

"You just don't like my people. Or the Racani. Tribal folk in general. Even the ones you've never met. Totally not racist."

"It's not racist if you have a good reason to—" Lanca caught himself, held up both open hands, and took another step back toward the door. "Forget it."

"Uh-huh," Kamaka said.

"I'm just..." Lanca bit his bottom lip, his face red. "This had better not happen again."

He stormed out and slammed the door behind him.

Suddenly, all eyes were on Kamaka. "What?" he said.

"Well?" the headmistress asked.

"Well, what?"

She flapped her hands at him with a look of quiet exasperation on her face.

"For the record, no," he told her. "I've thought about it, but no."

Chalk's cane rapped the floorboards as he strode to the lounge door. He locked it from the inside and turned to face the others.

"If we can get back to the matter at hand? I don't see any motive for Lanca to spy on our students, but I can't deny he's the only valid suspect." He paused. "Unless. Are we absolutely certain we don't have an outsider on the island?"

"Impossible," Chen Lan said. "I refresh the wards myself, *daily*. Firebreak has an alert system that warns me the second an unexpected portal opens anywhere on the island, as Professor Kamaka can attest."

Kamaka gave her a sheepish smile. She continued.

"This place is impossible to reach by interdimensional travel unless you know its exact coordinates — and I do mean *exact*, as the slightest miscalculation will send an invader to the depths of the ocean and, if they're very lucky, a quick death. That's why we chose this world in the first place. I'm rarely a hundred percent certain about anything, but I am about this: no outsider, since the Night Market's last visit, has set foot on Firebreak Island."

Professor Chalk leaned into his cane for support, ignoring the empty sofas. He could only sit more-or-less comfortably on a good day. The look in his eyes, as he regarded the headmistress, said this was anything but.

"Leading to the next necessary question," he said. "Are you equally as certain that the man hasn't slipped his leash?"

"My implant? Yes."

"Some reassurance would be nice," Kamaka said. "Beyond *yes*."

Chen Lan sighed. Her shoulders sank a bit.

"Do you remember, when we were hunting Lanca down, that Network kill-team we captured?"

"You said they were dealt with," Professor Mallory replied.

"They were all flunkies. Brainwash jobs, no intelligence of value. I offered them up on a plate to the Investors, who told me to toss them in the water and feed the mermaids. I may have...used them as the prototypes for Lanca's magical implant. Then I encouraged them to try to kill me, while I stood before them completely unarmed and defenseless."

"You *experimented* on *prisoners*—" Mallory started to shout, her voice clashing with Chalk's throaty growl: "Reckless and unacceptable. You could have been killed."

"I had to be sure," the headmistress said. "So yes. They were, in fact, dealt with. The mermaids got the chunks. Professor Lanca has been quite thoroughly neutered. Which doesn't mean he isn't our spy, but he's not in a position to harm anyone."

"Got a handful of puzzle pieces and none of 'em fit," Kamaka said.

Chalk nodded at him, stern. "We should delay the Night Market's next visit. Until we understand what's happening here, it's far too dangerous to add more moving variables."

"Can't be done," the headmistress said. "For security, the Racani have no way to contact me except face to face, and vice versa. They use a targeting key to arrive at a designated place and time, and once they get here I give them a list of all the supplies we need for their next visit. Nothing's ever done remotely, nothing that can be intercepted or traced by outsiders."

"Can we keep the students indoors at least?"

"And risk a riot? Everyone's flush with coin from their student jobs and looking to spend it. This is the highlight of the entire school year."

"They'll do as they're told," Chalk replied.

Mallory puffed out her wrinkled cheeks and slapped his arm.

"Morale matters. Can't ask these kids to work their hardest if we don't throw them a bone once in a while."

He narrowed his eyes at her. "So hold another one of your famous beach barbecues."

"Not good enough and you know it."

"In a state of emergency, Professor, pleasure must wait until peril has passed."

Kamaka put his beefy hands on his hips. "That what you're callin' it, Abe? A state of emergency?"

The lean, dark professor cast a stony stare at the faculty lounge door.

"I'm withholding judgment until I see more. All I know is this: the moments I've come closest to my inevitable appointment with Madame Death are those when I willfully blinded myself to the facts. These students are depending on us for their very survival. I will not fail them. And neither will any of you. Not on my watch."

# Chapter Forty-One

The sun sank below the forest canopy, turning the gathering gloom into a wonderland of spiderwebs and shadows. Colin hummed a happy song, a rare good memory, as he puttered around the greenhouse alone. The rest of the castaways were due in ten minutes or so for a bit of hands-on herbalism practice before racing to beat curfew. He knew his friends didn't mind a little mess, but he liked to make everything just right.

A shadow flitted past the wall of glass. He barely caught it, so low and furtive it might have been Murder Mittens on a hunt. He smiled and waved out into the dark, though he knew the illusion protecting the greenhouse would keep anybody on the outside from seeing him. Force of habit.

He had just pulled up a stool, opened his copy of the *Liber Scutum*, and leafed his way to chapter seven when the window behind him exploded.

He leaped up from his stool, kicking it back and sending it rattling across the soil-littered floor. He turned just in time to see a bottle sail through the broken window and break against the closest table of potted plants, a lit rag stuffed in its muzzle. As the bottle erupted in a breath-stealing wave of furnace heat, the air grew thick with the stench of burning gasoline.

*Oh God*, he thought, fighting the terror that froze him, locking his muscles tight. *Not like this. Not like this.*

Colin scrambled for the greenhouse door, but the plants were going up like dry kindling, flames spreading from table to table, riding dangling vines and catching along the rooftop. A hanging pot fell from a burning rope and splashed fire at his feet. He fell back, his only escape route cut off.

"Help! Somebody!" he shouted, doubling back. He picked up his fallen stool and swung it at the back wall of the greenhouse. The stool bounced off the reinforced glass, sending jolts of hot pain up his wrists, but the glass held fast.

Another swing and it glanced off twice as hard. The glass shook in its pane, but he wasn't strong enough to break through.

"Please, somebody, I'm in here!" he screamed. "*Help me!*"

\*\*\*

"Because seven ate nine," Bahati said, walking up the trail with Dalton, Amy and Vail.

"Still don't get it," Dalton said.

"Either the translation spell on this island is wonky, or you don't understand jokes."

"Of course I understand jokes," he said. "Okay, here's one: a sadist, a trillionaire, and a genocidal tyrant walk into a bar. The bartender says, 'Welcome, Overlord, want the usual?'"

Bahati stared at him.

"It's funny on *my* world," he said. "Of course, you can also get twenty years in a cube for that one—"

A panicked scream startled him. Olivia came tearing down the path, her uniform disheveled, face baked in sweat. She pointed back over her shoulder.

"Greenhouse," she gasped, out of breath. "Fire. Colin."

Dalton's eyes went hard. He broke into a run, the others right on his trail. They smelled the fire before they saw the first wisps of smoke above the treeline: acrid and foul, polluting the air with a chemical tang.

They heard Colin's muffled cries as they burst into the clearing. The greenhouse was burning, falling, letting out strangled metal groans as it listed dangerously to one side. The fires along the roof pierced the illusion of boarded-up windows and rot.

"We can't even see where he is," Vail said. She raised her voice. "Colin! Colin, we're here!"

"I can't break out," he shouted back, almost impossible to hear over the roaring flames.

Amy rushed to the wall of the greenhouse and felt along the illusory boards, yanking her hands back when they touched searing heat.

"Colin," she yelled, "hit the spot where you're standing as hard as you can, so we know where you are!"

A muffled *thump* echoed from the back wall of the greenhouse.

Dalton snapped his fingers. "Jackets. Everyone give me your school jackets. C'mon, *now*, damn it!"

"We can't smother the fire," Olivia protested even as she tugged off her uniform jacket, tears of panic glistening in her eyes, "it's totally out of control."

He took Vail's coat and slung it over one shoulder.

"Ain't for the fire, babe." He cupped his hands to his mouth. "Bro! Move to one side, get down on the floor and put your arms over your head!"

Dalton draped himself in the girls' jackets, pulling the last one over his head like a makeshift hood and mask as he backed up on the grass. Then he dropped into a sprinter's start, took one deep breath, and charged headlong toward the illusory wall.

The illusion shattered as he hit it with his entire body, shoulder first, and so did the real glass behind it, bursting into a spray of razor shards. Dalton hit the floor on the other side, inches from the spreading flames, and rolled to a stop. He dragged himself to his knees, suddenly swallowed by choking clouds of black smoke, and felt for Colin in the debris.

A trembling hand found his. Dalton yanked Colin into his arms, scooped up the smaller boy, and draped one of the jackets over his face. The greenhouse screeched, metal warping under furnace heat, and the ceiling over the front door collapsed in a storm of burning rubble.

Dalton carefully passed Colin through the broken window, both of them teary-eyed and hacking from the merciless smoke. Olivia and Bahati caught him on the other side, gently pulling him away from the fire and laying him on the ground. Amy and Vail helped Dalton out. He leaned into them, staggering, then collapsed to his knees with the fire at his back and dry-heaved until his throat gave out.

One last metallic groan, like the dying cry of some ancient beast, heralded the greenhouse's final collapse. The walls fell, crushing everything that didn't burn.

*** 

The blaze was almost out now, reduced to embers glowing in the twisted wreckage. The air still stank of dirty fire and all the things that shouldn't have burned.

Colin, Dalton, Bahati, Olivia, Amy and Vail sat in a ragged row on the grass, faces pale, uniforms stained with soot. Colin was still shaking despite the pair of blankets that swaddled him like a cocoon. Professor Mallory and Chen Lan stood over them.

"Some people mildly deface school property," Mallory said, utterly deadpan. "Congratulations on taking it to the next level."

"It wasn't our—" Colin started to say, then he doubled over in a hoarse fit of coughing. Olivia gently rubbed his back.

"I know," the professor said.

He looked up at her as the coughs subsided. "You do?" he croaked.

"Mr. Woodrue, if you had accidentally set the greenhouse ablaze, I feel safe knowing you would be the *first* to accept responsibility, especially if it meant sparing your friends from expulsion. If you say it was an attack, I believe you."

She shared a look with the headmistress. Amy couldn't read the unspoken message that passed between them, but she didn't need to. The gist was clear: *they already know things have gone wrong on this island. Maybe it was the camp we found, or maybe there's something they're hiding from us...but they know everything is going wrong.*

Dalton let out another hacking cough that ended in a desperate, strangled wheeze. Chen Lan leaned close to Mallory and whispered something. All Amy could make out was *smoke inhalation.*

"Of course I've got something for that," Professor Mallory said. "Okay, boys, come over to my hut. Going to introduce you to a new potion, the Universal Emetic. You're going to want to die for about ten minutes, but it'll clean you out from stem to stern."

"And ladies," the headmistress added, "you will go directly to your dormitory. No stops, no diversions. Do not test me tonight."

She pointed an accusing finger at the bobcat that lurked by the trees, keeping a careful watch on the young humans.

"And will *someone* please tell me why that animal is following you?"

"That's Murder Mittens," Amy said, less than helpfully.

"You're not bringing that thing onto campus."

"Don't worry about it," Vail said. "She won't go past the courtyard gates. She doesn't want to be civilized."

Chen Lan pursed her lips.

"I will refrain," she said, "from commenting."

# Chapter Forty-Two

Dalton was the last to return to the dorms. They'd all regrouped in Amy's room. He walked in with stubble on his cheeks and a thousand-yard stare.

"I just lost ten pounds," he said.

"Was it that bad?" Bahati asked.

Colin sat on Olivia's bed, trembling, while she held an arm around his shoulder in a death-grip and snuggled him by force.

"Not saying the potion was worse than the fire," Colin said.

"But let's spare a prayer for whoever has to clean that up," Dalton added. He flopped onto his back on Amy's bed.

"You're just going to—" she started to say.

"Yes. Until my legs stop wobbling, yes."

"*Jellica*," Vail snapped. She'd been pacing the creaking floorboards since getting back, and she wasn't slowing down. "She couldn't...she couldn't just let us have one thing. Just this *one thing*."

"We don't know it was her," Amy said.

"Don't we?"

Amy frowned at the floor. She would have been more than happy to blame Jellica for the fall of Rome, if she could justify it, but the clues didn't fit.

"She's a thorn in our side, but there's a heck of a jump from bullying to attempted murder."

"If you hadn't come along when you did," Colin said, his voice still weak, "it wouldn't have been 'attempted' anything."

"Maybe she thought it was empty," Olivia said. She clutched Colin like a mother bird afraid of dropping her baby from the nest.

"Okay, so...arson?" Amy said. "We know the school is protecting her, or at least the 'investors' behind it are, but that's going too far. Even if they can justify letting her run wild, blasting school property with a fireball is just—"

"It wasn't magic," Colin said.

Amy fell silent. Everyone turned his way.

"Wasn't magic," he repeated. "They threw something through the window. A glass bottle, with a lit rag stuffed in the top."

"A Molotov cocktail?" Amy said.

"Where I come from," Dalton said, "we call that a party-starter."

Now it clicked for Amy. The fire, the smoke, the *smell* had all been wrong. An angry reminder of her own past on a world without magic.

"That shouldn't be possible," she said.

"Pretty easy really," Dalton said. "Just fill a bottle with something that burns good and hot, stuff a rag in it, light it up, and give it a throw."

"That's what I mean."

She was thinking about her first time working in the stables with Mr. Orris. How he'd explained why they relied on horses for emergencies on the island and showed her the Vapor-Lock spell that could stop a car or a gun dead in its tracks.

"Gasoline," she said. "That's what I smelled. Gasoline. But there *isn't* any gas on the island. There's no need for it. No cars, no generators, and all the lights and such at the Academy are fueled by magic.

Where did someone get the ingredients to make a Molotov in the first place?"

Vail stopped pacing. She sat on the edge of her bed.

"Doesn't make sense," she said. "If *I* can harness magical fire, it can't be that hard."

"Hey," Amy said, a warning in her voice.

"Okay, okay, it's kind of my specialty, I guess. But still, you can't tell me any of the professors or an older-year student couldn't do the same thing. So what's with the low-tech weaponry?"

"I know I'm sounding like a broken record," Olivia said, massaging Colin's shoulders, "but the answer's pretty obvious, isn't it? There's only one reason I can think of for a magician to use gas and a lit match when they could use a spell and do twice as much damage twice as fast."

Amy got it. She didn't want to, but she got it.

"Because," Amy said slowly, "they can't use battle-magic at all."

"Because they've got an implant that'll kill them if they try," Vail added.

Olivia shrugged as if to say *well, see?*

"You know what the other professors will say if we tell them," Colin said.

"Sure," Dalton replied. "'Leave it to the adults.' But none of *them* nearly got killed tonight, so I say they don't get a vote."

"What if it was payback?" Amy said. "Vail and I found that camp. We ruined it for whoever was lurking up there. There's no way they can go back again."

"I don't think that contradicts my theory," Olivia said.

Colin tried to squirm out of her grip. She held him tighter, yanking him back against her chest.

"You don't really need to do that," he croaked.

"You scared me," she said into his shoulder. "Don't go anywhere alone again, okay?"

"None of us should," Amy said. "It doesn't matter who did it: we're being targeted, and the person behind all this is willing, if not eager, to kill us."

"So we get them first." Dalton caught their expressions and paused. "I don't mean *murder* the dude, I mean let's find proof that the school can't ignore and shut 'em down before they take another go at us. Next time we might not get so lucky."

"It would be nice if people actually listened to me once in a while," Olivia said.

Bahati sighed. "I can't believe I'm actually agreeing with Olivia, but she's right. We've got one suspect. If this was a murder mystery, it'd be all over by the second act. Looks like Professor Lanca's trying to get his old job back."

"If he ever really lost it," Vail said.

Bahati tapped her curled knuckles to her lips.

"But we need proof. For instance, a look through the man's personal effects?"

"In his office?" Colin asked.

"I was thinking more like his bedroom."

"No way," Colin said. "They'll expel us for sure."

"I know a way to do it without getting kicked out."

Bahati's earth-brown eyes gleamed, and she held up a finger.

"We just don't get caught."

\*\*\*

Once they'd made up their minds, Dalton summed up.

"This plan," he said, "calls for maximum chaos."

They passed the next few days with their heads down, traveling everywhere in pairs, doing their best to stay above suspicion. They'd decided on the perfect moment to strike: the morning of the Night Market's arrival.

"Mr. Orris never leaves the stables on the day the Market comes," Amy said, "because the horses get upset when portals open on the island."

The castaways had gathered in the library, huddled like thieves over a hand-drawn map of the Academy grounds, which Colin had inked across a string of looseleaf pages. Amy circled the stables with her pen, writing *Orris here* inside the ring.

"Chen Lan spends most of the day meeting with the head of the Market," Bahati said, "putting together her orders for their next trip and bringing all the new cargo to the kitchens and the storage rooms downstairs."

"Does she meet them here or on the Market grounds?" Vail asked.

"No idea, but I can try to find out."

Vail leaned over the map and drew crosshatching over the head-mistress's office, the storage rooms, and the halls leading to both.

"Call these danger zones, then. She'll be in *one* of these areas, so we'll have to be quick or have a solid excuse if we get caught out of bounds in the faculty wing." She drew a small circle at the western edge of the hatch marks. "This looks like the riskiest spot. Bahati, can you stand watch here and keep her busy if she shows up?"

"I might already have an idea or two brewing," she said.

"Perfect. Then all we need is an entry point that'll get us all the way to the faculty wing and back without being seen, just in case something goes sideways."

"What about the pavilion behind the school?" Olivia offered. "Those windows lead right into Professor Chalk's lecture hall."

Dalton stared at her.

"And barging into Chalk's turf on a clandestine mission sounds like...a good idea to you?"

"Of course not. But on Night Market days he goes down to the clearing to supervise setup. We just need to put someone here—" She drew a circle near the courtyard gate. "—to stand watch. Once he leaves school grounds, we're clear."

"Not safe, though," Bahati warned. "The clearing where they host the market is only a three-minute walk from the school gates. Even with that cane, he can get back fast if he has a reason to turn around."

"But he probably won't, and Professor Mallory doesn't set foot on campus unless she has to," Amy said. "That leaves Kamaka and Lanca."

Vail sketched more warning hashes over Professor Kamaka's office and private quarters in the faculty wing.

"Problem is," Colin said, "that's Kamaka's day off. He could pop up anywhere."

"He is deceptively quiet for a dude that big," Dalton said. "There's gotta be a way to corner him somewhere and keep him busy."

"Maybe we could just tell him what we're up to? Kamaka's a good guy."

Dalton shook his head. "He's a good guy, sure, but he's not *doing* anything. Dude, you almost died, and the best they can tell us is that they're 'handling it.' I don't see anyone handling anything, and I'm sick of waiting. We'll come clean once we've got ironclad proof that Lanca's dirty."

Colin took a deep breath and closed his eyes.

"What's in your head, little bro?"

"I know how to distract him," Colin said, "I'm just going to hate it. Trust me: I've got this part handled."

"And then there was one," Bahati said.

"Okay," Amy reasoned. "So we have to figure his door will be locked."

Dalton jabbed a thumb at his chest. "Leave that to me. Electronics are a different story, but I've never seen a mechanical lock I couldn't finesse. My crew used to call me Slippery D."

"Dalton," Bahati said.

"Yeah, babe?"

"Nobody has ever called you that."

"Logic says the burden of proving otherwise is on your shoulders," he said. "See? I pay attention in class. I learn things."

"Odds are that Lanca's implant will stop him from laying any magical traps," Amy said, "but that's not something I'm willing to roll the dice on. How fast do you think we can put together a working Spellchoke, just in case?"

"We all know how, Professor Chalk made sure of that," Olivia said. "If we divide and conquer, I bet we could brew one up in time."

Amy stared down at the makeshift map stretched across ripped, tattered notebook pages. She set her pen to the page and drew a line that snaked from the back pavilion through the lecture hall, around the crosshatched danger zones, straight to the faculty wing.

She circled Professor Lanca's bedroom.

"Now all we need is the perfect distraction. Something that's guaranteed to keep Lanca out of our hair until the job's done. We get in, we get out, we leave no trace behind. If we're right and we find proof, we bring it straight to the headmistress and come clean. If we're wrong or there's nothing to find...well, that's why we leave no trace."

"Alternatively, and hear me out on this," Dalton said, "we put all the evidence together, leave it outside her office door, then knock and run away really fast."

"Probably a better idea, now that you mention it," Amy said.

A sly smile spread across Vail's face, dimpling her freckled cheeks.

"I know exactly how to send Professor Lanca in the wrong direction," Vail said. "Trust me. This will be *satisfying*."

"Okay," Amy said.

She took a deep breath. She found her resolve, and Vail's hand under the table.

"By the time the Night Market leaves, our future will be decided one way or another. Nobody's coming to the rescue and nobody's going to help. It's all up to us. All in?"

She held her hand over the table. One by one, the others stacked their hands atop hers. As one, they brought their hands down, Amy's palm slamming against the sketch of Professor Lanca's bedroom.

# Chapter Forty-Three

*N*ow, Bahati thought, keeping her body pressed to the wall. As voices drifted down the corridor, her focused expression blossomed into a thousand-watt smile.

"I need you to be more diligent about checking the canned goods," Chen Lan was saying, floating along the hall with her slippers softly dragging on the flagstones. "Mistakes happen, but last time we had to throw out an entire crate of peaches. Minor dents are fine. Botulism is not."

"Of course, of course," said her companion. He was broad-shouldered and olive-skinned, with a handlebar mustache and bright brown eyes, dressed in swirling robes of burgundy and gold. "Apologies, we've had to change suppliers recently. One of our usual stopovers has become...unstable."

Bahati launched herself away from the wall, almost running right into them, blocking their path.

"Headmistress, I have an idea."

"That's...that's excellent, but I'm in the middle of a meeting—" Chen Lan started to say.

"With? Oh!" Her eyes lit in mock fascination. "You must be the man in charge of the Night Market."

The ostentatious stranger took her hand and offered her a courtly bow.

"It is my honor to lead the troupe, young miss, as my father and my father's father did before me."

"Charmed. I'm Bahati. Yes, that Bahati. Don't pretend you haven't heard of me."

His eyes went wide. "'All the Broken Pieces!' A most excellent album!"

The headmistress tried to protest, but Bahati slung one arm around each of their shoulders, talking a mile a minute as she steered them back the way they'd came.

"You know what this place needs? A *show*. I'm talking about a real spectacular. Headlined, of course, by me. Who else? The first Bahati concert performed for an interdimensional audience."

"A lovely idea," Chen Lan said, "but we really don't have time right now—"

"No, no," the Racani said. "I want to hear more."

"Darling, I just knew you would," Bahati gushed. "First, let me tell you all about my vision for the stage..."

***

Professor Lanca's head was on a swivel. He speed-walked the Academy halls, watching his back, as if he expected danger at any moment. His hand trembled against his office door, making the antique knob tremble in its socket.

The door groaned wide, and he froze.

His office had been destroyed. The drawers were ripped from his filing cabinets, folders and papers scattered all over the floor and filthy with trampled dirt. His desk lamp was a puddle of shattered green glass, and his appointment book had been reduced to a shredded pile of wet confetti.

A message just for him adorned the wall, scrawled big and bright in ivory paint: *Jellica Rules.*

A vein throbbed in Lanca's temple. He took a step back, surveying the disaster, and fixed his gaze on the wall.

"Of all the stupid, insolent, insufferable—" he said through gritted teeth, then raised his voice to a shout of raw fury. *"Jellica Barnes, come down here this instant!"*

\*\*\*

Crouched outside the windows on the cobblestone pavilion, Vail couldn't help but snicker as they heard Lanca's howl.

"I almost feel bad," she said.

Dalton cocked his head. "Do you really, though?"

"I do. Now that I know her damage, I feel more sorry for Jellica than anything. But there's a cosmic law at play here. Works the same all over the multiverse, I bet."

"Payback's a bitch?" Dalton asked.

"And so am I," Vail said with a satisfied smile. "Hold on, we gotta wait for the all clear before you jimmy that window. Let's hope Olivia doesn't buckle under the pressure."

\*\*\*

Olivia sat in the school courtyard under the shade of a stunted tree, pretending to read a textbook. She kept her eyes on the Academy doors, watching students come and go, waiting for her target.

Professor Chalk emerged, stately and lean, his cane tapping as he walked to the courtyard gates. He spotted Olivia and favored her with an emotionless nod. She answered with a nervous smile.

As soon as he was halfway through the gates, on his way down to the Night Market's clearing, she tilted her head back and called out, "Ba-*whoo!* Ba-*whoo!*"

Chalk stopped mid-stride. He turned, slowly, leaned into his cane, and stared at her.

"Miss Renn? What...was that?"

"Oh, uh," she said, a hot blush coloring her cheeks. "I'm working on my natural-magic homework, Professor. Professor Mallory has us learning bird calls."

He closed his eyes and pinched the bridge of his nose.

"Remind me to have a talk with that woman. Do not neglect your self-defense assignment, Miss Renn. What you learn in my class will serve you far better than anything you learn in hers."

He turned and kept walking. She waited until the wrought iron gates had swung shut at his back, the professor almost out of sight, then took a deep breath and cried "Ba-*whoo!*" at the sky two more times.

*** 

"I told her," Dalton grunted, leaning into the window and jamming a whittled wooden shiv under the jamb, "not to do the stupid bird calls."

Vail stood at his shoulder, keeping a lookout. "Cut her some slack, she's really proud of her talents."

"That's a talent?"

The window rattled upward with a quick pop of air.

"She thinks so," Vail said. "Besides, everybody had to have heard that."

"The *ocean* heard that."

"If everybody's on track, Colin should be taking Professor Kamaka off the board right about now. I still don't know what he's planning to pull, though."

Dalton poked his head into the empty lecture hall. Then he slung one lanky leg over the sill.

"I do," he said, "and his heroic sacrifice will be remembered for all eternity."

\*\*\*

Colin scurried through the Academy's halls like a mouse in a maze. Everyone was counting on him to get this done. Trusting him. Never in his life had he felt this kind of weight on his shoulders.

It felt good. Better than good. And scary, but now he knew he could handle the fear.

He rounded a corner and nearly barreled into Professor Kamaka. Kamaka looked down at him with a curious smile.

"Careful, little guy. Almost ran you over."

Colin's heart pounded. *They need me*, he thought. If he couldn't keep the professor distracted until the end of the break-in, his friends would be in danger.

"Sir? Could I ask you a question?"

"Sure kid, shoot. What's up?"

"Sir, I've been thinking a lot about what you've taught us and..." Colin looked up at him, utterly earnest. "I want to get *strong*."

Kamaka hesitated. Then he broke into a wide, lantern-jawed grin. He threw an arm around Colin's shoulders and pulled him close, almost hauling him off his feet.

"Young man," he said, "you will remember this as the most important day of your life."

He stretched his other arm out before them, his hand sweeping across the school hallway as if he was a director with a vision.

"Because today is the day you embraced...*peak fitness*. You know what I'm gonna do for you? I'm going to let you use my private gymnasium. And lucky for you, I haven't had my morning workout yet. C'mon, let's go. I wanna see how much weight you can press."

*And this is how I die*, Colin thought as the professor hauled him off.

***

Olivia sprinted through the hallways, her pleated skirt flaring out behind her, stopping cold at every intersection and checking the corners like a spy in a war zone. She'd earned a key to the basement storerooms by helping Professor Mallory take inventory, a job mired in tedium, dust, and spiders. Today, she didn't have it — she'd slipped it to Amy, hours ago, to prepare the way for the next leg of the attack.

She hopped down the dusty staircase and was about to knock on the oaken door at the bottom when it swung open. Amy grabbed her wrist and pulled her inside.

Amid a jumbled clutter of supply crates, old soggy cardboard boxes, and shelves bearing unreadable tin cans, Amy had set up a makeshift ritual space. A lit stick of sandalwood incense filled the dingy store-room with a smell like an Egyptian temple, and beeswax candles glowed against the dark. Oils and perfumes lay alongside dark stones of jasper and jet and a pair of open textbooks.

"I'm almost done with the bracelet," Amy said. "I need you to consecrate the stones while I finish up."

"On it," Olivia said.

They worked together in near silence, breaking the stillness only with whispered, wispy incantations that fell from their lips, blending in the dusty air before fading into the forgotten, cobwebbed corners of the basement.

Olivia looked on, nervous, as Amy carefully strung the beads onto the finished wire.

"Perfect," Amy said. "Now I've got to meet up with Vail and Dalton. Do me a favor and run ahead of me. If you spot the headmistress coming, sound a warning. If I make it, head back out to the courtyard and keep watch in case of trouble."

"Aren't you going to test it?"

Amy blinked at her.

"We can't 'test' it, Olivia. It's a Spellchoke. Only one use, then it breaks. Just gotta have faith."

A flood of expressions flickered over Olivia's face. The one she settled on looked...*devastated*, Amy thought.

"But I made half."

Amy slipped the bracelet onto her wrist. It was a perfect fit.

"Yes, and?"

"You..." Something glinted in Olivia's eye. "You really trust me?"

Amy took her firmly by the shoulders and looked her in the eye.

"Olivia, this is not our time to have a tender moment. You're every bit as good at this as I am. Even Professor Chalk says so. So please, can you hold it together and we can do the heart-to-heart thing *after* we bust into Lanca's office? Really need everyone to focus here."

"Right. Of— of course."

Olivia wiped her sleeve across her eyes, turned, and led the way upstairs.

***

Olivia scouted ahead, but the headmistress was nowhere to be found. Hardly anyone was — most of the student body was eagerly mustering in the courtyard, excited for the Night Market's arrival. Up a darkened hallway, Vail gave them a frantic wave.

"That's my cue," Amy said. She squeezed Olivia's arm. "You did great."

"But—" Olivia started to say, again on the verge of tears.

"Tender moment *later*," Amy reminded her. "Get down to the courtyard and keep an eye out, just in case. Clock's ticking."

She raced to meet up with Vail and Dalton, heart pounding. Above her somewhere, she heard Professor Lanca, still bellowing at the top of his lungs.

"*Stop screwing with the stairs, Jellica!* I am a professor of this Academy and you can't keep me from accessing the third floor! We are going to have *words*."

A chorus of hysterical laughter answered him. *The Blades won't be laughing when they figure out why Lanca's so angry*, she thought. She figured the confusion should buy them a good fifteen minutes, so she gave herself ten, at most.

Dalton was already crouched in front of the door to Lanca's private chambers, working the antique lock with a pair of makeshift picks.

"Few more seconds and we're in, nice and smooth," he muttered, clenching a third pick between his teeth.

"I'm not rushing you," Amy said, looking up and down the empty corridor.

"You're standing over my shoulder," he replied, shifting the spare pick to the other corner of his mouth.

"Sorry."

"Don't be sorry, just don't rush me."

"Remember, once you get it open, let me go in first." Amy pulled back her sleeve, showing them the newly minted Spellchoke. "Better safe than sorry."

***

Olivia was marching to the Academy doors when she entered the foyer and stopped cold.

Professor Chalk was back.

He paused, greeting her with a curious look. "Miss Renn."

"You're, uh, here!"

"Left my coin purse in my quarters," he said. "I have no particular issue with the Racani's insistence upon trade for trade, but they won't even answer basic questions without a bit of silver changing hands. Thankfully, it's a short walk."

As he moved past her, she did the only thing she could think of.

"Ba-*whoo!* Ba-*whoo!*"

He paused, turned, and gave her a dour look.

"Just practicing," she said, and gave him two shaky thumbs up.

"Miss Renn, you aren't by any chance...ingesting any of the odd herbs that Professor Mallory sends you hunting for, are you? Or perhaps smoking them?"

"No, sir. Just doing my homework. And following the rules. You know I'm a stickler for the rules. All of them. I love rules."

Professor Chalk's lips parted, as if he was about to say something. Nothing emerged but a withering sigh. He turned away and kept walking, heading straight for the faculty wing.

# Chapter Forty-Four

D alton had just jimmied the lock when Olivia's frantic hoots echoed up the hallway. Amy led the way into Professor Lanca's private sanctum, and Vail shut the door behind them before twisting the lock.

"Who do you think?" Dalton asked. "Lanca? The headmistress? Somebody's coming and we'd better be gone before they get here."

Amy's generous ten-minute allowance had just been slashed to ribbons. She looked around the room and her heart sank even deeper. Lanca's quarters looked more like a boutique hotel room than an evil wizard's lair, with a neatly made four-poster bed under a draped canvas canopy, an antique dresser, a rolltop writing desk, and a leaded window that offered a view of the fighting ring behind the school. An open door looked in on a cramped bathroom.

Vail ran over and gave the window a tug, trying to pull it up. It rattled in its frame.

"It doesn't open," she said. "Can't get out this way."

"We should call this off while we still can," Dalton said.

Amy's eyes narrowed to slits as she studied the innocent-looking room. She couldn't shake her intuition. It screamed in the back of her mind, telling her there was something vital here, something real to be found. And this might be the only chance they ever got.

"You two go," she said. "Whoever's coming, try to stall them and buy me some breathing room."

Vail snorted. "No way. You'll never get done in time. Dalton, check the dresser. I'll search the bathroom."

Amy focused on the writing desk, but the unlocked hutch rolled up to unveil nothing but schoolwork, a few stray books from the Academy library, and a collection of old, chewed pens in a coffee cup.

*Wasting our time*, Amy thought. *He wouldn't keep anything incriminating where anyone could just stumble across it. He's smarter than that.*

"Dalton," she said, "don't bother going through his dresser drawers. Check the backs and bottoms for a secret panel. Vail—"

"Already on my knees looking under the sink," Vail called from the bathroom. "Nothing but dust bunnies."

Amy rotated in place, taking in the entire room, trying to see past her assumptions and the million what-ifs assailing her fevered thoughts. Then she spotted it.

The canopy over the professor's four-poster bed was firm, ringed with ruffles. Amy took hold of both ropes, gritted her teeth, and pulled as hard as she could.

The next thing she knew, she was flat on her back with her ears ringing and the back of her head throbbing. Vail was helping her sit up, cradling her, but her voice tripled in Amy's swimmy ears and she couldn't understand. The wreckage on the floor said it all. Her Spellchoke lay in a twisted, black, smoking ruin, the stones shattered into a hundred jagged shards.

"I'm pretty sure that was supposed to kill whoever pulled it down," Amy managed to stammer, slowly getting her senses back.

"Yeah," Dalton said, pointing, "and now we know why."

The canopy had billowed down onto the bed below, still held up by the back posts so that it draped along the headboard and down over the sheets like a makeshift cork board. Maps and scraps of paper and notes littered the thing, a web of conspiracies.

It was the work of months, maybe longer, a wall of paranoia linked by colored string, and Amy couldn't help but picture Professor Lanca obsessing over every last detail by moonlight before furtively hoisting the canopy back into place each night. He slept under his secrets.

"That's a map of Gadfly Beach," Vail said, pointing to one corner of the string labyrinth. It was hand-drawn but unmistakable. Lanca had circled the abandoned camp in blood-red ink. The professor's notes scrawled beneath it read *Camp #1. Pen testing.* A second, later note in black read *Do not go back!! Kamaka found it, probably being watched now.*

"Pen testing?" Amy asked.

Dalton exhaled a puff of air. "Pen. Short for penetration. As in, staking out a target and figuring out where the weak points are."

"He was watching *us*," Vail said.

"Uh-huh. Like I said. Figuring out the weak points."

Another sketch depicted the greenhouse from above. Arrows curled like a diagram from a football game, pointing to where the fire began.

"*Non-magical incendiary*," he wrote. "*Mallory's hut is warded against attack. Greenhouse is just illusion-masked. Soft target.*"

"This is where he planned it," Dalton growled. "And damn near got Colin killed."

Amy looked across the sheets of obsessive logs in Lanca's crabbed hand, tracking his fellow professors' comings and goings, a stalker's manifesto. Her gaze drifted to another hand-drawn map, this one cruder than the others. *X* marked a spot just northwest of Mallory's hut and the ruined greenhouse. The note beneath it read:

*Watching me now because they found the surveillance post. They won't let me out of their sight and I can't throw their suspicion off anymore. Need to find a way to get to camp #2 and take care of business before I run out of time.*

"And that's where he must be keeping the goods," Amy said.

Dalton grimaced. "Like gasoline and empty bottles?"

"And anything else he's hiding," Amy said, gesturing to the ruined Spellchoke at their feet. "Maybe he can't use battle-magic anymore, but clearly he can rig a trap or two."

"That's a fifteen-minute hike from here if we cut through the woods," Vail said.

Suddenly, they heard slow, steady footsteps down the hallway, and the rhythmic rapping of a cane.

"'In and out without a trace' is off the table," Vail whispered, looking from the shattered Spellchoke to the fallen canvas. She shot a pointed glance at the back window.

Amy jumped on the bed, grabbed the canvas and pulled, hard. Tacks popped as it tore from its mountings. She and Vail worked to gather up the awkward bundle. Meanwhile Dalton rushed to the writing desk. He snatched one of the professor's hardcover books and hurled it as hard as he could, breaking a big, jagged hole in the window. He used another book to knock the loose shards of glass from the frame, opening an escape route.

The bedroom door jiggled. Then it began to shake.

Dalton scooped up Amy and pushed her through the window with the stolen canvas in her arms. Then Vail. He hurled himself out after them, landing on his shoulder and rolling along the grass. The three of them scampered toward the fighting ring and dropped into cover on the far side.

"That," Amy gasped, "was way too close."

"But we know where to go next," Dalton said.

Vail squeezed his shoulder. "Amy and I are going. We need you to stay."

"What? You're gonna check out Lanca's shady little hidey-hole without me? Don't think so."

"She's right," Amy said, understanding Vail's intention. She held out the folded canvas bundle to Dalton. "Lanca's planning something, and we don't know when it's going down. Might even be tonight. We need you to take this, round up Colin, Olivia and Bahati, and tell them everything. We should be back in less than an hour. Once we are, depending on what we find at the second camp, we can make an action plan. It won't be long before Lanca realizes the mess in his office was a cover for stealing his secrets, and he's going to go ballistic. Get everybody, and this bundle, someplace safe. Wait for us."

"And what if you stumble onto another deathtrap?" he demanded. "You just blew your one Spellchoke."

"Got another one in your back pocket?" Amy asked.

"Well, no…"

"There you go," she said. "If there's any evidence at the second camp, Lanca's next step will probably be to burn it all. That's what I'd do in his shoes. We can beat him, but only if we leave right now. Please. Rally the troops, and whatever you do, keep that canvas safe."

"Fine, fine." Dalton flipped a tired salute. "I don't like it, but you're not wrong. I'll hold things down here. Just get back fast. And hey."

Amy and Vail both looked his way.

"Don't get dead out there," he said. "We all made a promise to graduate together. Let's keep it, okay?"

***

Murder Mittens joined Amy and Vail outside the Academy walls and trailed them through the forest. She started to fall back after a while, though, and let out a hesitant, nervous growl.

Amy felt it too. The trees grew thick and dark and dead, their trunks riddled with fungus and disease, the brambles underfoot sprouting thorns that tore at her school trousers and drew bloody welts along her legs. The air was oily here. It smelled of rot, like a boatload of fish left to putrefy under the summer sun.

Her skin crawled, and one glance told her Vail felt the same way.

"It's...wrong here," Vail breathed, as if afraid to raise her voice above the whispering wind. "What did he *do* to this place? It doesn't feel anything like the rest of the island."

A long, rough slope led down to a forest basin. Beside a stagnant pond, the sickly green water coated in streaks of algae, a lonely oilcloth tent stood beside the dead remnants of a campfire. Vail crouched and sniffed, holding her hands over the charred kindling.

"Not fresh," she said. "From last night, maybe."

Amy studied the tracks in the mud. They were odd, confusing, shoeprints mingling with the tracks of something that looked like an overgrown animal.

"What is that, a bear?"

Vail peered at the tracks, frowning.

"Dunno. See how deep the tracks sink down, though? Whatever it is, it's *heavy*."

Amy looked at the tent flap. She hunted down the longest stick she could find, snapping a bone-thin branch from the lowest bough of a dead tree. Vail gave her a dubious look.

"I know," Amy said. "It's not high magic. But if there's something nasty on the other side of that flap, at least I won't lose my fingers."

*Probably*, she added in her head.

She poked the flap. It wriggled a little. Nothing else happened. Cautiously, she used the stick to peel it back, opening up the tent. Empty, but a bit of clutter and a faint metal gleam in the back corner caught her eye.

Amy crouched and wriggled into the tent, her nose wrinkling at a smell like wet, dirty gym socks. The tent was a humid, dark cocoon, and she carefully kept one foot outside as if she was afraid it might swallow her whole. She poked her stick at the far corner, trying to drag the shadowy objects closer to the light.

Outside, Vail crouched beside the campfire. Her fingers trailed over the impressions in the mud.

"Hey, Amy? How sure are you that Professor Chalk is one of the good guys?"

"Ninety percent on a bad day," she called over her shoulder. "Why?"

She reeled in her haul like a fish on a line. The objects slid halfway across the tent, catching the sunlight and glittering.

Amy froze.

"Because of these tracks," Vail said. "Look at this. Step, step, indent. Step, step, indent. Something round, like a cane. Chalk's the only person on the island who uses one."

Amy scurried from the tent, eyes wide, her lips parted. Her face was waxen, bloodless.

"We've got to get back. We've got to get back and warn the others, right now."

"Why? What did you find in there?"

"We were wrong," Amy said. "We were wrong about *everything*."

# Chapter Forty-Five

V ail held Amy's arms and pulled her closer, trying to calm her trembling.

"Talk to me, hon."

"We were looking for a spy. Had to be someone we knew. Nobody can get on or off the island outside of the Night Market visits, except through the Arch, so it *had* to be someone we knew."

"Okay," Vail said, uncertain. "Not seeing the problem."

Amy held up her catch from the tent. A pair of discarded trinkets, cheap talismans dangling on tarnished chains. One was a perfect twin to the one Olivia had bought at the Night Market.

"We know one other person who uses a cane," Amy said.

Vail shook her head. Her brow furrowed.

"But he was with the Night Market. They left months ago."

"We know the Network is hunting for this place. They destroyed the first version of the Academy, thanks to Professor Lanca, and now they want to finish the job. What if they infiltrated the Night Market? Hitching a ride from world to world, hoping they got lucky?"

"Elmer," Vail breathed. "The Jangly-Man."

"*He never left*." Amy leaned in, close. "He didn't go with the Night Market. He slipped away, and he's been camping on the island ever since. Hiding out and spying on us. He didn't *need* to open a portal to get here. He just used theirs."

"But why? Wouldn't he have run straight to his bosses and told them where to find us?"

Amy shook her head. "That's what I thought at first, but remember Lanca's notes? Penetration testing. That's what Elmer's been doing. Drawing maps. Making notes on the students and the staff. Probably testing the wards and protection spells and everything else they slapped on this island to keep it safe."

"Figuring out the easiest ways to kill us all," Vail said.

"So when his masters arrive, they can steamroll this entire island without breaking a sweat."

"And the professor..." Vail took a breath. "He's not helping Elmer. He's trying to *stop* Elmer. He didn't cause the greenhouse fire, he was figuring out how it happened."

"I'm not ready to go that far. There's another possibility: what if he thinks Elmer is his ride out of here? Straight back to the Network, where they can remove his implant and turn him back into good old Red Lanca."

"Either way..." Vail said. Her voice trailed off as the implication sank in. "The Night Market is tonight."

"Elmer is *leaving*, with or without Professor Lanca. And if he gets off this island and reports back..."

There wasn't anything left to say. They turned and tore back through the underbrush, racing for the Academy gates.

∗∗∗

"Where are we—" Vail started to gasp, both of them bathed in sweat as Amy led the way down the winding path that circled the Academy.

"Stables. I've got an idea."

She wasn't the first. They burst into the stables only to find Comet's stall open and empty. Prince, the black stallion, flicked his ears and stomped his hooves in irritation.

"Mr. Orris!" Amy said, rushing across the musty, hay-littered floor. Orris was slumped against the wall of the stable, groggy, rubbing the back of his head.

"Was it Professor Lanca?" Vail asked, standing over them.

"He actually apologized, can you believe that?" Orris slowly got to his feet, wincing, as Amy helped him up. "Said he didn't have time to explain. Hit me with some kind of whammy in a perfume atomizer."

"How long ago?" Amy asked.

"Best guess, maybe five, ten minutes. No idea where he went."

Amy and Vail shared a look. They knew.

"Are you going to be okay?" Amy asked.

"Ayuh, leastways until he comes back and I give him something to really be sorry about. Might bruise my knuckles then. Damn punk." Orris massaged his scalp. "Took a little bump but I'll be fine. What are you ladies doing here, anyway?"

"We need to borrow something," Amy said.

Her gaze drifted to the loft, and to the wall of tools.

"Two things," she added.

\*\*\*

The last rays of the sun vanished over the horizon, the storm clouds rippling faster than usual, spurred on by dark, cold winds. Lightning crackled, slashing down across the eternal black sea.

Amy and Vail burst from the stables on Prince's back, Amy holding the reins, Vail's arms wrapped tight around her waist. The catspaw, Mr. Orris's five-barreled hunting rifle, dangled from a sling across Amy's shoulder. The stallion's hooves thundered down the path, circling around to the courtyard where Dalton and the others were waiting.

Amy gently tugged the reins and Prince reared back, front hooves slashing the air, then came down with a thunderous crash.

"It's the Jangly-Man," Amy called. "He's the Network spy. We can't let him leave."

"What about Lanca?" Dalton said.

"He stole a horse, and he's going down to the Market to either fight him or join him. We'll know when we get there." Amy glanced back. "Sorry, only room for two."

Bahati nodded firmly. "We'll be right behind you. Go!"

"More running?" Colin said, looking pale and shell-shocked.

Dalton put his arm around Colin's shoulders. "More running. C'mon, dude, it's like a quarter-mile."

"Doesn't mean I have to like it."

Prince kicked up dust as he charged down the forest path at a breakneck pace, muscles rippling, like an engine hell-bent on speed. Amy ducked as gnarled branches whipped just overhead.

"Are you controlling the horse," Vail shouted in her ear, "or is it controlling you?"

Amy leaned into the wind, eyes sharp, hand firm on the reins.

"Call it a partnership," she yelled back.

Murder Mittens loped after them, growling as she leaped through the underbrush.

"Do we have a plan?" Vail asked.

"Stop Elmer from leaving."

"That's a goal, not a plan. And what about Lanca?"

"He gets one chance to prove himself," Amy shouted over the wind. "He's either on our side or he isn't."

"And if he isn't?"

*Then this is about to get seriously messy*, Amy thought.

\*\*\*

The Night Market was in full swing. There were stalls and booths and games by torchlight, exotic music drifting from striped tents, and the smell of street food and spices in the air. A fire-eater dressed in scant silks slid a torch between her parted lips and belched flame to the delight of a crowd of students. And further back, at the far edge of the clearing, stood the sleeping caravans and RVs converted for trans-dimensional travel.

Lanca reared Comet to a halt at the Market's edge and slid from the saddle. He patted the horse fondly, then slapped it on the flank.

"Go home, boy."

As the horse turned and trotted off, Lanca fixed his eyes on the crowds ahead, hunting for a familiar face. Slipping silently through the crowds, keeping to the shadows, he found his target in the outer ring of campers.

Elmer the Jangly-Man peered over his shoulder as he hobbled along, his deer-antler staff whispering as trinkets and amulets rubbed together like wind chimes. He looked back head, and stopped short.

Lanca stood in the middle of the lane outside his run-down RV, feet squared like a gunslinger.

"You stole my whole playbook," Lanca seethed. "And then you half-assed it, you dung-eating lackwit *hack.*"

Elmer recovered from his surprise. His lips curled into a sick little smile.

"This doesn't have to get unpleasant, seeing as we're both professionals here. Colleagues, even." Elmer nodded casually at the silent, rusted-out RV. "Come along. I've got room for three, and you'd be welcome. I know some people who would be very glad to have you back, Red. Glad enough to give you anything your heart desires. I'd be happy to leave you to rot, make no mistake, but my superiors would reward me for recovering such a...valuable piece of property. I want to go home. So do you. Let's work toward our mutual benefit, yes?"

***

Prince charged at full gallop down the Night Market's main boulevard, sending people screaming and scattering, throwing themselves into the dirt. A stilt-walker staggered back and tumbled, catching himself on an awning only to fall as it collapsed under him and the whole booth came down with a crash. A stray hoof from Prince kicked a standing torch, sending it rolling across the dirt shedding orange-hot sparks.

"Sorry," Amy called out. "So sorry, coming through."

They took the long way around, angling for the rows of caravans behind the market pavilion, until Prince reared to a stop with a ferocious whinny. Murder Mittens had veered off at some point and was nowhere to be seen, though distant screams suggested she was taking a shortcut through the bazaar.

Amy dropped down from the saddle, then reached up and helped Vail down. They stood side by side in the middle of a quiet, dark lane flanked by campers and caravans.

Elmer was ten feet ahead of them. And past him stood Professor Lanca.

"Stuck between a rock and a soft place," Elmer mused. "This should be fun."

"We know who you are, and we know what you did," Amy told him.

He faked a clown's grimace, pulling down the corners of his mouth with his fingertips.

"I thought they were raising *smart* students at this school," he said. "My dear, never give a man a reason to kill you if he doesn't already have one."

Professor Lanca stood, watching, utterly silent.

"Well, Red, old pal?" Elmer asked, gesturing to the girls. "How about we tie off these loose ends escape to much greener pastures? We'll have that implant out of you in no time, and you can get back to your old tricks."

Amy looked Lanca dead in the eye. He looked, she thought, like a man facing a terrible choice.

# Chapter Forty-Six

L anca stepped sideways, closer to Elmer's RV, blocking the door with his body.

"Think I'm happy where I am for now," he said.

"Nonsense," Elmer said, though Amy couldn't miss the hint of fear in his eyes. "There must be something I can tempt you with. If not your freedom, what? Money? Pleasure? Pick your poison."

"And I get it tomorrow, right?" Professor Lanca asked. "Never today. Always tomorrow. See, that's how the Network operates. They promise and they promise, but they never deliver a thing. I saw the truth and I got out. But you? You just dance like a puppet on a string."

Elmer snorted. "Lies. You were defeated. Beaten like a dog, chipped, and leashed."

A tiny smile quirked one corner of Lanca's mouth.

"I don't know," he said. "Was I? Or was that my exit strategy? What do you think, Elmer? Do I have a reputation for being predictable?"

Flustered now, Elmer took a hobbling step back, closer to Amy and Vail. He shot looks back and forth between them and Lanca, as if he wasn't sure who the bigger threat was.

"Whatever the truth," Elmer said, "you can't deny what Chen Lan did to you. You can't use battle-magic. You're helpless without me. Powerless."

In response, Professor Lanca brought his hands together and cracked his knuckles.

"Now what would make you think," he said, "in this world or any other, that Red Lanca needs *magic* to kill a man?"

"You...do appear to have me at a disadvantage, sir."

Amy and Vail spread out, circling Elmer, the three of them surrounding the spy.

"*We* do," Vail said. At her side, Amy unslung the catspaw and held the weapon in a ready grip, barrels pointed at the dirt.

Lanca gave them a sharp nod, then fixed his gaze on Elmer. He slapped his open palm against the side of the RV.

"This is your hopper, right? Sorry. If you want to run home to daddy, you'll have to get past me first. And to give credit where credit's due, those young ladies behind you are no slouches either. I know who I'd bet on tonight."

"Then, sir," Elmer said, "I dub you a superior warrior and an inferior gambler. I said I had room for *three* on my ship."

Lanca had a second of uncertainty before Elmer looked to the RV and shouted.

"Mr. Shaddock! *Feeding time!*"

The RV door blasted open, knocking Lanca aside as a monster in ragged, flea-bitten robes squeezed his bulk through the open doorway. Half a man, half a rat, his scarlet eyes flashed in the dark and his jagged, yellowed teeth dripped with yellow drool. He was fast, faster than he should have been with that much muscle, and he effortlessly grabbed hold of Lanca's throat and hoisted him in the air.

"Red Lanca," Shaddock growled as the professor struggled against his iron grip. "This is the best killer your species has to offer? With every passing day I'm more disgusted by human frailty."

He tossed Lanca like a rag doll. The professor rolled in the dirt, clutching his throat and gasping for breath. Elmer turned his back on Amy and Vail, confidently striding toward the open doorway.

"A good night to you both, ladies. I doubt we'll ever meet again, but some friends of mine should be arriving to keep you company in very short order."

They charged him. Vail was almost on him when Elmer lifted one foot, spun like a ballerina, and swept out his staff, catching her behind the knees and flipping her off her feet. Then he twisted the other way and used the head as a battering ram, driving it into Amy's gut. She dropped to the dirt, winded and gasping.

Amy grabbed his ankle, holding on with all her might as he dragged her along the dirt toward the open door. He lashed out with his other heel and kicked her in the face, a starburst of pain erupting in her cheek and forehead, and she felt a trickle of blood dribble down the curve of her chin. She still hung tight, scrambling in the dirt, trying to climb up his leg.

"Vail," she shouted, "I'll hold him. Take out the hopper!"

"Might as well try to hold back the tide," Elmer said. He kicked her in the face again, and she saw stars. Her right hand fumbled in her trousers pocket, while her left still clung on with fingers that grew weaker by the second.

She brandished the tiny curved harvesting knife from their natural magic class, reached up, dug it into his thigh, and *ripped*. The blade tore downward, shredding fabric and flesh. His hot blood spattered her upturned face. Elmer screeched, fought free, and rammed the tip of his staff against her shoulder until she finally let go.

Shaddock had Lanca by the throat again. He lifted the professor up and slammed him down into the dirt. Lanca was barely conscious, arms and legs dangling, and the rat-man let out a wet, burbling laugh as he hoisted him high for a third and final time.

"Barely a shadow of your reputation," Shaddock grunted. "Where is the great Red Lanca, hm? Where is the Network's champion? He must have died and given his name to this worthless milk-drinking maggot."

Lanca's eyes snapped open. He bared his bloody teeth and gums in a feral rictus.

"He's right here."

He opened his hands and brought his palms crashing together against the sides of Shaddock's head, bursting the rat-man's eardrums. As Shaddock howled, Lanca's forehead connected with his, ripping skin and fur as both warriors baptized each other in hot blood. Shaddock dropped him. Lanca hit the ground hard, gritting his teeth as his ankle turned, but he forced himself to roll to safety before Shaddock's huge paw-foot descended like a sledgehammer where his head had been a split second ago. Lanca sprang back up, on his feet but wobbly and favoring his left, and he spat a mouthful of scarlet onto the dirt at his feet.

Amy struggled to rise to her hands and knees. Elmer limped away from her, determined to reach the RV's open door, trailing blood behind him. Amy sagged, the last of her strength fading, she slumped to the dirt.

But a new arrival stepped from the shadows to stand in Elmer's path. Dalton punched his fist into his palm.

"You like hitting girls, huh?" Dalton said. "Try me instead."

Elmer paused and contemplated his antler staff, then spun it in his hands with the grace of an Olympic acrobat and hurled it with a flick of his hand. It flew like a spear. The butt cracked against Dalton's forehead, launching him off his heels and knocking him flat on his back in the dirt.

All pretense was gone. The old man act, the hobbling gait, vanished in the blink of an eye. Elmer launched into a cartwheel, spinning effortlessly away from the fight. Then Colin hit him from behind with a flying tackle, grabbing Elmer around the waist with both arms, clinging on for dear life. He wasn't big enough to knock Elmer down, but the spy reacted with sudden confusion, trying to throw the smaller boy off him.

"Hey," Bahati said from his left. "You a fan of mine?"

"What?"

"Wrong answer," she said, and swung a chunk of driftwood like a slugger. The makeshift club smacked Elmer across the side of his head and sent him reeling, Colin still clinging to his waist.

Meanwhile, Professor Lanca and Mr. Shaddock were trading air. Lanca threw out a punch and the rat-man effortlessly snapped his head to one side, dodging. Shaddock dropped into a spin-kick, his filthy robes flaring beneath him, and Lanca leapt over the sweep of his leg before trying to drive his knee straight into Shaddock's drool-matted muzzle. The monster blocked Lanca's knee with both paws, caught his leg, gave it a hard twist, flipped him, and threw him down on his belly in the dirt.

Lanca groaned, eyes glazed, and tried to push himself up again. Shaddock kicked his elbow, driving him back to the ground, and planted one foot on the small of his back.

In front of the RV, Olivia tackled Elmer from the side and hooked an arm around his neck. She and Colin strained to drag him down as he staggered, step by painful step, closer to the door. He flailed in all directions, raining wild punches, but his acrobatic tricks were useless with a pair of teenagers attached to him like dead weight. Bahati pulled Dalton to his feet, and together they attacked Elmer from the other side. Bahati swung her driftwood club up between Elmer's legs, drawing a squeal of strangled breath.

"Anything," he gasped, still fighting toward his escape route. "Give you...anything. You can come, too. They'll make you a god. The Network can make you a *god*."

"Then why didn't they make *you* one?" Dalton asked.

Elmer had a mere second to think about that before Dalton's fist pulped his nose.

Head still spinning, Amy rose to her knees. She gripped the catspaw and used it like a crutch, hoisting herself to her unsteady feet.

They had two priorities: stop Elmer and stop the rat-beast. Her friends had Elmer. She had to trust them. Without his battle-magic, Lanca wasn't winning this fight, and judging by the look on his half-dead face he knew it. So did Shaddock. The rat-man leaned his weight into the foot on the professor's back, grinding his heel in, taking his time.

"That's the sensation of your spine beginning to break," the rat-man growled, something almost like lust in his voice. "I'm not going to kill you, Red Lanca. I'm going to leave you broken instead. You aren't worthy of a warrior's death."

"How about me?" Amy said.

Shaddock turned, his scarlet eyes narrowing to slits. He saw the five-barreled rifle in Amy's hands and belched a wet laugh. He lifted his foot from Lanca's back, leaving him dazed in the dirt, and turned his back on the professor, focusing all his attention on Amy. He took a step toward her.

"Is this what the Saunders Academy teaches? To bring a gun to a mage-fight? I pity you, fledgling. You were poorly served by your so-called professors." He contemplated her, in no particular hurry to rescue his partner. "I think I'm going to rip your arms off."

Amy thumbed back the hammer and raised the weapon, taking aim. Her hands shook. The barrel swayed.

The rat-man's grin widened. He spread his clawed hands wide.

"Go ahead, child. I'll give you the first shot. Let me show you the error of your ways."

She aimed for center mass and pulled the trigger.

The rifle went *click*.

"The Vapor-Lock," Mr. Shaddock chortled. "A cantrip a child could learn, and you've never even heard of it. Might as well toss that stick aside and come at me with your fists, girl. You might actually hit me that way. Once."

*Oh, I know all about it*, Amy thought, cold sweat trickling down her spine.

*That's what I'm counting on.*

# Chapter Forty-Seven

Vail searched the back of Elmer's RV, hunting for something, anything she could use to stop his escape. It didn't look anything like a dimension-hopping vessel, more like a ramshackle ruin propped up on cinder blocks, but she knew by now that appearances deceived. Then she rounded the corner and spotted a cage made of two-by-fours near the RV's power line, hooked to a standing propane tank with three others, spares, clustered tight inside.

She took a step back and breathed deep. Everyone was counting on her now. On her and her magic.

She was the weakest of them all, she thought, but she knew a trick or two. And her friends had faith in her. Amy had faith in her.

Vail lifted a fingertip to her face. It sprouted a coil of blue-hot flame.

\*\*\*

Mr. Shaddock advanced slowly on Amy, rivulets of yellow drool dripping from his muzzle and spattering the dirt in eager anticipation, while the others ganged up on Elmer and tried to drag him away from the RV. The Jangly-Man was still on his feet, flailing blindly. He caught Dalton across the scalp with one frantic fist, splitting him open.

Amy spun the cylinder of the catspaw, shouldered it again, and pulled the trigger.

*Click.*

The rat-man chortled. "Do you know the definition of insanity?" he asked.

She spun the barrel to a third caliber, aimed, and pulled the trigger.

*Click.*

"Doing the same thing again and again and expecting it to turn out differently in the end," he sneered. "And look at you. I could do this all day, child, but you're nearly out of options."

She steadily backed up as she twisted the barrel again, feeling the shadows deepen here, at the farthest edge of the market. There were trees at her back, swaying in the dark, whispering in the night wind.

Fourth try. *Click.* Behind Shaddock, Professor Lanca was starting to rouse. He pushed himself up, biting back a groan of pain, and got to his feet. Amy kept backpedaling and Shaddock matched her pace, clearly enjoying every second of this, ignoring the threat at his back.

"One more try," he taunted. "Would you like to put it right up against my forehead before you pull the trigger? I'll be happy to let you, but...it's my turn next."

"Won't need to," Amy said.

"It only took you failure after failure to figure it out. Humans *can* learn."

"This?" Amy glanced down at the rifle. "No, I knew this was never going to work. It wasn't supposed to. I was just buying time."

Shaddock frowned, suddenly realizing just how far she'd led him from the fray. Behind him, Elmer howled, crying for help as he wrestled with the teenagers that clung to him like lampreys and Dalton hammered his belly with punches.

"Time for *what*, girl?"

Behind them, Vail's voice sang out.

"*Fire in the hole!*"

\*\*\*

Vail retreated to the cover of the forest, all but her eyes and her spinning helix of flame vanishing into the shadows. She dug deep. No time for fears anymore, no doubts. Her friends needed her.

*Amy* needed her.

She pointed her finger and let her feelings flow.

A torrent of blue fire streaked through the night like a knight's lance, the tip of the spear aimed straight for the propane tanks behind Elmer's RV.

\*\*\*

For a second, the black skies over the marketplace turned to high noon. There was a metallic *crump* and an eruption that swallowed the world with the sound of an earthquake as the RV ignited in a white-hot fireball, spitting gouts of black smoke into the sky. It rocked on its side, teetering, as the windows blew out and showered the lane with shards of broken glass. The fire spread, licking along smoldering steel and scorching the grass. Screams erupted across the Night Market.

Amy was dazed, her ears ringing, but she still managed to get to her feet.

Flat on his belly, with Colin, Dalton, Bahati and Olivia pinning his arms and legs to the dirt, Elmer stared up at the ruins of his only way out and shrieked at the top of his lungs.

"Sorry," Amy told Shaddock. "I don't think the Network's going to be hearing from either of you any time soon. You lose."

He stomped toward her, seething with fresh rage.

"And yet," he hissed, "you did nothing to protect your own life. If you wish to be a martyr to a pointless cause, it will be my pleasure to grant you the suffering you desire."

Amy's shoulders sagged. She tilted her head at him and let out a long-suffering sigh.

"Really? Do I look like somebody who would *martyr* herself? I'm a seventeen-year-old high school student, not a medieval saint."

"A bright future, I'm sure," he said, looming over her. "But a future about to be torn limb from limb."

"I think it's a lot brighter now than it used to be. I just had to shuffle my priorities around."

She glanced left and right, inviting Shaddock to notice where she'd lured him with the catspaw ruse. They were in the forest proper, a few steps outside the Night Market's bounds.

"Did I mention I was going to be a veterinarian?" she asked.

With a screeching roar, Murder Mittens exploded from the underbrush. She hurled herself at Shaddock, latched onto him, claws out, hungry, and raked at his face, ripping long furrows along his muzzle as he screamed. Professor Lanca, getting a second wind thanks to Amy's distraction, hit Shaddock from behind with a kick that brought him crashing to his knees in the mud.

\*\*\*

"Give up," Dalton snapped at Elmer, who still squirmed beneath them. "It's over. You're done."

One of Elmer's hands fumbled across the dirt. His fingers closed on a shard of razor-edged glass from the broken RV window. He clutched it so tight that blood began to gutter down his wrist.

"Something you'll learn about me soon enough," the Jangly-Man said to Dalton, their eyes locked. "I always have a backup plan."

He twisted his wrist, escaped Olivia's grip, and brought the shard slashing down across her forearm. She cried out and fell back, clutching the jagged wound. Elmer stabbed at Dalton, aiming for his jugular, and Dalton had to let go and leap back to protect himself. That was all the Jangly-Man needed. He shook off Colin and rammed an elbow into Bahati's face, forcing her to let go of his leg. He lifted the bloody shard of glass, reared his arm back and hurled it.

The shimmering bloody dart buried itself in the small of Professor Lanca's back. He stumbled, grabbing at the glass jutting from his skin. Shaddock spun on the ball of one foot and lashed out with a kick that sent Murder Mittens sprawling, the bobcat hissing in the dirt. In the same smooth motion he whipped off his flea-bitten cloak and sent it sailing toward Amy. The heavy, stinking shroud hit her in the face and wrapped around her like a net, dragging her to the mud as she fought to untangle herself.

Elmer took a wary step back as the rest of the castaways spread out in a semicircle to cut him off. Vail joined them, her fingertip still trailing sparks like a constellation of falling stars.

"I'll remember you," Elmer said, his gaze drifting from face to face as if marking each one.

"You'd better," Vail told him.

No one saw the thin, smoke-filled flask in his hand until he hurled it at the ground. It shattered on impact, washing the world white in a blinding burst of light that fried their vision and left spots behind their eyelids.

When they could see again, Elmer and Shaddock were gone. Their trail vanished into the depths of the forest. Alarm bells and gongs were clanging across the Night Market. A bucket brigade materialized. Water splashed and fire extinguishers hissed as the Racani fought to contain the spreading blaze. The RV, Elmer's escape, was nothing but an empty burned-out shell.

Amy flung Shaddock's cloak aside and lay flat on her back for a while. It was almost peaceful, staring up at the smoke and the clouds. Eventually, though, she knew she'd have to face the music.

They all would.

# Chapter Forty-Eight

"Pay for damages?" demanded the headmistress, her voice loud enough to reverberate through the closed conference room door. "They allowed a Network spy to infiltrate their ranks, and they want *us* to pay for damages? This happened because of— Yes, yes, but that's not the *point*—"

The castaways sat in a row of chairs outside the conference room. Olivia's sliced-up arm was wrapped in a plaster poultice. Bahati and Amy both sported black eyes, and Amy's tongue kept worrying at a loose tooth in her aching bottom jaw, courtesy of Elmer's heel. Colin and Dalton were both scuffed-up messes, their school uniforms disheveled, ties torn. They all looked like they'd just walked through a tornado together.

Eventually, the door opened. Amy braced herself.

Professor Lanca stepped into the hall, looking just as worn out as the rest of them, limping a little. He almost passed by, then stopped. He turned to look at Amy.

"Professor—"

"No." He held up a finger. "I'm the professor. I talk first."

He took a breath, wincing as his lungs swelled.

"I know what you kids did. And you know what?" He gave them a wan smile. "I would have done the same thing. At least...I like to think I would have."

Amy almost apologized. Then she remembered how he'd hesitated before the fight. How he'd looked from Elmer, to her and Vail, and back again. Maybe she'd misread the expression on his face...but she trusted her gut on this one.

He'd been deciding which side would win.

"I think," he said, "that this is one of those situations that could benefit from a wiping of the slate all around. So, let's just...start there, okay? Then maybe we can see what happens."

He jerked a thumb over his shoulder.

"They want you all in there. Good luck. Hope I see you tomorrow."

\*\*\*

The students found another row of chairs waiting for them, this time in front of the inquisition. Or at least, the headmistress and a trio of grave-looking professors, all of them dead silent until Amy and her friends shuffled into their seats.

"Leaving school grounds without permission," Chen Lan announced, as if reading from a royal scroll. "Vandalism of school offices. Breaking into a professor's personal quarters. Oh, and burning down the Night Market."

Colin held up a hand.

"Yes, Mr. Woodrue."

"It wasn't even half, ma'am."

The headmistress arched a thin eyebrow.

"The Market," he clarified. "Barely even half really got burned, and 'burned down' is a little dramatic, I mean, it was mostly smoke damage by the time the bucket brigade got there—"

"That will do," she said, firing a glare at Dalton instead of him. Dalton elbowed him in the ribs.

"Needless to say," Professor Chalk intoned, "any one of these offenses, plus the several others I barely care to list, is worthy of immediate expulsion."

"It was pretty cool, though," Professor Kamaka said.

The other professors stared daggers at him.

"What?" he said. "I'm just being honest. Yes, expulsion-worthy. But cool. Both things can be true at the same time."

"My friend and colleague," Professor Mallory, "just unwittingly hit on the crux of the matter."

"Nope, it was totally wittingly."

She ignored him. "You six have managed to make Academy history, for sheer property damage caused if nothing else." Mallory held up a finger. "*But*. You also exposed the deadliest threat we've faced in years. If Elmer had managed to escape with the school's coordinates after six months of studying our security and every possible way to attack us... 'Disaster' is far too light a word for what might have happened."

"You saw something wrong, you stood up and made it right." Kamaka shrugged. "Puts you in my good books, whether we kick you out or not."

Professor Chalk held his silence for a moment. He locked eyes with Amy. His verdict was short, soft-spoken, and to the point.

"I told you what I expect to see in a leader," he told her. "Now you're learning to follow through. Learning. You have a great deal of room to improve, and I want to see more of that improvement."

All eyes in the room turned to the headmistress.

She rose from her seat. And kept rising, taking to the air, levitating gently a few inches above the floor.

"There are times," she said, "when the rules of our Academy and the mission of our Academy do not necessarily align. And in those cases, our founders have made the verdict clear: the mission comes first."

She drifted back down to the floorboards.

"And in this situation, we have two Network operatives cut off from their home and running amok somewhere on Firebreak Island. They can't leave, which is a mixed blessing. We are still safe from their masters, so long as our fugitives don't find another way off-world."

"On the other hand," Kamaka said, "they're out there, they're tough, and the Network trains their people for guerilla war. They know how to hide and live off the land. We'll hunt 'em down, but it won't be easy, and they're going to try and take as many people as they can down with them."

"Meaning, to my eyes," Chen Lan said, "it would be beyond foolish to banish six promising students who could lend their skills to the school's defense. The founders would never forgive me if I wasted resources like that."

"I'm afraid you're just going to have to stay with us for another year," Professor Mallory said.

Professor Chalk nodded in agreement. His cold gaze swept over them all, landing once more on Amy.

"Who knows?" he added. "We might make real magicians out of you yet."


***

The students walked in a pack down the hallway away from the conference room.

"Did...did we just graduate?" Colin asked.

Dalton clasped his shoulder. "One year down, three to go."

"What even *was* that rat-thing?" Olivia shuddered. "Do they have more of those?"

"Probably," Bahati said. "Hey. Who wants to hear about my chat with the headmistress? While you were busting into Lanca's office, I was making my pitch for a new concert series."

Vail gave her a sidelong glance. "You know you were just supposed to distract her, right?"

"I distracted her with a great idea. Any of you play a musical instrument, by any chance?"

"Harmonica," Dalton said.

"It's a start," Bahati replied. "How about drums? Anyone? Cymbals? Cowbell? I *need* some percussion for this."

Amy and Vail shared a look, then found each other's hands.

"We'll catch you all in a bit," Vail said. "Me and Amy need to...check something out."

Olivia looked perplexed. "But if you need help, we can—"

Dalton poked her arm and whispered something in her ear. She blinked and fell silent.

Down the hall, out of earshot, Amy leaned close to Vail.

"What are we checking out?"

"Oh, I don't know," Vail said. "Adelaide says there's this broom closet in the east wing, and it's usually unlocked. We should go investigate for any signs of trouble."

Amy couldn't keep herself from giggling. Her hand tightened around Vail's.

She wanted to think of the Saunders Academy as a new start, a new life. Life didn't work like that, though. She still dragged the chains and the baggage of her past with her, and she couldn't flip a switch and leave it behind any more than Vail could wave a wand and make her own trauma disappear. They were who they were, the total of their histories, the good and the bad.

That was all right. She liked Vail a lot. And for the first time in her life, Amy Nettle was starting to like herself, too. Just a little bit.

"Lead on," she said.

# Afterword

I was getting dinner with friends when the subject of magic school stories came up, which lead to the question of whether a school of magic could exist in the same multiverse as the *Daniel Faust* and *Harmony Black* series. How would it work? What would that even look like?

Reader, I took that as a dare.

The ideas started to flow and soon I had an outline for a five-book series, the first of which is in your hands. I hope you're enjoying the ride so far! There are lots of mysteries to explore and questions yet to be answered. It's going to be fun, and weird. Very weird. After all, it's a strange cosmos out there, and it's just about time for a field trip...

This book wouldn't exist without the top-notch work of my team. Special thanks to Jay Ben Markson, my fantastic editor, and Rebecca Frank, my fabulous cover designer. And of course, thanks to you for reading! If you'd like to be notified when new books are released (such as, for instance, the sequel to this one), you can hop onto my mailing list over at https://craigschaeferbooks.com/mailing-list. Thanks again, and stay safe out there.

www.ingramcontent.com/pod-product-compliance
Lightning Source LLC
Chambersburg PA
CBHW051942240626
47153CB00005B/1601